ORDINARY MIRACLES

ORDINARY MIRACLES

Linda Crew

For Margaret—
I have loved knowing you
and treasure our friendship
probably more than you realize!
Love,
Linda
1993

William Morrow and Company, Inc.
New York

It is the policy of William Morrow and Company, Inc., and its imprints and affiliates, recognizing the importance of preserving what has been written, to print the books we publish on acid-free paper, and we exert our best efforts to that end.

Library of Congress Cataloging-in-Publication Data

Crew, Linda.
Ordinary miracles / by Linda Crew.
p. cm.
ISBN 0-688-11409-1
I. Title.
PS3553.R43907 1993
813'.54—dc20 92-13643
CIP

Printed in the United States of America

First Edition

1 2 3 4 5 6 7 8 9 10

BOOK DESIGN BY LYNN DONOFRIO

For Herb

ORDINARY MIRACLES

Chapter 1

If you go for the kind of story where the husband calls the wife "darling," we better stop right here. Because Gil has never called me darling in his life. I'm lucky if he calls me Betsy. Mostly he doesn't call me anything. Why should he, he probably figures. I'm the only other person in the house. Who else would he be talking to?

More to it than that, of course. I read a study once about the differences in the way the two sexes talk. Men launch right in, expecting people to listen, while women are never sure anybody's paying attention. With us it's always, "Gil? Gil, guess what happened today?" I mean, why waste breath until you hear the grunt that lets you know he's at least halfway tuned in?

But I'm making Gil sound sort of Neanderthalish, which is not the case.

When I first met him, I asked my mother if she thought it was true about still waters running deep, assuming that as another person who talks a lot, she'd automatically join me in my admiration for people who know how to keep their mouths shut. But she surprised me. "I used to think that," she said. "Now I think some of those still-water types just don't have much to say."

I didn't care for this response. I was already falling in love, and I was counting on Gil having unplumbed depths. Just a hypothesis, but then, aren't all marriages begun on the basis of a hypothesis? *We're guessing the two of us can make it together.* Ha! Then all you have to do is start living through a bunch of stuff to see if it proves true.

So I liked to think of Gil as one of those legendary men of few words. I liked to think that deep down he was bursting with sensitive feelings. I liked to think that maybe someday I'd hear about them.

And today might just be the day, I remember thinking that winter morning. A guy's got to say something when you tell him he's going to be a daddy, right?

I hummed as I slid the first roll of wallpaper out of the bundle. I slit the cellophane and pushed it off. Lush, old-fashioned roses. What a fool of a landlady I was turning out to be! You don't put Laura Ashley paper in a rental house. But what the heck. I spent most of my days hanging wallpaper picked out by my customers; once in a while I deserved the fun of working with paper I'd chosen myself.

I poured a cup of coffee from my thermos and rolled up my flannel sleeves. Ouch. The left one caught on the surgical tape holding the cotton wad to my inner elbow. I considered, then gave it the quick rip my mother long ago convinced me was preferable to some slow, torturous pull. Tossing the cotton wad at the garbage sack, I checked my vein, which bulged with a purplish bruise.

Nifty, these blood tests for pregnancy. Cost more, but a pregnancy can be detected so much earlier. None of this waiting around for two weeks before you can even try it the way you had to with a home urine test. At five-thirty tonight I'd call the clinic and that would be that.

Gil was going to be so tickled. Actually, he'd been the one all gung ho on the baby thing. If I hadn't been concerned about being able to get pregnant in the first place, who knows how long I might have stalled? *Let me tackle one more house*, I could easily imagine myself saying.

Well, sometimes there's no faster cure for ambivalence about which door to choose than finding one of them locked. Just watch, that'll be the one you'll decide you have to beat down. By now, after several months on fertility drugs, I was more than ready to fling open the door marked motherhood and charge on through.

Every once in a while I'd stop for a moment and put my hand over my belly, thrilled with the idea of new life. Then I'd go back to work, wonderfully energized. I almost had this place wrapped up, and maybe with a deadline I could get myself to finish the last nagging details on the remodeling of our own house. You know how it goes—once you find you can live three months with no knob on the pantry door, what's to say you couldn't go on that way forever?

But a baby coming—that made you want to have everything perfect.

So I buzzed along, mentally rehearsing how I'd deliver the great news to Gil. I loved having a secret. People like me usually do—we have them so rarely. To have a secret means not talking about something for a while, and who can do that? Amazingly, for two days, I'd managed to keep my suspicions to myself. Gil didn't even know I'd gone for the test.

Now, as I worked, I didn't think I could be any happier. This day, I thought, January 23, 1984, is the happiest day of my life.

Of course I'd said that lots of times before, and usually Gil and I would get in a fight about it. When I felt I couldn't possibly be any happier, I always wanted him to admit that, no, he couldn't possibly be any happier either. Only he always thought he could. He thought he'd be happier, for instance, if Josh Brewster's father wasn't coming in for a parent-teacher conference after school that day to see why Josh had racked up sixteen detention slips. Or he'd be happier if it had rained just *after* he got his peas planted instead of just before.

"Okay, you can always find something wrong," I'd say. "Or think of something that could be better. Like if they said on the news that all the nuclear weapons were being destroyed. But I'm not talking about things being better. I'm saying that after a certain point, you can't get any happier."

"Well, wouldn't you be happier if they chucked out the missiles?"

"Of course, but—"

"Then you *could* be happier."

Well, you see how this goes. If you don't watch out, an argument like this can put a damper on the best day of your life pdq, so I'd give up trying to explain. But what I meant was, if I wake up feeling fine, I'm looking forward to working, nothing terrible is happening to us, and the coffee tastes okay, well, that's about as good as it gets. And if there's some little bit of nice news for frosting on the cake of everyday good stuff—hey, I don't mind calling that the best day of my life. What more could you want?

So I thought I had it all that day. The baby news for toppers and meanwhile, working away in my best broken-in overalls, hanging the most beautiful wallpaper, turning a dump into a place where people would love to live. Okay, so we weren't going to change the world like we used to think—at least I was making this one little corner better.

And this was my favorite sort of day for hanging wallpaper too—miserable outside, cozy in. Dawn had brought the nastiest of Oregon weather—freezing rain, which always perked up *Coffee Break*, the local radio talk show. Everybody up in the coast range west of town took turns calling in. "Awful slick on the hill at Crestline," someone would say ominously, pleased at being the first to report it. To the north, people on Timber Mountain (just a glorified hill, really) were either stuck up at their houses or stuck down below, their BMWs useless on the steep, icy streets that looped through the trees. Callers speculated on how much worse it might get and which community programs would be canceled. Hey, if it froze again tonight, they might cancel school and Gil could stay home.

When the talk show was over, I switched to NPR. I didn't know much about classical music, but some of this Vivaldi stuff made pretty good work music—upbeat, happy, triumphant. Certainly fit my mood today, anyway. I was so jazzed, I finished the wallpapering by four. I gave myself a few minutes to admire it. A page right out of a magazine, that's what it looked like—exactly that antiquey golden glow I wanted.

I pulled off my bandanna and shook out my hair. Cleaning up, I sang and boogied my way around the room. "Oh, I got a twenty-dollar gold piece says there ain't nothing I can't do. . . ." I gathered the sticky paper scraps and stuffed them into my garbage sack. "'Cause I'm a woman, W-O-Oh-M-A-N . . ."

I was still humming as I swung my tray of tools into the back of the pickup and latched the door of the homemade shingled canopy. The icy patches on the street had long since thawed, so before heading home I detoured a couple of blocks toward the university to swing by the McBee houses.

We didn't have too many genuinely old houses in Mary's Bend. We're only talking a hundred and twenty years since settlement and unfortunately, during that time, far too many city fathers had been far too enthusiastic on the subject of urban renewal.

A bit belatedly, some of us were fighting back.

Last summer, as the big McBee house was being renovated, everyone had been amazed to watch an old-fashioned carriage house and walled garden go up next to it. Together they filled half a block. The garden alone was a wonder, with its latticed grape arbor and arching rose trellises. Imagine putting all that money into a house so close to downtown! Ostentatious, some said. Claimed the garden walls were an invitation to trouble. Graffiti artists, will you sign in, please? But I loved the whole thing. It showed faith in the future of Mary's Bend, I felt, and a certain generosity for the owners to beautify this corner instead of some hidden compound on Timber Mountain. After all, there was no charge to pass by, and the walls dipped low enough in places that we'd all get a peek at the roses, right?

I had my eye on the smaller McBee house next door, though, which was still owned by Jennie McBee Nellers. It had exceptionally nice gingerbread trim on the outside and I'd heard that the inside was all done in quarter-sawn oak, never painted. If I could get my hands on it, I'd try for a historic designation and a tax break on the remodeling.

I pulled up at the curb behind the yellow Norgren Construction van and let the engine idle. Leaning down, I peered out the opposite window at the smaller of the houses. I sure hoped Jennie Nellers would make up her mind pretty soon. Now that she'd moved over to Heritage Manor, this place would go downhill fast, left vacant this way, maybe even heatless through the damp winter . . .

A knock on the driver's side window startled me. Eric Norgren. He opened the truck door.

"Hey, Betsy."

"Jeez, you scared me to death."

He grinned. "Sorry."

I'll admit right off he's good-looking—nice teeth, bushy blond hair, reddish beard. But he made me uncomfortable. Like right now, the way he sort of hung there, too close, between the door and the truck cab roof.

"Moss sure is getting out of hand, isn't it?"

"What? Oh, the roof? Yeah." I wished he hadn't caught me here. He was the number one remodeler of vintage houses in the area, and I knew darned well he was interested in the little house too. I nodded toward the bigger house. "How's it going here?"

"Fine. Come on in. I'll show you around."

I was tempted. Eric and his crew did fine work. I might not get another chance to see the results of it in this house.

"Thanks, but I'd better not. Gotta get home."

He wiggled his bushy eyebrows. "Hubby waiting?"

He seemed to specialize in making innocent remarks sound suggestive.

"Yeah, I better hit the road." It would be dark pretty soon, and I had a couple other places to check on.

Still he didn't move.

"Eric? Excuse me?" I tried to reach around him to pull the door shut.

"Oh right. Sorry. Catch you later."

Next I drove by the house my grandfather had built on Sixteenth Street back in the twenties when that was the edge of town. Not for sale now, but if it ever hit the market, I hoped to buy it, both for sentiment and because it was the sort of place I'd decided to look for—a small, affordable fixer-upper I could rent to married grad students.

Thinking of Grampa Stroh, I considered stopping at the nursing home to check on him, then decided to wait. I'd go tomorrow when I could give him my news. His first great-grandchild—that ought to go over big.

I drove the long way home to the farm, checking for new FOR SALE signs in the gathering dusk along River Road. I couldn't help it, it was like a game. The Monopoly Queen, my sister, Stephanie, called me. Of course, that's an exaggeration. One rental house makes me a real estate baron? I guess this goes back to when Dad was still alive and loaned me money to get into a fixer-upper that I later sold for a surprisingly good profit, due more, I'm the first to admit, to the rising price of real estate than to my cosmetic improvements. But I made money, and it was probably the first thing I ever pulled off that truly impressed my business-minded father. I guess that bugged my sister. Later, after he died, she got the same financial settlement from the sale of his store that I did, and their house overlooking Yaquina Bay was a lot fancier than ours. Also I'm sure with her husband, Matt, being a loan officer and knowing what was what, he had their money socked away in good investments. Still, whenever she'd bring up my interest in houses, I'd hear it in her voice, the way it ate at her. I think she saw ownership as a self-satisfied, relaxed affair; she never saw the work I did.

When I got home, I opened our back door to the rich aroma of pot roast, the very dish Gil had first used to seduce me way back when. I love this scene—Gil whistling at the kitchen counter, chopping carrots while he does a little sock-foot shuffle to a zydeco record. I know, I know, if you turned it around, it'd sound awfully sexist—the little wifey in the kitchen, happy in service. But maybe we're too hard on guys. Maybe all it boils down to is wanting to come home to somebody who's happy. Happy with you, happy with your life. Wouldn't anyone appreciate that? Just the simple reassurance that the other person isn't ready to fling the stirring spoon and yell, "*That's it, I'm outta here*!"

"Hi," he said over his shoulder.

"Yum!" I kicked off my boots and spread my damp parka on the bricks in front of the wood stove. "What could be nicer than this?"

Since I've mentioned that Eric Norgren is good-looking, it's only fair to comment that my husband is too. At least I think so. One time my sister said she guessed Gil had the sort of looks that had to grow on a person. I didn't know what she was talking about. I'd been knocked silly by those eyes of his from the word go. They were the sunlit golden brown of the smooth streambed stones you see through running mountain water. His hair was dark and loosely curled and just right for poking daisies in, although of course even back when people were doing that sort of thing, Gil never would. He tanned without trying and his cheeks were a ruddy red. Once, at the farmers' market, a flirty woman in Birkenstocks told him how wonderfully healthy he looked. "I can tell you're a vegetarian," she said, letting her Indian cotton blouse slide off her shoulder. "Nope." He smirked, more than pleased to disabuse her of this assumption. "Nothing I like better than red meat."

Anyway, I don't know why Stephanie couldn't see what I saw in Gil, but to each her own. And I was glad to claim Gil as my own. None of this he-man stuff, but he could put snow chains on tires and chop wood, and although I couldn't seem to interest him in doing the Rhett carries Scarlett up the staircase scene, I think he could carry me if I broke my ankle or something.

More important, he could cook.

"We'll have to eat a little late," he said, "but I felt like doing pot roast."

"Definitely worth waiting for." I slipped my arms around him, laying my cheek against the soft flannel back of his shirt.

"What's up?" he said, pleased and a little surprised at this display of affection. Usually I burst in, already yammering away about something that's made me mad or sad or particularly glad—forget the hug. Like I said, we're not much on "darling this" and "sweetheart that."

"What're you so happy about?"

"Oh nothing." Brother, I can't lie worth beans.

"Papering go okay?"

"Yup." Still the same dumb grin. "Looks great."

He put down his knife and looked at me.

"How was school?" I said quickly. "Bike path slippery this morning?"

"Couple places. Not too bad." He peered even closer at me. "Come on. What? Jennie Nellers said she'd sell you her place?"

"No, no, no!" I spun away, dancing like a nervous child. Then I stopped. What the heck. "Gil!" I whirled to face him. "I'm pregnant!"

He jerked back, comic book style. "You are?"

I nodded.

"Are you sure?"

I clapped my hands. "Oh, I love it that you said that. They always say that! In the movies, the guy always goes, 'Duh, are you sure?' As if a woman wouldn't *know*!"

"But how can you tell?"

"Well, I didn't get a period."

"You *never* get a period."

"Gil, I mean on the drugs." When my periods had stopped for good not long after we were married, my doctor had assured me it wasn't the worst thing. No worries about birth control, and when I wanted to get pregnant, they had medicine for it. "This is the first cycle I didn't get a period after the Clomid." Theoretically Gil knew this, it's just that he never followed the details too closely. "Besides," I added smugly, "a woman knows her own body."

Ha-ha. This was funny coming from me, who used to be big on men and women not being so different, it was just how we were raised and all that. Now I was reveling in the differences. Especially the idea of men being kind of dense and out of it and women being in the know, closer to the heart of things, keepers of the mystical secrets of life.

"So this is it then?" he said.

I nodded, flushing happily.

He gathered me up. He hugged me. He kissed me.

"Let's call my folks," he said.

I pulled back. "Don't you think we should wait for the official word? I went up and did the blood test this morning and I can call for the results at five-thirty."

He eased his grip on me. "I thought you said you were sure."

"Well I am sure. I'm just not *sure* sure."

"Oh."

"But I'm still sure!"

The phone rang. I lunged for it. Maybe Dr. Lowell couldn't wait to congratulate me . . .

"Oh, hi, Mom." Just a check-in call. The usual. We'd always kept in touch, and since Dad died we phoned each other across town nearly every day.

Gil was peeling potatoes now, his green plaid back unreadable. Darn, I should have waited for *sure* sure.

Mom rattled on about how hectic budget meetings at the university had been—she's an administrative assistant in the forestry department. Finally, because she knows me too well and alarm bells probably go off when she notices herself talking without me interrupting, she said, "Honey, is something wrong?"

"No, no, everything's fine."

When I hung up, Gil said, "I have to admit, I'm amazed. You not letting her in on all this."

"Well, she's got enough to worry about, taking care of Grampa's stuff and all. I just haven't wanted to tell her anything until it could be good news." I started dancing again. "Can't wait till tomorrow. Think I'll go right up to her office first thing. Or maybe we could zip over to the house tonight."

It hadn't been easy holding off on this when I'm used to talking to her about everything, but I think Gil appreciated it. He's the private type. He wouldn't dream of driving around with a bumper sticker advertising his politics or a license plate spelling something cute, and he hasn't worn a T-shirt with anything written on it since he was a high school junior. *Surf's Up!* was his final public message to the world. So it wasn't exactly a shock to me that he wanted our attempts at reproduction kept between the two of us.

I opened the kitchen drawer and pawed through the half-used masking tape rolls, Super Glue tubes, and miscellaneous flashlight pieces, pulling out a screwdriver. "I," I said, setting my chin, "am going to fix the pantry door once and for all."

"Whoa! Stand back, boys!"

"That's the way it is when you're pregnant, see? You get this urge to fix everything up, feather your nest."

"How do you know?"

"Gil! Women know these things. Women talk to each other. You'd be amazed at what women tell me while I'm wallpapering their houses. Or at the pool locker room? You wouldn't believe it."

"Oh. Well, am I supposed to get this fix-it bug, too?"

"No! I mean, you can. It'd be nice. But we're talking hormones here. I've heard of women actually sorting out their junk baskets—the ones with buttons and pins and paper clips and bits of broken plastic from stuff they've kept so long they don't have a clue what it is anymore."

"No kidding. Think you might get the urge to tackle the shed?"

"Never know," I sang.

I guess I looked fairly convincing as a hyperdomestic pregnant person because Gil was grinning again, singing a ditty about the cake in my oven as he added more water to the meat.

I smiled even as I struggled and swore at the pantry door—it was a recycled number with the rusted lock mechanism still inside. Prying the darn thing out was the hard part, the hitch that kept this project from ever being crossed off the To Do list.

Every once in a while I checked my watch.

At exactly five-thirty, I dropped the screwdriver and dialed the clinic. Gil watched me, having a tough time keeping the lid on his grin.

"This is Betsy Bonden. I'm calling for the results of my pregnancy test?"

While I listened to the rustling of papers, Gil and I gave each other the thumbs-up sign.

"Mrs. Bonden?"

"Yes?"

"The test was negative."

"Oh." I stood there. I hadn't even considered this a real possibility. "Are you sure?"

She was sure.

I hung up the phone and stared at it a moment. "Well shit."

"Negative, huh?"

"Yeah." I didn't want to look at him. Today's daydreams—a stream of bubbles from a child's wand—were popping even as I remembered them. Telling my mother—*ping*. Telling my grandfather—*ping*. The nursery we would decorate, the baby quilt I would piece, the two of us becoming the three of us in time for next Christmas—*ping, ping, ping*. "I can't believe it," I said. "I *feel* pregnant."

Gil came around to face me. "Could it be a mistake?"

Well, he broke my heart, looking at me that way, so trusting, so willing to believe me instead of the lab.

"I doubt it. The blood tests are supposed to be real accurate." I went over and picked up the screwdriver. I stared at the empty doorknob hole. "Damn it anyway."

"Well, if it's not positive this month, it will be another month."

"I s'pose." But it hurt a lot more than I expected, the splattering to earth of all those little dream bubbles.

Gil opened the pot and dumped in the vegetables.

I leaned against the pantry doorjamb. "I'm really sorry, honey."

He turned in surprise. "What's to apologize for?"

"Well, I feel so stupid."

"Come on. You didn't get a period, so you thought you were pregnant, you had a test and you're not. So what?"

"So what?" I stood up straight. "Well, for one thing I guess we can forget women's intuition."

"Aw . . ." He waved his spoon dismissively. "Never believed in that anyway."

But he didn't fool me. For a few minutes there he *had* believed.

I looked at the screwdriver. I looked at the stupid jammed door lock. I marched over and tossed the screwdriver in the drawer. Then I shoved it shut, and when it jammed with a bunch of cardboard packaging, I didn't even bother to stuff it back in.

To Do

Work

Wed—Jacobs
Post business card new paint store
Return sample books
Send in bonding renewal

Call Dr. Lowell
Hist. Pres. meeting—Mon 7:30
Fix pantry door
Visit Grampa

To Buy

Paste
Razors
Fabric for rental curtains

Chapter 2

I'll bet when I start in about my gynecologist, you're expecting to hear what a jerk he is. You think I'll complain that he never remembers my name, he's cold, uncaring, an insensitive clod, callously checking his watch as I pour out my heart, striding over to fling open his door and stand by it as if to say, *"Time's up, lady!"* Or worse, he's calculating, sadistic, he learned his stirrup-side manner from some Nazi . . .

Sorry. No doctor bashing here. Call me a cockeyed optimist—I'm not the type who suspects all gynecologists of secretly hating women and taking up the practice with the express intention of torturing us.

No, I'm sure Dr. Lowell stumbled into it with a certain innocence. Sounded like a nice mix—office exams, a few baby deliveries, the occasional surgery. What he hadn't counted on were these soaring malpractice insurance premiums. And the way he would never have enough time to listen long enough to the problems of all these women. He hadn't counted on his wife having four daughters, who, as soon as they got old enough for pelvic exams, would come home saying, "Eeeuuw, Daddy, how can you *do* that for a job?"

I know these things because he tells me. It's important

to keep up the chitchat during a pelvic exam. Otherwise you might start thinking about what he's actually *doing* down there.

The best evidence of Dr. Lowell being a decent guy was probably his wife, who was not your stereotypical doctor's wife, hanging out at the country club or whatever. She wouldn't join all the socially acceptable charitable organizations either. Not Liz Lowell. She was one of the leaders of Save the Forests and too busy raising ruckuses at government hearings and getting herself chained to giant Douglas firs. Also—and I loved her for this—it was rumored that their Timber Mountain house was a housekeeping nightmare. No way would it ever be on the Shepherd of the Valley Hospital Foundation's Christmas Starlight Tour of Homes. I guess she wasn't into interior decoration, and even though I was—or thought I might be if our interior ever got to the point of decorating—I admired her go-to-hell attitude.

Gil was always running into Dr. Lowell at Safeway. He told Gil the gigantic new Ace Foods on their side of town gave him migraines. But stranger than finding him down our way, stranger than the fact that he was actually shopping for groceries was this: From the comments he made about a certain recipe for salsa, it seemed he planned to go home and actually cook dinner himself!

Because of these things, I forgave Dr. Lowell his little slips, his contention that it was somehow natural he should call his patients and the nurses by their first names while he remained Dr. Lowell to us. We winked at each other and humored him. Why not? My point is, a guy can get away with saying all sorts of politically incorrect things if he says them while he's whipping up a dynamite dinner!

I didn't know all this about Dr. Lowell when I came home from college and needed a gynecologist, though. He became my doctor by default. I had been a patient at the Mary's Bend Clinic all my life and one of the other ob/gyns—Dr. Beemer—had actually delivered me. Stephanie too, and she still came over from Newport to see him for her checkups. But in high school I had dated Dr. Beemer's son, and I thought I'd feel funny, discussing birth control with him. The other one—Dr. Kidd—had performed my first pelvic exam when I was thirteen with such a total lack of sensitivity (I still remember him pushing my knees apart) that neither my mother nor I had ever forgiven him. (Okay, maybe just a *teensy* bit of doctor bashing.)

With Beemer and Kidd ruled out, I was left with their new and rather handsome young colleague, Dr. Michael Lowell.

I sat now on the end of his examining table, wrapped in a sheet and shivering, naked except for my green knee socks. My bare arms were goosebumpy. I'll bet they use these fluorescent lights to make sure every woman will look as purple and blotchy and unappealing to the doctors as possible. Which is fine, except it doesn't do much mentally for a woman not exactly at a high pitch of self-esteem. I studied the chart on the wall outlining the success rates of various forms of birth control—success here of course meaning no conception . . .

Finally Dr. Lowell swung in, bursting with good humor, as if a sufficiently jovial manner could fool you into thinking this was fun. After the polite preliminaries, he ceremoniously unfolded the paper I handed him—a chart of my daily before-getting-out-of-bed temperatures for the last month, along with an arrow marking each dutiful act of, as the chart directions so charmingly put it, coitus.

When I'd first started on Clomid, I remember asking him exactly when and how often we were supposed to put these arrows on the chart.

"Well, ideally . . ." he started out, and then, as if the subject were simply too delicate for words, he stopped and penciled tentative arrows in every other box around the middle of the month.

"Okay, you got it," I said. "I'll give Gil the word."

"Oh, don't tell him!"

"Don't tell him? You want this to happen or not?"

"Well, of course, but . . . you don't want to give him the idea that . . ."

"That we mean business here?"

"Well, yes."

"But we *do* mean business."

"Yes, but I'm sure you can come up with a better approach, Betsy." And then he'd actually winked!

Now he took out a little ruler and penciled two lines,

checking to see if the second half of my cycle showed, on the average, the normal temperature rise.

He frowned, then tossed his pencil back on the built-in corner desk. "No, this graph is all over the place."

"But if I'm not pregnant, why didn't I have a period?"

"I don't know. Sometimes that happens."

"But with Clomid?"

"Oh sure. Not the typical response, but . . ."

Neither of us said anything for a moment.

"This is getting kind of old," I said, "you know?"

"Actually, you've held up better than a lot of my patients. It's not easy being infertile."

My green-socked feet stopped swinging. "It's official, then? I'm infertile?"

He blinked. "Well, Betsy, you're taking fertility drugs . . ."

"I know, but I just—" *Infertile.* Guess I never really thought of that label stuck on me, not as a permanent diagnosis.

"Let's have a look," he said, "shall we?"

I sighed. *I guess we shall.*

He helped me lie down on the examining table and I stuck my heels into the fuzz-covered metal stirrups. Once, after a batch of letters to the paper complained that the clinic wasn't responsive to the needs of women, he informed me in very hurt, indignant tones that it was he, Michael Lowell, who'd obtained the very first stirrup mittens in town. How dare they accuse him of insensitivity!

Now usually his gloved hand sliding into me triggered a stream of chatter, some weird Pavlovian response, anything to block it out. But today I couldn't talk. I could only stare at the perforated ceiling tiles and mull over this business of being infertile. Not that I could claim anything close to true shock, but until now it had never really hit me on a gut level.

Without my usual defensive chatter, I was left at Dr. Lowell's mercy as he calmly narrated the exploration of my inner regions. Please understand, I realize this is the currently accepted practice. It's modern. Women want to be informed. But honestly, sometimes it's bad enough having these things done—do we have to hear about them too?

"And now I'm putting my finger in your rectum . . ."

Oh please. My jaws clenched. Muzak emanating from a

silver disk on the ceiling mocked me with a smarmy version of "Feelings." "I hate this," I said between my teeth.

He tsked with a certain determined cheer. "That's what most women tell me." Finally he finished and stripped off his gloves. "Little tiny uterus. Definitely no pregnancy. No cysts on your ovaries, though, that's good."

I sat up, nodding. Had to be grateful for the things that *were* going right. He'd told me often enough about another patient of his who'd sprouted a baseball-size cyst from taking Clomid. It could happen. That's why I had to put up with these stupid exams every time I came in.

He took a long time going over my previous charts, stopping once to polish his wire-rimmed glasses, then looking at the collection of zigzaggy lines again. Finally he shook his head. "Five cycles, Betsy. If the Clomid's going to work, we usually get a pregnancy within this time frame."

I stared at him. "Are you saying I'm not going to get pregnant . . . ever?" I managed this in a rather straightforward tone, I think, except for a slight cracking on the word *ever*.

"Oh no, we've just begun to fight."

"Yeah?" Somehow I was having trouble matching his upbeat mood. "Hey, how come you didn't warn me? You know, that this might be some big deal?"

"Didn't I?"

"No. You just said I'd have to take these pills."

"Well, what good would it have done to get you all worried back when you weren't ready for a baby anyway?"

I plucked at the sheet draped over my lap.

"And before now you weren't ready, isn't that right?"

Grudgingly, I nodded. Once, I'd thought I was pregnant and practically freaked out. We'd only been married two years and our drafty old farmhouse was hardly fit habitation for us, let alone a baby. Honestly, was there anything so ambiguous as a pregnancy? It could be the biggest disaster or the greatest thrill . . .

"Come on, Betsy. Don't look so glum."

"You expect me to be happy about this? I don't have all the time in the world, you know."

"Well, we're a long way from the end of the line."

The end of the line? I shivered. Looking back, I think maybe this was the first time I considered the real possibility of failure. Maybe it was at this moment, wrapping my goosebumpy arms around myself, that my annoyance at all this cranked up into full-scale alarm. I was almost thirty-three. My whole life wasn't in front of me anymore. A good chunk of it was gone, and the rest of it, especially the reproductive rest of it, had suddenly telescoped up into not much at all.

Chapter 3

Pedaling up the road toward the house, Gil could see that the truck wasn't in the driveway—Betsy wasn't home yet. Where could she be? Oh yeah, the doctor. To say his heart sank in recalling this would be an exaggeration, but an evening spent analyzing the advice and predictions of Dr. Michael Lowell was not a monthly ritual he anticipated with great pleasure.

He braked his bike in front of the tilted mailbox, straddling the mud puddle gouged into the gravel by the mail truck's tires. The box used to be fancy, but the rains of ten Oregon winters had long since weathered away the "trailing vines and dew" Betsy had painted in honor of one of his favorite Taj Mahal songs, the one about moving to the country and painting your mailbox blue. The door opened with a creak of rust-encrusted hinges. Junk mail mostly, and catalogs. He stuffed it under his rain slicker and pushed the bike up the gravel drive. Then he dragged the bike up the steps onto the porch.

Out of the rain now, he looked through the catalogs. Great—Park's Seeds. And Stokes. He loved a long winter evening with his feet propped near the wood stove, idling through seed catalogs, imagining summer gardens.

Inside, he hung his dripping rain suit over the tub, put on a zydeco record, and got ready to start dinner.

Funny how his taste in music had changed over the years. Used to be he listened to nothing but the blues. When he'd first come to Mary's Bend, right out of college, he spent the rainy autumn evenings listening to B. B. King records, fooling with his harmonica, reading kids' papers. Sometimes, if he hadn't heard from her, he brooded over Marsha, wondering if maybe even a lousy relationship was better than none at all. (From the first get-acquainted faculty barbecue at Rivergreen Middle School, it was clear this was not a great town for being single.) But whenever one of her glorious sunshine and tequila postcards would arrive, he knew he'd done the right thing finally calling it off with her. The cards were as calculated as the string of guys she'd paraded past him in an apparent attempt at goading him into a commitment, a strategy that had completely backfired. Why would he want to sign up for life with someone who liked to run around?

Sometimes at night he just sat there, nursing a beer, staring at nothing, unwilling to move. Maybe he hadn't quite recovered from his hassles with the draft. First he had failed to convince his draft board that all those years of forced Sunday school attendance actually translated into firmly held convictions concerning the immorality of war. (Had somebody snitched on him? Reported how he'd spent his years in the junior high section of the sanctuary helping his peers pile the collection plate with envelopes marked "Elmer Fudd" and "Who Wants to Know?") He hadn't made any points voicing vague thoughts on preferring to grow things rather than kill, either. But finally he had drawn a lottery number just high enough to find himself suddenly safe, and with this anticlimactic resolution, the adrenaline that had pumped for several years over this had stopped, leaving him drained.

Suddenly safe. Suddenly free of Marsha. Somehow it didn't feel as good as he'd imagined. Yearning for ties, he started a vegetable garden that first spring at his rented house. Kept him going through the summer anyway.

Then, with the tomatoes all canned and the corn cut off the cobs and frozen, the wet gray winter threatened to drag him back to gloom. For in spite of his protestations to Marsha that he was no longer the California surfer she seemed determined to imagine him, he had not entirely adjusted to Northwest winters.

Then Betsy had exploded into his life. He had liked her right off. She had just the right amount of sass. Not that he'd tell her. Sass, he decided, requires a delicate balance. Why upset it by making her self-conscious? Also he liked her looks, especially the long brown hair. She wore makeup, he figured, but she didn't draw those lines around her eyes like Marsha used to. That was nice. And when she talked about what she wanted out of life, he noticed a welcome absence of any reference to a craving for continual sunshine. Never once did she mention a desire for a tan. She even had a healthy suspicion of California surfer types and delighted him by claiming she just couldn't picture him that way. He wasn't even blond! He found himself confiding that he'd only used a belly board, never ridden a wave standing up, something he hadn't actually explained to Marsha.

Anyway, thanks to Betsy, he lost his taste for the blues. He started favoring corny country-western music, not so much the down-and-out, hanging-around-in-the-bar numbers, but the mushy ones about true love, the ones that tended to rhyme "wife" with "life."

And now lately, with his teaching job, the farm, and more projects than he ever had time for, he'd taken to blasting zydeco, better than black coffee for keeping you moving.

He had the chicken in the oven and was stoking the wood stove when Betsy pushed open the back door.

"Hi," she said, barely audible over the music.

She took off her jacket. She was wearing a dress. Plaid flannel, not fancy, but since when did she have to dress up for the doctor at all?

"Boy," she said, "I just about lost it on the way home. Almost ran a red light coming through downtown. My mind was just . . ." She waved her hands to indicate a space-out attack and dropped on the sofa.

"What's the deal? Something the doctor said?"

She gave him a bleak look. "He says the Clomid's not working."

"But you knew that when you went over there."

"Yeah, but this is like it's not working as in it's not *going* to work and we'll probably—Hey, do you think we could turn your music off? I can't even think."

He headed for the stereo in the living room. The Cajun accordion and fiddles did seem suddenly oppressive in their exuberance.

"Thanks," she said when he came back. "That's better."

They sat there a moment, recovering from the audio assault.

"He's not saying you'll never get pregnant, is he? Isn't there some other treatment to try?" Up until now Gil hadn't wasted any energy trying to figure exactly how bad it would be if they had to face never having a baby, and, furthermore, he was all for postponing this crisis as long as possible.

"Yeah, there's this new medicine. You know how my prolactin level's always high?"

"Uh . . ."

"Gil, I've told you that."

He glanced away. He'd never seen any point in clogging up his brain with all these details. And as long as he came through in bed on the right nights, he didn't think she had much room to complain.

"Well, anyway . . ." She gave him the story about a high prolactin level possibly suppressing ovulation. The new medicine—bromocriptine—might lower the hormone level and make her ovulate on her own.

"Is it as spendy as the Clomid?"

"Gil! Is that all you can think about?"

"Well, I'm sorry. Am I not allowed to ask?"

"Sure, but does it have to be your first question? Aren't you even concerned what the side effects of this stuff might be?"

He sighed. "I imagine you're going to tell me."

"Oh heavens no. I wouldn't *dream* of boring you." She stomped up the stairs.

On the counter lay the pharmacy sack. Inside he found the drug company insert she had no doubt demanded from the pharmacist. It listed each and every possible side effect . . . nausea, headache, dizziness, fatigue, cramps . . .

Swell, he thought. Fun times, straight ahead.

Chapter 4

Forgive me if you know some saint, some contradiction to what I'm about to say, but in my experience there are two kinds of people: those who dislike visiting nursing homes and don't, and those who dislike nursing homes and visit anyway.

"You're so good at it," my cousin Laura always says to me. "Somehow I've never been able to handle anything to do with hospitals and sickness."

Right. I love confronting mortality. And the smells—food and disinfectant and body odors all mixed together. Sure, Laura. Makes my day, walking that wheelchair gauntlet of crumpled human forms.

But some of us are handicapped by low guilt thresholds, so while she writes nice notes from her home an hour down the freeway and chides my mother and me for not keeping her better informed of Grampa's condition, I'm putting "Visit Grampa" on my To Do list every week. I'm standing at his sink, toothbrush in hand, getting bossed through the cleaning of his dentures. Don't get me wrong, my attitude certainly disqualifies me from anything even approaching sainthood. I lack the proper purity of motive, not to mention that this item is usually the last one left unchecked on my list and sometimes even has to be shifted to the following week. But I try.

The Mary's Bend Care Center is generally regarded as the best in the area, although as anyone who's ever signed in a relative knows, a nursing home—even a good one—is not a place likely to inspire enthusiasm.

Six years earlier, my grandmother had died here, in a room right down the hall. Alzheimer's kills slowly. After four years of gradual decline at home, she lingered three more here, during which the rest of us had taken turns providing daily visits. Grampa established the precedent: *Grandma will be fed dinner by a loved one.* The love wore a little thin occasionally, like the time Mom and Grampa were both sick and Dad was off fishing. At this point, my sister, Stephanie, had already married Matt and moved to Newport, so I was it. But Gil and I were in the middle of reroofing our house, and by that I mean we'd ripped off three previous courses of shingles and were down to bare rafters. The attic was completely exposed to the early October sky—still blue, but only tentatively so at this late date. Couldn't Grandma make do with an aide like everyone else for just one dinner? Well, of course I went anyway—not so much for Grandma as because I didn't want to be the family chain's weak link.

After she died, Grampa did a slow slide from his house to a retirement apartment and finally to Mom and Dad's for a year. But after Dad died, Grampa had to move out. He kept falling, and Mom couldn't lift him back up by herself.

Now his address was reduced to this: Bed 2, Room 234.

Lord, if I ever end up in a nursing home, I hope my memory fails me completely. I wouldn't want to remember and know how hard it is for my visitors to step inside these doors. I probably would remember, though. I remember things too well.

"You look so beautiful!" Grampa would rave whenever I appeared around the curtain room divider. "So healthy!"

And I probably did. Only a few minutes before, I might have been feeling wearily middle-aged as I steered the pickup through the swarms of college students on Monroe Street. I could have been wishing I didn't remember so well how old thirty-two seemed back when I was in college. But each time I pushed open the glass doors of the nursing home, the first inarticulate cry seemed to magically bring the bloom back to my cheeks. My Nikes always felt unforgivably springy as I passed the wheelchair-bound patients in the hall.

"My granddaughter," Grampa would say to an aide, clutching at me. "Doesn't she look wonderful? Lord!"

I would cringe and give the aide an apologetic smile. Why shouldn't I look wonderful? I was breezing in from the fresh rain, from picking strawberries or canning tomatoes or pasting rainbows on a wall; these women had just come from emptying someone's bedpan—if they'd been lucky enough to get there in time. Often they'd be coming from a worse mess, and here was my grandfather, expounding on my wonderfulness, demanding they confirm it. No wonder their nods were sometimes sullen.

But Grampa never picked up on this. He would rave about me and rave about them—"Angels of mercy, that's what they are!" But heaven help me if I devoted thirty seconds and a dozen words to these angels. "Nobody ever listens to me," he'd mutter the instant he realized I was dividing my attention. "I'll just shut up. I'll be damned if I'm going to talk anymore . . ."

Well, that'd be the day.

A listener, that's what he wanted. That's probably why I often came here when I was down. It didn't cheer me up, but at least I could play audience. He didn't care if I was bright and witty. Didn't even notice. A witty visitor might have cramped his style, in fact, breaking up his monologue with too many unnecessary comments.

Maybe that's why I was here now. I felt lousy on these new drugs. Sitting here was the extent of my usefulness. Perching on the only available seat, the closed lid of his portable commode, I prepared for the strange ride his ramblings always took me on. One minute he'd make me want to weep with his fond memories or his blunt, no-nonsense talk of death, the next he'd be boring me with complaints concerning the incorrect manner in which the kitchen staff persisted in cutting his toast.

Today he began with his usual chronicle: the bedsore on his heel, the humiliation of incontinence, and how long he'd had to ring for pain pills before he got anyone's attention the night before last. (The moment they left his room, the Angels of Mercy mysteriously transformed into the Goddamnest Bunch of People You Ever Saw.)

"Look here." Grampa lifted a gnarled hand. "Can't even zip my own zipper anymore."

Thick purple veins twisted around shadowed hollows sunk between the bones in his hands, hands that had coaxed decades of flowers into bloom, harvested seasons of fruit from his carefully tended trees. Stephanie and I grew up on the produce he took pride in delivering, the variety names scrawled on torn bits of old envelopes and tucked into the corners of the bulging boxes. Red Haven peaches, Blue Lake pole beans. Sometimes we were even allowed into his garden to pick berries, but we usually blew our welcome. It wasn't the gorging of the raspberries that threw him, it was our carelessness in eating them before the number of pints had been duly noted. "For cryin' out loud, you kids! You'll louse up my production records!"

Now, after cultivating the best garden since Eden, he was stuck here, where the posted activities schedule in the elevator carried the listing "Basic Gardening" with a smile-faced daisy. What could they do here? Poke a pumpkin seed in a paper cup of dirt, kindergarten style?

Grampa had moved into another old story now, something about a car he'd bought back in 1958. "That Oldsmobile outfit, they always did right by me . . ." He talked on, staring off as if seeing everything he described. "Just like cutting my legs off, taking my car away, telling me I couldn't drive anymore . . ."

My eyes drifted to the wallpaper behind his head. Lousy match job on that seam, and it was already curling at the ceiling. They should have taken my wallpapering bid instead of just going for the lowest.

A framed needlework picture Stephanie had cross-stitched hung there, a still life of garden produce. I can't believe the hours those things must take—thousands of tiny, perfect stitches. Wonder she wasn't blind already. One she'd made for me bore this Bible verse: "Whatsoever thy hand findeth to do, do it with thy might." I'd mentioned once that I thought this just about hit the nail on the head as far as my philosophy of life went, and the next thing I knew, I had my own wall hanging of it, all done up in fancy stitched letters. That's how Stephanie is, always so thoughtful. She'd die before she'd forget your birthday, and even has this little notebook for jotting down everybody's favorite colors and clothing sizes. But cross-stitched pictures are her favorite gifts.

I tried one of those kits once, but as soon as I was half finished and saw that, sure enough, it was going to look pretty much like the picture on the box, I lost interest. I like doing patchwork quilts, where the outcome holds an element of surprise.

"Now tell me," Grampa was saying, evidently winding down. "How have you been? How's that good husband of yours?"

"Well, he's—"

"How are things out on the farm? You know, I tell so many people, 'That's my granddaughter and her husband, running that outfit.' I get such a kick out of you kids, selling those strawberries and raspberries all over town. I shouldn't say it, but I thought you were halfway nutty when you bought that run-down old place. You bragging about all the blackberry thickets and how many pies you were going to make. Not even knowing how those things can take over. And marrying a hippie . . ."

"Oh, Grampa, Gil wasn't a—"

"No, Gil's all right. I've got to give him credit, he's turned that into a pretty good little sideline business. But at first I thought he was kind of odd, with the long hair and the wooden bumper on that van thing he used to drive. But I tell you, honey, you've got a good one there."

"Well, I like him, Grampa, he's—"

"One of the little aides here, she's just as cute as she can be, but, oh, does she have a time with her bum of a husband. Ought to leave him, that's what, but they've got three kids already. Well, people have such problems with their families. Criminy! When I hear it, I just have to thank the Good Lord for my blessings. I've had a good life. A good family. I look at my pictures up there and I think, 'Fred, quit your complaining now. You've got so much to be thankful for.' "

I stood and pushed aside the commode, moving closer to the wall at the foot of his bed that was covered with pictures of all of us, everything from his own formal wedding portrait to a snapshot of Cousin Laura, with her dark gold hair glowing in the candlelight, taken just this past Christmas.

"Now that's Laura, isn't it?" Grampa said.

"Uh-huh." He was working hard, these days, to keep it all straight.

"Well now, what do you think? I got a note here from her says she's starting a new book."

"That's what I hear." Laura was a professor in the English department at the University of Oregon and had already published two biographies of little-known but very interesting women writers. Mom and I had been quite impressed.

"I thought maybe she'd have a baby. What does she need with another silly book?"

"Grampa! You don't really think her books are silly, do you? Aren't you proud of her?"

"Well sure. I'm proud of every one of you. I look at those pictures, honey, and I think, 'By golly, they've got my genes.' "

Not bad genes to have either. I'd be grateful for his skin genes anyway—he was remarkably unwrinkled for eighty-nine. My mother, too, looked young for fifty-seven. But probably I just got the talk-a-lot gene.

"Yup, every one of you—bits of me. Life goes on."

I peered into the eyes of all my family members. Maybe I *wouldn't* want to lose my memory if I were lying in a nursing home. Maybe that sense of things going on would make it tolerable. Seemed to be the thing he clung to.

And then my heart banged hard with a surge of adrenaline—like death remembered.

What if a person ended up with a blank wall?

Chapter 5

Of course I'd heard about Carla Holcomb. Who in the building trades hadn't? At the mere mention of her name, carpenters and bricklayers cast their eyes heavenward, as if begging divine protection. "I hear you've been summoned by Her Majesty," one of the electricians said when he heard she'd lined me up for some wallpapering.

I tried to withhold judgment. These guys can be pretty hard on women with strong opinions about what they want. On the other hand, maybe she had it coming. When somebody moves to town, buys a house that's practically brand-new, and then proceeds to rip it apart with remodeling, it's not too surprising she gets a reputation for being tough to please.

I knew she was this new Dr. Holcomb's wife and about my age, which was sort of unsettling. How could anyone my age be married to a doctor? Okay, it's not that amazing. I'm not a kid anymore. But I still feel like one.

Now whenever I go up to Timber Mountain for a job, I always have to fight the urge to greet the homeowner with the revelation that this used to be *my* woods. That's how I think of it, anyway.

"Do you realize," I want to say, "that this used to be all forest? We used to play here. I had my first *kiss* here." Sure,

I know they've done nothing but innocently buy a listed parcel. In my heart, though, I want them to at least be mindful of what's been lost.

But as usual I kept my mouth shut that February day when Carla Holcomb opened one side of her massive double doors and motioned me to follow. Her distracted manner made it clear right away that, at the moment, wallpaper selection was more minor irritation than major concern.

"I don't know what to do in here," she said, waving at the acreage of her living room. The plush carpeting still had that brand-new smell. "What do you think?"

I was thinking she had the most striking coloring—one of those dark-haired types who can get away with red lipstick. I was thinking her house sure did have a drop-dead view of the valley. I was wishing this killer headache of mine would go away.

What I said was, "Why don't I go ahead and measure first?"

"Whatever." She sipped her coffee and flipped through a wallpaper sample book, her hair falling forward.

This particular hairstyle she wore has always intrigued me—the one where it's parted on the side and constantly falls over one eye. Wouldn't that bug a person? I put it in the same category with long fingernails and high heels—might look good but sure as heck makes it tough to get any work done.

I measured, jotted down numbers, and multiplied. God, I felt awful. Every morning was like this on the bromocriptine. Accomplishing anything before ten A.M. was unthinkable. My day couldn't start until the metal band cinching my skull loosened and released my brains. Now, by eleven, I was on my feet, but that was about it.

Seemed like any drug that made you feel this bad had to be powerful. You'd think it would work, right? But after three weeks of daily headaches, my temperature chart had so far done nothing but meander up and down at random, no sign of the clear, sustained rise indicative of ovulation. And although theoretically, a break from a schedule of optimum target dates for sex should have come as a welcome relief, knowing that any day could be Egg Day had made me crazier than ever. *Just have sex as you normally would*, Dr. Lowell instructed. (But make sure it's at least every other day, indefinitely. Ha!)

"So can't we just toss the chart?" Gil wanted to know.

"Oh no! If I *did* get pregnant, I'd need to figure it out right away and quit taking this stuff. They aren't sure about possible birth defects . . ."

Carla hefted the sample book to show me a page. "What do you think of this?"

"Yeah, that's a nice one." I totaled my numbers. "But it's up to you. I don't pretend to be a decorator. I just hang the stuff." Oh, I might try to steer somebody away from Mylar, which is miserable to hang, or grass cloth, which, like the little girl with the curl, is very good when it's good, but horrid when it's bad. Beyond that, I try to keep my mouth shut. As a result, I'm here to say I've pasted up some of the ugliest paper ever manufactured. And afterward stood there with my customer, smiling, accepting thanks for a job well done, and agreeing that, no, there's nothing cuter than sea horses on the wall of a bathroom.

Now lots of women, when you show up to give estimates for a job, will act halfway apologetic, go into a song and dance about having hung wallpaper themselves in the past, but now, with the kids, and so little time . . .

But Carla obviously wasn't the type to feel guilty about paying somebody to work for her, even though as far as I could see, she didn't have the usual excuses—kids, a job, arthritis. Her husky voice had the authority of a born delegator. It was easy to picture her telling a batch of caterers exactly how to handle her dinner party, and I'll bet she had people to clean her house too—they probably used a riding vacuum cleaner.

When I finished measuring, she offered me a cup of coffee in the kitchen. She had a television in a custom cabinet tuned to the Olympics.

Sports don't interest me normally, but the Olympics are different. While Gil makes fun of the "Up Close and Personal" segments, I eat up the details about each athlete: what she wants, why she wants it, why it's so darned hard to get it. And—will she get it?

"You ski?" Carla asked, eyes on the screen.

"Used to. Now just cross-country. You?"

"Oh sure."

"Mount Bachelor?"

"Sometimes, or Hood. But mainly British Columbia.

Stan's into helicopter skiing. You know, where they drop you off at the top of a mountain and you ski all the way down."

"Gee, that's a new one for me." I pictured Carla hopping from a helicopter in a hot-pink-and-electric-blue ski getup, her dark hair spilling out over one of those stretchy headband things, mirrored goggles curving over her eyes.

On TV, a blonde in a sleek silver suit rocked on her skis in front of the starting hut. Barely recovered from her third knee surgery, the announcer said, she was determined to win a medal. Her father, who had coached her, was dying of cancer. Yeah, okay, I could relate to that. Now she was flying down the mountain, whooshing around the flags, spraying snowy fantails. Excitement charged the announcer's voice as the seconds ticked. Great time, so far. And then, *yow*. She cartwheeled.

"Oh shit," Carla said.

A tangle of legs and skis and dashed hopes. We watched the spill in replay.

"Not *her* favorite day," I said. Two bits says her knee was wrecked again. Would she be sorry she tried? After all, a gold medal wouldn't cure her dad's cancer. Honestly, the things people stake their hearts on . . .

When I came back a month later to actually hang Carla's paper—bold stripes in blue, green, and maroon—she talked to me the entire time I worked.

"What do people *do* in this town?" she asked, staring out the big windows as I stood on the ladder, adjusting the upper edges of a paper strip.

"You mean like for fun?"

"For anything!"

I'd been hearing this lament about Mary's Bend all my life. What the heck were people so hot to do that they couldn't do here? Go to nightclubs? Eat sushi?

I stopped to take in the view myself. So pretty, the way the giant firs framed the valley. To the east, clouds hung in the shadowy foothills of the Cascades. To the south, the light greens and pink blushes of spring stood out among the town's dark evergreens. I could see the red roof of the courthouse clock tower downtown.

Living here forever meant I not only knew all the stores

down there, I also knew each one's mercantile history. The Stork Shop, for instance, used to be athletic shoes, before that, very briefly, antiques, before that for many years fabrics, and way back in the distant past I remember it as part of Nolan's Department Store, whose smooth rounded name I associated with the fat pillars flanking the corner entrance. My earliest memories of drag-along shopping are centered here. I remember the candy counter, where my sister and I would be rewarded for endurance, and the pattern counter where I first wrestled with one of life's great mysteries, the disappointing fact that dress pattern envelopes contained only marked tissue paper and not the pictured dress itself. Which wouldn't on any account, my mother tried repeatedly to explain, look like the picture anyway because we'd be using different fabric . . .

Beyond the central business district, on the other side of town, would be our farm, although actually I couldn't at this distance distinguish it from neighboring trees and fields. Off to the right I could see the high school where I'd gone, where my mother had gone too. In that building, beside a drinking fountain just outside the gym, my mother first spotted my father, a college boy, in a sharp-looking yellow V-neck sweater . . .

"This place is practically dead," Carla said.

"Uh . . ." I cleared my throat. "Must seem quiet after Portland."

"Ha! To put it mildly."

Well, quiet was fine with me. I had a million things to do—hang wallpaper, fix up my own house, mind my rental, grow a garden, can fruit . . . We had the Willamette River, clean enough, I'm proud to say, to jump into on the hottest August days, and a public library full of more books than I could ever find time to read. I don't claim I never got bummed out, but I was never bored.

"I thought I'd like the change," Carla said. "I can't believe the traffic here compared to Portland."

"Yeah, it's been getting worse, though."

"Oh please. What do you want? Dogs sleeping in the middle of Main Street?"

I laughed. I guess it's all relative. To me, bad traffic is not being able to make it through downtown without getting stopped at a light. I hope it'll stay that way in Mary's Bend. I like living in a town small enough that when you're driving along and the car radio reports a car accident, your first reaction is still *Oh my God, who got killed?* as opposed to *Damnit! That wreckage better not be blocking my route.*

"Maybe I'm not being fair," Carla said. "Maybe I'm just grouchy about this place because things aren't working out like we planned."

Ah yes—one of those leading remarks where you're not sure if you're supposed to ask for more or not. I hesitated, measuring a new length of paper.

"Maybe I should go ahead and look for a job here," she said.

"You worked, before?" Snip, snip, snip.

She nodded. "Consulting. Personnel. You know."

Actually I didn't. The term *consulting* always mystified me. What did these people actually *do*? I understood things like growing a flat of raspberries and selling it, or being paid to hang wallpaper for some timid soul who had watched too many slapstick comedies where guys got tangled in sticky paper, their feet stuck in buckets of glue. But consulting? I stood in awe of anybody who managed to get money just for their advice.

"Not a lot of openings for personnel consultants in a town like this," Carla said. "But then, I hadn't planned on working. I planned on getting pregnant."

"Oh." I stopped, my glue brush poised over a fresh strip.

"Everything was going to be so great. Stan being taken on as a partner here, getting his practice going. Finding this house. Only, according to my plans, by now I should be pregnant with kid number two. Instead, I can't even get started on number one." She sighed. "I should probably find a job—anything, just for sanity's sake. But I keep thinking, oh why start now—I'll be pregnant by next month."

"How weird," I said. "I'm having trouble getting pregnant too."

"No kidding?" She looked at me as if for the first time. Then she was off, spilling her tangled medical history, which included questionable ovulation and the discovery of at least one tube damaged by an attack of pelvic inflammatory disease during college. Also, her mother had taken DES when she was pregnant with her, a nasty factor—seemed to screw a woman up in ways the doctors hadn't even begun to understand.

"My therapist says I have all this anger. I can't help thinking that if Stan had let me try to get pregnant back when I first wanted to, I wouldn't have had such a hard time. But oh no, he had to be completely finished with med school and into a practice before we could have kids. Which is ridiculous. Lots of people have kids during med school. Sure, they struggle, but so what? Now they've got their kids whereas all I've got is this great big empty house. I mean, who cares?" She glanced at me. "I suppose you think that sounds ungrateful."

"No." Then I qualified it. "Well, I wouldn't go making that complaint to some homeless person on the streets . . ."

"Of course not—"

I sponged down a strip of paper. "On the other hand, you'll never catch me arguing that a big fancy house is better than a baby."

She looked surprised. "I appreciate you saying that. Really. I'm so tired of people who think a person can't possibly have a problem if she's got plenty of money."

"But that would be stupid. That's like saying money *is* everything."

Then she smiled. Maybe for the first time. At least it was the first time she'd smiled broadly enough to reveal this disarming gap she had between her front teeth.

"So what's *your* story?" she said. "I want to hear *every* detail."

Should I have told her? To this day, even knowing how it all turned out, I'm not sure. But at that point, an invitation to spill my guts on the subject of baby craving was an invitation I was in no condition to decline.

"Well," I started in, "we've known for quite a while I might have trouble getting pregnant . . ."

Chapter 6

When we were first married and the farm was new to us, I couldn't walk back up the gravel driveway after getting the morning paper without thinking how incredibly lucky I was. I'd look at our old clapboard house sitting among the oak trees and I'd think, *this is ours*. Our place, where we're supposed to be. All the unchanneled energy and vague ambitions of my college years had coalesced into one wish—to make this place a real home, a thriving little farm.

We hadn't been married a full month before I ripped into the living room, prying away cheap paneling, tearing off wallpaper so old it was glued to burlap over boards. Outside, I loaded the entire, thirty-year accumulated contents of the previous owner's private trash heap into huge dumpsters, and since widespread concern about overloaded landfills was still in the future, I watched the disposal company's trucks winch those bins up and haul them away with nothing but the purest satisfaction. For days on end I hacked wild blackberry vines which Gil forked into big piles for torching. Evenings, after the fire had burned down to campfire size, we roasted hot dogs and ate them with orange pop. We were like little kids, throwing ourselves at everything with more energy than brains, playing house, playing farm, playing the game Stephanie and I used to call Big Life.

The first winter we had the best time trying to drain our swampy fields, stomping around out there with shovels, connecting one trench to the next, trying to coax the standing water into the ditch along the road, both of us going at it like kids at the beach, completely absorbed in our miniature dikes and aqueducts. Even when it became clear we were getting nowhere, we hated to quit. It was just too much fun! I was almost sorry when Gil discovered the government conservation program that would help pay for the laying of buried drain tiles by machine.

And then there was that first time I marched into the county courthouse to plunk down the property taxes on our farm. They weren't much at that point. The assessor had placed our house squarely in the hovel category. I used some money I'd earned from my flower shop job. Proud? Hey, I thought I was Scarlett O'Hara in green velvet curtains, hanging tight to Tara.

It wasn't all fun and games, of course. The pride of ownership wears thin when you discover that what you own is a failing septic system. Also, Gil and I did not always work that well together.

Once, in a sweet, rather rapturous letter, his Gramma Emma wrote how she loved to think of us working together on our farm, how it reminded her of those lovely weekends she and Grampa used to spend on their Orange County fruit ranch.

Well, I loved to think of us that way too, but the truth is, our cooperating skills weren't that great. Gil and I argued over every little project. He was mainly interested in his ever-expanding garden and berry plantings and viewed with suspicion each brilliant suggestion I offered for improving the house. I had to convince and cajole him every step of the remodeling way, and I believe he would have lived happily in the house exactly the way it was when we first moved in. Until the night he and the bathtub crashed right through the rotted floorboards, that is. And if I tried to get in on the farming or yardwork decisions . . . well, Lord knows if I so much as walked outside and picked up a pair of pruning shears he'd start right in bossing me.

So maybe Gil and I weren't meant to do every last thing together, and this is probably why I began to long for a project where I wouldn't need Gil's continual approval, and so convinced my dad to loan me the money for that first fixer-upper. The thing is, though, after ten years, we'd figured out this was okay.

What I'm trying to say, I guess, is that even if we were no longer exactly starry-eyed, on a glorious April morning like the one I'm remembering, I could still get that old feeling. *Grateful* is the word, I guess. We had this place, we had each other. The orchard was blooming. Birds twittered. The air smelled fresh, and I had a wonderful sense of being at the beginning of things.

That morning I was heading for what promised to be a first-class estate auction, and then Gil and I'd have the rest of the day to putter around the farm together. Hey, if I didn't know it would probably start an argument, I could have announced to Gil that this was the best day of my life!

Now nothing gets my adrenaline going quite like a good estate auction. All those one-of-a-kind treasures, pieces of history—some family's history anyway. Like the walnut-framed love seat I bought out at Jefferson one time. Every time I sit on it, running my hand over the indentations on the carved grapes, I picture the little culprit, somebody's long-ago toddler, standing on the velvet upholstery, idly teething.

Gil gives me a hard time about auctions. He's forever trying to make me promise to stick to my list or not go over a certain dollar limit. You'd think he'd give it up. How am I supposed to know what I'll do in the heat of bidding? Sometimes things get bought by accident.

"How on earth can you buy a major piece of furniture by accident?" he'd demanded the time I showed up with the Hoosier cabinet in the back of the truck. "And without even getting a good look at it first."

Okay, failing to check out something first is a definite no-no, but that cabinet was going so cheap! And it did turn out to be a nice piece—the only trouble being the five or six layers of thick white paint that had to be gooped off before the niceness actually appeared. But I did the gooping. And without griping either. I couldn't. Not with Gil just waiting for me to start so he could say "I told you so."

Driving to town, I hummed along with Jesse Colin Young on the tape deck, a song we'd played at our wedding, the one about the morning sun and a life that's just begun. I wasn't thinking about the words, though. I was thinking about the newspaper ad. *Contents of vintage house, eighty-year accumulation.* Hot dog. But when I'd almost reached the listed downtown address, I realized I had to go to the bathroom. Well shoot. I'd never make it past the previews unless I stopped at the library rest room.

A few minutes later, locked in the cubicle, I discovered the blood.

My period? No fair! How could it be? My temperature was still up this morning! Even if it was going to drop, it wasn't supposed to do it for several more days. Well, damnit. Blood was blood. Another month down the tube. Shoot. And this time, taking Clomid again on top of the bromocriptine, I'd really had my hopes up.

Not that I had even admitted it to myself. Waking this morning, feeling so happy and optimistic, I had barely acknowledged it had anything to do with my temperature chart. No, I wanted to think I was just bursting with energy because it was a beautiful spring day. But now I had to face it. Life looked great, assuming I was pregnant. If I wasn't, a sunny day might as well go gray.

I didn't even feel like going to the auction now. I'll go home, I thought. I'll go home and crawl back in bed.

But then, I couldn't just crash every time this happened, right? Life's too short to get bummed out over something the rest of the world seems to agree is not all that high on the scale of Bad Things That Can Happen. Hadn't Dr. Lowell's nurse clued me in to this just the other day? "Believe me, Betsy, not having kids wouldn't be the worst thing in the world." And she should know, right? She had three teenagers who were giving her a terrible time. So buck up and all that . . .

In the driveway at the auction site, people jostled each other in the narrow aisles between the tables and crowded at the door of the house itself. I signed up for my numbered auction paddle, then fought my way through, jotting down likely pieces in my notebook—a solid little kitchen table with turned legs, a nice Eastlake table.

In a small, slant-ceilinged bedroom upstairs I found a single-size brass bed—perfect for a child's room. Simple styling—fine for a girl or a boy. I took out my trusty magnet and held it against one of the corner cylinders. It didn't stick. Solid brass. Boy, I'd love to tackle this. I ran my hand over the metal, smooth but tarnished to a deep brown. Three cans of Brasso, hours of elbow grease, but it would be absolutely perfect in the room we were saving for our kid. I imagined it polished golden and spread with a bright patchwork quilt . . .

I stopped, remembering that this month's brief time of hope was over. The GO sign for kid room decorating was now at least a month in the future.

I'd never get away with telling Gil the bed was for the rental, and I couldn't very well hide something so big. To the extent he felt he could issue orders, he'd decreed that I not buy things for this phantom child of ours. "If we can't get pregnant," he'd said (and he didn't want to have to repeat this because it was such a drag, actually putting the prospect of failure into words), "if we can't have a baby, it's going to be bad enough without you stocking up on a lot of props to cry over."

From down in the parlor came the sound of someone trying out an old pump organ. I recognized the plaintive strains of "Long, Long Ago," a piece I'd enjoyed playing on the piano as a child. What had I found to be sad about back then?

Suddenly I felt so tired. I had cramps. Maybe if my period had held off, I could've bowled over Gil's objections to the brass bed with dauntless optimism. But I could never stand up to him like this, defeated.

I clumped back down the stairs. Often a so-called estate sale turns out to be nothing more than the leftovers of an ambitious spring cleaning. This sale was an honest-to-goodness lifetime accumulation; unfortunately, today, it was wasted on me. I kept thinking of that Bible verse, something about the folly of laying up treasures on earth.

At the foot of the stairs, I shuffled through a box parked on a cedar chest—dusty letters and picture postcards with spidery greetings. I found a photo in a crumbling cardboard folder. My throat tickled. Dust, I thought. Then I realized: No daughter would have left this wedding picture. No granddaughter would have turned down her grandmother's cedar chest—not unless she was so hard up she absolutely had to have the money. And even then, wouldn't she have made an appearance here today, if only to give the liquidation some semblance of dignity? I glanced around, stepped aside for more buyers heading up the stairs. No tear-glazed eyes here. Only the hard glitter of acquisition anticipated.

Clearly, this was the house of people who'd had no children.

This is it, then, I thought. This is what'll happen to our things if we don't have kids. I looked at the wedding couple. Had they wanted children? Did people have any choice one way or another in those days? My mom tells a story about one of my great-grandmothers who, after the difficult delivery of my grandmother, declared that one baby would be quite enough for her, thank you very much. And that's all she had. But what did she do? Kick my great-grandfather out of bed? Books hint of birth control back then, but rarely spell it out. Somehow the secrets of women aren't printed, for saving. The best, the ones that clue you in to someone's true feelings, are always the handed-down stories, the ones the men never hear.

I put the picture back in the box. My sister, Stephanie, would have children. I might get nieces and nephews, anyway. But then I pictured some future niece, a miniature Stephanie, picking over my life's legacy. "Oh, Mom, what would I want with Aunt Betsy's dusty old stuff?" The imagined comment sprang easily to mind, probably because it was more or less what Stephanie herself had said when we went through Grandma Conklin's things. It bugs Stephanie now that I took home the bits of old lace and cutwork tablecloths she didn't want. Antique linens have become chic. I suspect she'd like to do that scene over again.

Now I made my way back outside, wondering if I even wanted to stick around for the sale. What did I need with more junk? Wasn't my fix-it list long enough? Maybe I should go home and do something useful. Like the dishes.

Then I spotted my old friend Susan looking over the rusty tools leaned against the detached garage. No mistaking that fat brown braid swinging to the small of her back. She had her new baby in a front pack and her little girl was getting into everything. What was the girl's name? Something odd, I forget.

Susan hadn't turned around. I stooped to a box of embroidered tea towels, buying time. Should I pretend I hadn't seen her and beat it out of here?

Come on, I was beyond freaking out at the sight of an infant. Wasn't I?

Sure, it's hard, that first time you see a baby after you've figured out you may not be having one—ever. People are having babies all over the place; odds are good you'll run into a perfectly adorable and heartbreaking example somewhere between the doctor's office (where you've just been clobbered with your pessimistic reproductive outlook) and the clinic parking lot.

And I hadn't done too well at Gil's faculty potluck last month when I turned and for the first time saw him with somebody's newborn in his arms. That look on his face, that soft, unguarded expression, a smile so sweet he'd have a fit if he realized he was wearing it in public.

Well, it turned the blackberry pie in my mouth to glue.

But he only smiled when he saw me watching. No flash of sadness or guilt, no furtive hot-potato handoff of the guilt-wrapped bundle. "Want to hold him?" he said.

Was he kidding? Didn't he know I couldn't trust myself within a whiff's distance of a newborn baby?

But after these initial hits, I had sincerely hoped for a certain toughening up. Unfortunately, it seemed any toughening I'd managed had been effectively offset by the growing desperation of the wait.

So, truth was, I could never predict a baby's effect on me. It depended. Was my chart looking good? Was I optimistic, confident my own baby was just eight and three quarters months away? Or was I down, like today, dark blood flushing away hope?

I stared at the embroidered pattern of dancing plates, forks, and spoons on a towel, thinking it was probably a good day to just make a discreet run for it . . .

"Betsy!"

Oops. She who hesitates . . . I stood, preparing to act surprised, only to be surprised for real.

Susan's right nostril sported a tiny red jewel.

"Susan!" Yow. Was it punched right through? "How's it going?"

"Great. You?"

"Fine. Fine." Darn. I never know how to react to this sort of thing. Am I supposed to ignore it? Compliment it? Try to fake a certain erudite interest, as in *Ah, I see you've adopted the custom of the women of the Pandeeshi Marajii.*

"What are you up to these days?" she said.

"Oh, same old stuff." I laughed nervously. Shock had silenced me in the first critical moments after noticing the nose ornament; beyond that I could hardly pretend I had suddenly become aware of it.

Her little girl held up an old rhinestone button she'd found. "Yook!" she said. "Beaufital!"

Susan gazed at her daughter, charmed, and glanced at me, inviting me to be charmed too. "Yes, Freya, it is, isn't it?"

Freya. That was it.

I gave her a tentative smile. A three-year-old child did not have the same devastating effect on me as an infant. Mine was a case of baby hunger; I had trouble even thinking of a baby and a toddler as part of the same species.

Still, the suspicious stare she returned unnerved me in a different way. Had she somehow zeroed in on my maternal deficiencies?

Susan stooped with difficulty, one arm around her strapped-on baby, retrieving dropped buttons from the lawn. I helped her.

When we stood again I said, "Let me see this little guy. What's his name?"

"Anson. It means 'of divine origin.' "

"Oh." Humble City. Well, to give her a break, maybe all kids were?

I steeled myself as she pulled back the blanket.

"Oh, how cute!" My enthusiasm was actually intense relief in disguise. No danger of going to pieces over utter perfection here. Anson not only did not look divine, even *cute* seemed charitable, what with the foul-smelling green goo she had smeared over his cheeks.

"He's got a rash," she explained. "I think he's allergic to something." Her lips poked out, her voice slid into that talking-to-Baby tone mothers use. "Something man-made and nasty. So we're all fixed up with a nice comfrey salve."

He responded with a major squall, making conversation temporarily unnecessary.

Have you ever noticed how hard it is to talk to mothers of new babies? They are abysmally poor at eye contact. The baby must be cooed and jiggled. The baby must have undivided attention or it will grow up warped. Being the onlooker reminds me of the way you feel when your college roommate embarks on a passionate romance. Love takes priority! Love requires privacy! Love needs this room! (So disappear, sister.)

I watched Susan do her mother thing. Mothers are in love too, I guess. They're gone, lost to you. No cure for it but to get a baby and fall in love yourself.

I stood there, conscious of the occasional person doing a double take at Susan's nose jewel. This is not the sort of thing we see too often in Mary's Bend. I tried to steal a closer peek. Maybe it was just glued on?

She looked up and I quickly shifted from nostril to baby. "So. How many does Anson make now?"

"Three." It came out like a sigh, a combination of fatigue and pleasure.

"Three, that's right. I'm pretty sure I'd heard you were pregnant." Over the years I had followed her story through the grapevine. She'd had two marriages, although which husband was the father of which of these kids I could never keep straight. At one point I thought she was on her third, but it turned out her husband had given himself a new name when they went to live at Rajneeshpuram for a while.

We'd been best friends in junior high, and were, to all appearances, peas from the same pod. The same middle-class homes, closets full of clothes we'd sewn with our moms. We spent the summers tanning at the high school pool, trading boyfriends back and forth. Once, after coming down from my first kiss in the woods that later became the Timber Mountain development, I'd fled to her house, where we shared a hysterical half hour, giggling on her bed, snorting over poor Jeff Slaney's terrible technique. Positively reptilian, we agreed, the way the tip of his tongue flicked in and out.

"Why didn't you *warn* me?" I kept shrieking.

"Serves you right for stealing him!" she threw right back.

And another time, later, after experiencing kisses more satisfactory, we'd spent an afternoon flopped across *my* bed, listening over and over to the same record: "Take my hand, take my whole life, too/For I . . . can't . . . help . . . falling in love with you. . . ."

We swooned at the ecstasy of surrender, the power of fate to sweep us to our inevitable destinies. Love, marriage, babies . . . it wouldn't be long now.

We were both appalled when a school assembly featured a woman journalist who advised us each to plan our life—we could hardly believe our ears—as if there would be no man in it! If one came along, fine, she said, but don't be counting on it. Well! What could you do but write her off as a dried-up old biddy?

Looking back, I see that what the woman said made perfect sense, but to us, in 1968, it seemed incredibly radical and, frankly, unbearably pessimistic. Plan your life without a husband and babies? Hey, that *was* life.

At least that's what I thought until I hit college and read *The Feminine Mystique.* Shoot, I'd started it expecting a how-to on developing allure. Instead it was an alarm clock, buzzing me from my swoony daydreams. I woke, bolting upright with the realization I was headed straight for indentured housewifehood. From then on, I kept my eyes wide open.

Susan, however, elected to swoon. Not that I didn't do my best to enlighten her during that freshman year we roomed together. In fact, by spring term, she was fuming that having me around was like living with her own mother.

We both understood this was not meant as a compliment.

But the funny part was that although she'd steered clear of the middle-class, suburban swooning style of the mother she sneered at, underneath it was the same thing—always letting some guy call all the shots.

Now, with both of us back in Mary's Bend, we ran into each other occasionally, but we could never return to the days of that black-and-white snapshot I still have—the two of us with our arms around each other, getting ready for my first boy-girl birthday party, getting ready for our lives.

"Three kids." I shook my head. "Amazing. I remember when you had Jesse. I just couldn't believe anybody my age was a mother."

"I *was* pretty young. And when I look back, it seems younger all the time. I definitely did not know what I was getting into."

I remembered running into her at the food co-op, the awe I felt at the sight of her billowing dress, her long hair falling over her shoulders. For years we had done everything together. Now she had moved on without me. It was all terribly mysterious and amazing, but certainly not something I had the slightest inclination to try myself for the present. Gil and I had only been married a year. We had jobs and a farm and a lot of work to do.

"Remember when I visited you in the maternity ward?" I said. "That was before they even built the new hospital."

"What a nightmare. Thank goodness I managed to have these two at home. You'll have yours at home, won't you? I mean, when you do?"

"I don't know." And then, because we have this history, this connectedness, and because I fairly ached to talk about it, I took a deep breath and plunged in. "The thing is, I'm trying to get pregnant, but I'm not having any luck."

Her face lit up. "But you're trying?" This was only the first instance of something I was to experience again and again. Nothing warms the hearts of mothers like the news that you want to join the club. Beneath their fatigue, they're full of this secret joy, and all questions of flakiness aside, I'm sure Susan was sincere in wanting me to have it too.

"So what's happening?" she said. "How long have you been trying?"

"I've been taking fertility drugs for months."

"Oh." Her glow faded. "You really want to mess with those? They're so unnatural."

I shrugged. "My body's unnatural. It doesn't get pregnant."

"But maybe there're other things you could try. I have a

friend who couldn't get pregnant and finally she went to this naturopath. The very next month . . ."

For a good ten minutes she happily spun stories about boards under mattresses to straighten spines and correct ovulation problems, big toe massages to get pituitary glands back on track, herbal teas combined specifically to promote wholeness, wellness, and fertility. And of course, diet, diet, diet.

"Oh, Betsy," she concluded, laying her hand on my shoulder. "We need to get you back in sync with the universe, that's all."

That's all?

"Susan, I'm not ovulating. I don't think the universe cares."

The expression she beamed at me was open and loving and I hated it. I hated it the way I hated those touchy-feely encounter groups we did in college. This indiscriminate radiance always made me want to back away, made me feel I was hopelessly uptight for not at the very least responding with some minimum of warmth and appreciation.

"But *why* don't you ovulate?" she said gently, earnestly. "Why is your body holding back on you? Everything's connected with your mind, you know."

Oh please. Funny how you can almost forget why you stopped getting along with someone. Funny how fast it can all come back.

Freya was going through another box. I turned to her, my voice unnaturally bright. "Finding anything good in there?"

Grinning, she seized a hose trigger nozzle and aimed it at me like a gun.

"Freya." Susan blushed, peeling the child's pudgy fingers from the nozzle. "We never give her toy guns. I don't know where she picks this up."

Freya howled.

"So," I said over the noise, "are you bidding on anything?"

Susan struggled with Freya. "We're just here—ow—we're just here for fun. Freya, stop it! If you're angry, please use your words, not your kicks."

"Gimme that back!"

Susan ignored her. "We don't have any money anyway."

"Well, if it isn't the beautiful Betsy Bonden."

I turned. "Oh, hi, Eric."

Believe me, his greeting had nothing to do with me being beautiful and everything to do with him being full of it. He threw his arm around me and squeezed tight. As I've mentioned, he is good-looking and not to be ignored, so Susan took this in with obvious interest. And okay, I'll admit it—maybe because of those long-ago rivalries with her, I was enjoying this to a degree, but strictly for the impression Eric made, not out of any genuine craving for his attention. That's not to say there haven't been times since I married Gil when outside reaffirmation of my attractiveness has been welcomed. Who doesn't go for that occasionally? But attractiveness wasn't high on my list of concerns these days. I was too preoccupied by my lack of the right stuff reproductive-wise.

"When are you coming over to measure for paper at the McBee house?" Eric said.

He pulls this constantly, leaves me hanging, wondering if he wants me for a job, then acts as if it's been settled long before.

"Eric," I said, "all you have to do is call for a bid like everyone else does."

He looked hurt. "I thought we had an understanding."

"Hmm." I used to think so too, but the one time I showed up at a house of his on the assumption he wanted me to measure for paper, he put me down, said he hadn't even decided if he wanted to go with paper yet. Ever since then I've hung back, even though in the end I think I've done all his jobs for him.

"They've got the paper all picked out," he said.

"Fine." Now I was wishing he'd take his arm away. Big lug. He had to feel the stiffness in my shoulders, but when a guy doesn't want to get your message, it's amazing how impervious he can be to even the most obvious body language. But we women are raised to be nice, taught not to make a fuss. I don't know, maybe there's some cute, flirty way to get out of situations like this, but I never learned it. For me it's either "get your hands off" or pretend not to notice.

I think Susan would have enjoyed sticking around to see if this went anywhere, but Freya was dragging her away. "I have some pamphlets about fertility," she called back over her shoulder. "I'll put them in the mail for you, okay?"

Eric grinned. "Fertility, huh? Sounds interesting."

The auctioneer's voice crackled over the mike as he tested it.

"Oops, looks like they're going to start," I said, making a break for it. "I've got a job Monday but I'll come by Tuesday, okay?"

I found a lone folding chair at the end of a row where Eric couldn't join me.

The auctioneer wore a cowboy hat on his greasy black hair and his gut hung over a tarnished silver buckle. His son and daughter—straight out of the same mold—held aloft the various items for the audience while their mother sat at a makeshift desk, smoking cigarettes and writing down the sale prices and buyer numbers.

I usually succumb to auction fever as readily as the next person. You get excited, you get competitive, you end up buying things you wouldn't bother carting home for free if you had three minutes to think calmly about it. But today my adrenaline refused to pump. I didn't even care when that obnoxious woman from Forget-Me-Not Antiques got the Eastlake table.

"Okay," the auctioneer said. "A box of letters! Historical memorabilia! Good postcards. Lots of nice stamps in there for you collectors!"

The daughter scooped up a fistful of envelopes from the box I'd found on the cedar chest.

"Who'll give me twenty-five?"

No paddles.

"Who'll gimme twenny gimme twenny gimme twenny?"

No paddles.

The girl held up the wedding picture.

"Fifteen?" sang the auctioneer. "Come on, folks!"

I stared at the portrait. I couldn't stand it, nobody wanting those two. "Ten," I said, flashing my paddle.

He surveyed the crowd. "All in and all done . . . sold!"

Now they were hauling out that little brass bed. One last time I pictured it in our spare room. I imagined the fuzzy head poking out from under the handmade quilt.

But somebody else's child was going to sleep in that bed. Not mine.

I didn't want to watch them sell it.

I paid for my box of discarded memories and headed home.

Chapter 7

Gil shut off the Rototiller and stood for a moment in the backyard patch he'd tilled, enjoying the quiet, the sun on his shoulders, the smell of the freshly turned earth. He shook out his wrists, which still tingled from the machine's vibrations. Then he stooped and raked his fingers through the dirt, pleased at the way it had crumbled beneath the tines. Always impatient about letting the dirt dry out, he often as not ended up with mud balls.

His tradition of jumping the gun dated from the very first spring they had the farm. On the first day it stopped raining that year (barely into March) he had driven his ancient John Deere tractor out into the big field, where the front end promptly sank like a horse going to its knees. Their new neighbors hung on the fence and took it all in like a show. *Don't that beat all? Know-nothing hippie.*

By now he'd finally lived it down, and picked up some good money tilling gardens for people along the road. But every spring he'd go out there and sink the tractor to the axles again. He became something of a local weather vane. Nobody else even ventured into his field or garden until word got around that Gil Bonden had his tractor out for at least the second try of the season, if not the third.

Now he raked the rich, black dirt smooth. Lettuce, tomatoes, sugar snap peas, sweet corn, watermelon—he was ready to start marking out the rows when, through the apple blossoms in the front orchard, he saw their pickup slowing for the turn. He glanced at his watch. Home already? He heard the truck door slam, then the front door of the house.

He kept on hammering in stakes, tying them with marking string. She'd come out pretty soon. Tell him who she'd seen at the auction, what she'd bought, whether she figured to strip it or paint it. He just hoped she'd kept all the medical bills in mind when she was flashing her bidding paddle. That song and dance she'd always do before leaving about the nice, reasonably priced items she hoped to get for the rental . . . Who'd she think she was kidding? She'd come home with whatever she'd gotten excited about, period.

After a while, he glanced at the house. What the heck. Mildly curious, a little annoyed at feeling obliged to stop work, he dropped his dirt rake and headed for the back door.

In the dim interior, he strained for light as his eyes adjusted. From the clank of plates and rush of water, he knew she was loading the dishwasher. It smelled stuffy. Must be time to put up the screen door.

"'Lo," he said. "Aren't you coming outside?" On a day like this she'd usually want to be out hacking blackberries or blasting every structure and vehicle in sight with a rented power washer.

"I will in a while."

"We can clean this up later if you want."

"That's okay." She still hadn't turned around.

"So where's the stuff?"

"What stuff?"

"From the auction."

"Oh. Over there." She jerked her chin toward a cardboard box out on the sofa.

He took a quick look. "This is it? Come on, you've got some monster chest I've got to go back and haul or what?"

"No. Really. That's it."

"Betsy Bonden went to an auction and didn't buy any furniture."

"So send it to Ripley's. You ought to be happy after your tight-money lecture."

He went over to the window seat and opened a window to the sweet, fresh air. Out in his garden, birds were hopping over the dirt, pulling at worms.

"Hey, here come the deer." He never got tired of the constant parade of wildlife. With no pets to scare them off, animals were forever creeping from the forest and browsing through their yard. Quail laid eggs against the house; brown rabbits watched from the grass when Gil brought the milk in from the front porch. Every summer there was a new spotted fawn or two. "Better hurry. They're taking off. Don't you want to see?"

But Betsy didn't turn from the sink. She really *was* in a funk.

"So," he said, "was the auction a bust or what?"

She shrugged. "Guess I wasn't in the mood." Her face was hidden from him as she kept scraping the dishes.

He brought the last of them over from the table. "Since this is the first time in recent memory you haven't been in the mood for an auction, you'll have to forgive me for being a little curious here."

"I don't know, for once it all just looked like . . . stuff. Just somebody's leftovers with everybody picking through it."

He got a can of beer from the fridge. "That's what an estate sale is, all right."

"But what's the point? They accumulate all these things, then they die and that's that."

"As opposed to what? Living forever? Not accumulating things?" He popped open the beer. "You're mad at them for leaving stuff behind?"

"Not mad. Sad." She was staring at the vaseful of dead daffodils on the counter.

"It's sad they had chairs to sit on instead of sitting on the floor all their lives?"

"Oh, Gil."

Hell, he knew what she was getting at, but why encourage gloom? He took a drink of beer. The sun was out and he had a garden to plant. Why waste time discussing the transitory nature of existence?

"If you're going to be like this," she said, "maybe I should have bought this little brass bed I wanted."

"Well, why didn't you?"

"Oh, I'm sure you would've loved that. If I'd come home and said I'd bought it for our baby."

Is that what all this was getting around to? "Look, as soon as you're pregnant, you can go hog-wild, okay?"

She shut the water off. "I got my period today."

"Oh." Hormones, then. Good grief. You could spend hours trying to sort it out and in the end it all boiled down to chemistry. "That's too bad."

She turned on him. "Is that all you can say?"

Jesus! She hardly gave him a chance to absorb the news.

"Sometimes I wonder if you really want a baby the way I do."

"I want a baby," he said. "As I recall, I'm the one who first said we ought to go for it."

"Okay, okay."

"But don't try to get me arguing about who wants one more." Just because it wasn't taking over his life like it was hers didn't mean he didn't want one. As a matter of fact, somebody had handed him a newborn the other day—he couldn't even remember where or whose it had been now. But he remembered thinking as he held the amazingly lightweight bundle, *Yeah, okay, this would be good. This would be worth trying for.* Not a negative feeling. After all, they were going to a lot of trouble to get one of these; he liked being reminded it would all be worth it in the end.

"Come on, hon," he said. "Haven't I said I'd go along with whatever you want to try?"

"Yeah, and I appreciate it, but—don't you ever get discouraged?"

He shrugged. "I just figure it'll work out." He put his arms around her. "Sooner or later." Most things had so far. Why imagine the worst? He gave her a pat, thinking of the huge pile of seventh graders' papers he was supposed to be grading, the broccoli he wanted to get in the ground.

She pulled away. "I hate that."

"What?"

"When you start patting my back like that. Like I'm dismissed. You're done hugging me and you can't wait to get on to something else."

"Oh come on!" Jeez, you had to be so careful with her.

If she wasn't picking apart every word he said, she was reading his mind.

She turned back to the sink and flipped up the tap lever. She grabbed those dead daffodils, aimed them stem-first down the drain, and switched on the disposal. The blades chewed the stems and the brown-edged heads twirled grotesquely, jerking and spinning for the longest time before they were finally yanked down.

Chapter 8

I couldn't get over the shock of it, me desperately wanting a baby. Me, who, like I said, went practically rabid after reading Betty Friedan at the tender and volatile age of eighteen. Me, who sparred with the college president on the subject at an honors banquet.

I'm not sure how it began, but I was seated next to him, and I remember observing that surely the expensive education offered by his institution was hardly necessary if one was to be limited solely to a future of housewifery and reproduction. Au contraire, he replied. How could a woman expect to maintain civilized relationships with her neighbors without a solid grounding in International Relations?

I am not making this up!

Anyway, after taking on this guy, I came home for summer vacation itching to fight anybody who dared suggest motherhood as a suitable career for anyone with a triple-digit IQ, starting with my poor father, for whose benefit I found myself tossing off a lot of newly learned cracks concerning men as the oppressor class.

"Now hold on," he said one night at the dinner table, "if this is me you're talking about, I'm still the member of the oppressor class who's paying for your education."

"Exactly. And wouldn't it be a big waste to spend so much and then have me turn into some dumb baby machine?"

Stephanie gasped.

Dad drew back as if I'd called his own mother a dirty name. "You listen here, young lady. I happen to think motherhood is the most important profession there is."

Right. What bunk! Motherhood on a pedestal. If men really thought raising kids was so great, they'd be in there hogging the job for themselves.

"And exactly what is it you're so eager to do instead of having a family?" Dad went on, his blood pressure rising visibly. "If that's not too presumptuous of me to ask?"

I summoned the defensive tone commonly used at that time by liberal arts majors across the country. "Is there something that says I have to decide right now?"

Mom hurried to intervene. "She's young. She has lots of time to think about it."

I appreciated this. I *was* young. Young enough to feel that the three years until graduation were forever. And besides, the future seemed formless, frightening. I mean, *please*. He was making me nervous.

"I've always thought people who didn't have kids were selfish," my father said. "After all, somebody raised them. Don't they owe something to the next generation?"

"Dad, with overpopulation, it's probably more selfish to *have* kids."

"She does have a point," Mom said.

"But . . . but . . ." Dad was all but sputtering, enraged at having the two of us gang up on him. "Society has . . . values to maintain. We have to encourage certain things. Family and . . . well, *family*."

"Of course, I never felt like I had a choice," Mom said, musing along her own lines. "After the war, everybody had babies. Nobody questioned it, not out loud anyway. Frankly, I wasn't that thrilled with the idea. If it had been up to me, the girls might never have been born."

"Shirley!" Dad's eyes darted to me and Stephanie in alarm.

"Oh, don't look so shocked," Mom said. "They've heard me say that. And I feel I *can* say it because they know I'm glad they *were* born."

Dad harrumphed. "Doesn't that prove my point? If it weren't for society's encouragement, you'd have missed out."

"Well, I was lucky. But what about the people who have kids and then find out they're not cut out for it? All I'm saying is, we shouldn't make everyone feel they ought to have kids."

"I want to have lots of babies," Stephanie put in. "You'll have plenty of grandkids, Daddy."

"Stephanie," I said, "you've really got to read this book. If you're counting on babies to be your total fulfillment, you're gonna wind up on the shrink's couch!"

"Oh, Betsy . . ."

"I'm serious. That's what's happening to women all over this country."

Dad turned to Mom. "Where is she getting this stuff?"

Mom shook her head, trying to look innocent. She'd been reading *The Feminist Mystique* too.

Not much hope for Stephanie, though. Well, fine. Let her do the glorious motherhood thing. I had better plans. Vague maybe. But better.

Deep down I must have figured I'd eventually want kids, though. When I look back, it seems like my relationship with Gary Randall started its slow slide down the tube at about the point where he informed me he had no intention of ever changing diapers.

"Somebody changed your diapers," I reminded him, probably sounding a lot like my dad.

He shrugged. "Sorry, I still think it's disgusting."

Well, he was entitled to not want kids, but his above-it-all attitude toward the basic facts of life struck me as a grave character flaw.

Gil, on the other hand, when given this litmus test question, "Would you change your baby's diapers?" simply said, "Sure," and then added, "What's the alternative? Let the kid sit there in its poop?"

This was after I'd graduated and come dragging home to Mary's Bend. Leaves you at loose ends, breaking off an engagement a month before finishing college. I hate admitting this politically incorrect fact now, but my plans had been hinging on Gary's, and I hadn't done one lick of job hunting for myself. I wasn't even sure what sort of job I wanted.

I quickly came to the solution arrived at by so many of my contemporaries: grad school! It was time to get specific. Architecture maybe? But that didn't seem quite right. I liked *old* houses. I decided to work awhile and think about it.

Dad offered to let me ring up duck decoys at his sporting goods store. Actually, I wouldn't have minded except for the embarrassment of publicly presenting myself in such unliberated circumstances—working at Daddy's store. To salvage my pride, I decided to look for men's wages and eventually found myself pushing a broom down the hall of the junior high I once attended. The pride-saving aspects of this job were questionable. Imagine how much I enjoyed running into the puzzled looks of my eighth grade teachers. My face rang a bell, I'd see them thinking. But no, couldn't possibly be Betsy Conklin. She was a *good* student, wasn't she?

Well, you know how these things go. What looks like a less than promising situation might turn out to be the luckiest . . .

I had always been sort of curious about the person belonging to the incredibly messy desk in Mr. Gil Bonden's room. All I'd learned in my first two months on the job was that he apparently didn't hang around after school one minute longer than he absolutely had to. But on this particular day when I pushed my broom through his open door, he was sitting there grading papers.

"Oops. Sorry," I said.

"That's okay."

"I'll come back."

"No, I was just going to leave."

I remember just sort of standing there. He sure didn't look like the other teachers. He was younger, for one thing, and while the rest of them seemed grayish, this guy had been rendered in living color—ruddy cheeks, curly dark hair long enough to give the principal pause.

Suddenly I wished with all my heart I was not wearing overalls and a faded bandanna.

He'd stopped what he was doing too and was giving me this self-conscious little smirk. *Look at me pretending to be a teacher*, he seemed to be saying. Naturally I took this as an invitation to start chattering, because suddenly it seemed crucial he realize that I, too, was in disguise. *I'm really a princess*, I wanted him to know, once again abandoning any semblance of ideological correctness. *Kiss me and see.*

Over the next months, he seduced me by cooking the world's best pot roast and by listening to me at length on the subject of sexual equality. Such a clever technique, the way he would keep nodding so agreeably, watching me with those liquid brown eyes, his mouth curved in a sweet and distracting smile. Soon I'd have trouble keeping my anger focused. How could I feel threatened by this gentle person who declared right up front that women shouldn't have to do all the housework (with a judicious omission, the fact that he didn't much care if *anyone* did it)? Before long, I'd get bored with my own raving and—the heck with it—I'd start in kissing him.

While we were going together, we talked long and dreamily about what we wanted out of life: a little farm somewhere, a peaceful, laid-back existence. Kids might be part of it, but that was way off in the future, somewhere on that lengthy and optimistic master To Do list which also included such items as "Clean up the environment" and "Work for world peace."

But maybe there is something to the idea that, ultimately, people pair up with an eye toward reproduction. Some women look for strong genes, or smart genes. Sensing I was not supermom material, I was probably unconsciously drawn toward good-daddy genes. I needed a hero willing to haul himself from a cozy bed in the middle of the night if a little voice came wailing. Not just somebody who'd be Mr. Fun, the occasional horsey ride across the carpet. I was in the market for somebody who'd scrape the strained carrots off the ceiling without expecting a star on his chart for it. Just a hypothesis, but I had a feeling Gil might be that sort of somebody.

The one time I remember flat out asking him about it we were sitting beside a driftwood fire on the beach at Neskowin.

"Think you want to have babies?" I said. "Someday, I mean?"

"I'd like to have babies with you."

Well, falling in love sure does have a way of filling up a vague-looking future with a lot of promising visions, and somehow Gil had made the proposition of having children—

anathema to me only two years before—suddenly seem like a reasonable idea. A terrific idea even.

These weren't just any kids we were talking about, after all. These would be *our* kids.

Or so we'd assumed.

Chapter 9

Have I mentioned we talk a lot in our family? At least on my mother's side we do. In my grandfather, I had seen this tendency toward loquaciousness manifest itself in more than a simple enjoyment of conversation. Two years ago he had talked, his doctors claimed, straight through hip surgery. Then for days afterward, in a drug-induced haze, he endlessly strung phrases together, fragments of old monologues adding up to nothing comprehensible. What it boiled down to was this: If someone stood at his bedside and looked at him, he had to talk. It was an obligation.

This streak runs right through the generations. On the transatlantic crossing from Europe, my great-grandmother no doubt bored silly everyone in the steerage compartment, and if I ever had a baby, it would probably take a postdelivery gasp, flush pink, and immediately start discussing its first impressions of the hospital's new birthing room.

Unless it got Gil's "still waters" gene, that is.

Now not to knock the contemplative life, but being a bunch of motor-mouths does have its advantages. Talking can be a great way to kill time, although I hate that expression. Seems a sin. Life's too short. But once in a while you hit a stretch that's hardly tolerable, let alone something you'd want to savor. That's where the gift of gab comes in handy.

Like the time Stephanie and I chattered away six long months with Mom when she was in the hospital after a car accident. What did we talk about? Nothing. Everything. We speculated on the future and endlessly rehashed the past, telling stories, comparing memories.

"I'll never forget that time Dick Reed was supposed to take you to the Rainbow Formal," my mother would say. "I'd made you the red velvet dress? That was the *worst* fabric—the way it kept slipping under the presser foot . . . And then he backed out and told you he'd already promised Debbie Cornell? Oh, I could have killed that kid with my bare hands."

"But I went to that dance with Craig Bates."

"Yes, but that was *after* the Dick Reed trauma. Oh, Betsy, don't tell me you don't remember! You had the whole house in an uproar."

And then we'd be off, trading forgotten details. Stephanie used to go up to the hospital and do the same thing. "Terrible times we've survived" seemed to be our favorite theme, probably because we were trying to reassure ourselves we'd make it through this too, although clearly nothing so far had come anywhere near the seriousness of our mother hovering near death, hooked to machines with no unhooking in sight.

Well, she did recover, five or six grueling surgeries later, but through it all she claimed time and again that talking worked better than morphine.

So, with "Get pregnant" high on my To Do list, my inclination was, naturally, to talk about it. And not just to Gil, although I certainly did plenty of that. It's really nice, after all, to have someone who will willingly hash some obsessive subject over with you long past the point where there's a single new word to be uttered. But as the months passed, I began to sense a certain straining of his patience. Also, I got fed up with his constant steering of the discussions toward the financial impact of all this. What a bummer that the insurance wouldn't pay!

"If you want to quit," I'd snap, "why don't you just say so?"

"I didn't say I wanted to quit."

"It's only been—what?—eight months we've been trying. That's not so long." Pure bravado, of course. Eight months with medical intervention was not your normal eight months of trying, and it felt like forever.

"All I'm saying is, I think we ought to have a plan. Like pick a point in the future and just say, okay, if we're not pregnant by then, we quit."

"But I can't *do* that. You *know* I can't."

Living my life was like watching a movie or reading a novel; I never knew how I'd react to some hypothetical future situation. One time, for instance, while driving up our road, we chanced to spot a guy taking my grandmother's chairs from his truck. Yes, *our* chairs, the ones we'd just discovered missing from the shed. I made Gil stop, jumped out, confronted the guy, and started loading the chairs in *our* truck. Lord, to this day I can't believe I did that. People get shot over less. Anyway, the point is, how's a person like me supposed to predict, much less promise, what she'll do in a tight spot?

Ordinarily my mother would have been my likely confidante, and I longed for the sympathy she'd be sure to dish out, but she was overdue for good news, not more problems. My infertility would be her grief too. The children I couldn't have were the grandchildren she couldn't have.

And there would be no telling my sister without it getting back to Mom.

Mostly I found myself talking to Carla. The first time she called me was the day news of the abandoned baby in Grants Pass hit the paper. A freezing newborn had been found beside a mountain road, placenta still attached. Barely alive, he died on the way to the hospital.

That was a first for me. Not the first story like that I'd ever read, but the first since I'd realized there might never be a baby for us. At other breakfast tables across the country, people were shaking their heads over their newspapers at the utter waste, the callousness. But for the first time, our house joined those where more anguished cries went up. "Not fair!" we howled by the thousands.

I imagined a hierarchy of grief. The women who'd just started their periods cried especially hard, but the ones who'd recently miscarried cried even harder. And the mothers of stillborns—did they read about the abandoned baby and feel even worse? Or was it like my theory of maximum happiness in reverse? Maybe everyone was just as purely miserable as they could possibly be.

I wept and raged that day, detailing to Gil at length the many flaws in nature's perfectly lousy baby distribution system. Look here, we could give a baby a snug little bed in a snug little room in a snug little house. But oh no, here's God, dropping them on people who dumped them in the mud. The stupid stork could do better, for crying out loud! And I *was* crying out loud.

When Carla phoned, I could tell her whole morning had been wiped out too.

"I just had to talk to somebody who'd understand," she said.

But the next time a similar story appeared, she seemed almost annoyed when she called and it turned out I *hadn't* been crying. Another baby in a trash can. Okay, it was sad, it was awful, it made me sick. But emotionally I just couldn't afford to flip into full-fledged hysteria every time a story like this showed up on *Eyewitness News*.

Nevertheless, Carla and I got into the habit of phoning each other, to compare notes, to commiserate. Sometimes, though, it seemed as if her discouragement and bitterness were actually contagious.

"Why do you keep calling her?" Gil asked at one point. "Every time you talk to her, you seem to feel worse."

"Well . . ." Like most people, I don't appreciate having my irrationality held up to me. Then suddenly I figured it out. "Maybe it's that even though she doesn't say the *right* thing, at least if I tell her this is really getting me down, I know she isn't going to give me some line about relaxing, or it's all for the best or any of that."

Gil grunted. "I guess that's something."

"Well yeah, it means a lot. Beats talking to people like Pat."

He rolled his eyes, remembering how upset I'd been when the "just relax" bromide had first been offered over the phone by an old college roommate, who also thoughtfully assured me that she and her husband felt confident that if they hadn't been able to produce the darling boy and girl they had, they could have easily adjusted, easily found other satisfactions in life to make up for it. Hey, that had perked me up no end.

I guess at some point, during some pelvic exam (they all blur together), I must have complained to Dr. Lowell about my sense of isolation and said yes when he asked if I'd like to talk to another infertility patient, because one Saturday afternoon I got an unexpected phone call.

"My name is Ann Sether. You don't know me, but I used to be an infertility patient with Dr. Lowell. He asked me to call you, just to talk. Is this an okay time?"

"Sure, sure. Hang on a sec." I settled myself on the love seat in the dormer at the top of the stairs. "That was nice of him."

"Yes, Michael's wonderful, isn't he?"

Michael? She calls him Michael?

"You *used* to be an infertility patient?" I said. "Does that mean . . . ?"

"Oh yes, I got my babies. I have to tell you, I think the world of all the doctors in that group. You really are in good hands."

"Yeah, I know. Dr. Lowell's a great guy, but it's just so frustrating—"

"Oh, you don't have to tell me. I know what you're going through. I was struggling for years trying to get pregnant. Of course I already had my oldest, so that made it even worse. I got pregnant once. Why couldn't I do it again? I took Clomid for a whole year. Michael simply could *not* figure it out because my charts looked so good. You're doing temperature charts, aren't you?"

"Yes, but—"

"Well, mine looked perfect. So why wasn't I pregnant? I swear, it was the strangest thing. It wasn't until the month my husband got sick. And we had that bad freeze? A pipe broke and flooded the kitchen. For the first time in ages, getting pregnant was the *last* thing on my mind, and what do you know, I did."

I shifted uneasily. This was a woman who'd been through it. She couldn't possibly wrap this up with—

"I can't help but think relaxing really helped."

No. I stared out the window. She didn't say that. She couldn't have. "Uh . . . don't you think maybe your number just finally came up? I mean, this whole relaxing bit—"

"Oh, I know what you're going to say. I was sick of hearing it too. But maybe I should have listened, because in the end, for me, it was true."

I looked at the receiver in my hand. Would it be tacky of me to hang up on her?

"Naturally I never mentioned this to Michael. He was so happy. I wanted to let him think the pregnancy was entirely thanks to his little pills."

"Relaxing's got nothing to do with it in my case," I said. "I haven't had a period on my own in years. If I relax and do nothing, nothing's going to happen."

"Oh." Ann Sether contemplated this for a good second and a half. "But let me tell you the real kicker of my story. After Michael delivered David—that's my Clomid baby—he asked if I wanted my tubes tied. I said, 'You can't be serious. After all the trouble I've had? Why bother?' So guess what? At my six-week postpartum I'm pregnant again. Of course, this time I wasn't happy at all. We never planned for three, so I was practically hysterical . . ." She went on to describe at length the ironic flip side of infertility, the unwanted pregnancy, how she threw up every day and her feet swelled monstrously in the summer heat . . .

While she talked, I studied the mossy roof below the window, noticing the terrible condition of our gutters. Wet, crumbled leaves had sifted through the mesh guards and composted there. Weeds sprouted now, fresh green oak leaves pushed their way from deposited acorns. When I reached in to clean them out, I knew I'd find all sorts of bugs too. Lord, everything around here but me was so incredibly fertile. Left alone, even our gutters would support entire ecosystems.

"But in the end," Ann Sether was saying, "my little Cindy is the sweetest of them all—a whole headful of golden angel curls." She sighed, a pause honoring the beauty of this glorious child. "You know, Betty—"

"Betsy."

"I truly feel for you, and if you'd ever like to come over and talk about it, I'd love for you to see my kids."

"Thanks." I could hear them squabbling in the background. "I'll keep that in mind."

I wrote down the number she gave me. Then, after we hung up, I thought, *What am I doing?* and crumpled it into the wastebasket.

I went into the living room, where Gil was grading what were apparently some very amusing English papers.

He looked up, still smiling.

"That call? It was a patient of Dr. Lowell's." I flopped onto the sofa and reeled off a summation of Ann Sether's monologue. "I don't know, Gil. Other people's failures depress me and so do their successes."

"Nah! You're not depressed because that woman had babies. You're depressed because she didn't listen. You're depressed because she told you to relax. You're depressed because she wasn't getting pregnant even when her charts were perfect and your charts aren't that hot."

"Yeah." I brightened. "That's right." Somehow this cheered me, having my gloom properly analyzed. "At least I hope that's right. I don't want to start being mad at everybody who has kids."

"You won't. You're not like that."

"How do we know what I'm like if I can't have a baby? I've never failed at this before. And already I'm not doing a very good job of feeling happy for other people. Shoot, I thought I was going to start bawling right there in Gibson's when Sharon Carlson told me she was pregnant."

"Sharon Carlson?"

"Honey. You know, the woman who orders all my wallpaper?" I waited for some glimmer of recognition. "The one who steers so much business my way?"

"Oh, okay, sure."

"Sometimes it seems like everyone's pregnant. And Sharon was complaining about it, too."

"To *you*? Hey, I don't claim to be Miss Manners, but isn't that pretty darned insensitive?"

I shrugged. "She doesn't know we're having trouble."

"Huh. I thought everyone knew."

"No, Gil, everyone does *not* know. What do you think? I automatically blurt this out in the first minute of every conversation?"

"No! I know you better than that." He flipped a paper facedown and picked up a new one. "I'm sure it's usually at least the second minute before you get going."

"Thanks."

I sat there, somehow reluctant to leave, and he went back to reading. He chuckled.

"What?"

"Oh, some of these kids. Essays on 'When I'm a Parent.' "

Gil noticed I wasn't leaving. "So how come Sharon's not happy about it?"

"Oh, she's sort of happy. It's just that it's six months earlier than she planned, see. She doesn't want to be big and heavy during the hot weather."

Gil rolled his eyes. "Shit, Bets. Nobody says you have to be happier for these people than they are for themselves. Anyway, what's going to make you happy is getting pregnant yourself. And whether other people get pregnant or not doesn't have anything to do with us."

"Hey, that's right," I said, this somehow striking me as a clever new concept.

"This isn't the Olympics. There's no fixed number of medals."

I was smiling now. "You know what makes me feel better?"

"What?"

"You!"

"Well thanks," he said, mildly surprised. "You mean I actually said the right thing for once?"

"Yeah. Big shock, huh?"

He looked pleased. "Hey, why don't you call Amy?"

"Really?"

"Sure. I'll bet she'd at least *listen* to you. Seems like that's what you want more than anything else."

Given this impulsive permission to leak news of our dilemma to his side of the family, I looked up the number of his sister, who still lived in L.A., where she and Gil had grown up. Amy would understand. No secret she and Ed had been wanting a baby for several years now—once you start having miscarriages, it gets harder to keep it to yourself. "Poor Amy,"

Gil and I would say to each other every time news of yet another loss reached us. Only now, though, was I beginning to have some inkling of what she'd been going through. I'm afraid a good deal of the sympathy I'd felt for her up to this time was actually pity for her pathetic determination. Why couldn't she see the writing on the wall?

Believe me, I've paid for these thoughts many times over since then, wondering if that's what people were saying to each other about me. *Why doesn't she wise up and quit?*

Anyway, I phoned Amy. She listened to my story as Gil had predicted and then, as if her mind were some computer, called up related tales of women she'd known over her own years of trying, women who had fertility problems similar to mine, women who had eventually become pregnant.

Now this was more like it. This is what I wanted to hear.

"Do you think I should try to find a support group?" I asked her. "Didn't you say you were in one once?"

"Yes, I used to be. It helped for a while, I guess, but . . . well, whenever someone announced a pregnancy, you just knew everybody was thinking, *I wish it were me.* The pregnant person would almost feel guilty. That's what happened to me. Then when I had my first miscarriage, I felt funny going back. After that if I needed to talk about it, I'd just phone somebody. I still had a couple friends from the group."

We talked a little more and then I thanked her for playing shrink and said I'd better not run the long-distance bill any higher.

"Betsy?"

"Yeah?"

"Um, one more thing. Actually, I'm pregnant again right now."

"Yeah?"

"Six months."

"Six months!"

"I know," she said, acknowledging my surprise that she could be so far along without us hearing. "It's just I didn't want to tell anybody, because . . . you know." Her voice hummed with a quiet excitement. "I've never made it past twelve weeks before, so it looks like maybe this time . . ."

"Amy, that's terrific." To my intense relief, I realized I

meant this. I wasn't envious, just happy for her and Ed. So maybe Gil was right. Maybe I hadn't yet reached the point of abject personality deterioration.

After that, whenever Gil saw me flipping through our little book of phone numbers, he'd kid me with his nasal operator's voice: "You have reached the infertility hot line. At the sound of the beep, please leave your name, temperature, and your husband's sperm count. We'll get back to you as soon as we can."

"Will you shut up?" I'd say, but I'd be laughing as I dialed, knowing the relief of spilling my guts to Amy was just moments away.

To Do

Work

Bid—Copper Pot Coffee Shop
Tues—Smith-Wartons
Thurs or Fri—Finstads
Call Eric re check

Clean gutters!
Pick up Rx
Fabric—Amy's baby quilt
Clean up perennials
Pie Fri—faculty picnic
Pay property taxes
Pay bills
10th St. rent
Mother's Day cards
Fix pantry door
Visit Grampa

Chapter 10

Michael Lowell pulled the chart labeled BONDEN, BETSY from the rack on the examining room door and glanced at the most recent note: menstruating—Clomid check.

He pushed open the door. "Hello," he said, the absence of his usual joviality acknowledging what was bound to be her less than perky mood.

"Hi." She handed him her temperature chart.

He held it up by a dog-eared corner. "What have you been doing with this?" The sheet's soft, soiled creases were ready to tear with repeated foldings.

She ducked her head. "Studying it a lot, I guess."

"And these extra dots?"

"Just trying to see if there was any correlation with my temperature later in the day."

"Betsy, once a day's enough. You don't want to get obsessed with this."

She glanced up.

"It happens," he said a bit defensively. "I've had patients go into actual clinical depressions over this."

"No." She bugged her eyes at him. "Really?"

Oh, so that was it. Faring somewhat worse than he'd realized. Interesting, she'd never struck him as the type to go off the deep end. Not for lack of a baby, anyway. But then, you could never predict in these cases. He ought to know that well enough by now.

It never ceased to amaze him just how strong this urge to reproduce could be. Back when they'd had so much trouble with the Rh babies, they'd see women deliver and lose baby after baby on the slim chance that one might finally make it. Senseless, but as an intern he'd learned the lesson fast: Never count on rationality when it comes to women wanting babies.

He frowned at the chart for quite some time, more because he needed time to think than because this particular combination of dots and lines required lengthy analysis. Maybe it was time for a bit more aggressiveness. He cleared his throat. "Let's try something, shall we? I'd like to see if we really are getting an ovulation here."

"I thought you said we definitely were."

He affected innocence. "Did I?" He probably had. Why not present things as optimistically as possible? That was his usual approach. And perfectly reasonable, too, until you ran up against one of these patients who saved every casual comment on a mental recorder and played it back at you later. "The thing is," he said, "you're not getting pregnant."

Her voice was cold. "I'm aware of that."

Good God. She must be hell at home these days. Sad to see this deterioration. Before, she'd been the type to rush in for her annual exams and rush out, always on to something more interesting. Now he had the feeling that, given the chance, she'd sit here and grill him for answers all day.

Of course, all of his infertility patients were in varying states of misery; many of them he'd never known any other way. They came in depressed initially, and each time they returned without having conceived, they were naturally *more* depressed. Rumor had it these women occasionally experienced flashes of optimism between appointments, but he never saw it. He had no idea what some of them had been like before they found themselves in the grip of this obsession. It was only in dealing with someone like Betsy, who'd been his patient for over ten years, that he was reminded of the fact that these women no doubt had remarkably different personalities before they had unwillingly become professional infertility patients.

He chose his words carefully. "I just meant, Betsy, that if we got a pregnancy, we'd say, 'Okay, here's where she ovulated, this little blip on the graph.' But since we aren't we have to keep wondering what's wrong."

She blew up a stream of air, puffing out her bangs. "So what is it you want to do?"

Okay. He exhaled. Moving on to the next argument . . . "It's called an endometrial biopsy. We take a little section of the uterine lining and check the hormone level."

She winced, clamping her knees together. "A little section?"

He nodded, keeping his face blank. Actually, he probably should have done a biopsy sooner, but he'd been hoping she'd turn up pregnant before he had to.

"Wouldn't that mean going through the cervix?"

"That's the only way in *I* know." He truly disliked this procedure. During his residency, his first biopsy patient had terrified him with her screams. He thought sure he'd put the curette right through the uterine wall. No one had ever screamed like that during one of his biopsies again, but the memory of it, and the reports of pain from subsequent patients less demonstrative, certainly kept this from being a test he suggested casually.

A few minutes later Betsy's feet were straining against his fuzzy stirrups.

"This may cramp a bit," he said, inserting the curette.

Her shocked eyes flew open. Her teeth clenched. "Don't I at least . . . uhhn . . . get a bullet to bite?"

"Oh well, we could look into that, I suppose." Maybe he should have given her a local. But then they usually weren't exactly wild about the idea of a shot in the cervix either. "Hold on now. Don't go away."

She growled. "I hate that. Every time you get me like this you have to say that. *Don't go away*."

Uh-oh, she was starting to cry. Eyes squeezed tight, tears dribbling down to her ears. Damn. Definitely should have used the anesthetic. Well, he was almost done . . .

"Here we go." He withdrew the curette. "That's it." He helped her sit up. "Okay?" She was sniffling, trying not to. He set a box of tissues on her knees. She set it aside. So what's this? You're not officially crying as long as you don't use a Kleenex? Oh, don't do this. He could handle women who cried. It was the ones who tried so hard not to that got to him.

Suddenly she was blinking at him, in a puzzled way. Her eyes seemed to sink back. "I'm . . . a little dizzy."

He steadied her. "Breathe deep now." She'd gone a bit gray. He buzzed for his nurse. "Let's try a wet cloth here." Surreptitiously he glanced at his watch. Over at the hospital, Stacey Winters was probably nine centimeters dilated and wondering where the hell he was. He'd debated cutting out earlier but gambled instead, first in seeing Betsy, then in going for a biopsy. He'd counted on her being the type to sail right through the procedure. *Come on, come on.* He couldn't walk out on her now. Not that there was any real danger here, but . . . damn. He never seemed to have the luxury of time. The longer he hung around here playing Dr. Sensitive, the angrier Stacey would be when he finally showed up in delivery.

At last a little color crept back into Betsy's cheeks. She pulled herself up. "You didn't tell me it would hurt like that."

He sighed. "I know."

"You could have warned me."

He glanced at his nurse. "Thanks, Rose." Then he added, "Check on Stacey, will you?" After she'd gone he turned back to Betsy. He'd lost his train of thought. Those accusing eyes . . . oh yes, he hadn't warned her . . . "But what if it doesn't hurt as bad as I lead you to expect?" he said. "Then I've scared you for nothing. And women are all different. I can't always tell. What's excruciating to one is no big deal to another."

"Oh, so I'm one of the wimpy ones?"

"No no, not at all. Look, if it makes you feel any better, I had one patient who'd had all sorts of tests—hysterosalpingograms, hysteroscopies, laparoscopies, you name it, all operating room procedures—and she claimed her endometrial biopsy was the worst. So, no, you're not wimpy. It really can be very painful."

She blew her nose and hurled the wadded tissue in the wastebasket.

"Come on, Betsy, even if I'd said, 'Look, this is going to be the worst pain you've ever experienced,' I'll bet you'd have done it anyway."

"How do you know?"

He regarded her sadly. "Infertility patients *always* do it anyway."

Then, trying to sound upbeat again, he hustled through an explanation of a new treatment regimen that might be interesting—ultrasound scans combined with properly timed shots of HCG—human chorionic gonadotropin—to help trigger ovulation.

He never doubted for a moment she'd go for it, but sometimes he did wonder about the wisdom of pulling every single new medical technique out of his little black bag. Twenty years ago most of these patients wouldn't have had a prayer for a pregnancy. Or, more accurately, prayer would've been *all* they had. But they'd go out, adopt, and be relatively happy. These days, however, in the name of helping, in the name of advancing medical science, he and his colleagues had to offer everybody the chance to try all the latest treatments. Then they had to sit back and watch half the women win big and the other half go bankrupt and psychotic hoping to. It was one of the few instances where he felt the gift of knowing the future would have proved truly useful.

Think of the grief he could spare the losers.

Chapter 11

An ambush, that's what it was. I'd walked into the clinic expecting only the usual indignities and instead found myself the subject of a surprise torture session. Lord, doctors must take some sort of class—Useful Euphemisms—where they learn to say, "This may cramp a bit," when they really mean, "This is gonna hurt like hell."

My innards didn't stop quivering with shock all the way back to the farm. But before Gil even came home from school and could hear my biopsy story, I started wondering if I'd been exaggerating the pain. For me, physical pain fades fast. So while I could remember that during the procedure I'd been thinking the pain the worst I'd ever endured, I already couldn't quite reconstruct it in my mind. And it *had* been mercifully brief. I'd certainly heard of women going through a lot worse.

I was following dozens of life stories now, thanks to Amy and Carla. Tales from the trenches, I thought of them, women's war stories. Medical histories filled with accounts of stressful tests, repeated surgeries, difficult husbands. In comparison, I'd been through very little.

Well, except for the brain tumor incident. That had to count for something . . .

Our adventures in baby making had gotten off to a hair-raising start last fall when Dr. Lowell sent me for brain X rays. This was nothing new, exactly. I'd been under a tumor watch for years, ever since I'd stopped having periods and discovered droplets of milk at my breasts. What a bizarre sign of infertility! Milk for a baby you can't even get started. But sometimes, they tell me, this spells tumor, so once in a while I'd humor the doctor with an X ray. Other times it was thanks, but let's pass on the radiation this year. Then the hospital in Eugene acquired a fancy new X-ray machine. Somebody had to use it, right? Somebody had to pay for it.

That's how I ended up flat on my back, eyes shut, listening to this state-of-the-art machinery whirring and clicking over my head, capturing slices of my brain on film.

I'll never forget the exact moment the call came the next day. I was hanging wallpaper under our kitchen cabinets. I remember staring at one particular little flower as Gil tried to sort out the news over the phone with some endocrinologist we'd never even met.

Something showed on the X ray. Looked like a tumor. These pituitary tumors tended to be benign, so the effects depended on what it pressed against as it grew. Blindness . . . paralysis . . . severe personality disorder . . .

Oh God. My personality disordered instantly. How did we get into this? One day I was in the doctor's office, cheerfully announcing that, yes, we were finally ready for that baby we'd been putting off, ready to take those fertility pills he'd always promised would be the answer when I wanted to get pregnant. Now, a week later, I was scared for my life.

Fear feels terrible. Makes you sick. I couldn't eat. I lost six pounds in the six days we waited for the follow-up appointment.

Then the machine whirred and clicked over me again. This time the technician, a guy about my age, did not joke around with me as he had the first time. This was serious. This time I'd get the verdict immediately. Some mysterious Wizard of Oz doctor hid behind lead doors, studying the films while I remained alone in that vault, lying on the slab of a table in case he wanted more films.

When the door squeaked open, my stomach lurched. The technician stood over me.

"It's okay," he said. "You can go."

I sat up. "No tumor?"

He shook his head, lips compressed.

In one huge rush I started breathing again. "Hot dog!" I waited. Was this all he was going to say? And then I noticed: He was blinking off tears. This *mattered* to him. Can you beat that? A man who X-rayed people every day without turning into part of the machinery?

He swallowed. "It was just a shadow."

I jumped off the table and hugged him quick and hard. Then I split. Entirely too much waffling around here. I'd make my break while the verdict was life.

Choked silent by the force of joy, I pulled Gil up from his waiting room chair and started dragging him out.

"I'm okay," I managed, swabbing at tears. "Just a shadow or something."

"A shadow? They put us through this for a shadow?"

"Gil." I fell against him. "Gil, I was so scared!"

Clinging together, we ran out of the hospital into one of those dramatic autumn afternoons where the sun lights the trees against blue-black clouds. We dashed through pelting rain into a Victorian-house-turned-café and ate lunch, grinning at each other like we'd just that morning fallen in love.

Whoosh! The future had opened up in front of us again. For a minute there I'd been worried. For a minute I'd been afraid that life was about lying on cold tables, shivering under the impartial eye of a machine, waiting for dreadful news. Silly me! Now I remembered that life was about gold leaves dripping jeweled rain. It was about shafts of sunlight hitting stained glass and blazing into rainbows. It was about eating the most delicious food I'd ever tasted with the best husband in the world . . .

It was about the pinch-faced woman at the next table who couldn't keep her eyes off of us, probably wondering what the heck we were so lit up about.

Finally I couldn't resist. I leaned toward her.

"I don't have a brain tumor!"

Chapter 12

I was sitting in a dressing cubicle in Shepherd of the Valley's X-ray department, flipping through a *Glamour*. Skinny bodies, pouty lips . . . I tossed the magazine aside. Should have brought a book from home. I stood up. I sat back down. What the heck, I couldn't have read anyway. All that mattered right now was getting this ultrasound scan over with so I could go to the bathroom. I pulled aside the curtain and peeked out.

Nobody.

I sat again, squirming, crossing my legs. Ultrasound scans are painless, they'd told me. Just like an X ray. Oh, there's a little discomfort with your bladder so full. But other than that . . .

Other than that. Wasn't that enough? Good grief, where was that woman? I stood up and yanked the curtain. Had they forgotten me? Maybe I should hang around outside, be more visible. I clutched the hospital gowns around me. They'd given me two—front and back. Maybe they'd finally seen enough hospital gags about the embarrassment of exposed rears.

Still, a getup like this could only make a person feel pathetic. I shivered. It was cool here in the air-conditioned bowels of this building. Even crossing the sun-warmed parking lot outside I'd felt a strange chill tingling, filled as I was with the four prescribed glasses of water. A definite mistake, drinking it ice-cold. I shifted from one foot to the other. Come on, come on. One of the doors was tantalizingly labeled REST ROOM. Never before had the words looked so appealing. My bladder must be as rock-solid as a loaded water balloon, I thought. If I sat down hard, it'd burst.

The hall door banged open and a girl in a gown bellied her way through and into the rest room.

The older woman in jeans who followed her waited behind. She turned and cracked a hard smile at me. "She was about to bust, needing to pee."

I nodded, clamping my thighs.

Her hair was stretched back tightly from her temples with combs and fell down her back in a cascade of damp-looking ringlets. She reeked of cigarette smoke. From the way she tapped her cowboy boots I guessed she couldn't wait to get outside for another.

The girl came out of the bathroom. "God, what a pain. I am *not* going through this again."

"Oh, take it easy. Nobody said you'd have to."

"Mo-om! Didn't you hear the doctor? He said I might."

"Well, don't gripe to me," her mother muttered. "You didn't have to go through any of this, remember?"

I couldn't help glancing at the girl's hand—no wedding ring. She looked incredibly young. Fourteen? Fifteen? Young and miserable and, unlike her skinny mom, chubby even before pregnancy. Not the type who was always hearing how pretty she'd be if only she'd lose weight, either. You could picture her saying yes to some guy—*Okay, I'll let you*—with a vague hope for something, anything.

Did she want to keep the baby? Was she absolutely opposed to abortion and planning to put it up for adoption? What if we applied and this was the baby we got? Would it turn out like us or would it be like this girl and her mother?

Beep! Beep! My internal alarm went off: *Wrong Thoughts! Wrong Thoughts! Curiosity concerning a potential adoptee's genetic inheritance will not be permitted!*

Oh well, maybe the babies given up for adoption carried a gene for intelligence by definition. At least their mothers had to be smarter than the ones who seemed to think of babies as nothing more than cleverly animated dolls, the ones who kept them just long enough for their new boyfriends to beat them to death in fits of potty-training frustration . . .

Stop it. I was supposed to be past that—dwelling on babies left in trash bins, babies fed a steady prenatal diet of cocaine . . .

The technician came in. Sandy, her plastic name tag read. She had an athletic look about her, boyish almost, with a freckled face and Peter Pan hair.

She handed the girl a small square of film. "Now this is the head. And see? Right here is his little bottom." She glanced at me on her way out. "I'll be right back for you."

I nodded. She looked vaguely familiar but I couldn't quite place her.

The pregnant girl dropped the negative into her mother's palm. "I want to show this to Nick. Maybe then it'll seem real to him." She checked my wedding ring. "You pregnant too?"

I shook my head no. Now the two of them eyed me as if wondering which ghastly disease was gnawing away at my insides.

"I'm *trying* to get pregnant," I explained, feeling obliged to spare them their dire imaginings. "They're using ultrasound to measure my eggs and see if they're ripe."

The girl looked puzzled. Was it possible she hadn't even heard that getting pregnant had to do with eggs?

"Well, good luck," the mother said, and then with a sideway glance at her daughter added, "I guess."

Almost a grandmother, and she couldn't have been much older than I was. Weird these days, with people having first babies anywhere from fifteen to forty-three.

The girl went into her dressing cubicle.

"I'll wait for you in the car," the older woman said, taking off.

The technician pushed open the hall door. "Doing okay?"

I nodded, gritting my teeth.

"Bladder full?"

"That's the idea, isn't it?"

"If it's uncomfortably full you could empty it a little."

"I could?"

"Sure, wait just a sec."

Oh thank you, thank you.

She went out and reappeared with a plastic urine sample cup. "Fill this halfway, but no more, okay?"

"Right." I pushed open the heavy rest room door. Oh, it felt so good to go. But darn, the cup was half full before I knew it. My bladder still hurt. How could I stop? But I *had* to stop if I wanted this test to work. I had to if I wanted a baby. Well, maybe I didn't want a baby *this* bad. For a good thirty seconds I seriously considered forgetting the entire concept of progeny and happily peeing my way to total relief. But no, we'd come too far.

I *would* have kids. Grandkids and great-grandkids too. I pictured them at my knees, their cherubic faces turned up to me as I, the proud matriarch, regaled them with the chilling story of how close they had come to not being born at all. How one day way back in 1984 I had saved them with an act of sheer heroism, staunchly resisting the world's most powerful urge to pee.

The technician was waiting outside. "Better?"

"Sort of."

"Okay, follow me. Bring your purse."

Right. The only thing that feels dumber than wearing these gowns is wearing these gowns and carrying a purse. I followed her trim figure down the hall.

"Do you swim at the Aquatic Center?" I asked, speaking to the back of her spotless white dress.

"Yes, I do." She pushed the door open for me.

"I thought I'd seen you somewhere."

Inside, the ultrasound monitor displayed a grainy picture of what was presumably the girl's baby. In the corner of the screen, Sandy had somehow lettered "Hi, Mom!" in a cartoon speech balloon.

I dropped my purse on a chair and climbed up on the sheet-draped table.

"How old was that girl?" I asked.

Sandy fiddled with the knobs and the screen went blank. "Sixteen, I think."

"Wow. Half my age. Can you believe that?"

"Yeah, although you're pretty young-looking for what? Thirty-two?"

"Thirty-three now, but what I meant was, can you believe anybody that young having a baby?"

"Well, not too much surprises me here anymore. And actually, Mary's Bend is tame compared to what's going on other places. I have a friend who does this same thing in Portland. You wouldn't *believe* some of her stories . . ." She turned back to me. Apparently she had the machine ready. "Okay, now this is going to be cold." She pulled up my gown and started smearing gel over my stomach.

"I sure hope this works," I said. "Do you do many of these?"

"Every day."

"Really? And it works pretty well, pinpointing the ovulation?"

"Oh." She punched some buttons on the machine. "No, what I meant was, I do a lot on pregnant women. Using it in infertility cases is fairly new."

"But it works?"

"Well . . . we see the eggs ripening and all. But conception is so complex."

"Unless you're sixteen and unmarried."

She didn't comment. Maybe snide remarks about other patients weren't allowed. Well, hell. I was just making cracks to keep my spirits up. Wish she'd hurry. I was going to wet this table if she didn't.

"We did have one patient who got pregnant."

"Only one?"

Again she took her time answering, sliding a little plastic box over my belly and watching the screen.

I focused on the neat gold ball fastened through her earlobe. I was beginning to get the picture, and I don't mean the one she was trying to tune in. Dr. Lowell never gave me any statistics on how often his patients got pregnant on this treatment because there weren't any. I was his first guinea pig.

"There might have been more," she said at last. "We don't always hear what happens to people. We're just one part of it here."

This is crazy, I was thinking. I'm just the warm body that gives them an excuse to play with their fancy toys. They'll probably order anything as long as we keep paying . . .

"Okay, there they are." She pointed to a couple of black dots in the grainy, fan-shaped picture. "Not doing much yet, but it gives us a baseline."

I rolled my head to the side and looked at the screen. Little black dots. Suddenly I found myself staring in fascination. One of those could be the start of our baby. While Sandy's little arrows zipped back and forth across the screen, measuring, I looked at those egg dots as hard and as carefully as eyes can look. It seemed a solemn moment to me; I was determined to remember it. *I saw you*, I would tell our child someday. *I was watching for you. From the very beginning.*

Chapter 13

Gil and Betsy carefully disengaged. Mission accomplished, Gil thought, sinking back with relief that was as much mental as physical. Betsy's hand, reaching across the darkness, patted his chest with gratitude. After a moment she flicked on the bedside lamp, hugged her knees to her chest, and squinted at the ceiling.

"Swim, little suckers," Gil said. "Go for it."

Betsy laughed. "My thoughts exactly." She reached over and pawed her chart and a pencil from the nightstand. Holding the paper against her palm, she marked the arrow in one of the boxes. "Okay. I really think this is it. The egg's supposed to pop twelve to twenty-four hours after the shot and now we're ready for it. We've never had a chance to ace the timing quite like this before. So if my temperature will just go up tomorrow . . ."

Gil shut his eyes. He'd done his bit. Her temperature was beyond his control. One more arrow on the chart. He hadn't blown it yet, but it nagged at him, the fear that some night he might not be able to deliver, some night when the director of this project informed him it was particularly crucial. Was there a special punishment for husbands who failed?

Jesus, just the thought of your wife sitting there, explaining the empty grid of boxes to her doctor . . .

Actually, sex on schedule hadn't been so bad at first. When you had a wife who never got anything done unless it was on her To Do list, having sex at the top of it wasn't the worst thing in the world. Beat the hell out of "Sort recycling stuff" anyway.

But lately the demands of the chart sometimes turned sex into a chore. So much was up to him. Coming on to her when maybe he wasn't much in the mood. And all her rules about gravity and the optimum position . . . As far as he was concerned, the optimum position was also the least interesting. Sometimes it took him so long to come, he was sure he must be hurting her, and suspected this was the reason she'd taken to turning the lights off, wanting to spare him the less than encouraging sight of her gritted teeth.

Well, so much for those nights of honest loving the country-western song celebrated. And yet he knew she didn't want him to ask if he should stop. The arrow had to go on the chart—this was their tacit agreement. They loved each other and they wanted a baby. Silence was a kindness; a moratorium on verbal analysis only made sense.

He patted her and pulled the pillow over his head. Besides, it wasn't all *that* bad, not always. She claimed the pills made her feel sexier at ovulation. Could just be in her head, but when she started in on hormones, he wasn't about to argue, especially if she was talking sexy hormones as opposed to freak-out hormones.

He had come to look forward to this time of each month, the point where Betsy figured she'd ovulated. It meant at least a week ahead of them where she would have her hopes up, be her old self again for a while. A week or two of relief from gloom. And maybe this time, with all Lowell's new high-tech tricks, they'd get lucky.

God, he hoped so, because it was alarming, how this was beginning to get to her. A couple of weeks ago he'd come in from cultivating the new strawberry patch and found her painting in the extra bedroom, standing transfixed in front of a film on public TV, cream-colored paint dripping from her roller. At first, looking at the screen, he didn't know what she was watching. Then he realized those wriggling tadpoles were sperm surrounding an egg, vying to be the first to penetrate it. The background music sounded churchy—organs, heavy on the holy awe, thundering to a crescendo as the fated sperm pushed into the egg.

Betsy had burst into tears.

"What's the matter?"

"What's the matter?" She stared at him. Her normal alto went high soprano. "What's the matter?"

Seemed like a logical question to him.

"It's just such a miracle," she said.

Well, actually, he thought, as miracles go, it was fairly ordinary. And to some, not a miracle at all: Big-eyed eighth grader Kyla Taylor, slouching into his empty classroom during lunch hour on the last day of school in an oversized denim jacket and a cloud of killer perfume, telling him she was pregnant, crying, begging him for advice. For a crazy instant—maybe stunned by the power of the perfume?—he thought she had somehow heard about their troubles. Just as quickly he realized the ridiculousness of this, but he'd been thrown off long enough for the idea to flash across his mind: *Give us the baby*.

Then he'd gone ahead and given her the standard policy line—*Discuss it with your parents*. But since neither her mother nor her father had turned up for a parent-teacher conference all year, it was hard to have confidence in the soundness of this advice. Desperately wishing he could offer more, he rummaged through his files and gave her phone numbers of the local social service agencies that offered counseling to pregnant teens. It all seemed so inadequate though. And somehow he felt guilty, vaguely cowardly, for reasons he couldn't even define. He kept remembering how disgusted he'd been to hear a couple of his fellow teachers making cracks about her in the teachers' lunchroom—references to the surprising size of her breasts. This was a thirteen-year-old child they were leering over! Why hadn't he told them off?

He'd considered telling Betsy about Kyla. It would interest her, sure. He'd get points for producing a story on the number one subject of the day. But did she really need to hear about one more person who was pregnant and didn't want to be?

It was all so weird. They had a problem; Kyla had a problem. Seemed like it would be simple to be each other's solution. He wouldn't mind getting a baby this way. A baby was a baby. But it could get sticky, adopting a baby whose child-mother would always know exactly where it was. . . .

Now he was dozing off. What the hell, maybe this time would be it. Wouldn't that be great? Not that he could actually imagine the happiness of a positive pregnancy test, but he certainly liked thinking in terms of skipping the monthly crash and burn . . .

"Shit!"

He jerked up. "What? What?"

Betsy sank down, pulling the covers up over her face. "Oh, Gil, you're gonna kill me."

He shook his head to clear it. He pulled the covers away from her face. "What's the matter?"

"The thermometer. I think I broke it."

"Huh?"

"I was shaking it down, and it . . . well, it just flew out of my hand. Over there by the dresser."

Grumbling, he threw back the blanket, got up, and went to the foot of the bed, retrieving the two halves of the thermometer. "How many of these have we gone through, anyway?"

"Mmm, that's the fourth."

"Well, if you're going to be so damned obsessive about taking your temperature, how about learning to hang on tighter?"

"Sorry."

"Hey." He put the broken pieces on the dresser. "No big deal." He climbed back into bed. "What do you think? I'm gonna hit you?"

She winced. "You might feel like it when I ask you to go into town and get a new one."

He raised up on his elbow. "Now? You want me to go *now*?"

"Tomorrow's the day my temperature's supposed to go up."

"It isn't *not* going to go up just because you don't have a thermometer to check it."

"But I have to *know*."

"Come on, it's almost midnight!" He had a big day tomorrow too—orders for forty flats of strawberries, and the extension agent coming to see why that one patch of raspberries looked like somebody'd been busy with a blowtorch.

She gave him a hopeful look. "Safeway's open."

"Oh Jesus."

"Well, I'm sorry, honey. I'd go myself but I can't get up. You don't want me to blow the whole thing, do you?"

"I thought the doctor told you that was a bunch of bunk."

"Well, fine. He can say that, with all these patients of his who could probably get pregnant swinging on a trapeze, but I can't see how it'd help our chances for me to stand up and let it all run down my leg, can you?"

"All right, all right." He swung out of bed, pulled on his boots and jeans.

"I'm *sorry*, honey."

"Yeah yeah." *Swim, suckers*, he thought. *This is definitely getting old.*

To Do

Work

Mon-Tues—James (take lunch clothes) Steamboat Landing 12:15
Wed—Robinetts
Measure Croft bathroom
Call Eric re check

Buy spare thermometer
Pick up Rx bromocriptine refill
Fix pantry door
Strawberry jam
Anniversary card
Turn compost!
Recycling center
Visit Grampa

Chapter 14

Following Carla to our table at Steamboat Landing on the day she'd persuaded me to "do lunch" (the first time I'd heard this expression), I felt like an imposter. Peanut butter and jelly in a brown bag is more my speed, and if I do grab a deli sandwich, it's more likely to be from one of the little places on Second Street, where I'd run into the guys I work *with*, as opposed to here, where I might see the business and professional people I work *for*.

"The lighting in here helps a lot," I whispered when we were seated. "When I hung this paper it really looked ghastly with the booth upholstery."

She looked up from her menu and glanced around. "You did this wallpapering?" I couldn't tell if she was impressed or embarrassed.

"Yup." I looked down at my hands. I had paint around my cuticles. "I've papered stuff all over town."

"That's amazing. It must be fun to see your work everywhere you go."

"It is, actually. Except when I hate the paper people pick out."

"Oh." She considered this darkly. "You know, I couldn't

do that. If I hated the paper, I'd have to tell them to get someone else."

Right.

"Did you know Eric Norgren did this place?" I asked. She'd mentioned that he'd been the contractor for her remodel. "It used to be the train station—the very place my grandfather first laid eyes on my grandmother. Saw her stepping off the old Red Electric, coming here to college."

"You're not kidding about having roots here." Then she frowned. "Aren't the train tracks over on Sixth Street?"

"Right, and that's where this place was. They were going to tear it down for the new city hall. Everyone said it was impossible to move a stone building. Then Eric did it. Sort of established his reputation. Now he's got a hand in on just about every restoration project in town."

The waiter came to our table. Drinks? Carla ordered white wine. I passed. I never touched a drop after the day when I thought I'd ovulated, at which point I began treating myself as a pregnant person as far as alcohol or medicines. Wouldn't even pop an aspirin. I knew Carla followed the same routine, so a drink order probably meant another month down the tube for her.

"I like your outfit," I said. It was a skirt and top with a loose jacket, all purple knit stuff, drapey and dramatic—the sort of thing it took a tall woman to wear, the sort of thing that on me would look like a circus tent.

"Thanks. It's incredibly old. I have *got* to go shopping, but there's just nothing in this town, is there? I mean, where do you go?"

I shrugged. "I sew. Or order from L.L. Bean or Eddie Bauer. And anyway, I mostly wear jeans." Today I had on my nicest chambrays and a cotton sweater, my standard warm-weather outfit for giving wallpapering bids. Not fancy, but a distinct step up from the painty overalls I'd been wearing this morning. "The other thing is, I'm a sucker for those catalog descriptions. *A one hundred percent cotton sweater, perfect for the farmers' market, for raking leaves, or for simply relaxing by a cozy fire.* I'll read that and go, yeah, they've got the picture. But when I walk into a store full of clothes on racks, I get confused. Who's gonna explain to me what's so special about each thing?"

Carla smiled. I don't know why I liked that gap between her teeth so much. Maybe it was just the idea that she hadn't run right out in a panic to get rid of it.

"The truth is," she said, "I've had plenty of chances to shop in Portland, but I just keep thinking, Oh, I'll be buying maternity clothes by next month."

I nodded. I knew about putting things on hold. Only a few weeks back, during my period, I had finally broken down and rolled a coat of nice, neutral, all-purpose off-white paint on the walls of our extra bedroom, this after months of putting it off, figuring I would surely be pregnant soon and wanting to pick out wallpaper.

"Oh, here's my latest." Carla pulled out an envelope of snapshots—their recent windsurfing vacation in Hood River. Turned out they'd bought a house there just for weekends.

"You look great in your bikini," I said. "Who took all these?"

"Stan. Who else?"

Gil never took pictures of me. No, wait, I take that back. There's that shot of me standing by his new tractor, to give it perspective, he said. And the one where I'm kneeling in the soybeans to make them look taller. (By the way, you cannot, as we found, grow soybeans in the Willamette Valley.)

When I complained, Gil would say he was looking for before and after shots. Growth records.

"Well, I'm growing and changing too," I pointed out one time. "I'm not always going to be twenty-eight, you know!"

And see, here I was, already thirty-three.

The waiter came and took our orders. Then we got down to the main purpose of this lunch. First, the status reports.

I had finally finished the grueling treatment cycle which wound up including five ultrasound scans in five days plus the complication of a urinary tract infection which I was convinced had resulted from the unnatural process of spending a good portion of the week with a painfully full bladder.

"What am I supposed to do?" I'd wailed to Dr. Lowell. "You're not supposed to have sex when you've got this, right? But I've *got* to have sex!"

Apparently no other patient had ever been stupid enough or unlucky enough to find herself in this particular set of miserable circumstances, and other than quickly putting me on sulfa drugs, he honestly didn't know how to advise me.

"I suppose when you're trying this hard to get pregnant," he said, "it's different."

It certainly was.

Bromocriptine, Clomid, two drugs for the infection, and now an HCG chaser. My poor bloodstream was totally polluted.

"So how was the shot?" Carla asked. She knew I'd been dreading it.

It's silly, but shots, for me, are right up there on the ick list. When I was a kid, I single-handedly launched a major panic at the county polio clinic by being the first to pitch a fit at the sight of the needle.

"Not too bad." Because really, I had no business even *thinking* of trying to get pregnant if I was going to freak out over one little shot. Pregnancy, after all, has been known to frequently lead directly to the not-necessarily-pain-free experience of childbirth. "It was the rear end kind, though. I hate that. And the nurse was some older lady they'd pulled in from Dermatology. She acted totally blown away by the idea of this shot. I mean, I'm standing there with my pants down and she's making these comments about how in *her* day if a woman couldn't get pregnant, she just had to take God's word for it she wasn't meant to be a mother . . ."

"I think I've run into her too! Red hair?"

"No," I said. "Completely white."

"Must be a lot of them running around."

After the injection and the crucial coitus arrow, my graph line had shot up more definitively than it ever had before. My temperature had been up six days now. I hadn't felt this optimistic in ages.

As for Carla, she'd had her period but had now crawled out of the monthly depression pit. She hesitated (to my relief) as the waiter set down our green salads, then, when he was gone, explained that her doctor had suggested artificial insemination with Stan's sperm.

"Basically," she said, "I don't think he knows *what's* wrong." She pointed a forkful of salad at me. "Do you realize how *lucky* you are, having your problem be so obvious? I hope you appreciate that."

I shifted uncomfortably. Ever notice how sharp-eyed people are in noticing the good luck of others? How generous in their willingness to point it out?

Maybe because of the implication I'd always had it so easy, I told her my brain tumor scare story.

"But how can you sound so cheerful about it?" she said when I'd finished. "God, I would have been scared to death."

"I was. But the point is, I *didn't* have a tumor, and the relief was terrific. I mean, I was ecstatic."

"But that's like the bit about hitting your head with a hammer."

I laughed. "No, see, a crisis just throws it in your face—Wake up! Life's precious! Love each other now!"

"Hmm," she said. "I still think happiness ought to be more than relief."

"Hey, don't knock relief," I said. "Beats the heck out of the alternative. Anyway, for me, once the bad stuff's over, it's over. As long as it ends happily, whatever it took to get there is just an interesting detour."

"Yeah, and I'll bet *Pollyanna* was your favorite Disney flick as a kid, right? Tell me something. How did you get this far in life and still have this . . . this *cheery* attitude?"

Cheer, her expression made plain, was, in her book, rather pitiable.

Okay, so maybe I *was* naïve. On the other hand, what did she have to be so cynical about? I hadn't been handed such a rough life, but then, neither had she.

While we waited for our food, she briefed me on other incidents of interest—the friend who'd unwittingly confided about her recent abortion (Carla handed her own story back on a platter of guilt), the birth announcement from a friend she hadn't seen since high school (straight in the trash can), her sister's miscarriage (she already had two kids, so Carla couldn't feel *too* terrible). And then, of course, how she'd cried and cried last week when her period started.

"The shittiest part is the way Stan's acting. I wouldn't be surprised if this splits us up."

"Carla! Really?"

"Oh yeah, it happens. Did I tell you about my friend Cheryl, up in Portland? Seven years it took her to get pregnant. Seven. She got the positive pregnancy test on the day she was supposed to sign their divorce papers."

"Oh great. So what did she do?"

"Cried. Divorced him. Had the baby."

"Boy," I said. "After all that time, to not be able to be one hundred percent happy about it. That's . . . *tragic.*"

"Oh, I don't know. Not in the end, really. She loves that kid."

The waiter brought our lunches—a plain turkey sandwich for me, some sort of fancy pasta for her.

"Even if Stan and I split," Carla said when he was gone, "I still want the baby. Maybe I'd *rather* have the baby."

"Carla." I tried to picture trading Gil in for some faceless little bundle.

"Husbands can be so temporary. The two of you aren't actually related. Not by blood. But your parents are always your parents, and your baby will always be your child. Of course we're not supposed to say that. The marriage is supposed to come first. But look at all the divorces and tell me which is the lasting bond."

"Yeah, I see what you mean," I said. "I met this woman at the pool the other day. Thirty-nine when she accidentally got pregnant. Her husband wanted her to get an abortion, but she said forget it. So he took off. But it's like your friend—she's not sorry at all. The baby's worth ten of him."

"So do you think it was really an accident? Her getting pregnant?"

"Hey, like I said, I'd just met her. I wasn't in any position to pin her down on details. Besides, I always have such a hard time relating to these stories about birth control failure."

"Oh, I *know.*"

"I just—well, when the system refuses to work for you, and you start studying up on everything that has to go right for conception to take place, doesn't it seem amazing that anyone *ever* gets pregnant, much less anyone who's supposedly trying *not* to?"

"Exactly."

"And anyway, the point is, even though she's totally worn out being a single mom, she was still acting like, *My God, to think I almost missed this.*"

We were both quiet a moment, picking at our food, me

wondering if telling that story had been such a hot idea. If Carla and I were going to miss motherhood, and not by choice, we didn't need to be haunted by reports of unimaginable bliss.

"Well, I'm not going to miss it," Carla said. "If Stan won't cooperate, I'll find somebody who will."

"Carla!"

"Is that so terrible? Unmarried women are going out these days and getting themselves artificially inseminated. Why should I have to put up with a husband who's actually handicapping me?"

"You're not serious, are you?" I was imagining Gil's reaction to this. He always seemed incredibly threatened by magazine and newspaper stories about artificial insemination.

"Oh, I wouldn't really do it," Carla said.

I had to wonder, though. Was she just backpedaling because I was so obviously shocked?

"Maybe I'm an incurable romantic," I said, "but I still like the idea of babies being conceived in . . . well, you know, like an act of love."

"Oh please. I don't even remember what that is. I mean, be honest. Isn't this the worst sex you've ever had?"

I surprised myself by blushing. Isn't that funny? We were supposed to be the liberated generation. Sex would never be a hang-up with us. We could talk about anything. And back in college we did. But there was something about getting married that shut the door on that. References to sex had become oblique.

"I mean, really," Carla went on. "I'm going, 'Come on, Stan, tonight's the night,' and he says, 'Well, I'm too tired.' Why does he have to say that when he knows we've got to go through with it anyway? Sometimes I think he's *trying* to make it harder."

"I know what you're saying," I said, consciously lowering my voice a notch, "but considering all the pelvic exams and different tests, sex is still one of the nicer things happening to my body these days."

"But Stan and I are both so bored. God, I'm even bored with my fantasies!"

I laughed a bit nervously, glancing around, hoping she wasn't going to start spelling them out. I didn't enjoy the feeling that heads were turning our way. Also I was wondering, as I sometimes did, if I were deficient in the fantasy department. I've never understood this bit of pretending you're in bed with some movie star or whoever. I always thought the point of making love to Gil is that it *is* Gil. Why would I want to think about somebody else? No, if my mind strayed during sex, I was most likely thinking of something on my To Do list, or the secret stash of baby things under the bed.

Somehow I didn't think Carla wanted to hear about the positive aspects of my sex life, though. "We haven't been trying as long as you," I said finally, trying to be diplomatic.

"Hmm. Well, just wait."

She reminded me of a neighbor girl I'd grown up with who was always making ominous predictions. "Straight *A*'s in sixth grade? That's nothing. Wait till you get to junior high."

But maybe I was being too smug. Maybe I was just feeling optimistic, assuming Gil and I were on the verge of success, that our problem was about to be relegated to the nostalgia file, romantic in retrospect.

"This is wearing me down so bad," she said. "Sometimes I wonder if I'll be happy even if I *do* get pregnant. I'll probably be so paranoid. And when you've had all this extra time to let all your fantasies build up, all these stories we tell ourselves about how wonderful it's going to be . . . Maybe it's almost dangerous for people like us to succeed past a certain point. You realize, don't you, that we'll probably smother the poor kids."

"Oh come on. You'd be so busy just being a mother, you'd forget all this, don't you think?"

"I doubt it. I have this label now—INFERTILE. Asking a baby to take away four years of inferiority . . . ?"

"But if you had the baby, you wouldn't feel inferior anymore. Wouldn't you just feel . . . blessed?"

"Blessed? That I had to go through all this?"

"Well yeah. When I get pregnant, I bet I'll appreciate it a lot more than people who get pregnant so easy. I was thinking about this, Carla. You know how you have the world's greatest view from your living room?"

She shrugged. "If you say so."

"Well, it is. But you know what? When there weren't any roads there and we had to hike up to see it, it was even better. More special somehow. Don't you think it'd be the same with going after a baby?"

"Maybe," she said. "Unless the climb kills you."

Then, as we started in on coffee refills (decaf for me), two pregnant women were seated on the next tier down from us. We looked. We took in their big bellies, their charmingly embarrassed grimaces as they struggled to tuck shopping bags under the table.

"I can't stand it," Carla mouthed at me.

"That'll be us," I whispered. Such an ordinary little outing. Pregnant, shopping with a pregnant friend, loading up with booty from the Stork Shop and then stopping for a leisurely lunch, discussing whatever it is pregnant women discuss. To us, it looked like heaven. "Seven months from now, Carla."

"Right." She was already digging around in her purse for tip money, anxious to get out. "Oh, why don't restaurants have pregnant and nonpregnant sections, anyway?"

"Come on, Carla," I said gently. "It's not as if people are getting pregnant just to make us feel bad." I think maybe I could talk this way that day because deep down, where I was hardly even admitting it to myself, I just knew that I was about to join their exclusive club. Those women couldn't make me feel bad; I expected to be one of them very soon.

Outside it was a beautiful early-summer day, the air full of the smell of blooming things, a warm breeze wafting up from the river.

We walked toward Carla's slick-looking car. I don't know one make from the next, but it was that creamy yellow color you only see on expensive models. I looked over at our little red pickup. I hadn't noticed until now how filthy it was.

"I have to say it, Betsy. I really am worried about you. It's obvious you're working awfully hard to block out a lot of your negative feelings. And that's so unhealthy."

"Hey, I admit it. This has been a bummer."

"But you're trying to tell me you see somebody pregnant and it doesn't get you upset?"

"Those women being pregnant's got nothing to do with whether *I'm* going to get pregnant or not." I thought a moment. "Okay, sure, it gets to me, but I don't know, maybe you really do feel worse."

"Apparently," she said, separating each syllable. "I can't wait to see how *you're* doing in two years when you're still not pregnant."

I sighed. "Carla, I'll be the first to say you've been through more than I have, okay? You win. Only they aren't handing out babies based on who's the most miserable."

Her face colored. She opened her mouth to say something, then apparently thought better of it.

"Carla? Come on now, I'm sorry. Don't be mad. Please."

"Oh, okay." She hooked her over-the-eye hair behind her ear. "I don't know why I'm taking it out on you anyway. You're the only one who really listens to me on this." She gave me a quick, stiff hug and got in her car.

"Keep me posted," I said. As if she needed any encouragement.

And then I had an awful thought. How was I ever going to break the news to her when, two weeks from now, I got my positive pregnancy test?

Chapter 15

With the golden light slanting from the west and the sweet smell of ripe berries warmed by a day in the sun rising all around, it's hard to imagine a more pleasant place on earth than our strawberry patch on a summer evening. A fresh-picked strawberry has a glorious sheen long gone by the time it reaches the grocery store cooler, gone by morning if the berries sit on the kitchen counter overnight. And the taste! Let one of these dissolve in your mouth and you will never want to go near those mealy, imported-from-California imitations again.

When Gil first got the idea of selling our extra produce, we thought we'd pick it all ourselves. (Self-sufficiency was In.) This plan had exhausted us in one season and now, with more acreage in berries, we relied on a half dozen twelve-year-olds who bicycled out each summer morning for the harvest. (At eleven A.M. under a hot sun, they do not find this nearly as romantic and pleasant as I do at sunset.)

But as I said, at sunset, it's lovely. The evening after my lunch with Carla, I was out there picking a few boxes for jam. Gil had driven to Salem for a truckload of berry pints, and I was on my own. Between the berry rows, the mobile phone lay next to my carrier along with a pad and pen.

When the phone buzzed, I picked it up expecting another berry-order call.

"Hi, I have some wonderful news."

"Oh." I fumbled mentally. "Hi, Mom."

"Your sister's going to have a baby."

I dropped the order pad. "She is?"

"Yes, I just found out."

"Well, that's . . . great."

"Isn't it? Oh, I'm so happy for her. Well, and for me, too, of course. But I think this is such a good sign, you know, that she's starting to, well, get over losing your dad. Frankly I thought she'd have had a baby long before this, but I think his . . . I think losing him just depressed her so much that she couldn't seem to get on with it, and then of course she feels bad she didn't do it before he died . . ." My mother sighed, then perked up again. "Anyway, she said it was all right if I told you . . ."

She went on with all the details of Stephanie's first symptoms, the home test she'd used, how excited Matt was. I half listened, staring off to the end of the field, poised between elation and despair. This would be so terrific, if I turned out to be pregnant too. Matched-up cousins. But if I weren't . . .

"Now, honey, you *will* call her, won't you?"

"Well . . . sure."

"Because you know how she is. It always means so much to her, whatever you've got to say."

I hesitated.

"Just call her, okay?"

"Okay."

My sister was going to have a baby.

I had no business being shocked. If I'd been thinking, I would have realized we were due for this news. Okay, so Stephanie was younger. Two years—big deal. Her clock was ticking too. And it was no secret she'd always wanted children. We'd both loved dolls, but when we played Big Life, it was Stephanie who always wanted to be the bride and take care of the babies. Stephanie who played school with the younger neighborhood kids and later helped out in the church nursery. Stephanie who was always asked to baby-sit first.

A baby at twenty-five—this had been on her schedule as

long as I could remember. But first her timing was thrown off by Jerry the Jerk, and then after she married Matt, she kept postponing it. She had a certain line of baby furniture in mind, she said, and wasn't about to get pregnant until their savings account would cover it. And then the grieving over Dad . . .

But sooner or later she was bound to go for it. And it wasn't as if she needed my permission, or had done it to spite me. Our discussions about kids had always been her saying she couldn't wait; me saying I most certainly could. Officially, as far as she knew, I was still lukewarm to the whole idea of motherhood.

"I've got to call her," I told Gil after he'd arrived home and I'd given him the news.

"Why?"

"To congratulate her, I guess."

"Okay, so call her."

"It's not that easy."

"So don't call her."

"Gil!" Mostly I was annoyed that it all felt so complicated. Shouldn't it be easier between sisters? Shouldn't I just pick up the phone, bursting with joy?

Gil always says that meeting Stephanie for the first time actually sticks out in his mind more than first meeting me. It was so much more dramatic.

It was the Christmas after I'd graduated from college and I was working my janitor job, camping out at my folks' house. When Gil came to pick me up for our first date (*The Way We Were*—Robert Redford and Barbra Streisand), Stephanie was in a state of hysteria because just two weeks before their wedding, Jerry the Jerk had bowed out.

"He can't *do* this!" she kept shrieking. "Everything was all set." And then, as if it were proof positive she deserved better: "I signed up that caterer six months ago!" Poor Stephanie. It wasn't fair. She had played by every rule and now this.

Gil appeared stunned at the sight of a girl shredding her Perfect Wedding Planner notebook, and since normally my sister is rather sweet-tempered—occasionally a bit pouty at most—I, too, was mesmerized by this almost Shakespearean demonstration of grief. Her chestnut hair was still long then, carefully, gorgeously curled on the ends, and I must say she flung it around to great effect.

Of course, looking back, Stephanie was glad she wasn't stuck with Jerry, but at the time, well, all those carefully laid plans—the gorgeous winter gown trimmed with white fur (size 6—she had starved herself for that), the red velvet bridesmaids' dresses (eight!), the white roses, and poinsettias for the church. And the cake! Oh, the cake was going to be a wonder, tier upon tier . . .

But canceling and returning all this was easy compared to the embarrassment of disinviting three hundred guests. I remember my mother flipping through etiquette books, consulting friends on the phone. How did people handle this sort of thing? Dad ranted around for days. With any encouragement at all, he'd have grimly presided over a shotgun wedding.

Opening a pile of presents is a lot of fun. Packing them back up isn't. But at least for me, packing Stephanie's gifts wasn't painful, just tedious. Once in a while over the three-day course of this project, Stephanie would come stand at the family room door and watch me, red-eyed. "Oh, I *loved* that," she'd say as I wrapped an enameled teapot in tissue.

Darn that Jerry. I hadn't felt so protective of my sister since Scotty Baker chased her around the neighborhood with a dead, gut-spilling salamander. Too bad I couldn't take care of Jerry like I had Scotty, with a good punching out.

So this is how "the Jerk" got added to Jerry, and this was the state of things when Gil first met my family. Lucky for me he didn't just head the other direction, fast.

Our wedding the following summer was, in contrast, a rather hastily organized affair, a picnic at our new farm—that was the plan anyway. My folks found us suspiciously casual about it and, maybe because of Stephanie's disastrous experience, were not convinced until the last minute it was actually going to happen.

Stephanie was depressed to find herself cast as maid of honor. According to her life schedule, she should have achieved the status of matron by now. And even with a two-year head start, I don't think it ever occurred to her I might marry first. Bummer. Well, what was I supposed to do? Call it off until she got a new guy lined up?

Besides, I was used to Stephanie being annoyed with me. I'd even given up trying to figure out why. I do know it all goes way back. Mom still has the old alphabetical address file with the sliding metal pointer we used to love playing with. Under *B* is Stephanie's childish scrawl: *Betsy gets favered!*

Why she thought that I don't have a clue. I never felt favored. The whole idea was ludicrous. She was the sweet one, the one who behaved and didn't give them any trouble. Why on earth would any parent of sound mind favor me? If anything, she was Dad's favorite, his idea of what a girl ought to be.

Stephanie didn't care for the bridesmaid's dress I sewed for her—long, cotton, and decidedly farmy. And her nose wrinkled when I announced the elimination of the formal receiving line. "It's your wedding," she kept saying as our plans unfolded, the unspoken implication left hanging in the air: *Go ahead, be tacky.*

Our invitations featured a photo of us striding purposefully across our field together, our Walk the Proud Land picture, I called it. Walk the Proud Fifteen Acres anyway. Okay, maybe it was a little hokey, but people were doing stranger things in those days. One of my college roommates said "I do" (or some vague equivalent) in a white minidress and platform heels, and lots of people were going the barefoot-in-a-dewy-spring-meadow route. (Sounds better than it probably felt. Maybe you had to be stoned.)

It was only later that I realized the point of a strictly traditional wedding: The photos won't be so embarrassing later. Your white satin album will stand the test of time even if your marriage doesn't. Well, nobody was having much luck selling tradition to our generation at that point, as I recall. Just making the sex legal seemed conventional enough.

Still, ten years later, nothing about our album looked too funky. The wedding itself turned out fine, except for a couple of glitches, like my failure to warn Gil that a photographer would be taking a few formal shots right after the ceremony. Why hassle him ahead of time, I thought? As a result, our photos show all of us smiling except Gil. *I* know he's scowling because by this point, he imagined he'd be enjoying that promised pastrami sandwich, not having his picture taken, but when our great-grandchildren find this book—that is, if we have the children to have the grandchildren to *have* those great-grandchildren—they'll surely conclude their family was founded under extreme duress.

Then there were the corsages I made for all the guests from flowers around the farm. Gorgeous, but I blew it by storing them in the fridge overnight with Mom's homemade potato salad. Every last petal soaked up the oniony odor, and I caught more than one person plunging in her nose for a deep whiff, only to back off in puzzled distress.

Oh, and of course the minor matter of moving the whole thing to the grange hall, our alternate site, when we woke that morning to rain. Did I care? Nope. We were married, that's what counted. This was the year of the long lines at the gas pumps, and one of my main concerns for months had been making sure Gil and I were in the same place when that last drop of gas was gone. Now we would be.

The following summer, Stephanie married Matt in what everyone swore was the loveliest, most picture-perfect ceremony they'd ever seen. The flowers smelled sweet; Matt smiled for the birdie. Careful plans, perfectly executed. A triumph for Stephanie. Her one regret was having to reconcile herself to a size-ten gown.

Now she was going to have a baby. For some reason, I kept thinking of the phrase that pops up in saccharine magazine articles: *Then little Billy was born and our happiness was complete.* Is that for real? Complete happiness? Even when I argued with Gil about being as happy as I could possibly be, I thought of it as transitory, a brief, peak moment. But *complete happiness*? Sounded so permanent, as if once you'd grabbed it, you could hold on to it forever.

But things were always changing. Look at our picture albums. This shot, taken at our wedding—Gil and I and six grandparents. Click. This shot, ten years later—Gil and I and two grandparents. Click. How could we hold on to happiness when our lives were clicking away in snapshots?

I didn't call my sister.

I'm not proud of this; I believe in doing what I say I'll

do. But each time I'd think of it, I'd make some excuse. I might interrupt their dinner, or it was probably Stephanie's nap time.

We were restocking our little roadside berry booth one day when Gil asked if I'd phoned her. I went the old offense-as-defense route.

"She could call *me*, you know. Shouldn't she be giving me the news herself?"

"I don't know. Is there some kind of etiquette on this?"

I shrugged. "Anyway, I'll be seeing her at Neskowin."

"Won't that be harder, in person?"

"Yes, except . . . Oh, Gil, think how great it would be if I were pregnant too! Then it would be total celebration all the way around."

He put our "honor system" cash can on the counter. "Think you might be?"

Oh, I loved that hopeful note in his voice.

"Well," I said, "my breasts seem a little tender. I felt kind of yucky this morning and my orange juice tasted strange . . ." I went on, happily noting all the minute physical changes I had observed. Then, when he looked thoroughly convinced and excited, I added the disclaimer that I might, after all, just be imagining things.

"I know," he said, but as I headed up to the house, I could hear him behind me, whistling.

To Do

Work

Fri—Croft

Wash truck!
Camera film
L. L. Bean order
Fabric—Steph's quilt—
ask Mom colors?
Shortcake stuff for 4th
Fix pantry door
Call yard service re 10th
St.
Visit Grampa

Chapter 16

Shirley Conklin poured herself a second cup of coffee and sank into the faded chintz cushions of the wicker armchair, propping her feet on the hassock. Beyond the paned windows the ocean sparkled in the morning sun, and their American flag snapped in the breeze. Nice to just fly it again without all the arguments. For a while, during Vietnam, she hadn't been so quick to poke it into the rusty metal bracket the moment they arrived at the beach house. Why get Betsy and her dad going—Jack always struggling for control, threatened to his core by any questioning of his authority, Betsy feeling morally compelled to speak her mind. Thank goodness nobody had to take the flag as some pro-war message these days. Now it mostly just meant *We're here this weekend.*

She sighed contentedly. Neskowin was so good for her. Here, she almost felt like a kid, hardly a widow nearing sixty, a woman on the verge of grandmotherhood. Maybe it was the fresh, salty air, or the easy comfort of jeans and running shoes after the heels she still felt she ought to wear to work on the campus. Or maybe it was all the childhood memories the sagging shingled house held. Here she had a happy history that predated her husband, Jack, and now that he was gone, she found herself grateful for any hints of who she used to be, who she could still be without him.

Her sister, June, scanned the beach with binoculars, her "fun" Fourth of July firecracker earrings twinkling as her head turned.

"There he is," she said, spotting her husband. "Look quick if you want to see him standing up." Ray, formerly a dentist, was not coping well with retirement. Each morning while they were at the beach he'd get up and walk to the store for *The Oregonian*, then spend the rest of the day on the sofa asleep under it. June lowered the binoculars. "What time do you expect the girls?"

"Stephanie any time," Shirley said. "Matt's driving up later. He's got a golf date at Salishan. And Betsy just said sometime in the afternoon. What about Laura?"

"Around two. I know Dad would love to see her, so I'm hoping they'll stop at the nursing home on their way up. I dropped a hint anyway."

That'd settle it then, Shirley thought. Laura wouldn't stop in a million years. Why couldn't June ever figure this out? In spite of Laura's age and accomplishments (June said she'd just been awarded a new grant), it was Shirley's opinion that her niece exhibited an almost adolescent tendency toward contrariness when it came to her mother's "suggestions."

Shirley cocked her head at the sound of distant children's voices, glad shouts carried up from the beach on the wind. "You know, when I first came down this morning and heard that, I thought for a second the voices were from upstairs. It sounded just the way it used to when the girls played up there." She smiled. "Won't it be nice to hear that again?"

"Yes, it will. I always enjoy having the three girls here together. They get along so well."

Shirley hesitated. "I was thinking of our grandchildren, June." Odd how her sister still managed to speak of their daughters as if they were children instead of women in their thirties. And yet, she had to admit, there was, even now, this unexpected sense of waiting to see how they would all turn out. They were all still in the process of growing up. Somehow she'd imagined it would all be settled by now, but of course it never was. For anyone.

"You don't want to get me started on the subject of grandchildren." June shot Shirley a loaded look. "Or the lack of them."

Now anybody who follows Ann Landers knows that whether or not, when, or to what extent people intend to reproduce is absolutely nobody's business but their own, so in spite of the fact that she and her sister were alone, Shirley lowered her voice in an unconscious acknowledgment of the forbidden nature of this question: "Laura and Barry won't put it off much longer, will they?"

"That's the thing, you see. They're not putting it off." This with a clipped brightness. "They've made up their minds. No kids."

"Oh." Shirley couldn't suppress a note of alarm. It had long been obvious Laura was in no big hurry, but babies had been completely ruled out? This *was* news. "Have they said why not?"

"According to Barry, the world doesn't need any more children." June's earrings twitched with indignation. "And the place isn't fit for them now anyway."

"Well, for heaven's sake. Has it ever been?" Shirley herself had learned she was pregnant with Betsy just as the Korean War was breaking out. Burned in memory was her dismay at the ominous, unknowing remark made by an older woman at a church coffee. "Mercy," the woman had said, shaking her head, "wouldn't this be a terrible time to be bringing a baby into the world?" To Shirley, twenty-three and pregnant, the future had suddenly looked precarious all over again. It seemed they'd only just finished World War II and sent her sailor boy home to marry her, and now this.

But she'd certainly never been sorry she had Betsy.

Were things worse now, or did they just seem that way? Of course the world could never be as nice as you'd want for your children. When her girls were babies and so innocent, she'd hardly been able to bear the idea of them finding out about war, about poverty and suffering. When it turned out there was radiation in all the cows' milk because of the bomb testing . . . well, she'd been furious. And she felt guilty somehow, too. But none of it made her regret having her daughters.

June got up and started clearing off the breakfast dishes. Shirley helped her, then began squirting liquid soap into the plastic tub in the sink and running the hot water. At home she wouldn't have dreamed of going without a dishwasher, but here, with few other chores, there was a certain pleasure in it. She watched a hummingbird vibrating over the honeysuckle vines just outside the window. You really couldn't ask for more, she thought—this tiny wonder from the back window, and from the front, the pounding Pacific. Well, you couldn't ask for more given basic laws of nature, the futility of yearning for the dead to be brought back to life . . .

She slid another dish into the suds. "Did I tell you I've found a condo?" That awful chirping tone again. She'd hear herself using it whenever she had a bleak thought to shake.

"About time," June replied, sponging the counters. "Frankly, Ray and I haven't been able to figure out why you haven't made the move sooner."

Shirley held her tongue, but not without effort. June really had no idea. She seemed to think that a widow's properly managed life insurance policies and investments would automatically lead to a widow's efficiently managed emotions. She didn't understand what a huge chunk of Shirley's life had been ripped away, what it meant to lose a husband. She'd turn right around and start nagging at Ray just minutes after listening to Shirley talk about how badly she missed Jack.

"They always say," Shirley ventured, "that widows shouldn't make any big changes or decisions right away. And also I knew the girls wouldn't be too happy about it." She gazed out at the little glade surrounded by hydrangeas where Stephanie and Betsy used to play.

"I can't see why it would make any difference to them," June said. "They've got their own houses now."

"Yes, but that *was* the house they grew up in. I think they still have a feeling of wanting to come home, you know, at Christmas and all."

"They can't ask you to plan your life around that."

"I *know*, June." Stephanie and Betsy hadn't asked her to do anything; she just understood how they felt, that's all. "I do have to think about Stephanie, though. This *has* been hard on her."

"She and Jack were awfully close, weren't they?"

Shirley nodded, hanging the dish towel on the line behind the stone fireplace. "I don't think I even realized *how* close until he was gone." Jack's death, while initially bringing Shirley and Stephanie closer in a grief Betsy never quite seemed to share, later had pulled them apart. In the same way Stephanie would never listen to a word against her father when he was alive (her defense of him during the battle to get him to quit smoking came to mind), she had lately been cool and disapproving of any sign that Shirley was ready to get on with life, as if this constituted some sort of betrayal. Once, Shirley had remarked that she didn't care what those other widows told Ann Landers, one thing she did not miss was the snoring. Poor Stephanie couldn't have looked more horrified if Shirley had said she was flat out glad Jack was dead. "I just hope this pregnancy means she's doing better," Shirley told June, "and that it'll be something to sort of bring us all together."

Upstairs, the two women stood on the landing with stacks of ancient white sheets, debating.

"This one for Laura and Barry?" Shirley nodded toward the west-facing room with the sweeping view of the beach and Proposal Rock. It was a standing joke, Laura and Barry needing the biggest and best room because they were forever retreating to it in search of privacy.

"I suppose." June cracked open the window to air out the stuffiness. She stood looking at the rock for a moment. "Oh what the heck. Stephanie's the one who's pregnant. Let her and Matt have it."

Any of these beds was as bad as the next when you got down to it, Shirley thought as they put on the cold sheets, but it wouldn't hurt to give Stephanie the TLC of the best view. Next they moved into the smallest, south-facing room.

"I just can't accept it," June said. "I can't believe Laura doesn't want a baby."

Shirley pulled back the top quilt. "We have to let them live their own lives, June."

"Well. You wouldn't be so quick to say that if it was *you* who was never going to have any grandchildren."

Oh dear, Shirley thought, hearing in this a familiar old envy. Laura had been delivered in the breech position, and afterward June hemorrhaged, necessitating an emergency hysterectomy. June had never really forgiven her younger sister for the ease with which she'd given birth. She had a habit of letting it be known, usually after a second martini, that she certainly never would have taken it so much for granted, this talent for reproducing. And certainly never would have stopped at two. Now Shirley wondered: Would she be penalized for enjoying her grandchildren if her sister weren't likewise blessed?

"From the day the doctor told me Laura would be my only child," June said now, "I've been consoling myself with the thought of lots of grandkids. And Laura knows that."

Exactly, Shirley thought. Laura knows that. "Maybe she'll change her mind."

June shook her head. "She seems set."

"And she's what? Thirty-six?"

"Almost thirty-seven."

"Millie Berg's daughter just had her first at forty."

"Oh, but that's crazy. Shirley, can you imagine? Remember when Marge turned up pregnant with Jeffy at thirty-eight? We were all so embarrassed for her. I was the one who would have loved more, and I *still* felt sorry for her."

"But things are different these days. In lots of ways. You know, I've been preparing myself for years that Betsy might never have kids."

"Well, pardon me. Don't you see a difference here? I'm sure I could be more philosophical about Laura if I had another daughter who was already pregnant."

"Oh, I know, June. I'm sorry." She was wondering—which is harder? To envy or to be envied? She placed the pillows on the edge of the folded-back quilt, thinking of her two daughters. She hoped Betsy had called Stephanie. She wasn't sure Betsy realized just how careful they needed to be with her these days.

"Why are you doing that with the pillows?" June said. "I've never seen anybody put the open ends of the cases in the middle like that."

"Oh. Well, this is Betsy's room, right? I always do it this way for her." She explained that when Betsy was six, the two of them had been making a bed here, and when Shirley asked about Betsy's unusual placement of the pillows, Betsy explained it just seemed right to her to hide the open parts. Instead of correcting her, Shirley went along. Made as much sense as the other way, she said. At least that's how Betsy always quoted her. Shirley herself didn't remember the incident at all, yet Betsy claimed it as a pivotal moment, an important validation of the value of her own opinions.

"Isn't that amazing?" Shirley said, following June into the third room. "Here I wasn't even paying attention and I find I've made some momentous statement."

Other times when she'd self-consciously tried to convey something she felt really *was* important, she had failed utterly. Betsy had come to her at sixteen, stricken to realize she'd lost the faith of her childhood. Fumbling, even a bit shy about it, Shirley had attempted to explain how her own faith in God had somehow been renewed at Betsy's birth. "What on earth has that got to do with the price of rice in China?" Betsy had cried, leaving Shirley at a complete loss. Words weren't much good once Betsy hit that age where she had to question everything.

"Honestly, June, the whole time she was growing up, it was as if I couldn't tell her a thing, and now she spouts back every silly cliché I ever came up with. I would have been a lot more careful what I said if I'd thought anyone was paying any attention!"

"With Laura it's the other way around. I always thought she was listening. Now I realize she wasn't."

"Well, who's to say our advice is any good anyway? *I* certainly don't pretend to know how they ought to live their lives." Shirley checked the northern view from the tiny window. "Maybe it's a blessing about Betsy anyway—her not being that crazy to have kids. Because you know, she's got problems."

"Problems? She and Gil?"

There was a pleased spark to June's question, an eagerness that annoyed Shirley.

"No, no. She and Gil are fine. I mean with her system. Her periods stopped several years ago. I'm not sure she could get pregnant if she wanted to."

"I hadn't heard about this. Shirley, aren't you concerned?"

Meaning, *You certainly should be.* As if the correct degree of well-placed concern on a parent's part could solve a grown child's every problem.

"I can't see any point sitting around wringing my hands over it," Shirley said.

June pressed her lips together. Touché. For this was where the two sisters differed, and they'd been arguing their contrasting child-rearing methods since the girls were born. June had always accused Shirley of a certain emotional distance from her daughters. Bordering, at times, she implied, on neglect? Whereas Shirley felt June, for lack of anything better to do, simply enjoyed wringing her hands over Laura whether it did any good or not.

"Was that a car horn?" Shirley went back to the window in the big room where she could see the driveway through the branches of the gnarly shore pine. "Oh, it's Stephanie!" She hurried out, glancing into the other room in passing. "That's about it up here, isn't it?"

Without waiting for June's answer, she rushed down the stairs to her daughter and to her grandchild-to-be.

Chapter 17

Covered with an afghan against the chilly air, Stephanie reclined on the porch lounge, the canvas for a needlepoint wall hanging across her lap. Of course she'd been warned about the fatigue of early pregnancy, but she had expected perhaps a pleasant sleepiness, not this terminal torpor. At the rate the tiny stitches were going into this project, the frolicking animals would be ready to hang on the nursery wall about the time the baby qualified for senior citizen discounts.

Pregnant. She'd looked forward to this all her life, and now it was happening. Difficult to imagine, but by the Fourth of July next year, she'd be sitting here at Neskowin with a baby. And that's what she really wanted—the baby, soft and cuddly. Not like some of these women, who seemed mainly excited about pregnancy itself. Were they seriously suggesting a person should enjoy bloating up like an ongoing and ever-worsening case of PMS?

Down the beach to the south, she could see the waves crashing against what she and Betsy had always called Shark Fin Rock. Above it rose the steep, northernmost slopes of Cascade Head. There, in its curved protection, the fir trees stood straight to the sky. In the opposite direction up the beach, the low dunes lay exposed, and the wind bent and shaped the shore pines that arched over Neskowin's cluster of cottages.

At the creek which cut out through the sand between their end of the beach and Neskowin, she spotted two specks. She picked up the binoculars—her mother and Aunt June. Wouldn't you know it? Just talking away. She lay the binoculars down again. Would she and Betsy ever look that chummy to someone framing the two of them in a spying circle? Or would the places where they could never connect show up even at a distance?

She went back to watching the gravel road that divided the yard from the grass-covered dune at the edge of the beach. Betsy and Gil should be arriving any time.

Her stomach fluttered at this. Darn it anyway. She'd have sworn she quit caring what her sister thought long ago, maybe the year Betsy left for college and, for the first time ever, she could talk at the dinner table without having to fight for center stage. No more Betsy versus Dad, arguing them all into indigestion over the war or land-use planning. And how nice it was to let Dad call her "kitten" and not have to cringe, waiting for Betsy to mutter, "Jeez, what is this? *Father Knows Best?*" What a relief to come home with a problem and not have Betsy instantly eclipse it with something better and more dramatic. For if Stephanie had a friend who'd seemed a bit cool lately, Betsy had someone who was posting poison pen letters about her at school. If Stephanie had been reprimanded for talking in class, Betsy had been called into the principal's office over her guest editorial in the school paper. If Stephanie was a bit under the weather for the big football game, Betsy had a temperature of 103 the day before her SATs.

Stephanie still remembered that week in seventh grade when she had to have braces put on. Face it, she'd thought, staring at her tin teeth in the mirror. Life's over. Then Betsy had to go and break her leg skiing, which of course caused a much bigger commotion. Okay, she didn't do it on purpose, but wasn't she almost asking for an accident, taking on the head wall like that? All those hunky high school boys who'd carried the stretcher down the mountain . . . and back at school, the sweet, goofy little drawing Todd Baker had scribbled on her cast . . .

But that was kid stuff, right? What was she afraid of now?

Betsy's sarcasm on the subject of motherhood? No, surely her sister had outgrown that a long time ago too. Even a dismissive attitude would be hard to take, though, especially after Laura's barely concealed condescension.

"Well, isn't this *nice* for you?" she'd said when she and Barry were presented with the news on their arrival today. As if having a baby was a lovely idea for people who didn't have anything more important to do. As if Laura regarded pregnancy as just so *cute*. And then, the first minute she got Stephanie alone, launching into all the reasons she and Barry, of course, would not be indulging . . .

Indulging. That was a good one. Stephanie had already gained seven pounds and her face was broken out like it hadn't been since she was thirteen. So far, pregnancy felt more like a strange case of the flu than anything to do with a baby. It definitely did not feel like an indulgence.

Then too, she was still in shock. It had happened so fast. One month of not using her diaphragm and bingo. Madeleine, who did the bookkeeping at the dress shop where Stephanie worked, said it had taken her six months, and her doctor said that was perfectly normal.

Stephanie sighed. It might help if Matt were a little more attentive. Instead he kept forgetting. She'd be lying on the sofa, completely exhausted after putting in a full day on her feet at the shop, and he'd come home from the bank and say, "What's the matter?" as if it surprised him, as if she must be coming down with something serious if she hadn't started dinner yet. "I'm pregnant, remember?" she'd say. "It makes you tired." Maybe when it showed he'd be more sympathetic. Other people too. She looked forward to appearing obviously pregnant and not just fat.

Still, her mother's happiness almost made up for everything else. Stephanie had known she was pleased, of course, but until today, when Shirley had hurried out to greet her, Stephanie hadn't realized just how much this grandchild meant. And Aunt June right behind her, equally teary. Stephanie had felt like a person delivering a lovely picnic to some very hungry people. Heavens, if she'd known they were going to be so thrilled, she might have done it sooner.

She *should* have done it sooner.

She picked up the canvas, found her place on the pattern,

lay the fabric back down. If she had a boy, she would name him after her father. Matt wouldn't dare argue about that.

Stephanie tried not to notice how her heart thumped when the dusty red pickup rounded the road. She watched Gil park. Oh really, why didn't they get a new car? Surely they weren't so hard up they had to drive around looking like something from *The Grapes of Wrath*. Didn't it embarrass them, parking next to her sparkling clean Honda, not to mention Laura's Volvo? That homemade shingled camper top on the back . . . Stephanie thought Gil had realized the sixties were over when he cut his hair, but maybe not.

As Betsy got out of the truck cab, Stephanie fought the urge to rise. Let Betsy come to her, she thought. She was the pregnant one. She lifted her hand in greeting.

Betsy started up the stone steps, stopped and said something to Gil, then continued. She carried a Tupperware container. Probably sugared berries for the shortcake Mom mentioned. Too bad it didn't sound as good as usual. Her appetite had turned so strange. She watched Betsy climb the steps. Something was wrong, she realized. Usually she'd be six steps ahead of Gil, talking and laughing.

"Hi," she said, finally reaching the porch. "Hey, congratulations."

"Thanks." Stephanie nodded at Gil, who, in spite of his smile, looked distinctly uncomfortable.

"So how are you feeling?" Betsy asked.

"Okay." She laughed uncertainly. "Well, actually, not so great, but my doctor says it's within the normal range of yuckiness."

Gil's eyes flicked to Betsy. More than his usual shyness, Stephanie decided. Maybe it embarrassed him, acknowledging something to do with women's bodies.

"But everything's okay?" Betsy asked, paying no attention to Gil.

Stephanie nodded. Did strawberries always smell so strong? Actually, it seemed pregnancy was making everything smell strong.

"Well, great," Betsy said. "Hey, guess I'm going to be an aunt, huh?"

Stephanie listened hard for the barely stifled wisecrack. Funny, it didn't seem to be there.

* * *

A short time later, after everyone had collected back at the house and exchanged greetings (except for Laura and Barry, who raised eyebrows as usual by remaining upstairs with their door closed), Shirley and June started a late lunch.

"We just realized we're out of mayo," Shirley said. "Betsy, could I get you to buzz around to the store?"

"Sure."

"I'll come too," Stephanie said. "Let's take my car."

"Are you sure you want to drive?" Shirley said.

"Mom! I drove up from Newport by myself."

"Well, I know. I just thought, as long as Betsy's here . . ."

Stephanie rolled her eyes at Betsy, heading out. "Something tells me this is going to be a long pregnancy."

Driving the gravel road to the highway, Stephanie realized her mood was lifting. Maybe she'd been even more uptight about seeing Betsy than she'd realized. In fairness, her sister hadn't been anything but pleasant.

She stopped at the highway. "Laura's saying now she's not going to have kids. I mean ever."

"Yeah?" They waited for a couple of cars and a camper coming down from the run over Cascade Head, then pulled onto 101. "Is she saying why not?"

"Oh, *really*, Betsy, how could they? And risk their special, *special* relationship?"

As children, she and Betsy had shared an intense admiration for their sophisticated older cousin, especially during certain periods. Still completely flat-chested, they'd been awestruck, for instance, the summer Laura showed up at Neskowin with honest-to-God breasts. And whoever heard of a blonde tanning like that? They openly competed for her attention, with Stephanie usually winning. Her willingness to have life explained always meshed so neatly with Laura's need to do the explaining.

But after they'd all grown up, and especially after her marriage to Barry, a university physicist too brilliant to converse with ordinary mortals, Stephanie and Betsy had subtly united against her, partly out of envy (who wouldn't enjoy having her husband's eyes constantly following her like that?) and maybe partly because they'd never quite been able to forgive her for divorcing Christopher. Stephanie and Betsy had been bridesmaids at that first wedding; they had a certain sentimental stake in the marriage. Not to mention the way Christopher had charmed them with his wacky sense of humor, his completely on-target mimicry of everything from TV evangelists to the current occupant of the White House. Everyone hated to let such a rich source of entertainment escape from the family. And it was so annoying, too, the way Laura never felt obliged to voice regrets or say exactly why they'd separated. In light of her choice for hubby number two, Stephanie and Betsy could only conclude that Laura wanted a spouse she wouldn't have to share.

"Laura tells me the no-baby decision was not one they made lightly," Stephanie said. "She says she and Barry put it all down on paper, the pros and cons of parenthood."

"Oh right. Can't you just see them doing one of those little check-off tests in the women's magazines? *Are You Ready for a Baby?*' Betsy snorted. "As if deciding to have a baby could ever be a rational decision."

"Well, thanks a lot."

"No, I mean not rational as in it's a gut decision. If you really started thinking too hard about all those nights you'll be walking the floor with this crying baby . . ."

"Hey, do you mind? Don't get me all depressed. Anyway, I just can't believe her saying that to me, about her marriage being too good to risk. What does that make mine?"

"Maybe it's not so much her marriage being too good as being too fragile."

"Are you kidding? They're going on four years now and you've said yourself she makes it sound like one long honeymoon." They'd all heard about the vacations at cozy lodges in the mountains, the bicycling tour around the Olympic Peninsula. No way would Laura join the gripe sessions where they told my-husband-is-worse-than-your-husband stories. She had Barry on a pedestal and was obviously determined to keep him there.

Okay, Stephanie thought, so some of this was envy. But, really. Holing up in their room so they could read aloud to each other? Sometimes it all got too sappy to bear. Thank goodness she had Betsy to widen her eyes at ever so discreetly when Laura decided to once again favor them with some breathless hint of marital rapture.

"Maybe she's afraid having a baby would ruin her figure," Stephanie said.

"Oh, I can't believe anybody would give up having a baby because of that. Even Laura."

"Well, she's also got this whole spiel about overpopulation."

"Right. I'm sure. She's always so correct."

"Do you think I should be feeling guilty about that?"

"Don't be silly."

"Well, I just wondered what you thought. Didn't you used to wear a stop-at-two button in college?"

"Yeah, I wore flowers in my hair and talked about weaving my own clothes too."

"So you've quit worrying about overpopulation?"

"No, I still think it's a problem. I just don't think life's so black and white anymore. Anyway, I never said stop at none. If everybody stopped at none the human race would be gone in a hundred years, right?"

"Gee, I hadn't thought of it that way." Stephanie pulled into the store parking lot. "Hey, when did Laura start wearing those glasses, anyway? Is she trying for a more intellectual look or something?"

"That's sort of what I thought at first. Like she wanted people to take her more seriously. Remember that time she tried to tell us just how *difficult* it was, being pretty?"

"Like *we* obviously wouldn't have a clue about it."

Betsy laughed. "But anyway, actually I guess her contacts were bugging her. Did you notice how pretty her eyes are without them? That pale, pale gray."

"I guess." Stephanie's contacts were tinted turquoise. Sometimes she wondered if they were too vivid. "Oh, wait'll you see the ring Barry got her. It's one of those anniversary ones with diamonds all the way around."

"Yeah? Well, good for her. Has she checked into whether those South African diamond miners are being exploited?"

Stephanie laughed, and then after a moment said, "Well gee, Betsy, what about you? Seeing as how cousins are so much fun, is this baby of mine ever going to get any? I mean, what's *your* gut feeling?" Stephanie waited as her sister stared through the windshield. Why was the question such a stumper? "Come on, don't tell me you're still not giving any thought to this."

"Don't worry," Betsy said, turning away. "I think about it." She pushed her door open.

Stephanie got out her side and smiled at her sister over the top of the car. "It's just that it's so hard to believe, Betsy. For once, me actually beating you to something important!"

Chapter 18

I wish I could report that Gil and I held hands as we strolled back along the beach after the Fourth of July parade, but he isn't into hand-holding any more than he's into calling me darling. Sometimes for fun, I grab on and time him. His record? Forty seconds.

Carrying our shoes, we passed opposite the beach house, and by some silent agreement walked on toward the forest-crowned cliffs at the end of the beach. The morning's overcast had given way to blue sky, with the air holding just enough fog to mist the scene, soften the edges of the rock out-croppings. The fir tops of the highest ridge disappeared into the dark cloud that always seemed to hang over the head, hovering to swirl out at any time. How often had we strolled to the creek in sunshine only to be caught running home in the rain?

But if you waited for a perfectly clear, safe day, you'd hardly ever get out in the sun at all.

I had always loved this particular place, but today its majesty seemed strangely empty.

I thought of a study I'd heard about where they showed landscape paintings to people and tracked their eye movements. A human figure in the composition, no matter how small and insignificant, would always draw the eye, they found. You see, we say we love the landscapes, the vistas, the wild world free of humans, but most of us still love our place in the whole scheme best.

Once, on a cross-country ski trail the winter before we married, I'd been overcome with this feeling, watching Gil glide before me down a long slope, diminishing into a dot against the cold white expanse of mountain and sky. So much of what I loved in the world, my whole future it seemed, was contained in that figure, the only warmth in the entire picture.

Now Gil walked beside me, and for my future I wanted our child as the tiny human counterpoint, dancing out ahead of us.

I noticed children so much lately, it wasn't hard to conjure an image of our own. Naturally I optimistically endowed this child with every good quality, and beyond that, I pictured in her an extra glow, a joy I thought must surely be the birthright of a baby wanted so fervently that her parents had all but willed her into existence through longing alone. I saw her whirling across the sand, arms upraised, cartwheeling into a flock of gulls.

What if we never got to see this?

Never.

This word must be one of the cruelest in the English language. Certainly used to get our adolescent tear ducts going as we parted from new-made camp friends and boarded home-bound buses. *I will never see you again.* We enjoyed the crying then, I think, reveled in our newfound capacity for what we imagined to be adult-type emotion, conveniently overlooking the fact that we could probably arrange to see these friends again if our grief persisted beyond two weeks.

But now we were grown, and didn't move on to new hurts so quickly. The word *never* had more permanent possibilities, as in *Grampa Stroh will never walk the beach at Neskowin again*. As in death. As in this situation that felt curiously similar to death.

Which was worse? I wondered now. I will never see you again. Or I will never see you. Ever.

I'm still a great believer in crying, flushing out with tears the poison of sorrow. These days, when it built up in my chest to the choking point, I had only to flop across our brass bed and whisper one sentence to myself: *I will never have Gil's baby*.

Death. That's what it felt like.

But then, it wasn't really death, was it? So when the tears were all cried out, or sometimes even before they'd stopped, I'd get up and go on. I learned to do things like balance the checkbook even while crying. Very useful. I recommend it to anyone who finds herself becoming a frequent crier. Like my mother always said, you're bound to feel better in the morning. And then you'll be glad your checkbook's done.

We stood for a moment now in the shady cove, gazing at the ferns and clumps of yellow flowers that spilled from every damp crevice. What was the matter with me, even for one moment linking all this to death? We were alive. Why wasn't Gil enough? Was there something inferior about our relationship that it needed a child to complete it?

I tried a mental list of all the couples we knew who were living happy lives without children. Trouble was, there weren't that many. In the first place, if they were under forty, you couldn't really consider the matter closed, the way people were beating the clock at the last minute these days. And second, even if it was clear they definitely wouldn't have children and were definitely happy (I thought of Jed and Clair Compton, high school art teachers envied by all for their mutually supportive relationship, their welcoming home, their wilderness adventures), the crucial question for me still went unanswered: Had they *chosen* not to have children, or had they somehow found their way through the misery of infertility to some semblance of contentment beyond?

If only the whole subject weren't so darned private! The only person I knew who talked openly about it was Laura, and what comfort was that? Obviously Gil and I did not have the sort of cozy, self-contained marriage she and Barry bragged about.

We turned at the same time and headed back up the beach.

Watching the children in the Fourth of July parade earlier, I realized that no matter what I said in college, deep down I always assumed I'd have kids. I thought we all would. Laura too.

Maybe I even took a proprietary view of Laura's reproductive history. After all, it was me who first spotted the red stain on her shorts the summer she was thirteen. I'd thought myself pretty smart, knowing what it was, even though I was only nine. I'd been educated early on the subject after a shopping incident in which I had loudly asked about the contents of the pastel boxes with the pretty ladies on them. My mother's embarrassment only increased my curiosity—as well as my persistence. She spelled it all out as soon as we got home, mainly, I think, in hopes of avoiding such scenes in the future.

Anyway, feeling smug and excited about my discovery concerning Laura, I hadn't appreciated it at all when Aunt June swooped her into the bathroom, closing the door in my face. Later, when Laura came out looking supremely pleased with herself, she seemed to have completely forgotten who'd been good enough to clue her in to this historic event in the first place.

"Now I can have a baby" was all she said.

Same story when I started two years later, same for my friends. "Now you can have babies," we told each other, eyes aglow. "Now you can have babies," our mothers warned, eyes narrowed.

Always the babies. Even before I started my period, I remember weeping in the bathtub one night because I could not find this vagina thing my mother had finally told me about. (Her initial, euphemistic explanation, which relied heavily on the word *tummy*, had been clarified when she overheard me explaining to Stephanie about bleeding belly buttons.)

"I don't have a vagina," I wailed when she found me crying in the tub. "I won't be able to have babies!"

I'm struck now that even as a child, with no thought to what being vaginaless might mean to a person's sex life, I could already well grasp the sorrow of childlessness.

You Will Want Children. Was this something they conspired to program in us so early that we had no choice but to obey? Or did it go deeper, a biological directive, compelling us to keep swimming salmonlike up that stream, battering ourselves on the rocks, leaping the falls to lay those eggs at all cost?

And whichever it was, I thought, how had Laura managed to circumvent it so effectively? Because if I couldn't have kids, my second choice was to be like her and not *want* kids. I'd marveled at her apparent contentment at the beach fire last night. Didn't it bother her, watching the children at a nearby fire, knowing she'd never have one of her own to watch whirling in the hissing white light of a sparkler? For by now, older children were starting to get to me almost as much as babies, as if with passing time the true scope of our potential loss was becoming clear. I couldn't get a sulfur whiff of fireworks or taste a charred marshmallow without remembering my own childhood and realizing—if you couldn't get pregnant, it wasn't just this baby you held in your arms for a few months you'd be losing; you were losing an entire life.

I kicked along a line of pulpy debris, my shoes dangling from my fingertips.

"Not saying much," Gil pointed out.

"I've said as much as you have."

After another moment of silence, he said, "I told you we shouldn't have gone to the parade."

Yes, he'd told me. Over and over, in fact, starting back in Mary's Bend when I told him I'd gotten my period, and not letting up until the volunteer fire department truck led off the wacky procession here in Neskowin.

"What are we supposed to do, Gil? Hide out the rest of our lives? Other people's kids exist. We're bound to run into them."

"Yeah, but we don't have to make a point of going out looking for them, do we?"

It *had* been fairly overwhelming—swarms of costumed kids running around, the babies tucked in backpacks or frontpacks, pushed in strollers, hoisted up to shoulders, safely hidden, unborn, in big, proud bellies.

"Not that it's some major cosmic sorrow to me," Gil went on, "but what's the point of watching other people have fun?"

"You know, I was thinking about that," I said. "Remember the little girl, the fairy princess whose mother was pretending to fly her? I was trying to cheer myself up imagining someday I'd be doing that. How I'd make the greatest costume. And then I realized that when I'm doing that, when I've got my baby—well, there'll always be people watching who can't have babies. Then I'll be making *them* sad."

Gil winced, apparently at the unbearable stupidity of this. "Betsy? Uh, whaddaya say we worry about that one when we get to it."

I kept walking.

"If nobody could be happy until everybody was happy," he called to my back, "we'd all be miserable forever!"

But I couldn't help thinking about all those others. Sometimes when I got my period, I wondered how many women had just yesterday dared hope along with me that they were finally pregnant, only to come up disappointed once again today. Tears? Lord, I hate to think.

And somewhere, somebody who'd been trying to conceive for a long time found out that she finally had. Was she thrilled? Were she and her husband crazy with joy? Was she on the phone to people about it? Down at the store buying baby things? Picking out wallpaper for the nursery?

I dreamed of joy like that, held the hope of it up to myself, imagining it would be all the sweeter for having been so elusive. But in darker moments I wondered if Carla was right. Maybe these monthly failures did just wear you down until you didn't remember *how* to be happy.

Gil had caught up and walked beside me again.

After a while, I asked if he'd seen Laura's anniversary ring.

"No. What about it?"

"It's one of those with diamonds all around. The kind the ads claim is the only way to say you'd marry your wife all over again."

"Those ads are full of shit."

I laughed. "Yeah, but would you?"

"Would I what?"

"Marry me again? Even if you knew about all this infertility stuff?"

An annoying half beat for thought. "Sure."

I sighed. I figured that was the answer. But sometimes I

wanted words. More of them. Inside my sweatshirt pocket, I rubbed my thumb against my plain gold wedding band. On the inside was engraved "All my love forever." But those were *my* words, damnit, the ones I told Gil I had chosen when we'd gone to pick out our rings. I'd asked then what he planned to have engraved on mine.

"Well . . ." He considered. "What was that you said?"

"All my love forever?"

"Yeah, that."

"What about it?"

"That's what I'll put too."

"Oh come on! Aren't you going to make up something yourself?"

"Hey, all my love forever. What more do you want?"

Sometimes I wondered if I'd paid the jeweler to engrave on his ring "For as long as I jolly well feel like it," that's what mine would say too.

"Sometimes," I said now, "I just wish you'd *say* things more. All you ever say is 'sure.' Couldn't you elaborate a little? Stretch it out to six words, maybe?"

He sighed. "Yes, I'd marry you all over again." He thought a moment. "That's seven, okay?"

"Gil." I wondered: Were there women out there actually hearing what they wanted to hear, or was that just a Madison Avenue fantasy?

"Come on, Betsy, saying a lot of mushy stuff or buying a fancy ring would be easier than going through all this medical stuff together. And probably a lot cheaper, too."

"Huh. I thought talk was supposed to be cheap. I swear, you're tighter with words than you are with money."

The parade and flag raising must have ended. Down where the creek ran into Proposal Rock and divided around it to the ocean, people were gathering with their beach umbrellas and coolers, setting up mini-encampments for the afternoon. Children scampered around, tiny figures dwarfed and protected by the monolith. Damn! I wanted to be down there with them. To be fair, at a distance, the scene probably looked more idyllic than it really was. The wind and the ocean muffled the children's squabbling and the parents' scolding. So what? I even wanted in on the nagging—that's how crazy I was getting. One kid was the ticket into that world. One kid and you could be one of the mothers pushing someone in a park swing, or hugging that sweet, slippery flesh at the Aquatic Center pool. One child and you were a mother, down at Neskowin Creek, part of the club.

Coming toward us at right angles, a couple carrying a small child struggled down through the dry sand to the hard-packed strip where everyone walked. They set the baby down. Just taking its first steps, he toddled toward us, one pudgy hand grasping his mother's finger, the other his father's.

As we met, we nodded in the reserved way people on our beach do when they pass. The parents were about our ages. They smiled at us with a certain self-consciousness, aware, I guess, of just how cute their little boy was with his silky, bowl-cut hair and brightly colored jogging suit. Gil, I noticed, returned the smile automatically, easily. But I no longer smiled at children just because they were cute. I smiled because smiling at children is obligatory. A person who doesn't at least crook the corner of her mouth risks looking like a grouch.

So we passed, and because I was walking with my face down, I noticed their footprints, the larger ones on each side anyway. The baby was so light, he left no print, not the slightest indentation.

My head snapped around.

"What's the matter?" Gil said.

The baby still walked between them. "Nothing." I faced forward again. How could I explain that for an irrational instant I'd thought he might not really be there? Maybe theirs was nothing but a dream child too. A baby like ours, lighter than a wish, too light, too precious for ordinary footprints in the sand.

To Do

Work

Measure at Donnells
Tues—Griffith

Balance checkbook
Lunch w/ Mom?
Pick up Rxs

Fri—Andersen

To Buy

- Paste
- Razors
- Measuring tape
- Sizing

Raspberry ad to paper
Have film developed
Fix pantry door
Pay bills
10th St. rent
Work on Amy's quilt
Visit Grampa

Chapter 19

After we got home from Neskowin, I decided to make my big confession of infertility to my mom. Gil wouldn't like it, but with Stephanie pregnant and Laura openly torturing Aunt June with her decision to live child-free, pregnancy was a hot topic, tough to avoid. Besides, I was thoroughly sick of carrying around this grenade of a secret. That's how I thought of it anyway.

Imagine my surprise when I pulled the pin and—fzzz—no explosion.

The thrill of hearing I actually wanted a child after all seemed to render my mother impervious to the news that I wasn't having any luck getting one. "Oh, but you will," she kept saying, just too pleased and excited to willingly come back to earth.

Swell, I thought. Go looking for sympathy and what do you get? One more person you'll be letting down with your failure.

Believe me, I was more than ready for the distraction of some new project when the son of Jennie McBee Nellers called to say they were ready to discuss selling the little house.

Gil balked, of course, and fretted about the money. So I

got out the books and showed him we weren't in such bad shape. I could get a loan for the remodeling, and I wouldn't have any trouble getting a good monthly rent for the place to cover payments. It would only be tight for a few months. And besides, with any luck, I could get a historic designation which would eventually help on taxes.

He kept on about the medical bills, but actually I think money was just what he talked about when other things were getting him down.

"Look," I finally said. "I am *so sick* of feeling like a loser. Wouldn't a project like this make more sense than sending me to a shrink at seventy-five dollars a pop?"

"Well, yeah, I can see that . . ."

"And anyway, what's the worst that can happen? I have to put the house back on the market. So what?"

Actually, the worst was that I'd have to sell the house at a loss, but that wasn't likely. And any deal is something of a gamble. Can't get anywhere always playing it safe.

Finally he gave in. I'm sure the appealing prospect of a less mopey wife helped. God knows I'd been a drag. I do try to be choosy about the time and place for breaking down, but basically, crying comes as easily to me as laughing or breathing, whereas to Gil, crying is a phenomenon to be halted at all costs, immediately if not sooner.

So we bought the little McBee place. Call it an investment. Call it therapy.

This was my third house, not counting our own. The third time I'd pulled up in front of a place with my camera ready for the *before* pictures. My favorite moment. I'd seen the inside, of course, but the first time you arrive after you've officially taken possession is something different. You can walk through and really see what you've got—feel free to pull back a corner of the wallpaper, scrape a bit of painted woodwork to check the grain beneath.

It was a quiet July day. Warm, a little muggy. I unlocked the door and stepped in. The air was stuffy, thick with the smell of old, heated wood and ancient mice nests. I went around opening windows and then, before I so much as took out a broom, I snapped pictures everywhere. A *before* shot should be as bad as possible, right?

The house was unusual in having such nice woodwork and fittings for its size. Besides the main room downstairs, it had a small kitchen, one bathroom, and then, through an arch in the living room, facing the backyard, a neat little library with a window seat. The upstairs was one large bedroom with slanted ceilings and dormers. Best of all, it had been well maintained—rewired and plumbed fairly recently. Most of the improvements would be more or less cosmetic—things I could do myself.

But where to start? It would be nice to strip the old varnish from the woodwork while the weather was still warm and dry enough to keep the windows open. Those fumes could get pretty bad. But the roof and exterior painting needed to be finished before the rains too.

But first things first. I gave the bathroom—including the claw-footed tub—a good scouring. I could clean up right here for my clinic appointments instead of having to detour by the farm.

Several weeks and another failed cycle later, I was sitting on the front porch of the little McBee house, eating a tuna sandwich and listening to the news. I had stripped interior woodwork until I was sick of it and now I was halfway through prying the old shingles off the roof. My knuckles were raw, but I'd been enjoying sitting up there, Frisbee-tossing old shingles toward the haul-away bin I'd had the disposal company deliver. I was just about to get back to work when Eric Norgren's van cruised up. At first I thought he was going to the big McBee house next door for some final detail, but then he stopped right at the end of my cement walkway.

He got out and slammed the door. "Hey there. Heard a rumor shingles were flying around here. Didn't know it was you."

"It's me."

"So, the McBees hired you to get her in shape, huh?"

"Nope," I said. "I bought it."

His eyes widened just a flash. This one little place was nothing to him, but he felt entitled to his pick of every property in town.

"This mean you're giving up on the farmer and moving into town?"

"Eric! No, it doesn't. I'm going to rent it out."

I didn't care for the way he always referred to Gil as "the farmer." He started that a couple years ago, right after Gil's accident, the one that made Gil temporarily famous all over the county. The tailgate of his big truck had come loose as he rounded the corner of one of the main intersections downtown, and he has never truly recovered from the shock of finding that picture of himself on the front page of the newspaper, looking befuddled, surveying the damage. After that he never hauled chicken manure again.

Eric squinted up at the roof. "I've got some leftover shakes I could give you a good price on if you're interested."

"Oh thanks, but I've decided to go with composition."

He frowned. "Won't sell. People don't like the look."

"But they're so much safer—flammability and all that . . ."

"Well, sure, if safety's your top priority."

I stuffed my sandwich wraps in the bag and stood up. "Sometimes it is, sometimes it isn't."

"Well. Hey, you gonna be able to do that Forest Acres job for me next week?"

(As if he'd asked me previously, which he hadn't.)

"That one of your new houses?"

"Right. It'd be quick, clean. Fast money."

"Fast money? Excuse me, Eric, but there's no such thing with you."

"Hey, I'm paid up with you, aren't I?"

I narrowed my eyes at him. Actually he was, for the moment. First time in months, though.

"I don't know," he said. "Maybe you've got your hands full with this."

"Well . . ." I *was* cutting back some on the papering. I couldn't afford to drag out the work on this place too long. Still, money coming in was money coming in. "Yeah, I'll do it."

"Okay, great. Hey, there's a good auction up in Yamhill County this weekend. They're liquidating an architectural salvage place. All kinds of great stuff. Stained glass, carved doors, used bricks, brass light fixtures. You want a ride up?"

"Gee . . . stained glass . . . ?"

"Oh yeah. Everything. I'll be taking my big truck, so it'd be easy to toss on anything you wanted to pick up."

"Well, that sounds—"

"And it's right there on the winery route. We could hit a few of those too."

Okay, wait a minute here. It'd been a while, but I had a dim memory of this sort of ambiguous invitation.

"Uh, thanks, but I don't think so."

"Oh come on, why not? I thought you'd be hot for some great bargains. At the last one of these things I got a marble sink top for thirty dollars."

"Thirty dollars? Well . . ."

"I could pick you up here."

I cocked my head at him, wondering. Why not at the farm, if this was so damned innocent?

"Eric." I was looking over toward the big McBee house now, hating the fact that I was blushing. I remembered these dialogues. I remembered the utter impossibility of giving a graceful answer, one that would save face, yet extricate me in no uncertain terms. "Eric. Gimme a break. I'm married, remember?"

He laughed, shaking his head at his boots like he couldn't believe I was saying that. Then he raised his bushy blond eyebrows at me. "Married people can't go to auctions?"

My cheeks burned. "So call me old-fashioned."

"You? Come on."

See how this works? If I had agreed to go with him, I'll bet the rent he'd eventually be asking me something along the lines of why had I come if I wasn't interested in him? If I then pleaded to being just a hopeless sucker for a good auction, his answer would be the same: *Oh come on.*

"Don't you think that's kind of screwy," he persisted, "wanting to be the kind of woman who can take a crowbar to an old roof, then going and tying yourself down?"

I'll be darned. He really *was* trying to hit on me. I suppose he had been for quite a while.

I tried to laugh it off. "Hey, I hated dating the first time around. Why would I want to start in again?"

"Jesus, who said anything about a date? Is it against the law to offer a friend a ride?"

Oh yes, the part where the guy makes you pay in humiliation. Heavens! Maybe you misinterpreted his kind offer!

"Okay," I said, "have it your way. You weren't asking for a date. You politely offered me a ride. I'm politely declining."

Still that sly smile. "You," he said, "are such a good little wife."

I smiled right back. *And you*, I was thinking, *are going to make such an amusing anecdote at my dinner table tonight.*

But also, I have to admit, I was turning something else over in my mind. I couldn't help contrasting this guy's verbal persistence with Gil's lack of it. I wondered if this translated into delicious listening for the women Eric ultimately cornered. Maybe. And yet, whatever had gone wrong with his marriage, it apparently hadn't been helped by willingness on his part to discuss it.

"Eric? I've got work to do."

"Okay, sure." He eased in on me. "But, Betsy? You gotta learn to lighten up, okay? I can't believe you make such a big deal out of every friendly offer." He was standing so close I could catch his own personal scent mixed with the smell of sawdust.

Right then I saw our farm truck coming around the corner.

"What a nice surprise," I said sweetly. "It's Gil."

Eric the Innocent immediately arranged a more suitable distance between the two of us.

My face was flushing as Gil got out and slammed the door, not from any feeling of guilt, but from a consciousness of Eric's innuendos lingering in the air.

I needn't have worried. Gil had other things on his mind. He came toward us slowly, nodding at Eric without actually taking him in.

"Dad called," he said to me. "Uh . . . Gramma died."

Chapter 20

Much as I loved Gil's ninety-five-year-old Gramma Emma, I confess that my mind registered unadulterated sorrow for only a moment or two before flashing alarm: Flying to Los Angeles for the funeral meant I would not be in Mary's Bend for my HCG shot.

Gil and I drove the two trucks home, and as soon as he was safely out in the garden, I called Dr. Lowell. Could we arrange for the shot down there?

"Oh, Betsy, I don't know . . ." A long, depressing pause. "If it were just the shot . . . the thing is, your follicles aren't doing anything yet. I don't know how many more scans you'd need or when you'd be ready for the HCG."

"It just kills me, though, to waste the whole cycle."

"But it won't be wasted. You're both going to L.A., right? You can still have intercourse."

"Yeah, but if I don't get the shot . . ."

"Well, Betsy, we don't really know if the shots are helping anyway."

"We don't?" News to me. "My charts have been better."

"I know, but . . . Look, consider this a little break. Forget about ultrasound scans. Go do what you need to do in L.A. Have sex the way you normally would—"

"But—"

"And we'll see what happens."

Right. Sex the way we normally would.

If I could rely on some memory of normalcy from the distant past, I was pretty sure that normal for us was not what Dr. Lowell envisioned. Normal for us with death hanging in the air would be no sex at all.

Nothing makes me feel more like a true Oregonian than L.A. in August. Lanes of crawling cars to the right, lanes of hostile, impatient, swerving-in-and-out-for-position cars to the left. It's easy to picture the guns, the shootings. ("Bastard cut into my lane!") And the beach. Nice warm water, sure, but I cannot get used to facing thousands of miles of ocean and not being hit with a cool blast of fresh air. Something close to panic comes over me when those Santa Anas swirl the hot smog out over the water and I realize there will be no such thing as a clean breath until I'm home. The entire time I'm down there, one refrain pulses through me, low and barely controlled: Get. Me. Outta here.

March would have been better. Flying, as we did one spring vacation, from the soggy gray Northwest to the breezy sunshine of Pacific Palisades, I could understand why people might enjoy living here. Surprise! There are mountains out beyond the city. Residents get to see them for three days each March.

But August? Well, we can't expect people to schedule death with an aim toward nice funeral weather, can we?

It's always a bit strange, sleeping in Gil's boyhood room. Not that it's one of those shrines to youth or anything, but with its no-nonsense plaid bedspread and a couple of junior high sports trophies on the shelf, it still feels like a place off-limits to females. I can almost smell the grass-stained jeans and dirty socks.

Our first night there, I turned to Gil in bed. Might as well get it over with.

He patted me halfheartedly. "I s'pose this is an arrow night?"

"'Fraid so."

Well, of course we didn't feel like sex. I don't know why

it is that in so many books, death is supposed to be some big turn-on. Faced with it, fearing it, or simply smacked with the news of it, couples hop in the sack for a desperate, life-affirming orgy. Is this for real? Is it possible writers are just recycling the notion from one novel to the next? Maybe I'm weird, but I prefer sex accompanied by joy.

"Tired?" I said.

"Yeah. Um . . ."

"What?"

"Well, what do you say we give it a rest?"

I ran a finger along his jawline. "Is it Gramma? You're too bummed out?"

"No, that's not it." He hesitated. "But if you didn't get the shot . . ."

"Gil—"

"I've got that right? You didn't get it?"

"Yeah, right, I didn't get the shot." I raised up on my elbow. "But I did swallow fifty dollars' worth of pills and go through two ultrasound scans. I've had hot flashes and cramps and every time you turn a light on when it's dark the whole world wiggles with black lines like a bad TV screen and I worry I'm gonna go blind!"

He opened one eye at me. "Is this your idea of talking dirty?"

"Oh *please.*" I flopped on my back and stared at the ceiling. Amazing how insulted I managed to feel, given that I didn't want to make love one bit more than he did. I waited for some move on his part. It didn't come. I glanced over. Asleep! He let out a long, rude snore. "Well fine." I rolled over and curled up on the far edge of the bed. Maybe he really didn't care if we had a baby or not.

There I was, a thousand miles from home, longing to cry, in bed with a husband who would be nothing but annoyed if I did. It has come as a sorry surprise to me over the course of my marriage to find that some of the loneliest moments of your life can be spent lying next to the person you love best.

I pressed a fist against my mouth and I started thinking about my dad. Gramma Emma had missed Amy's delivery of the first great-grandchild, but Dad hadn't even lived to see his grandchildren. Or to know how much I wanted to give him some after all. What the heck—Gil's grandmother dies, and I'm the one lying here with tears dribbling into my ears. But Dad . . . Oh shoot. I've never been a person nagged by ancient regrets, the sort you wind up spilling out to a therapist. But when I remembered the smart-mouthed pronouncements made for his benefit, the ones hinting that only women of subaverage intelligence would consider bearing children, I knew I had a world-class case of Words I Wish I Could Take Back.

My father said people who don't have kids are selfish. What he meant, I realized only now, when it was too late, was that it killed him to think I didn't care to keep it all going, that I didn't want children to love the way he and my mother loved Stephanie and me.

The black spiral of dark night thoughts pulled me down. We're all going to die anyway—what difference does getting pregnant make? And that thing they say about each of us being born alone and dying alone? What a lousy arrangement. I don't want to be separated from the people I love—ever. I thought about Grampa Stroh, so confident that dying would mean reunion with Grandma.

I sure do hope he's right.

The next morning I stood in my slip, looking out Gil's window. We were dressing for the service with an amazing degree of lethargy, as if stalling would somehow make it all go away.

In the distance I could see a patch of ocean, the smudgy horizon. The window was open. I could not so much smell the auto exhaust as taste it. The pop-up sprinklers ching-chinged, flinging their droplets onto the lawn.

"The grass here is weird," I said.

Gil shrugged. "Different variety."

It always strikes me as oddly lacking in depth, like green felt glued over cement. You can't sink in. I watched the sprinklers. Where did that water come from anyway? The Colorado? Frankly, the whole idea of L.A. makes me nervous. It's so precarious. All those people parked there because it's sunny, sucking up the flows of distant rivers.

I don't know, maybe I'd like Southern California better if I weren't always there for a funeral. Maybe it would look different if we were taking our kids to Disneyland, or introducing them to an ocean you could swim in without turning blue.

"You're gonna be miserable in that," I said, referring to Gil's tweed jacket. "We really ought to get you a summer sports coat."

"To wear once every other year?"

He had a point. Still, even if he'd needed it, he wouldn't have bought one. Because even more than he hated dressing up, he hated shopping for clothes to dress up in.

I'll never forget the agony of outfitting him for Stephanie's wedding. He'd been relieved not to be included in the wedding party, but I'd groaned inwardly at the news, knowing a rented tux would be easier than shopping together for a decent alternative. Lord, looking back, I can't believe I actually got him to try on that baby blue leisure suit. I can still picture the incredibly dark look he gave me, how he barely glanced in the mirror, how he started to peel out of it the instant the salesman mentioned white shoes.

Now, after ten years, I wince at the memory. A polyester leisure suit! All I can plead in my defense is the newly wedded naïveté that makes brides somehow imagine their husbands have been simply *longing* for someone to arrive and help polish all those rough edges. I know now it's easier to tolerate ten rough edges than it is to polish even one.

I slipped on my dress and turned for Gil to zip me. "I'm just so sorry Gramma didn't get to see Amy's baby."

"Yeah. Well, at least she knew there'd *be* a baby."

More than we'd come up with.

I shoved one reluctant foot into a too-tight shoe. "You know, when Grandma Conklin died only a month after our wedding, I remember feeling so grateful we'd at least been able to have her with us that day." I put the other foot in the second shoe, equalizing the pain. "I don't think Stephanie's ever forgiven me for that—Grandma living to play the piano at our wedding and then dying before she and Matt got married the next year."

"Come on. That's supposed to be your fault?"

"Well, not really. I mean, she's never put it in so many words, not to my face . . ."

"But she blames you."

"Gil, you know how it is. Don't you think we all put a lot of energy into laying blame for things that aren't anybody's fault? Anyway, it just makes you think. About people dying. Being around for certain stuff and then dying and missing whatever comes next."

Gil was giving me a familiar look—the one that says, *Either I've missed your essential point, which I doubt, or what you've just said is truly astonishing in its total lack of substance or coherence.*

"Betsy." He spoke with exaggerated patience. "Whenever you die you're going to miss whatever comes next."

I sulked, wondering, as I often did, if I was really so poor at expressing myself. I seem to be able to voice similar thoughts—however spacey—to certain friends or to my mother and be understood. Why did Gil persist in finding me so baffling? Well, this was no time for the Why We Can't Communicate fight. He might just be cranky enough to start in with his most below-the-belt explanation—that everyone else must simply be humoring me. Who needed that?

I spoke carefully. "I just meant that some happy things, like a wedding or having a baby, are things you want to share. You hate to have people miss them."

"Well, one thing Gramma lucked out on." Gil tugged at the knot of his tie. "She gets to miss this funeral."

The mission-style chapel in Laguna Beach was not air-conditioned, and the muggy heat, heavy with the mingled scents of carnations and perfume, pressed on my face, melted my makeup. I hardly ever had occasion to wear panty hose, and an afternoon like this certainly made me glad of it.

Gil and I had attended too many funerals together, beginning with the service for my grandmother right after our wedding. Welcome to the marriage, I remember thinking, standing in the reception line next to my husband of one month (That word! *Husband!*) watching him accept condolences from strangers for the loss of this woman he'd met twice.

Three months before, he'd still been arousing in my family certain suspicions of the what-exactly-are-your-intentions variety. Now he was a certified son-in-law, and introduced with barely subdued pride. "Look," my mother was dying to say. "Someone married our daughter! No, not the sweet one, the one who swore she hated men!"

Now we're truly married, I remember thinking. Now we're starting our story, our history of things we've gone through together.

As the organist played now, my eyes kept drifting over to Gil's sister in the pew ahead of us and to the right. Pregnancy looked good on her. A fullness softened her throat. Whoever coined the cliché of the glowing expectant mother had obviously been thinking of someone like Amy. Her uplifted profile could have been captured in stained glass and set beside the angels in the sanctuary windows.

That afternoon, I swear I saw her as some sort of saint. Carla said infertility was wearing her down to nothing, and that's how I was beginning to feel too, but Amy . . . she'd come to some state of grace, it seemed, over and over saying yes to life, even when it kept saying no to her.

Are you bracing for me to explain that her saintly calm was a result of accepting God's will?

Nope. Actually, she wasn't religious at all. She just had a way of standing up to whatever came at her. The words *Why me*? didn't seem to be in her vocabulary. She didn't seem to feel, as so many people do, that she had some sort of inalienable right to be spared bad luck.

And now, as a reward for her patience, her goodness, she was being blessed. *Blessed with children.* Another great cliché, a phrase I'd heard without bothering to analyze all my life. "We've been blessed with three children" was just a sentimental way of saying, "We *have* three children," right? But now that word—*blessed*—held new meaning.

When the minister spoke of life going on in Gramma's children and grandchildren, Gil's mother turned and gave Amy, her own personal proof of it, a weepy smile. A lovely daughter, filled with life. Amy returned the look, and for a moment the two of them seemed encased in this bubble of joy.

Seeing it, watching from the outside, I suffered a pang of the purest, most poisoning envy. I thought of my own mother. And my sister. I glanced down, dropping a couple of guilty tears on my lily-embossed program. Gil saw them and our eyes met. His were red in that pathetic, I'll-die-before-I'll-cry way men have. How do they do it? How do they live their whole lives, choking it all back?

He took my hand and squeezed. He knew what these tears were about, and I knew why, for once, he wanted his hand held.

It's hard to accept the natural order of things; even harder to be out of step with it. Life and death—it was all moving on without us.

Sometimes I felt we were engaged in one long, private funeral. No flowers, no casseroles, no gathering of loved ones. Just a long, slow grieving.

Oh yes, and while you're grieving, be sure to keep your hopes up!

Gil and I clung together on the church pew, heads bowed. To anyone else, we probably just looked like devoted grandchildren, breaking up at the thought of never seeing Gramma again.

That word.

Never.

Chapter 21

Amy opened her eyes from the fast-fading dream. Must have been a bad one, to leave her with such a heavy sense of dread. She lay there, weighted against the mattress, the already warm morning air pressing down on her.

Well, of course she felt heavy. How else could you feel, nine months pregnant? Slowly waking, she blinked at the clock on the bedside table. Then she remembered. Gramma. Gramma Emma was dead. She thought she was used to the idea. Obviously not.

Rolling to her back, she tucked her hands into the nursing slits of her gown and rested them over her belly. Time had all but stopped in the last few days, or at least conspired to stretch out and pass only in the slowest ticks, like languid drips from a leaky faucet. At night she would rise and pace the quiet house, bare feet on the hardwood floors. Sometimes she'd go into the baby's room. Everything had been ready for at least a month. Bunny decals romped across the freshly painted furniture, diaper pins were lined up on the changing table. In the bureau drawers, nighties lay folded and waiting, having been carefully prewashed in the recommended baby soap. There was nothing left to prepare, not the slightest wrinkle to smooth. So she'd sit in the rocking chair, wakeful, watchful. She'd hear sirens in the distance and rock, wondering about the tragedies of strangers, wondering if each twinge in her belly was the beginning of labor or just another practice contraction. Would *this* be the night she would always remember as the beginning? At dawn, having seen the sun safely up, she would slip back in bed beside Ed and fall asleep as he got up for work.

She'd heard friends talk about the way the end of a pregnancy went on and on. But living it was something else. If only she hadn't let herself start thinking *anytime now* so early. Days separated into moments this way might last forever.

It was impossible to believe that this ripe roundness would ever be gone. Would she miss it? This part of her body to which she'd grown accustomed? This comfortable shelf to lay her arms across, the slippery interior somersaulting reminding her that someone she loved was very close? The little tap-tap-taps? *I'm in here, don't forget.* As if you could.

Now, in bed, she ran her hands over the taut skin of her belly. Not awake yet?

She rolled to her side and heaved herself up to sitting position. A practiced routine: rest there, get her bearings with a few deep breaths, then stand. She took an awkward step or two and pulled aside the home-fashioned fabric shade. Just outside the window, the bougainvillea was in full bloom. Across their adjoining backyards, she could see Mr. Murillo hosing his patio.

She went out to the kitchen, thinking she should eat something, but she wasn't really hungry. Was that a sign of labor's imminence? She couldn't remember. Eating was such a chore anyway with her intestines flattened to nothing. She poured a glass of milk and swallowed a prenatal vitamin. Then she switched on the radio. Maybe some upbeat music would help. Weren't you supposed to feel lighter toward the end, when the baby settled in for delivery? The baby was certainly quiet anyway. This she knew for certain as a sign of labor's onset. Maybe that's what this heaviness was all about. It was about to begin and she was supposed to be resting up.

She was standing by the kitchen sink when the first prick of alarm flicked the back of her neck. The baby hadn't moved yet this morning. But it was moving last night when she sat in the nursery, wasn't it? She couldn't remember. *No. No, now don't start thinking like that.*

She finished the milk, rinsed the glass. She went to the kitchen desk to look for the booklet they'd given her at the clinic. She needed to see it in print again, the part where it said a person shouldn't worry unless the baby hadn't moved for at least twenty-four hours. She found it. But now she was counting back. Had she felt anything last night after dinner? What about in the afternoon? She couldn't remember.

Her legs trembled. She sank down at the kitchen table, bracing herself with flat palms. *Come on, move.* Just a little tap, that's all she needed. She waited a long time, waiting for the thump that would jump start her own heart again.

But the huge mound of her belly remained still.

You are paranoid, one part of her brain told her.

What did you expect? the other part said. *You didn't really think you were going to get a baby, did you?*

The radio news announcer was talking about Geraldine Ferraro, but Amy hardly heard him.

Any minute this baby will kick, she promised herself.

She waited.

Nothing.

She stared at the telephone, thought irrationally of calling 911. Help. Please stop this from happening. No, it was too late. Besides, picking up the phone, giving words to her fear—that would be the first step in making it real, making it true.

She got up and walked around the kitchen. She even hopped. *Wake up. Oh please wake up.* Then she sat back down, with every passing minute sinking deeper into the dreadful knowledge.

Finally, as if she were outside her own body, she watched herself push up from the table and move toward the telephone. The doctor's number, penciled large, was taped next to it.

"My baby isn't moving," she told the nurse. No, she wasn't sure how long it had been.

They told her to come right in. Probably no reason to worry, but they wanted to reassure her in person.

Fine, Amy agreed, but without any real hope. She knew. Once again, it was all over. Yesterday she'd been bursting with life; this morning her veins ran with the sick, heavy chemistry of death. I won't be able to stand this, she thought, oddly calm. Not this time. This is too much.

Still she didn't cry. Crying would make it real, and she wasn't ready for that yet.

She watched herself getting dressed. She called the neighbor who would drive her to the clinic. She thought about calling Ed at work. Or her mother. No, let them all be happy a little longer.

I won't be able to live through this, she thought.

But then, she'd thought that before. She'd thought that every time she'd miscarried.

She wouldn't even have believed this was happening except for the fact that she believed it all too well. Wasn't this the way it would always end up for her? Surely by now she should have caught on.

Her neighbor's car was pulling into the driveway. She would have to go to the clinic now. She would have to let the doctors do their tests and make it official.

Oh God. If only she could soar above it all for a while. Or go to sleep and have them wake her up sometime in the future when the pain would be more bearable. Assuming it would be. It was appalling really, when you thought about it. If you intended to go on living, you had to live right through every part, even this. No vacations. No time off for good behavior.

Chapter 22

Our pantry is full of home-canned produce—fruits and vegetables in ancient blue jars given to us by Gramma Emma during the great canning jar and lid shortage of 1975. Our summers are lined up there—Italian prunes, split and pulpy, from 1977; questionable-looking pickles from 1979; and even, heaven help me, a jar of wild blackberries from 1975. The blackberries and I were still honeymooning back then. I had yet to recognize those thorny brambles as the enemy and felt morally obligated to pick and preserve every juicy berry appearing anywhere on our fifteen acres.

Obviously, the unappetizing and probably unsafe contents of these jars would never be eaten. And yet I hesitated to throw it all out. Every time I considered it, I'd think how good this food might look if it was all we had due, say, to some civilization-shattering catastrophe. From there it was an easy step to the troubling notion that clearing out these shelves might be just the thing to trigger a nuclear war.

If nothing else, however, the contents of the pantry served as documentary evidence of what *not* to bother canning in the future. We had reduced our efforts to only those items and recipes we felt confident of using up.

One evening, when Gil had just started back to work at the middle school, we were making my ever-popular tomato juice. We had one batch of jars jiggling in the boiling water bath; I was cooking down another pulpy potful. The house fairly steamed with the smell of tomatoes. Gil was in the middle of telling me about some new teacher when the phone rang.

He picked up the receiver, said hi to his dad, then made a noise like he'd been punched.

I turned and watched him lower himself into the rocker. As soon as I got the last hot jar out of the scalding water, I walked around to see his face.

"Yesterday?" He looked up and mouthed these words: "Amy lost the baby."

No. I shut my eyes. No. I dropped onto the sofa.

Face in my hands, I listened to Gil's short, flat answers. At one point, I went and turned off the burner under the tomatoes. Out the kitchen window, our mother deer and her fawn grazed lazily. My movement caught the mother's attention and she lifted her head to me, without alarm. We looked at each other for the longest time. We were still looking when Gil hung up. I turned. His eyes were wide, balancing tears.

"It stopped moving yesterday. They went ahead and induced labor today." He pushed up out of the rocker like he'd just aged twenty years. We sat down together on the sofa. After a while he said, "It was a little girl."

We watched the amber rays of late summer flood the room from the west, lighting the drying flowers of every color that hung from the beams above our heads. Life could look so good, so beautiful. It could beckon before you like a yellow brick road, and only after you started skipping down it did you find out they were for real—those poison poppies and wicked flying monkeys you hadn't wanted to hear about. Bad things could happen. Things no one should be asked to endure. And we couldn't protect each other. We couldn't protect the people we loved. We wouldn't even be able to protect our own baby—if we ever got one.

"I've never heard my dad sound like that," Gil said.

I waited. "How?"

"Just . . . broken up."

After a long time, when the room had gone dim, we got up, flipped on the lights, and cleaned up the tomato splatters.

I spoke with Amy the next day. Or rather I sat there, connected to her by telephone lines, and wondered, as people do in these situations, what on earth I could possibly say. Mostly I listened as she gave me the details in a strangely calm voice, told me a story about things I'd never even imagined.

"They brought her in to me, afterward."

I pictured this; tried not to picture this.

"It's supposed to help," Amy said. "You know, in the long run."

"Oh, Amy . . ."

"She . . . Betsy, she was perfect."

"Oh, Amy." That's all I could say. "Oh, Amy." I was going to cry all over again. "It's just so unfair."

"I know." Her voice caught. "She didn't get to live at all."

The baby's loss, not her own. She was forever shaming me with her goodness.

Ever since the news, I'd been racking my memory, dredging up my sins of envy, as if some less than supportive thought of mine had been her downfall.

"But that's crazy," Gil would say every time I started confessing.

I knew, but it didn't change how I felt. I just wished to God I hadn't sat there in the pew behind her and thought for even one split second that *I* wanted to be the mother of the first grandchild.

"Did you hear we named her Emma?" Amy was saying now. "We're going to have a little ceremony—sort of a christening and funeral together."

"That's . . . that's nice." Lord. I'd been hating the way our own situation dragged on with no finish, no funeral-style finality. But any fool could see that even the faintest hope was a whole lot better than the finality of a dead baby in your arms. "Do you want us to come?" Say no, I was praying, guilty again. If it would help, we'd have to, but I didn't think I could stand it.

"No, that's okay . . ."

I let out my breath, squeezed my eyes tight against the thought of a tiny white coffin.

"It's going to be small, just us. The counselors here thought it was a good idea. You know, to help us."

I nodded, forgetting she couldn't see me. I was thinking how little I'd understood about life when I was younger. I can remember hearing of people losing their newborns and thinking, *Well, at least they never had time to get attached to it.* I had no idea how much loving and dreaming went into bringing a baby to the moment of birth.

I was remembering the young mother brought by her relatives to the flower shop where I worked briefly when we were first married—she was supposed to choose the funeral flowers for her baby. Awed by the nearness of death, I showed her the pictures: a little cross of pink roses, a spray of baby carnations and forget-me-nots . . . When we'd gone through them all, she stared at me blankly. I wondered if she were deaf. Or maybe retarded?

"One pink rose," she finally said. "Doesn't matter anyway."

Pretty pitiful, I remember thinking, her not even caring. Now I realize she must have been in deep shock. Her baby was *dead.* What difference *did* the flowers make? Oh, I wish I could go back. I wish I could go back and be a person who understood, someone kinder to her at that moment, but I was so young. What did I know?

"How's Ed doing?" I said now.

"Oh, not too well. He's just—well, he's going crazy, raving about who he's going to sue. I think he's afraid if he quits being angry, he'll fall apart."

"Oh dear. Why don't men just cry?"

"He *is* crying," Amy said. "Sometimes crying's not enough."

I sighed. There was *still* so much I didn't know. Maybe that's how it would always be, life always surprising you, things never feeling the way you expect.

"Cousin Carol sent flowers," Amy said. "There was a note with them. You know what she wrote? She wants me to know that something like this can be a blessing in disguise."

"What?"

"Yes, because it can help prepare a person for the *real* tragedies in life."

"*Amy*. You're kidding."

"No! Can you believe that?"

"Oh, of all the—"

"I mean—" Her voice cracked with laughter or tears, I couldn't tell which. "If this doesn't qualify . . ."

"Amy, keep me away from her at the next reunion or I'll kill her. I swear I will."

"Keep you away? I'll help you."

"Oh, Amy . . ." Now both of us were hysterical. And I mean in the true sense—laughing and crying simultaneously. Did you know that the ancients considered this condition more prevalent in women than men and blamed our uteri?

Maybe they weren't so far off.

Chapter 23

Shirley Conklin could almost pinpoint the moment during the League of Women Voters retreat when her elation at Betsy's wanting a baby shifted to concern. Three or four of them were sitting out on a deck overlooking the Black Butte Ranch golf course when a woman on the farmland preservation committee began detailing her daughter's ordeal with infertility. The daughter had been trying to get pregnant for three years now and was, according to her mother, on the verge of a nervous breakdown. Listening to this medical history so similar to Betsy's, Shirley noticed her chips and dip suddenly weren't settling well at all.

After this, perhaps to compensate for her casual dismissal of Betsy's fears, she became a one-woman clipping service, scouring articles on the subject from newspapers and magazines—stories of persistence against all odds, miracles of modern medicine. She acted as censor too, discarding the accounts of futile efforts, weary resignation. Luckily, there were fewer of those. Magazines preferred publishing happy endings.

Whenever she heard a good personal story, she immediately got on the phone to Betsy.

"Mary Claridge's daughter adopted a baby last year, and now she's pregnant."

"Mom." A long pause. "Adopting a baby doesn't help you get pregnant."

"It happens. This isn't the first story—"

"Trust me on this, Mom. There just isn't any statistical correlation."

Shirley contemplated the phone line silence. Who would have guessed that your children, even in their thirties, could cause so much concern, make you feel so helpless. She had nothing to give in the way of advice. When she and her friends were young, anyone who couldn't get pregnant promptly adopted—none of this four-year-waiting-list business Betsy talked about. And as far as the question of how long to pursue these ghastly medical treatments, well, it was all just so brave new worldish, she had no experience, no precedents, nothing at all to offer.

Her one lame suggestion had been that Betsy consider coming back to church. Maybe she'd find some sort of comfort.

"What's so comforting about Father Peyton dragging out his favorite story again? I think every time he sees me sitting out there, he says, 'Aha! I'll do the story about the woman pounding the tent stake through the guy's head!' "

"Oh dear, I'd forgotten about that."

"Three times I've gone back and three times he's used those verses. I almost walked out last time."

Shirley remembered when she did walk out one year during the Christmas processional. They'd found her in the parish hall later, huddled on a sofa. It was too beautiful, Betsy had tried to explain. It just hurt too badly when you couldn't believe it. Well, she wasn't making much sense and mostly Shirley recalled her own impatience. Why did this daughter of hers have to *think* so hard about everything? Why couldn't she just *enjoy* it, or at least take what comfort she could?

Thank God Stephanie wasn't like this. Shirley had often thought she never could have survived two Betsys. Not that Stephanie hadn't been full of questions too. The difference was, she didn't feel compelled to argue every answer.

On a warm Sunday afternoon in mid-September, Shirley opened the screen door of her condo to her younger daughter, grateful that she, at least, was doing well. Safely into her second trimester now.

Standing back, she eyed her daughter's middle. "If I didn't know, I'd never guess."

"But I want it to show!"

Shirley laughed. "In a few months you won't believe you ever said that! But really, honey, you look great."

"Thanks. Actually I *feel* great. So much better than last month."

Stephanie always had the cutest haircuts. Right now it was sort of a vamp style, the sides dipping in a curve at the jawline. Betsy's hair would look good that way too, Shirley thought, but she always just let it go, said she didn't have the patience for a haircut you had to repeat every six weeks.

"Well, this was a fun idea," Stephanie said. "I feel like I'm coming to a slumber party."

"Here." Shirley took her suitcase. "I'll put this up in the guest room." She wanted her daughters to feel comfortable here, although of course Betsy wouldn't have much use for the room. She'd better not anyway. They had a longtime family rule against running home to Mama to escape each little marital spat. Shirley had never run away overnight, and unless they were being beaten, God forbid, she didn't expect her daughters to either. But it was nice for Stephanie to have a room at times like this, coming over from the coast for her doctor's appointment tomorrow.

"Maybe you ought to stay here when the time gets close," Shirley said, coming back down. "I worry about that long drive."

"It's just a little over an hour."

"An hour? You must be driving pretty fast."

"Mom, don't *worry*."

"But what if there's snow?"

"Lots of people come over from Newport to have their babies. I've never heard of anyone having any trouble. I promise we'll leave in plenty of time, okay?" Stephanie walked around, examining with renewed interest furniture she'd lived with for years. "I like what you've done in here. It's cozy."

"You think it's okay? It *is* an awful lot to cram into such a small place. But I'm enjoying not having that big old yard to worry about. In the spring I'll just do some planters for the deck. That'll be enough gardening for me."

Stephanie went to the sliding glass doors. "It's neat, being able to watch the river."

"Yes. 'Riverfront property.' Sounds ritzier than it is, but you know, with those trees, you really don't hear the highway out front that much. And it's such a short bike ride to the campus or downtown."

"It is sort of strange, you not being at the old house . . ." She let this drift off for a moment, then turned back to Shirley. "But if you're happy," she said, "I'm happy."

"Of course I'm happy. I'm going to be a grandma!"

"Right! So. Can we go to that baby store? The Stork Shop?"

"Sure. I've been looking forward to it. But first let me fix you some lunch." She went into the compact kitchen and took out the Oriental chicken salad she'd prepared earlier. "Guess what? Millie Swan's offered to give a shower for you."

"Really? How sweet! Who'll be coming?"

"Well, she'll need a list of your friends still here in town."

Stephanie thought. "Not too many anymore. Just Trish and Sally. That won't make much of a party."

"But she'll be inviting all my friends too, the ones who've known you since you were little. They'll want to do something for you."

"Oh." Stephanie's face had gone dark. "You mean all the people who sent the wedding presents I had to return?"

"Now, honey, nobody blamed you for that." Suddenly Shirley thought of Amy, Gil's sister, and wondered if people ever had to return baby shower gifts. No, that would be too cruel. Poor Amy. Now there was a story she would definitely *not* be idly passing on to Stephanie. She hoped Betsy would have the sense to keep her mouth shut about it too. Shuddering, she forced a smile. "Shall we take this out on the deck?"

The air was warm and still and smelled of the dry grasses along the riverbank.

"I'll bet everybody's completely forgotten about you and Jerry anyway," Shirley said when they were settled.

"Well, *I* haven't. I have never been more embarrassed."

For a few minutes, Stephanie concentrated on her salad and rapidly polished it off. "I want this recipe, Mom. It's so good. Boy, my appetite is back in a big way." She scooped out another helping. "Oh, and there's Betsy."

"Betsy?"

"My sister? Your other daughter? Mom! For the shower list." She stopped eating, her face earnest. "Unless you think she wouldn't want to come. Probably she wouldn't. I'll bet she thinks showers are silly. Will they make us play those games? She'd never let me hear the end of that. And if they take all the ribbons and make them into one of those paper plate bouquets . . . ?"

It never ceased to amaze Shirley what stock Stephanie took in Betsy's opinion. And it had been this way from day one. All those years of wasted breath, trying to convince Stephanie she didn't need to worry so much about her sister's approval . . .

"Stephanie," she said, "have you talked to Betsy lately?"

"Well, not real recently. I guess she phoned after they went to L.A. Why?"

"So she hasn't said anything about . . . ?"

Stephanie was waiting. "Anything about what?"

Oh dear. This clearly wasn't her news to tell, but now, facing the delicacies of baby shower invitations . . .

"Well, honey." She sighed. "The thing is, Betsy and Gil have been trying to get pregnant for quite a while. And they aren't having any luck."

Stephanie looked puzzled. "I didn't know she *wanted* a baby."

"Well, apparently she does. So this has been very difficult for her."

Stephanie dropped her fork on her plate. "Wonderful."

"Now, Stephanie—"

"So I'm supposed to think back and remember every stupid thing I might have said, every time I griped about how awful I was feeling and . . . Well, darn it. Why didn't she *tell* me?"

Shirley could sympathize. This seemed not unlike the time Dorothy Slater was undergoing chemotherapy and never told anyone, just kept turning down invitations with half-baked excuses until she had everyone thoroughly annoyed.

Then, of course, when it came out about the cancer, they all suffered the most punishing guilt.

Still, it was Dorothy's news to tell or not tell. The same for Betsy. Maybe trying to clue Stephanie in was just making things worse.

"At least now that we know," Shirley said, "we can all be a little more sensitive . . ."

"So you're saying I've been *in*sensitive?"

"No, I didn't mean—"

"How can you be sensitive about something if the person doesn't care enough to confide in you about it?"

"Oh, Stephanie, she cares. And I never meant to imply you've been insensitive. I just meant that, knowing this, we'll naturally want to . . . well, for instance, about the baby shower. I'm not sure what we should do. It might be pretty hard on her, all the fuss over baby things."

"We can't *not* invite her, can we?"

"Well no, that wouldn't seem right."

"How about an invitation that says, *We know you won't want to come so you don't have to*?"

"Oh dear," Shirley said. "Poor Betsy. Well, we don't have to decide right now." All the light had gone out of Stephanie's face. "Stephanie?"

"Hmm."

"Now, honey, you're not going to let this get you all upset, are you?"

"I'm not upset," Stephanie said, sounding very much upset.

"I honestly think she didn't tell you because she didn't *want* you to be upset. I think that's why she didn't tell me. And it *is* such a personal matter."

Stephanie took a deep breath, let it out. "So how long has this been going on?"

"About a year, I take it."

"Hm. Well, a year isn't so long to try. I know people who've had to try a year."

"Well . . ." Shirley said, shaking her head, "I think this is different. This is a year of fairly intensive treatments."

"Okay, but all's I'm saying is it's not so long she's got to completely freak out, right?"

"That was my first reaction too, but later, when I realized

that if you count all the years they've gone without birth control, you could say they've been trying *seven* years . . ."

"Okay, but—"

"And I wouldn't say she's freaking out, but I think she is beginning to wonder how much longer they should keep trying. Pretty soon here they may have to face the fact that there isn't much hope. I can certainly understand how that would be upsetting."

Stephanie's lips pressed tight. "Don't worry. She'll get pregnant." She stood and collected her dishes. "Doesn't she always get what she wants?"

Chapter 24

When we'd first started infertility treatments, a clinic appointment had been an annoyance, a time-wasting aberration in my busy life. Now, in spite of my efforts to occasionally pretend otherwise, clinic appointments *were* my life.

Before, I had resented the bother of having to change out of my overalls. These days, climbing down from the roof of the little McBee house, I bathed and dressed for ultrasound scans and clinic consultations as if purifying myself for some ceremony, as if my worthiness for motherhood were part of the examination.

Looking back, remembering these weeks, I will see myself standing there at the McBee house kitchen sink, drinking glass after glass of water as I stare out the window at summer drying into fall.

I will see myself sitting in waterlogged pain at the hospital's outpatient admitting desk, being reprocessed from scratch for each ultrasound scan.

I will see the black dots—my potential children—on the screen.

I will see myself trudging along the winding, sunbaked

sidewalk from the hospital to the clinic, wearing my caftan for its ease in slipping on and off.

I will see myself on the monthly day of highest hopes, driving up to where Shepherd of the Valley Hospital and the adjacent Mary's Bend Clinic building crown the hill, a citadel of holy knowledge and power, the place where a white-coated priestess performs the sacred rite of human chorionic gonadotropin, a mystical shot of medicine distilled from the precious urine of the blessed pregnant ones, an honor bestowed on me as a reward for patiently suffering the preliminaries.

I will see myself, ten days later, approaching the clinic reception counter, bleeding again, giving my name as if I'm not fully recognizable as the embodiment of our collective failure.

I will see myself sitting on the end of Dr. Lowell's paper-covered table, arguing on and on in a desperate attempt to avoid the truth: I am whipped.

In late October I was sitting there once again.

"But look at my chart," I said, as if somehow a properly rising line on a graph could overcome the hard fact of utter fruitlessness. "And those are genuine arrows," I added. "Not faked."

"Well I should hope so," Dr. Lowell said, throwing an arm behind his chair, leaning back from the built-in corner desk with a bemused look. "What would be the point of faking?"

"Oh please." This from the guy who openly advocated deception in dealing with husbands? "How would you like to put everyone through all this hassle," I said, "and then have to sit here and admit you didn't have sex at the right time because you got in a fight with your husband?"

"Ah. Well yes. It's awkward, I know." He handed me my chart.

"I mean, other people get pregnant by getting along for about fifteen minutes, right? We have to get along on schedule, every other day, month after month."

I had already had the obligatory pelvic exam. As Dr. Lowell jotted notes in my ever-thickening file, I looked at my graph. The arrow on the tenth—that was the day it was so miserably hot and we read in the paper that the guy next door wanted his acreage rezoned industrial. And then on the twelfth, Gil had come home from school all grouchy about the new student dress code they expected him to enforce. Let's see . . . the fourteenth—that was a pretty good one. Gil mellowed out on Friday nights. But the sixteenth, that argument about who was supposed to put gas in the truck . . . And also I forgot to unplug the phone and Carla called in the middle of everything . . . (She needed to unload, she said. She'd just found out that Greta Baxter, the wife of one of Stan's partners, was three months pregnant and hadn't told her . . .) When I came back to bed, Gil said it was all my fault for blabbing our personal life to every silly person who paid me to hang wallpaper. "Why do you always *do* this?" I said. "Why do you exaggerate? You *know* that's not true." But from there it was a quick jump to complaints about me phoning my mother all the time . . . on and on . . . Lord, I always think I want the guy to spill out his feelings, but when he does, I find I don't much care to hear about them after all. Well, really. Am I supposed to find being labeled a blabbermouth some big aphrodisiac?

I glared at the chart now for everything it represented. Damnit. Nations could negotiate world peace with less effort than it took to get the arrows into these little boxes. And all for nothing. How much more of this could we take?

Dr. Lowell did not seem impressed with what I considered the vast improvement in my charts since I'd started the HCG shots.

"Okay, I'll admit it doesn't look like this." I indicated the sample graph printed on the back of the sheet, the chart of a perfect woman who ovulated like a champ—her temperature dipping, then rising sharply after ovulation and staying up for exactly the specified fourteen days until her period started. "But I'll bet," I went on, "if you had a stack of charts from a bunch of real, live, normal women, they wouldn't all be perfect. I mean, can't there be some variation?"

Patiently—and clearly patience was something I was requiring a lot of—Dr. Lowell explained again the necessity of analyzing a chart more critically as the number of conceptionless cycles mounted.

"For example," he said, "I'd like to see your luteal phase go longer than ten days."

"But look how my temperature dipped and spiked up, right after the shot, just like it was supposed to."

"Yes, but—"

I nodded. Yeah, yeah . . . "—but I'm not pregnant." Lord, when would I ever learn? As Gil often pointed out, I had argued my way into plenty of things in my life, but I wasn't going to be able to argue my way into pregnancy.

"I'm afraid that's the bottom line, Betsy."

I sat there, arms crossed over my middle, holding the draped sheet closed. Somehow this felt as if we had reached a crossroads. Dr. Lowell allowed the silence to weigh down on us for quite some time, then he broke it with words I half wanted, yet dreaded to hear.

"Have you two discussed adoption?"

I sighed. "We've discussed everything."

He stood up. "Okay, tell you what. Why don't you get dressed and then we'll talk some more." He pulled the privacy curtain for me and went out.

I slid off the table and gathered my bundle of clothes from the chair. Was it time to quit? Cut our losses? This course of dogged persistence often felt like the slow, pain-maximizing technique for removing a stuck-tight Band-Aid, each individual hair follicle stinging as it pulled free. Maybe it was time for a quick, merciful rip.

I began to dress. Of course we'd talked about adoption. Gil thought it would be nice to have our own, but if we couldn't, well, a baby was a baby and he didn't give a damn where it came from. How admirable! What generous genes! Trouble is, this only made those genes seem to me that much more worthy of being reproduced.

Also, I'd been frightened by too many stories of pathological nature conquering careful nurture.

Aside from all that, what chance did we have of being awarded a baby anyway? To read the personals column, it sounded as if they were all going to the highest bidders. What could you offer? Pets? Grandparents? Music lessons? Ski trips? A Harvard education?

Actually, I'd sent for the papers from one agency, but I'd never shown them to Gil. All those personal questions. He'd have a fit. And as for me, certain parts of the application practically paralyzed me with guilt: *Applicants are strongly urged to prayerfully consider accepting a special-needs child.*

Now what sort of words could I cram into a half-inch

blank that would adequately express my feelings on this? How to explain and apologize for the fact that, unfortunately, God had not dealt me any moral superiority to go along with my infertility? How to admit my guilty secret: I was hoping for a healthy newborn.

Forget it. Surely there were thousands of women out there, better women than I, bent over these forms, neatly inking in the morally correct answers.

Hey, maybe it was a trick question? Only those who agreed to take any child would be offered a newborn?

The agency had immediately put me on their mailing list for a monthly magazine featuring stories of families who'd adopted hard-to-place children. God told them to, they were quoted, every last one of them. Wouldn't that be great? God never seemed to give me a clue about anything.

From out in the hall I heard the nurse, Rose, talking on the phone.

"And the spotting . . . ?" A pause. "Oh." Her tone was grave. "Okay, then, if that's the case, Dr. Lowell would like you to come in."

A heaviness settled in my chest at this. More tragedies. So many ways it could all go wrong, so many detours on the road to our happy endings.

And whoever promised happiness at the end? How slowly it had crept over me, the grim realization that there were no guarantees. Oh sure, I would have sworn I understood that from the beginning, but actually my lifelong faith lay in the gospel according to Walt. After *Pinocchio*, when my mother assured me that wishing on stars really did make dreams come true, I believed her. I carried with me the conviction that ultimately life was meant to be sweet, and happy endings are possible for those who try hard enough, long enough.

Get real.

When Dr. Lowell reappeared I pointed out that he had always promised to level with me when we got to the wheel-spinning, time-to-quit stage.

He nodded, not looking at all comfortable at remembering this promise. "Unfortunately, it's just not that cut-and-dried. We could fiddle around forever without getting anywhere—or you might get pregnant the very next try. Or six cycles from now for that matter."

"So you're saying I should keep trying?"

"I'm saying it's up to you."

I groaned. "I just want it resolved, one way or the other. And I don't feel I can quit until I've tried everything."

"Well now, wait a minute. Nobody ever said you have to try *everything*."

"I know, but if I don't, I'm so afraid I'll have regrets later on." I'd thought going on was the hardest thing. Now I realized quitting would be even harder. How could we quit when one more try might do the trick?

Dr. Lowell's voice was kind. "There's no shame to calling it a day, Betsy. You've already been through plenty."

I stared at the worn toe of my boot. If he didn't watch it, I'd wind up blubbering all over his office.

He waited. He was always so good about that. Most of my visits could have been wrapped up in fifteen minutes flat, but he always took time to let me talk. Or not talk.

"You know," he finally said, "sometimes I'll have a young patient with an unplanned pregnancy, and she'll ask me if I know any nice couples who could give her baby a good home."

I raised my eyes. Was he offering me a baby?

"I don't have anyone like that right now," he added quickly, "but it's something we could keep in mind if you'd want to consider it."

"Well, yes, we might. At some point." I was getting in deeper than I thought today. I needed Gil here. "The thing is, I wouldn't feel right adopting a baby like it was something to tide us over until we got what we *really* wanted. I wouldn't want to adopt while I was still hoping I'd get pregnant. I'd want those hopes done with. Otherwise it's not fair to the adopted baby."

"Why not just try for both and then go with whatever happens? I've seen people do that."

"Oh, it makes sense, sure. And I'm not criticizing them. It just doesn't feel right for me, that's all."

He nodded, not necessarily in agreement, but in resignation, acknowledging my right to my own feelings.

"What about the med school?" I said. "Pergonal and all that."

"You could try it."

"You don't sound enthusiastic."

"It has its risks."

"Sextuplets, you mean?"

"Among other things. If it interests you, you'd have to talk to the people up there. I'm not really up on the latest developments. But we are talking about extremely powerful drugs."

I nodded. This was sobering territory. Just the thought of going to the medical school in Portland had always put the fear in me. I carefully considered the phrasing of my next question.

"If a person got pregnant with quints or sextuplets," I said, "would the doctors . . . well, would they suggest a therapeutic abortion or something?"

Dr. Lowell colored.

"I mean, a woman's body isn't really meant to carry six babies, is it."

His eyes cut away from mine. "I'm sorry." He cleared his throat. "I'm afraid it's difficult for me to understand someone wanting babies so badly and then saying, 'Oh, this is too many.' "

Tears pricked my eyes. He couldn't understand that? He couldn't imagine the terror of hearing you had six babies getting ready to explode your body, something nature tried about once in a billion? I'd always known how he felt about abortion. Never begrudged him his stand, either. But come on, wasn't it a fair question in a case like this? Read the papers! What was so great about producing a hopeless litter of one-pound babies and watching them die in plastic boxes without ever being held?

Now I really wanted to bawl, having just blown us clean off his "nice couples" list before the ink could even dry.

Dr. Lowell cleared his throat again. "They do have something new they're trying up there."

"Yeah?" My ears were still burning.

"It's a portable pump."

"A pump?" I flashed on a picture of me and a piece of machinery engaged in some unnatural act.

"It's a battery-powered unit that delivers a constant dose of hormones. Hormones to induce ovulation."

I regarded him suspiciously. "Delivers it how?"

"An IV. They say the unit itself is very small. It'd be like carrying a pack of cigarettes around."

"But an IV? You mean like you'd have a needle stuck in you?"

"Well, yes."

"All the time?"

"Only until you ovulated."

"How long would that be?"

"Depends. A few weeks, I suppose."

"Wonderful."

"And there's some feeling that keeping it in for a couple of weeks after might be advantageous too."

This had to be the worst yet. I pictured trying to make love in a tangle of IV lines.

"It does have the advantage of being more natural than the Pergonal," he went on, "in that it doesn't up the odds for multiple births."

"That's something, anyway," I conceded.

"You'd be getting into more money. Something like five hundred a month."

"Dr. Lowell." I blinked at him. "We're into this for five hundred a month now."

"Oh really?"

Doctors! Honestly, sometimes they don't have a clue. It wasn't as if cost never crossed his mind—these last few cycles when I had so many office visits, he often checked no charge on the bill sheet out of pure pity, I'm sure. But he never totaled up the cost of everything he ordered.

"Isn't your insurance covering this?"

I laughed at his innocence. "Hey, insurance companies have caught on. This stuff is expensive. This stuff is elective, right? Babies are a *choice*. Our policy is full of exclusions. The only thing that's saving us is that the ultrasound scans are so new for this, they haven't figured out it has anything to do with infertility."

"I see."

"And please don't tell them!"

"Don't worry." He sighed. "So, the pump doesn't interest you?"

"I didn't say that. Hey, it's only money."

Now he turned upbeat, relieved, probably, that we had

steered clear of the touchy question of abortion. Maybe relieved at the idea of being rid of me. "Shall I give them a call and refer you?"

"Well, I'm not sure." I wasn't sure of anything at this point. Also, I was still smarting, wondering if I'd ever forget his making me feel like a criminal for daring that quints question. "I need to talk to Gil."

"Of course." He flipped back through the pages of my file. "We'll probably want to do another semen analysis on him." He explained that the first one had been long enough ago that a new one was in order. "The med school will want a more up-to-date count before they'd approve you for the pump."

I sat there nodding.

He studied me for a moment. "You do seem to be under a lot of stress with this. Why don't you consider just taking a breather? Even if you're determined to go on, nothing says you have to do it right away."

No, I had to be done with this one way or the other. You know what they say—when you're going through hell, for Pete's sake, don't stop.

To Do

Work

Call Eric re check
Mon—Stanfields

Make urologist appt. for Gil
Call med school for appt.
Note to Amy
Work on Steph's quilt
Fix pantry door
Property taxes
Visit Grampa

Chapter 25

Mary's Bend can hardly qualify as an everybody-knows-everybody-type town, but it is small enough that I can't go to Safeway without running into *somebody*. And one rainy afternoon in November when I came barreling around the egg racks, the cart mine nearly collided with happened to be that of my own husband.

"Well hi," I said, enjoying the little thrill the sight of him in a different setting could still give me. My own true love, right here in the pet food section. Sometimes when I hear friends wistfully speculating about the guy they probably should have married, I think what a blessing it is, knowing you've married the man you were meant to marry. Doesn't stop arguments about the proper way to sort laundry, of course, or guarantee against brief fantasies of jumping on airplanes for flights to destinations unknown, but it does prevent wasting valuable time actively plotting divorce. I dropped the box of instant muffins I was holding into my cart. "I thought I was doing dinner."

"Uh, I figured you'd forget." (Translation: "I forgot you said you would.") "You're not down here on your bike, are you?"

"Yeah."

"But it's pouring."

"I know," I said gaily, "so isn't it lucky I ran into you? You can give me a ride home. We can do our shopping together." I transferred cans of mushroom soup into his cart and parked mine. "There now, isn't this cozy?" I had temporarily forgotten that we absolutely cannot shop together. For half an aisle I walked contentedly beside him, pleased to be presenting a picture of the way I thought happily married couples ought to look.

"What's all the mushroom soup for?"

I declined to answer. He claims I never cook anything that doesn't call for a can of mushroom soup, so this was more a dig than a real question anyway.

"So what'd the doctor say?" I asked. Gil had left school a bit early for his long-awaited appointment with the urologist, and the health of his testicles certainly seemed a more interesting topic than my pathological dependence on Campbell's.

"Well . . ." He drew it way out. "I've got whatever that thing is you were talking about." He dropped the word from the side of his mouth. "A varicocele?"

"Yeah? How can he tell? I mean, what kind of exam was it?"

He made a sour face. "The pull-down-your-pants-and-let's-have-a-look kind."

"Oh." I suppressed a smile as we turned into the meat aisle. Gil had always been so great at reassuring me we were in this fight together, but so far, it had always been *my* body serving as the battleground. I was the one who was always in there pulling down my pants.

He tossed a couple of thick steaks into the cart. "It's like you were saying—this varicose vein heats things up and presto . . . cooked sperm."

"Sh!" I laughed, glancing around. So that explained the depressingly high percentage of wimpy-looking wigglers that had been documented during his recent test. Sort of creepy, those two-headed mutants . . . I turned back and gave the meat he'd chosen a critical eye. "Gil, if we're trying to watch the money, I think we could find some cheaper cuts."

"Hey, you expect me to grow good sperm on granola?"

I let it go. "So, does he think you should have the surgery?"

"Up to us, I guess." We pushed on down past the meat case. "I'm borderline. He says if you were real fertile I'd probably get you pregnant eventually, but it's kind of dumb to spend all this money and effort making you pop an egg if I'm going to be iffy."

"Well yeah—nice that they come up with this *now*, after all the rigmarole we've already been through. I mean, did he say anything about that first test? Have they got any explanation how you could have one test be perfectly good and then another so bad?"

"He says the first one wasn't that great—"

I was indignant. "They called it normal when you had it!"

"Yeah, well now they say it was in the low-normal range. I guess it's just that it wasn't bad enough to worry about when it seemed so obvious you were the one with the problem."

"But still . . ."

"Also, he says a guy's count and everything can go down with time. Oh, and something else." We had backed ourselves into a corner by the frozen corndogs. "I have a hernia. He'd like to fix that too."

I sucked in my breath. "Gil, that's great!"

"Huh?"

"The insurance! They might not pay for baby-making surgery, but they'll pay for a hernia. The doctor checks the right box and we're home free."

"Wonderful. Glad to be so accommodating."

"Oh, I'm sorry, hon. I didn't mean—"

"It's not exactly life-threatening. He said I could wait if I wanted."

"Oh." I put a pint of ice cream in the cart. "But how could you have a hernia and not know it?"

"Well, I thought something felt funny, but . . . what the heck."

I rolled my eyes. Men! They have to be dragged to the doctor for just about anything. And we've all heard stories of them chickening out on vasectomies, right? So I could hardly be shocked at his lack of enthusiasm for somebody waving sharp instruments in the vicinity of his favorite parts.

"So what do you think?" Gil said. "Should we do it?"

"You're asking *me*?"

"Well, we're in this together, right?"

He could still say this? I leaned across the grocery cart and laid my hand over his on the push bar.

He pulled away, embarrassed at such a gesture in the frozen food section. "Well really, how far am I going to get calling it quits now after everything you've been through?"

"Oh, Gil. I've never had to have surgery."

"It's not that big a deal. Check into the short-stay center first thing in the morning and leave by the middle of the afternoon."

I followed him to the checkout line. As far as I knew, he'd never had general anesthesia. What were the chances of being the freak case, the one whose system goes haywire on sodium pentathol? A baby was so ephemeral, an unknown quantity. I had no way of knowing what actually having one would be like. I only knew the wanting. But Gil was real. He was warm, alive, and right now. It was easier to picture the grief of losing him, the utter emptiness of life without him, than it was to imagine the mixed blessings of motherhood.

He got in line behind a woman with a cartload of toddlers who were busily putting items on the conveyor belt. Faces crumbed with the free cookies they'd been given at the bakery counter, they grinned at Gil, instinctively pegging him as the sort of grown-up kids could fool with.

I couldn't watch. Instead I checked out the lurid tabloid headlines: TEN-YEAR-OLD GIVES BIRTH TO BABY!!! Spare me. I glanced at the covers of the women's magazines—Princess Di with princeling number two, several other celebrities with their new babies. Shoot, reproduction was getting to be downright fashionable.

Outside it was wet and cold, with that ominous autumn wind that reminds you it's only going to get worse. We put my bike in the back of the truck and settled the groceries around my feet in the cab. "I figured I'd do it over Christmas vacation," Gil said, backing out, not looking at me.

I glanced at him. He'd already decided?

"He says I'll need a few days off work. And then it's three months before you get a new crop of sperm going."

I was calculating. We could go for the consultation at the med school next month—make sure we were cleared for the hormone pump before we put Gil through surgery—and then forget doctors and pills and shots and ultrasound scans and temperature charts until April.

We'd been like salmon, beating ourselves against the dam, desperate to get upriver for spawning, exhausting ourselves in the effort. Every time we'd think we were making progress up the fish ladder of medical technology, we'd wind up back at the foot of the dam, the overspill pushing us deeper. Maybe a rest would give us the leaping strength we needed to go on.

It scared me, though, when I thought about it—the way fish will die trying.

"Did I tell you Pam Carver's husband had this surgery?" I said.

"Probably."

"Maybe you'd like to talk to him."

"What for?"

"To find out what it's like."

"Guess I'll find out soon enough."

"I always feel like the more I know, the better."

"Hey, I'll have the surgery, but I'm not about to plug into the infertility hot line, okay?"

"Okay, okay."

A loaded Christmas tree truck pulled onto River Road ahead of us, rumbling south. The bound trees looked like furled umbrellas, ready to spring open in some California parking lot the day after Thanksgiving. I thought of the families, coming to choose . . . Maybe we should skip all that this year. Maybe by next year we'd feel more like celebrating.

"So. Did he give you some numbers?" I asked. "What kind of improvement we could expect?"

Gil shook his head. "Just said it might help and it can't hurt. Unless I croak from the anesthetic, that is."

"Gil!" I took a deep breath. "They put people to sleep up there every day. It's totally routine." As if it could ever be routine when it's somebody you love. "You probably ought to have the hernia fixed anyway . . ."

"I s'pose."

"The thing that scares me . . ." I stopped before the rest of the words got out. What if deep down he was scared too? Hardly seemed fair to make him reassure me he wasn't going to die on the operating table. "Maybe I'm just getting paranoid," I said. "Seriously. I mean, my mental state is . . ."

"Is what?"

"Well, I'm starting to feel like there're all these . . . *forces* out there. Gil? This *is* just a medical problem, right?"

"Yeah . . ." he said warily. "As opposed to what?"

"As opposed to we're in this big cosmic game of reward and punishment and God's trying to strike us down for something we've done wrong."

"Hell with that noise. Anyway, I thought you didn't believe in God."

"I never said that. I mean, okay, I didn't think I did, but now it's like I believe in God just enough to know He's against me."

"Oh that's great. Look, if you're going to get religious, couldn't you at least get religious in a way that would make you feel better?"

"Hey, just be glad we're not Jewish or Catholic, okay? All these articles I'm reading—the Jews with this guilt thing—they've got to have babies to make up for the Holocaust. And then the Catholics have the pope, always issuing pronouncements about the evils of infertility treatments. Big sin, right?—trying to have a family. At least all I'm dealing with is this vague notion of the entire universe being dead set against me."

"Give me a break. There's something haywire in your system, okay? That's all. You don't see me running around, trying to figure out why I'm being punished with sickly sperm."

I sighed. "What can I say? I wish I were like you, but I'm not." I truly admired the way he never wasted energy on useless emotions. I'd look out the window on a day when I was falling apart and there he'd be, planting bulbs to bloom next spring. Such a talent for simply getting on with it. Such faith! Half the time I couldn't even imagine spring anymore at all, much less hope and plan for it.

We drove in silence for a while on the rain-slick road. The world had a beat-up look this time of year. Only a few days ago, with the sun shining, everything was golden. But sometimes you don't realize how tentatively those last leaves are hanging on until the first big wind comes along. Now, overnight it seemed, they'd been ripped from the trees, and the rain-swollen ditches were floating old, bruised apples.

"He wouldn't give me any success rates in terms of pregnancies either," Gil said.

"Yeah, they never do."

"He said there're too many factors involved—how fertile the wife is, what other possible problems you might have."

Other possible problems—blocked tubes, for instance. I kept that thought pushed way back in my mind. Number one—lack of ovulation was the obvious problem. Number two—I'd never had a burst appendix or the sort of infection that scars the fallopian tubes. And number three—I couldn't even begin to deal with anything beyond the difficulties we'd already uncovered.

"I have to laugh," I said, "when I remember how I used to try to pin Dr. Lowell down on the HCG shots. I kept waiting to hear what percentage ovulated with this treatment, what percentage got pregnant, as if he had hundreds of patients like me. And then it turned out I was it. There *were* no statistics."

"But for me," Gil said, "statistics wouldn't have been nearly as convincing anyway."

"As convincing as what?"

"Aw . . . he had this whole wall covered with snapshots of babies. Shoot, all these little bald-headed guys. During the exam I was ready to puke, hearing where he wanted to cut and all. Then he takes me into his office and here's all these gummy grins."

"Good advertising, huh?"

"No shit. I forgot all about how much I hate hospitals and stuff. I just got mushy and went, aw, what the hell?"

"Gil." I looked at him. "Did you already tell him you'd do it?"

His eyes never left the road. "'Fraid so."

I watched the windshield wipers swish back and forth,

letting it sink in. "I guess you're not just doing this for me, then."

"Hey, I said right from the start I wanted a kid. Not my fault you never believed me."

I put my hand on his knee. His hand dropped from the wheel to cover mine. Maybe we really were in this together.

Chapter 26

Stephanie stood at the beach house kitchen sink peeling potatoes. Damp heat fogged the window, fogged the eyeglasses she now had to wear in lieu of contacts, thanks to some mysterious chemistry of pregnancy.

"Excuse me," Laura said.

Stephanie shifted so her cousin could reach the faucet to wash pears for her fruit plate. Lord, it was hot. She wiped the back of her wrist across her forehead. Why did they have to do Thanksgiving here every year, when the kitchen was so tiny and cramped?

"You okay, honey?" her mother asked. "Why don't you go put your feet up? We can handle this."

"No, I'm fine, really. Just my back aches, is all."

Laura gave her what was probably supposed to be a sympathetic look, but just the sight of Laura these days made Stephanie feel a good ten pounds heavier and rather cranky. Laura, with her clear skin and enviable ankles. Funny, Stephanie had never given one thought to ankles until the bones of her own had disappeared.

"I always thought seven months was the hardest time," Shirley said, looking at her daughter but directing her comment to her sister, June. "Didn't you?"

"Well," June said, opening the oven, releasing the aroma of turkey into the kitchen, "since I only got to go through it once, I mostly just remember being so thrilled."

Shirley and Stephanie traded glances. June could never seem to pass up a chance to remind them of her life's biggest regret: the raw deal of having only one child.

"At seven months," Shirley said, "you're just beginning to get really uncomfortable, but you still have quite a ways to go."

June's enameled turkey earrings dangled over the browning bird as she squirted it with the baster. "I do remember the heartburn," she said. "Toward the end."

"Is that what that is?" Stephanie dropped the last potato in the pan. "That sort of burning after you eat?"

"Oh, honey. You're having trouble with that?" Shirley started rummaging through a cupboard. "I was sure I'd seen some Tums in here somewhere."

"It's okay, Mom. It's not that bad yet, and I should ask Dr. Beemer first. You know, before I take any medicine."

Shirley stopped her search. "They're so careful these days," she said to her sister. "I guess it's good. But it makes you wonder how we ever managed to produce this generation in the first place, doesn't it? Cigarettes and martinis right through our pregnancies."

"Mom!" Stephanie said. "Did you really?"

"We didn't know any better."

"My doctor used to *tell* me to have a drink," June said. "To relax me. And really, if it was all so bad, wouldn't you think there would have been more birth defects?"

"But there were birth defects," Laura said, flinging back her hair. "And I'll bet the doctors told everyone the causes were unknown. Just because they weren't making the connections doesn't mean there weren't any."

June contemplated her daughter for a moment. "Isn't it a wonder," she said, "that with everything I did wrong, my daughter still turned out so much smarter than me."

"Oh, Mom," Laura said, and then couldn't resist muttering, "Smarter than I."

Stephanie hoped June and Laura wouldn't start one of their little pick-on-each-other sessions. June with her digs. Brags or complaints? You couldn't tell if June herself knew for sure. And then Laura, signaling her barely controlled impatience with her mother by holding her eyes closed a fraction longer than a regular blink would necessitate.

"What a great-looking fruit plate," Shirley hurried to say. "What are those star-shaped ones?"

Laura laughed. "Starfruit, of course." She dolloped cream cheese on her kiwifruit. "Haven't you ever tried it?"

What was wrong with a normal, traditional fruit plate, Stephanie wondered. She'd better avoid that cream cheese. What was it, a hundred calories per ounce?

"Stephanie, honey," Shirley said, "would you go get off your feet? I'll do your mashed potatoes. Now, please. You look like you're about to expire. Okay, let's see what we've got for serving plates. Oh dear. Are we going to have enough burners here?"

Stephanie lumbered out to the living room, smiled weakly at the men, and lowered herself into the wicker chair by the front windows.

Outside, the wind kept the flagpole creaking, and clouds scudded above the horizon at the clip of a time-lapse film. After an earlier rain, the sun had broken through, lighting the piled-up rows of breakers to a blinding white dazzle. Below, in the front yard, Betsy sat twisting in one of the swings that hung from a weathered wooden crossbar.

Stephanie watched her, wondering if her mother had managed to break the baby shower news like she'd promised. They'd certainly devoted enough telephone time to the subject in the last two months. Stephanie kept hoping she herself might mention the party casually to Betsy sometime, just toss it out there in passing, try *not* to make a big deal of it. But somehow she and Betsy didn't seem to be *having* any casual conversations. Actually, Stephanie thought, there'd probably been lots of two-month periods in the past where neither had phoned the other—but certainly none where she felt this conscious of it.

She watched Betsy drag her feet in the sandy depression under the swing. She looked like a little kid, her hair hanging forward, hiding her face. Poor Betsy, she thought. Poor Betsy can't get pregnant . . .

Right. Poor Betsy, who'd spent years making fun of her for wanting kids. Poor Betsy, who didn't seem to be noticing this pregnancy at all. You had to wonder if having a baby was really the big deal to her that Mom seemed to think.

Honestly, it wore Stephanie out, having to be so careful what she said. And who was being careful of *her*? Like that conversation this morning, Betsy telling everyone about her *big problem*, the contractor who'd been coming on to her every time she hung wallpaper for him, Laura chiming in about what she does whenever guys hit on *her*. Like it happens every day. Well. Stephanie had a solution for them. She wished them both pregnancies like hers. Then they'd feel safe. Men had been looking right through her for months. And it just kept getting worse, what with having to wear these glasses that she normally wouldn't wear any longer than it took her to get from her bed to the bathroom, where she could put in her contacts . . .

"Matt," she said, "couldn't you jazz that fire up a little?" Really, what was the point of having one if it wasn't going to be bright and crackly? Her father's beach house fires had always been a point of pride; nobody ever had to remind him to stoke them either.

Matt pulled back the screen and threw on another log. Smoke puffed into the room. Anyone could see, Stephanie thought, that the chunk was too big to catch without a little more fiddling. She wouldn't say anything though, she decided.

In the kitchen, the timer buzzed.

"Gil," Shirley called. "Your yams are done."

Gil pushed up from the sofa and went into the kitchen, where he was greeted, Stephanie noted, with a certain fuss. Gil and his famous candied yams.

He and Betsy had a pretty good thing going, all right. Nobody else seemed bothered by Betsy's complete failure to help with the cooking (usually she'd be talking real estate with Matt) and Gil always got extra points for it.

Hard to believe now, but at first her parents had liked Matt better than Gil. Who would've guessed she'd end up feeling almost apologetic for the way her husband sat around with Uncle Ray like this, lamenting the bowl game they were missing and joking about hunger pangs. "Sure smells good," they'd say, lifting their heads from the chair backs just enough to sniff the air. "Wonder when they're going to let us eat."

Maybe it was her father's death that had thrown everything off-balance. He'd been the one who'd always taken to Matt, enjoying their investment discussions. Not that her mother ever bad-mouthed Matt, but clearly she enjoyed Gil's help in the kitchen more than Matt's pronouncements on the economy.

Once, when Stephanie had admitted to feeling a bit wounded at this favoritism, her mother had protested that she loved both her sons-in-law.

"It's just that I knew someone wonderful would marry you," she said. "But you remember how . . . well, *bristly* Betsy was about men at that point. Gil appearing out of nowhere for her seemed like more of a miracle."

Stephanie sighed. Even now there was no denying that Matt's slightly offhanded attitude toward his approaching fatherhood did not play well against the revelation that Gil had actually volunteered for surgery to further *his* chances of having a baby. Lord, just reporting this had practically reduced Shirley to tears. Stephanie had been sworn to secrecy, of course. They weren't supposed to be discussing this. Gil was such a sensitive hero.

"Coming through," he was saying in the kitchen now. "This is hot." Stephanie heard water splash into the sink.

Soon, the aroma of hot butter and brown sugar wafted out from the kitchen. Why'd she even bother with the mashed potatoes, Stephanie thought. Who'd want plain old mashed potatoes when they could have candied yams?

Chapter 27

"Hey, Betsy." Laura was coming down the beach house steps. "How about a quick walk to the creek? They say we've got time before dinner."

I stood up from the twisted swing and let it unwind, the chains clinking. We clambered down the steep dune path to the beach and out onto the broad wet expanse of sand. Clumps of foam had been left quivering by the high wash of the winter tide; the air smelled of driftwood burning in stone fireplaces.

"We haven't really had a chance to talk," Laura said, matching my step companionably, leaning in close to be heard over the wind and roaring ocean. "June told me about this infertility thing. Sounds like a drag."

I should explain here that my cousin is one of those artful listeners, people who know how to prompt others to start talking and then keep them going by maintaining eye contact and nodding encouragingly at appropriate intervals. Leaving plenty of silent spots for the other person to fill works well also. For a year or two after she perfected this technique—probably to help in the research for her biographies—I was flattered, imagining she had for some reason grown particularly interested in me. Then I caught on—she was practicing this on everyone.

So I had mixed feelings about being another of her interview subjects. I shouldn't be talking about this anyway, I was thinking. I'm obsessive enough as it is. And Gil sure as heck wouldn't approve.

On the other hand, with the whole baby issue running through my head all the time anyway, what difference did it make if some of it came out in words? And since she'd already got the gist of it from June, Gil could hardly accuse me of spreading the story to a new audience. (Although he would undoubtedly see fit to make a nasty crack or two about the family grapevine.)

So we walked along, hunched against the wind, and I told her about the medical regimen we'd been on.

"I don't know how you could bring yourself to *do* that," she said when I'd finished. "Sex should be . . ." She squinted, searching the horizon for the right word, settled instead for a shiver that hinted of delicious intimacies. "Well, you know." She fought the blond strands away from her face. "I'm just saying I could never do that."

"Sure you could. You would if you wanted a baby." Even as these words of mine came out I heard them as an odd echo from the past and laughed.

"What?" Laura stopped and waited with one of those puzzled, let-me-in-on-the-joke smiles.

"That's just what you said to me the Thanksgiving you first clued me in about sex. Don't you remember? I thought it sounded awful. 'He puts his what in my what? Forget it!' And then you got this little know-it-all smile and said, 'You'll do it if you want a baby.' "

"Oh no! Did I?"

"Yes, and that made a big impression on me. Imagine my surprise when I figured out it was supposed to be fun!"

Laura had *always* been such a know-it-all. Whatever she was doing at the moment was the thing to do. Going steady in junior high, playing the field in high school, living with a guy in college—she never seemed to have qualms. I remember listening to her explain the separation from her first husband, how wonderfully it was working out, how she and Christopher were the best of friends, the romance had been rekindled, blah, blah, blah. She made separation sound like civilization's most enlightened social arrangement, never seeming to realize that what she was describing actually constituted her marriage's last pathetic gasp. But no matter—by the time that became apparent, she had already moved on to the amazing advantages of civilization's even *more* enlightened social arrangement—divorce!

Only in retrospect did this look flaky, though. In the middle of any given phase, Laura always seemed completely in control, her decisions well considered. So who was I to criticize her for always feeling good about herself and what she was doing? Maybe that was a sign of true mental health.

And certainly one that was eluding me.

The sky had darkened for another shower. We had reached the rain-swollen creek, broad and deep this time of year, floating the driftwood stumps and logs that would be our backrests and beach fires next summer. Next summer. Walking this beach *last* summer, I would have been appalled to see into the future and find our situation even now unresolved. What if it turned out we were still only at the beginning?

"Have you really thought about what it would be like to have kids?" Laura said. "Do you have friends with kids?"

"A few. Mostly people Gil works with." I knew what she was getting at. People always try to cheer up the infertile by detailing the downside of parenthood. I believed it and yet I didn't, if that makes any sense. I could acknowledge the truth of their stories while somehow imagining it would all be different for us.

"My theory," I told Laura, "is that people have to try to warn us how tough it is, having kids, but at the same time, we're supposed to ignore them. Otherwise, who would have the babies? I think Mother Nature just wants us to plunge in."

"Betsy! Isn't that one of the main points of the women's movement? That biology doesn't have to be destiny? We don't have to be controlled by these . . . primitive urges." Then she flashed me one of her overly intimate smiles. "Not that we shouldn't appreciate *some* of those primitive urges, of course."

Yes, Laura, we know: You have a great sex life. I looked off down the beach.

"I wonder," she said. "Do you think Stephanie's given any thought to this?"

"To primitive urges?"

"No, to why she wants children."

"She's *always* wanted children."

"Yes, but why? You see, I'm bothered by this blind acceptance of motherhood in so many women. People should go into this with their eyes wide open, make sure they're having kids for the right reasons."

"You want them to fill out questionnaires or something? It's not like reproducing is exactly abnormal, you know." I found it wearying, this constant call for analysis, maybe because, personally, I'd had far too much time to consider every ramification. Sometimes I just wanted to vent my feelings, not be forced to justify them.

"But in your case, for instance, since you *are* having so much trouble, wouldn't that make it that much more important to be sure this is really what you want?"

"Actually, I sort of resent the feeling that it ought to be. I mean, I see what you're saying, but I get sick of feeling like I ought to have superior reasons for wanting a baby just because I can't get one as easily as most people. Like putting us through this hassle means I've got to promise to be a superior mother."

"Promise whom?"

"I don't know. God? The doctors? The people on *Donahue* who feel moved to phone in and say that women like me ought to quit whining and accept the fact that we weren't meant to be mothers?"

"Betsy—"

"Because after all, that's exactly what *they* would have done if they hadn't been blessed with three beautiful children, praise the Lord."

She was giving me a funny look. "I have to admit, I'm surprised, this coming from you. Of course Stephanie's always been so traditional, but you—"

"Now *tradition*'s a dirty word?"

"Betsy! I'm just saying there are advantages to being child-free, that's all. Things worth considering." She took off her glasses and polished away the mist with the tail of the T-shirt she yanked down from under her parka. "Barry and I have our careers, of course, and our traveling . . ." She set her glasses back on her nose and blinked at me. "You don't think people have to have children to be happy, do you?"

"No, not at all. I'm sure some people are perfectly happy without them."

"I know I am."

"Fine," I said. "Great. It's just that I don't think it's possible to get where you are from where I am."

I was thinking how much had changed between the two of us over the years. Once Laura had been so much older; now we seemed the same age. I no longer bowed to her authority. I no longer thought she had all the answers.

I wished she did. I wished *somebody* did.

I swear, sometimes these family dinners completely exhaust my brain, all the sorting out of vibes zipping back and forth between people. You're tempted to just tune out and eat, but it's hard to ignore things like the routine Aunt June and Uncle Ray always do. She has a tendency to check out his every bite, clucking over second helpings, quoting his doctor. But then, in the event she manages to keep her mouth shut, he'll keep it going. "Now my wife doesn't think I ought to be eating this," he'll say, and back and forth they go. And then the way Laura is forever whispering to Barry. Rude? I can't *believe* it. Matt interrupts Stephanie until she slips into a pout. Barry and Gil don't say much at all, but as soon as one of them does, the other rolls his eyes—no big dramatics, but if you're watching, you'll catch it. You're always a bit on edge, worrying that someone will start on some topic that's a red-flag issue for somebody else . . . I don't know, maybe I was just in a bad mood that Thanksgiving. For all I know I was doing something that was driving the rest of *them* crazy.

Anyway, after the meal, I was more than willing to go solo on doing up the dishes, just for a chance at being alone. Maybe everyone else had had their fill of togetherness too, because suddenly people were off in different directions. Uncle Ray to the sofa, Gil to work on the garage woodpile, Matt into Neskowin. The rest bundled up for a beach walk, Mom pawing through the bread drawer for stale ends to feed the sea gulls.

I thought I might get my solitude until Stephanie insisted on staying to help me.

"You shouldn't have to do this all by yourself," she said.

"I don't mind. Really. After all, I didn't do any of the cooking."

"Come with us, Stephanie," June said, pulling on her stocking cap. "The fresh air will do you good."

"You shouldn't be standing up doing dishes anyway," I said.

"I'll just keep you company then," she said, and lowered herself into a chair at the tiny kitchen table.

The others left. Clearing the last few dishes, I looked out and saw Laura and Barry veer off and head the opposite way down the beach from Mom and Aunt June, who were being descended upon by gulls like some scene from Alfred Hitchcock.

In the kitchen, I started scraping plates with Stephanie watching me. I did not appreciate this feeling, this self-consciousness around someone whose presence I had taken for granted for thirty-odd years.

"So," I said after a while. "How're you feeling?"

"You want the truth? I'm dying of heartburn. It's not fair, I ate so carefully."

"Sorry to hear that."

"Oh well. Comes with the territory, Dr. Beemer keeps saying."

She watched me fill pans to soak. I had the uneasy feeling she wanted something from me, but what?

"Actually," she said, "I've been hoping for a chance to talk—you know—alone."

"Yeah?"

"I feel like I ought to be apologizing to you for being pregnant."

"Oh come on."

"No really. I mean, the timing couldn't be worse for you."

"Don't be silly. Nobody's asking you to put your life on hold for me."

"I know." She sat there picking fuzz pills off her pink maternity sweater. "But Mom says this has been really hard on you, so I'm sorry if I said anything—you know, before—to make you feel bad."

I shrugged. "Don't worry about it."

"But the thing is, I didn't know."

"Stephanie, it's okay." I was finding this tedious. "I *know* you didn't know."

"Maybe if you'd just said something earlier . . ."

"Look, you didn't say anything that made me feel bad . . ."

"But I mean, were you *wanting* me to feel guilty?"

"Stephanie! No!" How did we jump so quick from apologies to accusations? "Honestly," I said, "the last thing I want is for you to feel guilty. In fact, it's been bothering me that you really don't seem very happy about this pregnancy at all. I keep expecting you to act more . . . I don't know . . . lit up or something."

I wasn't looking at her when I said this, but I could feel her reaction. Or maybe it was hearing her sharp breath of surprise.

"Uh, excuse me," she said. "How can I, with Mom always shooting me these looks?"

"What—?"

"Be-careful-of-Betsy looks."

An uncontrollable warmth flushed up my face. I thought I was so great at vibe monitoring—guess I'd missed a few. "Well, none of that's my idea. I don't want to be a damper on everything."

"Oh sure, that's easy to say, but it doesn't change things. I mean, I can't win. If I complain about how tired or fat I feel, it's thoughtless whining. If I rave about how happy I am, I'm rubbing it in."

I sighed. She had a point. I was a damper by definition.

"I don't know, Betsy. I guess it's terrible of me to feel this way, but sometimes it just seems like no matter what I do, you have to top me."

"Huh?"

"You always have to have a better problem, or something more dramatic."

"I don't believe this. *You're* having the baby."

"Yeah, and I thought it was so neat that Mom would have something to be happy about—"

"She's thrilled—"

"Not the way she would be if she wasn't worried about you *not* having a baby."

"Oh, Stephie." I dried my hands on a dish towel. How can you be mad at someone so pathetic? "Stephie, Stephie, Stephie." I went over and put my arm around her.

That *really* made her cry.

Well, I clicked into mother mode and fixed her a cup of tea. Isn't that what you do when somebody cries? I'm always a big advocate of crying, but I'm hardly ever on this end of it. Does make you feel sort of helpless.

"Sometimes I just have to cry," she said. "You know?"

"Yeah, I know."

So I worked on the dishes while she cried, but I'll tell you, as pitiful as she looked, I wasn't exactly feeling sorry for her. For the first time in our lives she had something I wanted, knew something I did not. She could sit there and sniffle like a child, but in this one sense, she now seemed the older one.

"Could I ask you something?" I said when she'd calmed down.

She rubbed a palm up her cheek. "Sure."

"Well, what's it like? I mean when the baby moves."

She perked up a degree, pleased, I guess, at my interest. She reached for my hand. "Here. Feel."

"Oh no." I pulled back. "I'm all wet."

"So dry off."

I wished I hadn't said anything. She'd misunderstood. But I dried off my hands on a dish towel and let her place one on her stomach.

"There!" she said after a moment. "Did you feel that?" A small triumph. "Usually he won't kick when you want him to."

I nodded, fascinated as much with finally seeing a hint of joy on her face as with feeling the little thump. "But, what I—oh never mind. Uh, thanks."

I turned away from the sudden glow of her. Never had I felt so excruciatingly shy in front of my sister, so completely humbled.

What I wanted to know but couldn't trust my voice to say out loud was simply this: How does it feel when the baby moves and it's your baby and it's your husband's baby that's moving inside of you?

And then the question beyond this: Was I ever going to find out?

Chapter 28

I couldn't possibly finish the quilt I'd started for Stephanie by the day of the shower. And passing along the quilt I'd made for Amy hardly seemed right, invisibly personalized as it was by all the thoughts of Amy and her baby that had gone through my head and into the stitches.

To avoid the trauma of the baby store, I even briefly considered raiding my own contraband layette, the one I'd smuggled into the house piece by piece and stashed away under our brass bed. But every item I'd tucked away was a tangible symbol of faith. Giving up any of it would feel like giving up hope.

The Stork Shop seemed my only option.

The thing is, I was schizophrenic about that place.

On a good day, I used to be able to drift through in a warm fuzzy dream of ruffled nurseries with teddy bears waiting in cribs. And all those darling little clothes. Sure, I'd heard the rumors about real babies—the spit-up on everything, the messes. These hand-embroidered-in-the-Philippines dresses were good for a ten-minute photo session and that was about it. So what? I was in love with the dream, not the reality. No apologies here, either. Before the reality actually hits, what else have you got to go on, anyway? Yes, I could be a dangerous case, no question. *Why not snap up this darling little rosebud dress on sale?* I'd start thinking. *My chart's looking good. My breasts feel tender . . .* Honestly, it should have been against the law for me to enter a store like this under the influence of optimism. Gil would've had a fit if he'd known just how often I tantalized myself doing just this.

Give me credit for a tiny shred of sanity, though, because on bad days, times when hope was tentative at best, I wisely refused to so much as glance at the window display in passing.

What I'm saying is, up until now, I'd at least had a choice. But today was different, having to go in for a gift on what would normally qualify as a drive-right-by day. But you can't show up at a shower with an IOU, right?

I parked several blocks away and sat in the truck. Gathering courage? Stalling? Whatever.

I would be so damned glad when this baby shower was over. Even knowing I was not alone wasn't much comfort. Every day, I'll bet, women from coast to coast shed tears on pastel shower invitations until the carefully penned dates and times run all over the bunnies and bears. The more decisive simply toss them unopened into the garbage.

Then there's the opposite tack—always rushing in to be the first offering to actually *give* the shower. Carla told me about a woman who did that. The only infertile sister-in-law in a big Catholic family, she had hostessed showers year after year, carefully preserving the boxes of decorations for reuse when the guest lists didn't overlap too much. Once she'd been forced to bravely smile her way through the opening of the gifts a mere hour after discovering that once again she'd started her period. Why did she set herself up like this?

All I wanted, I told Gil, was some sane, middle-of-the-road route for getting through this. When he realized this meant, for me, attending my sister's shower, we had another big argument, essentially a rehash of the Neskowin Parade fight, him arguing against pointless masochism and me taking a stand for doing the right thing and making healthy adjustments and not hiding from life. I even wound up having to defend the invitation itself which he implied was in questionable taste. So I asked him what the heck pregnant people are supposed to do with pathetic cases like me. Invite us and we might flip out; don't invite us and we might flip out.

Well, swell. Now I not only had to go to the shower, I had to come home in the armor of cheer if I hoped to ward off his stinging I-told-you-sos.

Finally I got out of the truck and walked down to the pillars flanking the Stork Shop's corner entrance. Okay, lean against one and take a deep breath. Ready? Walk in. Come on, this isn't some scary medical procedure. Nobody's sticking you with anything. It's a store, for Pete's sake. Okay. The newborn section. Now. Reach out. Go ahead, touch the soft, yellow terry cloth. It won't bite you . . .

I heard a familiar voice. Carla's. But her husky laugh carried a ring I'd never heard before. I looked up from the rack of sleepers. She was back in the maternity section with another woman, smiling and pulling out a flowing fuchsia dress.

My insides cramped and heat flashed behind my eyes. She was pregnant. I just knew. Ten different emotions pulsed across my synapses, overloading every single one.

Nudged discreetly by her friend, she saw me and her jubilance froze.

I started pushing toward her through the mark-down racks, heart thudding, my legs on automatic pilot.

"Carla?" A question of condition, not identity.

"Betsy." She was red-faced now, her smile strained. "Um, I guess I should have called you." She glanced at my hands, her black brows going up hopefully. "Are you . . .?"

I looked down, found myself clutching a baby sleeper. "Oh no, this is just . . ." I lifted my eyes. "But you are, right?"

She nodded just once, triumph barely contained.

I swallowed hard. "So tell me about it," I said, horrified to realize I was in danger of crying.

"Betsy, this is my friend, Greta Larson."

I nodded, my face fixed. Dr. Larson's wife. The pregnant one. Pregnant friends, shopping together. "But when did you find out?" I said to Carla. "I want to hear all the details."

"Oh, I've known for a little while."

"Yeah? So what finally did the trick?"

She checked the fiber label of the dress. "Greta, we're just going to have to go up to that maternity boutique in Portland."

I blushed to the roots of my hair. She wasn't going to tell me? I'll be damned. After laying every detail of her ordeal on me, right down to the consistency of her cervical mucus, she was suddenly going to act like I was getting nosy?

"I meant to call you, Betsy," she said. "But I kept putting it off. I was afraid you'd be upset."

"Carla! I'm happy for you."

The two of them exchanged a glance that put it right between my eyes: I had been *discussed.* Obviously, the problem of Betsy Bonden had been the topic of at least one previous conversation between these two, maybe more. Well, fine.

"I'll call you," Carla said. "We'll have a long talk. I promise we will."

I hated the pity in Greta's puckered chin. Carla's lipsticked mouth bore the same expression. She was never going to call me. Why should she? Her misery didn't need my company anymore. Her success had turned me into nothing more than the hard-luck friend who would forever remind her of how she'd been at her worst.

Suddenly the store seemed unbearably stuffy. "Well." I jerked like I'd been zapped with a prod. "Guess I better get going." Backing away, I bobbed my head at Greta. "Nice meeting you."

I hooked the sleeper on the first rack I passed and I was out of there, heading blindly for the truck. *Damn her. Why didn't she call me? Why didn't she give me a chance? I wanted to be happy for other people, but how could I if they shut me out?*

Oh stop it. She was just worried how you'd take it. And see? She was right. You're jealous. You're mean and spiteful. Wouldn't matter how you'd found out . . .

Not true! the other side of me raged. *Of course I'm happy for her. I just hate her for cutting me out, that's all, mixing up all my feelings . . .*

Huffing along, my thoughts churned until I was passing the post office. Gradually I slowed my pace and began to hear again sounds beyond the pounding of my own blood against my eardrums. The courthouse carillon was chiming the first Christmas songs of the season. *What Child is this who laid to rest . . . ?* The newly strung lights in the curbside trees came twinkling on.

I blew a visible puff into the gathering dusk. So Carla

was pregnant. Good for her. She wouldn't be calling me with disaster bulletins anymore. Big loss. Anyway, maybe she had a good reason for not talking to me, not telling me something she might actually be planning to keep her mouth shut about—like it isn't her husband's baby. Well, however it happened, if she could finally get pregnant, maybe there was hope for me, too.

A woman about my age came out of the post office with a handful of letters. Descending the steps, she thumbed through them until suddenly her face lit up. She'd found the one she was hoping for. She hurried down the rest of the steps, smiling to herself. I stood there and watched her swing away down the sidewalk.

She got what she wanted.

That's what *I* want, I thought, turning away. I want to quit crawling and bounce again the way I used to. I want to go around smiling like somebody whose wish has come true. I opened the truck door. Or at least somebody who's still believing it might.

Chapter 29

I survived the baby shower, which actually wasn't so bad. Well, except for that one awful moment when Millie Swan wagged a finger at me and said, "Now see here, Betsy, when are you going to let us give *you* a baby shower?" I'll never forget the instant silence, the turning heads. In a flash I knew: Mom had clued everybody in to my problem. Everybody but poor Millie. Exposed, stunned, I stood there. In the end I must have mumbled something because I remember the sudden relief of the noise level once again rising protectively around me.

I also survived the Christmas Eve pageant at church. All those little girls in jewel-toned velvet dresses, white tights, and Mary Janes. Gazing at them, I couldn't help picturing myself at the sewing machine, turning a heap of fabric into a wearable confection . . . Oh dear, more wrong reasons for wanting children. Dying to dress someone in ruffles and lace doesn't qualify, right?

The high point of the service—or low point, depending—came when Mary and Joseph walked in and the congregation realized with one collective *aaahh* that the infant Jesus was not somebody's baby doll this year, but a real, live newborn.

Gil glanced at me. He needn't have. I absolutely was not going to cry.

The bathrobed shepherds paraded in and knelt at the manger, displaying the soles of their running shoes. They admired the baby to the count of ten, then made way for the Wise Men.

"But Mary kept all these things," the narrator read from St. Luke, "and pondered them in her heart."

I sniffed. Had to admire that. Whatever other saintly things she'd done to qualify for this position, they couldn't top this. An angel tells her she's pregnant by God, her baby is His son, people show up from all over to worship, and she manages to keep her mouth shut? Personally, I've never been able to ponder any big news in my heart for more than three and a half minutes without wanting to get on the phone about it.

Speaking of the telephone, do you ever play who's on the line? Your spouse/roommate/significant other answers the ring and you try to guess from his tone of voice who it is?

I thought I had Gil down pretty well by now, even though he was a tough subject. From his gentlest response, reserved for nine-year-old kids who called to see if they could work as berry pickers (too young) to the inordinant amount of time he'd give an annoying salesman before cutting him off, there was not a huge range.

But his response to that Christmas morning call instantly perked up my ears. Mainly it was the surprise in his voice that alerted me this was not one of our frequent callers. I rose from the clutter of wrapping paper—the two of us had been in the middle of opening our gifts—and padded after him.

He looked up. *Marsha*, he mouthed.

Marsha? After eleven years? What in the Sam Hill.

He shrugged to register bewilderment equal to my own.

Well, naturally I was dying to hear the whole conversation, both sides, but even lurking around to get in on his end of it didn't seem polite, so I went back to the living room. I couldn't really keep opening presents without him though. Really, she had a lot of nerve, interrupting Christmas!

I sat looking at our tree. Yes, we'd put one up, but it felt to me like a charade. No getting around it, we needed kids.

We needed a toy train and dolls opening their eyes as they're lifted from their boxes . . .

Marsha. What the hell could *she* want? Trust me, this was not one of those situations where we'd all been part of some chummy gang so why hold grudges. This was a woman who wrote letters containing the nastiest allegations about me, based solely on the evidence I was about to marry her old boyfriend. The only time I'd ever seen her was when she showed up at Gil's place a month before our wedding in a last-ditch effort to win him back.

Okay, I'll give her this: She throws a good scene. Secretly I found it sort of thrilling—her calling me a tart (so quaint, and nothing anyone had ever called me before, has since, or probably ever will again) and Gil defending me, more or less throwing her out. Well, he asked her to leave anyway, said he was going to marry me and that was that. Since I owed her no sympathy (she had cheated on him all over the place) I remember it, all in all, as a rather rousing episode. I wasn't looking for any opportunities to repeat it, though.

Out in the kitchen, Gil was still on the phone. This was getting ridiculous! I marched out, parked myself in front of the rocker where he sat, and crossed my arms over my chest.

"Yeah . . . uh-huh . . . sure . . ." He rolled his eyes at me in desperation.

This guy needed help. I crawled into his lap and started nuzzling his neck.

"Uh, Marsha?" I was making him squirm. "I better go . . . yeah, okay . . . no, that's okay . . ." Finally he managed to hang up.

"Well?" I said.

"Boy, was that strange."

"What'd she want?"

He stood, sliding me off. "I don't know."

I followed him into the living room. "So where is she?"

"Florida. I felt better when I heard that. And she's married."

"Good!"

"Said she was mad at her husband because his old girlfriend called him, so she decided to get back at him by calling me."

"What a great idea! Now I could call Gary. Then his wife

gets POed and phones her ex. Can't you just see it, the domino effect of Christmas-morning fights breaking out all over the country?"

"And don't break this chain or you'll be cursed with bad luck!"

"Right," I said. "Well, anyway, what did she say? And don't tell me 'nothing' because you were on there too long for that."

"Well, she says we ought to keep in touch. She wants to be friends."

"Nuts to that!"

"Hey, don't worry." He dropped into the armchair. He sat there for a minute, then he said, "I just think it's so weird. I can't understand why she'd do this."

"Oh, I can."

"Huh?"

"Same reason I phoned Gary a few years back. Don't you remember? Maybe women are just more curious. I am, anyway. I always want to know how people's stories turn out."

"Well sure, but—"

"So what *is* her story? Has she got kids?"

"Yeah. Boy and a girl." He wouldn't meet my eyes. "Here. Open another present."

"Gil." I flashed on a picture of Christmas in that faraway Florida house—dolls, toys, cherubic faces lit with wonder . . . "If you'd married her, you'd have babies by now."

"Betsy, if I'd married her, I'd have a custody battle by now."

Later that afternoon we drove to Eugene for Christmas dinner at Aunt June and Uncle Ray's—a holiday celebration preceded by the usual six weeks of negotiations concerning who would go where for which part of the holiday.

At the first opportunity Stephanie whispered, "I can't believe Laura and Barry split up for Christmas."

"I guess she and Barry's mom don't get along too well."

"So?" This said in a very exaggerated way, reminding me she was a bit short of sympathy here, seeing as how she had a rather provoking mother-in-law herself. ("I try *so hard* with her," Stephanie was forever saying.) She had already done her time with the in-laws on Christmas Eve.

Actually, I wondered about Laura and Barry too. No matter how entangled our annual debate became (Should we go to L.A. for Christmas? Could I leave my mother alone? Would Gil's parents come to Oregon? If they did, would Amy feel abandoned?), the one thing we never considered was not being together. Laura, of course, was casting this as another of her completely reasonable and civilized solutions to one of life's little dilemmas, almost as if it were a bit pathetic for the rest of us to go to such lengths to be together.

Not long after that, Laura pulled me aside. "Stephanie does not look well at all, does she?"

"Laura, she's nine months pregnant."

She gave me a withering look. "I'm just wondering if she shouldn't be sticking closer to home, being this close."

I shrugged. "It's probably not that much farther from here to the hospital than it is from Newport. Besides, she couldn't stand to miss Christmas."

My sister, the full-blown Madonna. Next year we'd be avalanching her child, our sole representative of the next generation, with gifts. I'd be smiling, acting happy. I envisioned years of Academy Award–winning performances . . . *To Betsy Bonden, for her role as the adoring aunt.* What else could I do? Be this blight on every celebration?

Okay, it hadn't been my favorite Thanksgiving, and now it wasn't my favorite Christmas. I seemed to be having a hard time putting up with Laura, in particular, and was wishing I'd never begun issuing installments on the continuing Eric Norgren harassment story in the first place. Now she was lecturing me on how I really ought to be filing a suit. I tried to explain he wasn't technically my boss, so how could that help? But she made it plain: In her book, I was a wimp. Well, nobody likes being pushed, you know? Also she started in again on both my mother and me for not letting her know often enough what was going on with Grampa Stroh. I don't know. Was her sweetsy needling worse than usual or was I just in an extra touchy mood?

But Laura failed to provide the worst moment of the day. That honor went to Matt, who turned to Gil at dinner and, in what he probably thought was an understated tone, said, "I hear you're going under the knife."

I could practically see the ham lodging in Gil's throat,

not so much at the thought of the knife as at the realization that his upcoming surgery was apparently common knowledge. He glanced around, saw everyone watching, mumbled something unintelligible.

"What's that?" Matt said.

Furious, Gil stonewalled it. We could all just choke on our food, too. He wasn't going to help us out of this.

My appetite was ruined. I'd be paying for this later. Well, take me out and shoot me! He needed perfect secrecy; I needed to get things off my chest once in a while. What are two people supposed to do?

Besides, is it my fault Matt doesn't know any better than to talk surgery at the table?

Fortunately, Stephanie chose this moment to announce that she judged her pains close enough now she ought to start paying attention.

"Pains?" Mom jumped up, knocking her chair over. "You're having contractions?"

"I think so. I—"

"Why didn't you *say* something?" June said. "Why, for heaven's sakes . . ."

You never saw people stuffed with food move so fast. In about two minutes we had Stephanie bundled into the car.

"Call me at home, Matt," Mom told him. "I'm going to head back now too."

"And you'll phone the doctor?"

"Right."

I watched their Honda round the corner.

"A Christmas baby," June said, following Mom in. "Wouldn't that be something?"

Everyone went back in except Laura and me. We stood at the end of the driveway, watching the empty street as if we might read some clue to Stephanie's outcome there.

"I hate that," Laura said. "When my mother gives me that look, like, *See how wonderful and exciting this is? Too bad you're not going to the hospital to have a baby*. How am I supposed to know what I want to do when she's always *on* me like that?"

"At least you've got a choice, Laura." Okay, I know. This is exactly what I hate having people do to me, but she had it coming.

"You think having a choice makes it easy? Try being an

only child, your mother practically on her knees for you to give her a grandchild. I just don't need this. Like I've always said, if I ever have a baby, it's got to be for the right reasons."

"Tell me, Laura. Exactly what are the right reasons?"

She looked at me.

"Seriously. I'm interested. You're always saying this. You seem to feel you know."

She pushed back her hair. "Well, it's very personal, of course."

"Very personal, but we sure as hell better be politically correct, right?"

"Betsy, I—

"I want a baby, okay? I want a baby for the wrong reasons and the right reasons and all the reasons in between. I want to make a baby quilt, is that okay? And I want a baby because—guess what?—someday I'm going to die. Maybe I'm like Grampa Stroh. Maybe I like the idea of things going on. Does that qualify? Or should I just rattle off the standard line about all this love I have to give?"

"Oh dear." She'd backed up a step to scrutinize me. "You *are* having a hard time dealing with this, aren't you?"

Did I have to answer this?

She sighed, and after a moment she said, "By the way, speaking of Grampa Stroh, nobody ever did say. How *is* he?"

"Oh, Laura." I kicked a pebble into the gutter. "Why don't you go up to the nursing home and ask him yourself?"

Chapter 30

I was all set to help Gil through his surgery—take care of him, reassure him, do and say all those things I'd have wanted myself, all those things I'd never been able to do because up to this point I had always been the patient. But that's the trouble with the Golden Rule, isn't it? We knock our lights out doing unto others as we'd want done, only to run smack into the reality of Different Strokes for Different Folks. Each Valentine's Day, for example, Gil receives a flowery, sentimental card from me and I get a goofy gorilla one from him. Does this make sense?

If he could have figured any way around it, I honestly think he would have preferred I not even drive him to the hospital. Minimum fuss—that was his aim. He'd brought one of his mysteries to read in case he had to wait.

As soon as he had on his blue hospital gown, he all but dismissed me. "You're not going to sit around here the whole time, are you?"

"Don't you want me to?"

"What for? I'll be dead to the world."

"Gil."

For a while, on Christmas, I'd been thinking I could do double duty today—bring Gil into the short-stay center, then visit Stephanie in the maternity ward. But she'd been sent home Christmas night. Labor, it seems, had not actually begun. On the phone the next day, fit to be tied, she made it sound as if the hospital staff had banned her from the premises forever.

"I did bring my swimming stuff," I told Gil. "I could go down to the Aquatic Center and do some laps."

"Yeah, that'd be good. You could even go now." He seemed almost unnaturally calm—only a hint of stiffness in his shoulders.

"But, Gil?" Maybe all my nervous questioning of the nurses and anesthesiologist had been bugging him. "Is it *okay* if I stay?"

An ambivalent beat of silence, then, "Sure, if you want."

"Just for a little while, anyway? Until they take you?"

A nurse came by and reminded Gil to remove his wedding ring. "Shall we put it in the safe?"

"That's okay," I said. "I'll keep it."

Gil twisted and tugged. "Don't think I've ever had this thing off."

On our honeymoon he'd been so conscious of the plain gold band, the first and only ring he'd ever worn. He wondered if maybe he should remove it when he worked around the farm. "No way," I'd said. "It's to be worn. So what if it gets scratched?"

He got it off now and gave it to me. I held it up for a look, then peered inside the band.

"Gil! It's gone!"

"What's gone?"

"The inscription. *All my love forever.*"

"Really?" He took it and looked. "I guess the grit that gets under there just wore it down like sandpaper." He handed it back.

Dismayed, I studied the ring a moment longer as if the words might magically reappear. Then I dropped it into the change pouch of my wallet. "I thought the engraving was supposed to be permanent."

"Oh well." But he saw that it bothered me. "Hey, it's just words. It doesn't change how I feel."

I gave his hand a squeeze. "I know."

After that he read his book some while I folded his clothes

and put them in the locker. I put his boots in too, noticing they were starting to crack across the instep. I would put greasing them on my next list. Then I took the solitary chair provided for each patient space and sat there watching the wall clock, listening to bits of conversation through the partitioning curtains. There wasn't much. Maybe I wasn't the only one scared chitchatless. Honestly, the medicinal smells alone were enough to bring back in a rush your every childhood doctor-visit nightmare.

"I wonder if you'll feel like eating tonight," I said.

"Have to wait and see."

I nodded. I had all my best recipes planned for the days ahead. And nothing with mushroom soup, either.

Gil had already been given one sedative by mouth. I stepped out momentarily when a nurse with a hypodermic came to inject him with something stronger.

"We'll be feeling no pain now," she promised cheerfully.

A few minutes later he was flat on his back, smiling. "The bed rails are waving."

"Yeah?" It was good to see him relaxed, anyway. "Well, have fun."

When the people with the gurney came, I fought the urge to beg for some final reassurance. Could they possibly understand what a special person this was, this man they were shifting onto their cart? He looked so vulnerable in his funny paper shower cap.

"Will somebody call me when he's out?"

"Sure will." They pushed the gurney away. "Hey, Nick, who you got for the Orange Bowl?"

I tried to catch Gil's eye, but by the time they reached the heavy swinging doors with him, I realized he wasn't going to let me. Or maybe he was just spaced out on the drugs.

And I was probably overdramatizing the whole thing, anyway. Nobody ever said we had to do this as a last-looks scene.

It felt strange, walking out of the hospital, leaving him. I can't help placing some indefinable value in being near a person at a time of crisis, as if psychic energy might actually help. So it was with a certain uneasiness that I got in the truck and headed for the Aquatic Center.

But this is exactly what Gil would have done. That's how he handled any ordeal—by simply going on with life. Probably did us more good in the end than all the hand-wringing and beaming of positive thoughts in the world.

My mother operated on this theory—years afterward telling me how she'd driven to Portland with a U-Haul trailer to collect her new sofa on the gravest day of the Cuban missile crisis. She figured if the world blew up nothing would matter anyway, and if it didn't, she wanted her business taken care of.

I admired this attitude; imitating it was something else.

At the pool I swam hard, releasing the tension. Afterward, while I was showering away the smell of chlorine, a young mother came in from the baby pool with her little girl, a two-year-old Asian doll.

I smiled at the child. "Cute," I said to the mother.

The mother smiled back. A compliment is permissible. A compliment is welcomed. Beyond that, I knew from reading Ann Landers, risked offense. It is not permissible, for example, to say, "By the way, I noticed that you are Caucasian and your daughter is Oriental so I'm naturally assuming she's adopted. So what's it been like for you? Did you feel like her mother right away? Did you try to have your own first? How long did you try? Was it hard to quit? Do you ever regret it? How long did you have to wait for this one?"

The adoption agency near us placed a lot of Korean babies. Well, if it came to that, I certainly liked the idea of the birth mother remaining safely on the far side of the vast Pacific. I just couldn't see myself happily hostessing monthly visits of my baby's birth mother as part of some open adoption arrangement. The agency literature indicated that the Korean mothers wanted to see pictures of the prospective American homes and help pick one for their babies. I already had the perfect shot, brilliant summer flowers against our cheery yellow house. *Yes, isn't this lovely? Send your baby to us . . .* No two ways about it, it certainly would have its appeal, being chosen, or at least having your home chosen, after this long streak of feeling like such a loser . . .

Combing out my hair, I glanced at the clock. Not even nine yet. I'd zipped back and forth in the pool so furiously, my half mile hadn't taken up nearly the time I'd planned. If I went back to the hospital, I'd just be sitting around.

I decided to stop and pay a visit to Grampa Stroh.

In the nursing home hall I encountered the usual wheelchair lineup—the man who whinnied like a horse, the one who liked to walk his chair along with his feet, the woman who spilled out such articulate streams of nonsense. *Excuse me, could you tell me the proper procedure for securing the rainfall data that Walter needs while he's waiting for you to come iron his shirts? Because if he doesn't mend that gate, one of those children is bound to get out.* More than once her calm earnestness had fooled me into attempting an answer, but in the end she only argued. I was left marveling—what long-abandoned closets was she cleaning in her mind?

I slipped past them and went into Grampa Stroh's room.

"Well, tell me," he said by way of greeting, "has that little Stephanie had her baby yet?"

"Not yet, Grampa. Don't worry, you'll be the first to know. So. How've you been?"

"Well, honey, I'm having kind of a tough time . . ."

I took a seat in his empty wheelchair and relaxed into his litany of bodily betrayals. My mother, Stephanie, and I often debated what was best for Grampa Stroh, conversationally. They both opted for teasing him along to more pleasant topics. I tended to let him complain. Partly I was lazy, and partly I thought it must make him feel better to talk about it. Otherwise, why would he persist?

So I sat there and listened, glancing at the clock occasionally, wondering if maybe my dad had been lucky, in a way, dropping dead of a heart attack. Died too young, true, but at least he got to skip all this. Which is harder on a family—the shock of instant loss, or the long grief of slow deterioration? Which is harder on the person who's dying?

On the window ledge, the front page of the local paper displayed a story about a five-year-old boy who'd been killed falling out a second-story window. Lord. That had gone down real well with the bran flakes this morning. Five years of life. And here's Grampa, saying every week he's ready to be with Grandma again, that he prays God will take him soon. Was anybody in charge of all this or not? Because the wrong people were checking out.

Finally Grampa directed me to run along, adding his usual admonition to take care of my good husband, my wonderful farm.

I kissed him on the forehead. For someone who'd never been one to traffic in open physical affection, he lately seemed surprisingly pleased when I'd do this. Maybe vulnerability had turned him tender. As soon as I was out in the hall, he slipped back into his plaintive chant: "Oh God. Oh my God . . ."

As I passed the wheelchair people, one of the women called to me. "Wait!"

I hesitated, reflexively, obediently.

"Esther!" she cried, raking at my arm, her open mouth revealing spaces between her teeth.

I mumbled apologetically and quickened my step toward the elevator. Clearly, this was no simple, please-pull-up-my-lap-robe request. I hit the button.

"Honey!"

The elevator opened. I hopped on, shuddering, then turned to find her shoving her chair toward me with shocking strength.

"Esther!" Her eyes bored into me. "Please, honey. Because you know, they've taken all my names away . . ."

Close, you damn doors. My smile had stretched to a grimace. My desperation to escape shamed me. Was I supposed to go back and pretend to be Esther? Did people do that? People of superior moral fiber?

The doors lurched. I raised my hand in a feeble wave. "Bye."

You are pathetic, I told myself as the elevator dropped me to the first floor, my stomach arriving a split second later.

That could be me someday, I thought—parked in a nursing home, crying for the phantom granddaughter who never showed up because I'd never been able to get pregnant with her mother or father.

Stop it. People *with* kids got parked and left. Kids were no guarantee. Still, kids were hope.

* * *

My mother's is the one place in the world where I can go unannounced and uninvited and know that I will always be welcome. No guarantees on her availability for a visit, but she would never be annoyed at me for showing up. One time, back when Dad was alive, I remember hesitating on their front porch in my overalls. Clearly a party was in progress, not the time for an intimate chat. So what? I was nevertheless pulled in and introduced around. Another time I stumbled into a rather heated argument between the two of them. No matter—my appearance seemed to put an end to it, for which my mother was grateful. She has an interesting theory, which is that *acting* normal helps return things to normal in fact. Makes sense. Beats escalating to the pot-throwing stage anyway.

Now she opened her condo door. "Betsy! I thought you'd be at the hospital this morning."

"You remembered." Gil might not value the psychic energy of others, but I did.

"Well of course. But why aren't you up there?"

I shrugged. "He told me not to hang around."

She nodded. "Sounds just like your father. Well, how was he doing?"

"Oh, fine, I guess. If he was scared he wasn't letting on. But you know Gil. He has to be hating this. I can't think of anything harder for him than having to put himself in the hands of strangers like that."

Again she nodded as if this were a familiar story. Then she perked up and said, "Well come on in. This is such a nice surprise. Let me fix you a cup of tea. I'm just in the middle of taking the tree down."

"Already?" My dismay at this surprised me. Was she supposed to keep it up just to boost my spirits? "Don't you usually wait until after New Year's?"

"Yes," she said, setting the kettle on the burner, "but I've got to do *something* with all this nervous energy. Between Gil having surgery and Stephanie having these contractions every day, well, I just want to be ready for whatever happens."

Wrapping ornaments in tissue, she talked about her concern over snow on Highway 20, the strangeness of Christmas in a condo, Grampa Stroh's impatience and excitement over his first great-grandchild.

I took down a snowflake ornament I'd glittered in grade school, a candle made from a cardboard toilet paper roll. "I can't believe you saved this," I said.

"Honey, you *made* that."

"I know, but look at this—it's still got bits of toilet paper on it. Don't you remember how you used to talk about having a fancy flocked tree someday when we were grown up and didn't care so much about all this homemade stuff?"

She shook her head. "Isn't that the way it goes? Now that I could, I don't want to."

The tea kettle whistled and I followed her into the kitchen.

"Hey, Mom? How would you feel about a Korean grandchild?"

She put tea bags in mugs. "That would be wonderful." She cocked her head. "This isn't an announcement, is it? Gil wouldn't be having this operation if you'd already made up your minds to adopt."

"No, of course not," I said, suddenly feeling guilty of a certain faithlessness. Didn't I owe Gil a measure of optimism on his surgery day? Was it bad luck to plan ahead for failure? Unfortunately, by now, failure had become a habit, success difficult to imagine. "I'm trying to prepare myself," I said. "In case. The pump really is our last hope."

She poured the steaming water. "You've ruled out those stronger drugs?"

"Well . . . every time we talk about it we end up arguing. It's just so scary, the thought of quints."

"Scares me too." She put our mugs on the kitchen table and we both sat down. She took a good long studying look at me. "So. How are you, honey?" she said. "Really."

I burst into tears.

"Betsy! What—?"

"Oh nothing, it's just that—you're so good at—" My voice had slid up to a squeak. "It's got to be one of the nicest things in life to have your mom give you a cup of tea and ask how you are and be able to know that she really does want to hear about it."

"Well, of course I do—"

"And it just hit me that I want to do that too, see? You've

been a good teacher. I want to do this scene with *me* as the mom."

"Oh, you will, honey. You will."

I rubbed the tears off my cheeks. "Oh bother." I sniffed and pushed up my sweater sleeve to check my watch. Only ten-fifteen. "This is the longest morning. I'll be *so glad* when it's over."

She sighed. "He's going to be okay, honey."

I nodded, as if that might help make it true.

We sat there for a moment and then my mother jumped up. "Oh, I've got something to show you." She went upstairs and when she returned, she had something hidden behind her back. "Are you ready for this? Ta da!"

It was my old Little Miss Revlon doll. "Oh, Mom. I thought that was lost forever."

"I found her when I was moving."

Almost thirty years before, in the dime store downtown, I'd stood with my mother before a wall of forty of these dolls in different outfits, without hesitation pointing at my favorite. She must have smiled. I'd chosen the very doll and outfit she'd already bought and hidden away for me. I liked this story better with each passing year. A true Christmas miracle—not the doll, but that I had a mother who knew me so well. Sometimes we retold the story to others, but for us, just saying, "Remember the Little Miss Revlon doll?" was usually enough.

"And we're saving this for your little girl, right?" she said.

"Right, Mom." As a child I had insisted on saving every single doll because it had always bothered me that my mother never saved any of hers for me. Gave her plenty of grief over it too.

We sipped our tea and passed another half hour with talking, the way we do at times like this, but we were having trouble sticking to the diversion of pleasant nostalgia. Too many happy memories had been rendered poignant by later events. Even the dolls you'd saved for your children weren't safe from sadness. And of course anything to do with Dad was tentative territory. My mother and I had both arrived at a point in our lives, I saw, where we had to think in terms of loss containment—how to stop our sorrows from spilling over and blotting out our joys.

Or maybe, in the end, that's all life was ever about? Loss containment? What a grim thought.

"Mom? Remember how you always used to say 'This, too, shall pass'?"

She smiled sadly. "That's easier to believe when you're talking about the flu or something embarrassing that happened at school."

Or even the heartache of a failed love, I thought, which might in fact pass rather swiftly if a replacement like Gil appears on the scene.

But death—how could that pass? Or the ache of wanting a baby and not getting one? That's something that would affect the rest of your life. How could that pass?

"Maybe the intensity of it passes," my mother said. "Maybe that's the best we can hope."

When I walked back into the day surgery waiting area, the receptionist nodded at me and picked up the phone. Gil's doctor appeared in green scrub pajamas, his face mask dangling on his chest.

"We've been looking for you," he said. "He's going to be all right." Something in his voice implied this had been in question. My eyes must have widened because suddenly he was giving me a closer look. "No one's told you?"

I chilled to my fingertips. "What?"

"Oh." He cleared his throat. "Your husband had a little problem. Has he ever had trouble with anesthesia before?"

I looked toward the doors leading into the holding area. "No, he's never . . ." I couldn't breathe. "What . . ."

"Unfortunately, he vomited while under the anesthetic. Maybe he forgot he wasn't supposed to eat after midnight?"

"No! We were really careful."

"Hmm. Well, we were worried he may have aspirated it, sucked it into his lungs."

Brain damage. I flashed on a TV movie I remembered where this very thing gave a woman brain damage.

"So we tipped him upside down and got an X ray."

"But he's okay?" My heart pounded.

"Yes, we're still keeping an eye on him, but he seems fine. And other than that, the surgery went well."

Other than that. My knees gave—fear after the fact. I sank to the waiting room sofa.

"He's out of the recovery room," the doctor said. "You can go in whenever you want."

I stood, steadied myself, and followed him through the swinging doors.

Back in the curtained partition, Gil was sleeping. Someone had pulled off the surgery cap, and his hair curled dark against the starchy pillowcase. I rested my hand on his arm and just stood there, watching his face. He has the most beautiful eyelids, sculpted like a marble statue's and tinted olive. His lashes are black and thick.

After a moment, I dug into my wallet for his ring. Then, being careful of the taped IV needle, I picked up his hand and slipped the gold band back on his finger where it belonged.

Chapter 31

In all my recent trips up to the hospital, I'd entered through the combination emergency/short-stay entrance on the lower level. But going to visit my sister and her new baby boy, I headed for Shepherd of the Valley's main door on the higher side of the hill. The walls of the entry room were papered with a huge, sepia-toned photo collage showing the succession of hospital buildings Shepherd had outgrown.

Not exactly eager for the maternity ward, I could have lingered among the potted ferns, studying the pictures indefinitely. But the entry chamber would not seem to allow it. Even when I tried standing in the precise center of the room, my weight on the tiles kept triggering the automatic doors, both sets, to the outside and to the hospital's main lobby.

No standing still permitted. Please move on.

Upstairs, I crept through the maternity ward, shyly glancing in each open door, half expecting beds filled with bloom-cheeked beauties in satin hair ribbons—Madison Avenue Motherhood. What is it with those ribbons, anyway, those pastel flags of newly conferred femininity the mothers always wear in the ads?

Instead, each room revealed a sacked-out woman or two

with hair at least disheveled if not dirty. The only ribbons hung from balloons and gifts.

At Stephanie's door, I hesitated. The rooms seemed so clean. Was everything sterile? I glanced down. This time of year, I always had a bit of the farm stuck to my boot heels. Her room was a double, but the bed by the door was empty. I tiptoed in. Beyond the curtain, Stephanie slept on her side, back to me.

Congratulatory bouquets filled the place. A ceramic lamb bearing white sweetheart roses frolicked on the wide windowsill beside a basket featuring daisies and a little teddy bear with a blue ribbon. Gift boxes spilled tissue and bits of blue clothing. To Welcome Your Baby Boy cards were taped to the wall along with the newspaper picture: First Baby of the New Year. A list in our mother's handwriting—the gifts and who'd brought them—lay on the rolling tray table.

To me, it couldn't have been clearer if the Mylar balloon tied to the foot of her bed had simply been lettered HERE LIES A WINNER.

I was tempted to dutifully set my gift on the foot of her bed and tiptoe out, but as I stood there, undecided, a nurse bustled in past me. She poked a thermometer on a cord into Stephanie's mouth and held her wrist for a pulse count. When she was finished, Stephanie shifted in jerks to her back. Seeing me, she grunted. Another visitor. I'll bet each time she'd opened her eyes she'd had a different one, judging from the array of gifts.

I hung back until the nurse had left, then moved around to the side of her bed.

"Hi," I said. "How are you?"

She took a breath that caught in her throat and triggered a coughing spasm. Groaning, she pressed her hands over her middle. "I keep forgetting . . . I can't do that."

"Rough time, huh?"

She made a face. "Well, Mom told you, didn't she?"

"Yeah." Sixteen hours of labor and a C section. No picnic. "So where is he? In the nursery?"

She nodded.

"Well," I said, "your timing sure was perfect. First Baby of the New Year."

"Not really. Matt thinks it would have been better to get the tax deduction since it turns out this is the first time the local merchants aren't giving the New Year's Baby a gift basket."

"Oh."

"It was kind of fun having the picture in the paper, though."

I nodded, eyeing the box of chocolates on her tray table. "Mind if I . . . ?"

"Please. Go ahead. Eat them all. I'm so fat, I'm never going to see my hipbones again."

"Come on."

"I worked so hard to keep that weight off before. And you know how I hate to exercise."

"I thought you liked dance aerobics."

"Oh please. And right now, the very thought of jumping is torture. What am I going to do with *these*?" She cupped her huge breasts. "My milk came in and they're hard as rocks. You never felt pain like this." She glanced at me. "Well, I don't know, maybe you have. But *I* haven't."

"Doesn't the baby . . . take care of that?"

"Not so's you'd notice. I'm supposed to be nursing on demand, but every time they bring him in here he falls asleep on me. The doctors walk by and see me holding him and say, 'Oh fine, fine,' and I'm going, what are you talking about? I feel like a little girl, sitting here pretending to nurse my doll."

"Our dolls were bottle-fed, as I recall."

"You know what I mean! I don't get it, Betsy. It's supposed to be so natural. And then, too, I'm worried about him. They keep telling me they have to take him back to the nursery to warm him up. His temperature doesn't stay up like it should. Do you think they could be hiding something from me?"

"Stephanie, no! They'd tell you if anything were wrong. Or Mom would have said something to me. But shoot, she's higher than a kite."

She plucked at the thin cotton bedspread. "I guess so."

I handed her my wrapped box.

"Betsy. You already got me that baby sac. That L.L. Bean thing."

I shrugged. "That was just for the shower."

She pulled off the paper, took out the baby quilt and ran her hands over it. Then she looked up with tears in her eyes. "I feel so guilty."

"No—"

"Look at this! Is it all by hand?"

"Mostly."

"Here I am, griping away."

"It's okay. Now come on. Don't be crying all over the quilt, for Pete's sake!"

"You know what's really making me sad?" Her face crumpled. She couldn't seem to get any more words out.

"Stephanie, what?"

"Daddy."

"Oh."

"That he's not . . . here for this."

"Yeah." Dad never getting to see his grandson—one of those Big Life nevers.

Neither of us said anything for a while.

Then Stephanie sniffed. "Sometimes I think you don't miss him at all."

"Sure I do."

"Not like I do."

I looked away, catching my own pained reflection in the silver backing of the Mylar balloon. "Maybe nobody ever misses anyone exactly the same. Anyway, *you were* his favorite."

"No, Betsy, he—"

"It's not like it bothers me. It's just the way it was." I walked over to the window. "I made him nervous. We never got along. You know that. Don't you remember how he was always needling me, saying stuff just to get me going?"

"Betsy, he tried to get everybody going. It's just that you were the one who always took the bait. And then Mom would be sitting there, silently cheering you on because you were saying everything she was always choking back."

I looked at her. Was that how it was?

"If Dad favored me, you have to admit Mom favored you."

Was I supposed to deny it? Apologize? What difference

would it make what *I* thought, if that's how Stephanie felt about it?

Imagine, having the bad manners to be favored by the one who didn't die.

"And anyway, as far as Dad, what about when you fixed up that first house and sold it? I didn't think we'd ever hear the end of it—how much money you'd made and all."

Yeah, I had to admit that won me a few points. Too bad they came so late in the game.

I turned back to the window. Even against the wintery, washed-out colors of the stubbled fields, the old white farmhouse and red barn on the next hill made a perfect picture. I imagined holding a baby up to it—what a lovely first look at the big outside world.

"Betsy, I'm not ready for this," Stephanie burst out.

I turned back to her. "Stephie—"

"I thought when the baby was born, I'd automatically know how to take care of it, but I don't. Every time they say something about me taking him home, I break out in a sweat. I can't believe they're going to let me do it. I keep thinking there must be a test or a license or something to make sure I know what I'm doing."

"Don't they give you any hints?" It sounded a little scary to me too.

"Well, they had a bath demonstration. I dragged myself down to that . . ." And then she was crying, silently, pathetically.

I sat on the edge of the bed and patted her. She needs to do this, I told myself, trying not to dwell on the thought that these tears were dribbling down the cheeks of a person with a healthy newborn baby down the hall. After all, I was the one always telling Gil how important it was to cry if you had to. This probably had more to do with Dad than with having a baby anyway.

So she cried and I kept patting and sort of spaced out. Only a few days before, I'd been standing beside another hospital bed—Gil's. Gil, who could have had brain damage or worse, but was fine. That made *me* want to cry. What a gift it is, I thought, to be made aware and glad of what you've got while you've still got it.

Maybe the whole thing had scared Gil more than he'd let on, too. Only seven days after the surgery, there he was, nuzzling up to me in bed. And we didn't even have any arrows to make! Just wanted to make sure everything still worked, I guess. Fortunately, it did.

"So," I said to Stephanie when her crying tapered off, "do I get to see this nephew of mine? Can you walk down there yourself?"

She groaned. "I have, a couple of times. It kills me, watching the ones who delivered vaginally waltzing around. I saw this one girl from my childbirth class—she'd only delivered four hours before and here she was—up!"

"Don't they have stitches or something?"

"I guess, but it doesn't seem to slow them down much. But with me, every time I stand up all the blood rushes to my incisions."

"But isn't it good to try moving around?"

"Yes, it is," a nurse sang out, bustling through. "The doctor wants you up more now that your IV's out."

Stephanie made a face, but then she said, "Well . . . okay," and started easing her legs over the side of the bed. "I hope you won't think he's funny-looking."

"Stephanie!" I laughed, handing her her robe. "Honest to God, you are hormonally deranged! I'll bet he's the cutest baby in there."

I slowed my steps to match my sister's as we made our way toward the glassed-in nursery, there to join a set of grandparents, another mother, and her husband. Their toddler daughter stood on the steps provided for a peek at her new brother.

"That one," Stephanie whispered, pointing at a bundle in a blue blanket.

I stared through the meshed glass at this little creature lying in the Plexiglas box.

"Stephanie, he is truly beautiful."

"Do you really think so?"

"Are you kidding? He's perfect."

Stephanie smiled now. "He is, isn't he?" Then she burst into tears all over again. "And I haven't even been appreciating him."

Boy, they weren't kidding about this hormone thing. I put my arm around her, conscious of the other family near us. But they gave us only the briefest of glances, absorbed, as they were, in their own baby.

"I'd better go back," Stephanie said. "I get so flushed."

"Okay, I'm right behind you. I just want to look at him a little longer."

I turned back to Jack. My nephew. Right there, working on that pacifier—that little person might be my closest genetic link to the future. Would any traits of mine show up in him?

Oh what the hell. Did it matter? All of these babies looked perfect, each a cuddly armful. The immediacy of them lying here together in rows, one after another, overwhelmed me. The nursery seemed like a store, the babies like goods displayed for the choosing. My brain, my heart, every fiber in me pulsed a single, power-packed message: *I want one.* I didn't care how it got born. So what if it was a gamble, taking on some other family's genes? Your own genes were a gamble too.

One of the babies was Oriental, a little boy. A happy fantasy formed—Gil and I at the Portland airport, watching the deplaning corridor for the adoption agency woman who would be carrying in her arms our son from across the sea. We could show him the world just the same as if I'd been pregnant with him for nine months, right? "Here it is," I'd say in my softest, talking-to-babies voice. "It's not perfect, but we're working on it for you."

Maybe that's the way this was meant to work out.

I noticed one of the nurses watching me. Did I have the crazed look of the barren woman who dons a lab coat, marches into the room of a nursing mother, and announces it's time to take the baby "for tests"?

Or maybe she noticed me for a different reason. Maybe, I thought hopefully, maybe I looked like I would make a particularly good mother. Another fantasy formed. I imagined her walking out, placing one of those babies in my arms, saying, "Yours if you want it."

What would I do? Could I love somebody else's baby? What would I *do*?

Walk away with it and never look back, that's what.

To Do

Work

Call Eric re Carter remodel
Measure at Atwells
Rent floor sander for McBee
house
Order wallpaper—McBee

Adoption agencies
Fix pantry door
Income taxes
Visit Grampa

Chapter 32

Shirley sat with her grandson in the rocker, watching the moving picture framed by the living room windows of her daughter's house—boats returning to the harbor, the sun going down beyond the arches of the Yaquina Bay Bridge.

She'd looked forward to this—her first time alone with her grandson while Stephanie and Matt had a much needed evening out.

So much was different these days, the way these girls had their babies. Or in Betsy's case, didn't have their babies. But some things never changed: the drowsy weight of an infant on your shoulder, the softness of his head, that newborn smell, unlike anything else on earth. She would try to appreciate it more this time around, now that she understood how fleeting it all was.

The baby started mewling. She lifted him from her shoulder and supported the tiny head against her hands.

"Whassa matter? Whassa matter now? I'm your Gramma, don't you know? Yes. Yes, I'm your Gramma."

Heavens, she hadn't used that cooing voice in years. She was not, after all, the sort to cootchy-coo every baby she encountered. But how quickly it came back now that she needed it. How easily it *all* came back.

She was already remembering what the girls had been like as babies. Betsy so feisty, so eager to push herself up on stiff little legs. After this first daughter, Stephanie had been a surprise, soft and passive, amazingly difficult to pick up. Not that she'd fight you the way Betsy did, or that she weighed so much more, but you couldn't get a grip on her. She was sweet, though, and always so eager to please.

And hadn't she turned out nicely? Now that she was over that initial touch of baby blues, anyone could see she was going to be a good mother.

Shirley glanced around the room. She'd had her doubts about this place when Stephanie and Matt first showed it to her two years ago. It didn't look like Stephanie's idea of a home so much as Matt's idea of an investment. Big. New. Good neighborhood. But Stephanie's loving handiwork had achieved the seemingly impossible task of turning the cavernous, white-walled rooms cozy, and the view *was* spectacular. Shirley would enjoy thinking of her grandson living here by the bay.

Oh dear, she'd have to remind Stephanie to write down all the cute things he was bound to say. She wished she'd done more of that herself. When you were in the middle of motherhood, your life seemed so filled with children, it never occurred to you that any of it—their flashes of delightful cleverness, or the hours of true tediousness—could ever be forgotten. But it could. Those early years were long in the living of them, but gone so swiftly in looking back.

The baby began to whimper again.

"Now don't you cry," she began automatically, and then stopped, suddenly remembering something she hadn't thought of in a long time—one of the things Betsy had said as a child that *was* remembered, initially because of the force of something so wise springing from a child, and then because the story had been repeated over the years.

Betsy had been four, and probably frustrated at the attention required by Stephanie. She'd been crying brokenheartedly about some silly thing and Shirley, completely out of patience, remembered saying, "Betsy, you are four years old, almost five, too old to be crying like this."

Betsy had stared at her, aghast. "But, Mama, *you* cry."

She'd searched her mother's face with an earnestness Shirley could still picture because it had cut right through her, and then she'd delivered this: "Don't you know we have to cry some at every age?"

If only that weren't so true. Oh, poor Betsy. She hoped . . . well, she didn't know what she hoped anymore beyond that one wish for a miracle pregnancy. Maybe her next hope was that if this ghastly pump thing they were talking about didn't work, Betsy would be able to put all the medical business behind her and move on. Shirley had even stopped passing along stories of other people's miracles, which would have seemed cruel at this point. She hated to encourage false hopes. But Betsy was so stubborn. "Remember what you always said, Mom," she'd taken to repeating every time Shirley hinted about other options. "If at first you don't succeed, try, try again."

But who could know that life would require so many caveats? If she'd had the vaguest hint of infertility treatments in her daughter's future, she'd definitely have revised this. Try until it's time to quit, she would have said, then quit.

Because maybe this time Betsy wasn't going to get what she wanted. Not that she always did, of course, in spite of Stephanie's views on this.

A person could argue, in fact, that Stephanie's record of getting what she wanted wasn't any worse than Betsy's. Shirley remembered when she was about five, how she'd longed for that little housekeeping set she'd seen at the dime store. Shirley had tried to dissuade her—a bunch of miniature detergent boxes weren't worth a dollar ninety-five. Determined, Stephanie saved a nickel a week and finally bought the set, which turned out to be, as Shirley expected, a big disappointment. Theoretically Stephanie should have learned something from this, but had she? Grown-up, she still seemed chronically disappointed with the very things for which she'd longed. Certainly she seemed pleased about the baby, Shirley thought, but still, with Stephanie there would probably always be that little something hurting just under the surface.

It was so hard, trying to know what to do. Even with grown children, the temptation to fix things for them remained. Only now they wanted what money couldn't buy.

They had spouses ready to resent your interference. The question of helping or even advising had become infinitely more complicated.

With Betsy's problem it had seemed obvious there was nothing she could do other than listen. Then the question of money arose. Now she felt uneasy about the loan she'd agreed to. Not that she begrudged her daughter the money, which she'd have given freely anyway. But Betsy didn't want Gil to know about it, and it went against Shirley's better instincts to put herself and money between the two of them. But one way or another, Betsy explained, they'd soon be finished with the medical treatments. Then the bills would end. To sell one of her properties now to raise cash, especially when the McBee house was almost ready for renting, would be foolish.

In the end, of course, Shirley couldn't bring herself to say no.

There just weren't any rules for this, that was the trouble. What was, after all, the correct answer when a daughter asks you to invest in the hope of a grandchild?

She looked down at the baby. "Because I wouldn't mind having lots more like you," she said, automatically cooing again. "Yes, if they could all be as cute as you."

Chapter 33

People claim to admire persistence. To be specific, though, what they admire is persistence after it has resulted in success. Persistence that doesn't seem to be getting a person anywhere is viewed as stupidity, not knowing when to quit, not being able to read the writing on the wall. If your luck runs bad long enough, persistence begins to look pathological.

But persistence with a positive outcome guaranteed wouldn't be any trick at all, would it?

Certainly no one was admiring *my* persistence. And I was no longer in touch with the people who might at least have understood. Carla was pregnant and presumably happy—she never did call. Amy was still grieving—I certainly couldn't complain to her. Gil had heard it all a million times.

I took an unprecedented step: I shut up about it.

The price of this unaccustomed silence was a spate of strange dreams. I dreamed of palm-sized babies, flat as paper dolls, who spoke in sentences from the moment of birth. "Is it supposed to be like this?" I kept asking people. I dreamed about cartons of broken eggs, trying to scoop the yolks back into the jagged half shells. (Okay, so my subconscious is not particularly subtle.) I spent one long night wandering a maternity nursery the size of our pumpkin patch, peering into each little bed, searching for Gil. And some of the dreams were nothing but feelings—me grieving endlessly, with Gil impatient to the point of anger at my tears.

I would wake to the comfort of Gil's arms and his absolute refusal to accept responsibility for anything he had done or had neglected to do in my ridiculous dreams. These were mornings of clear spring light, and days that included no doctor visits, no temperature taking. I tried to set my mind on real life, on finishing up the McBee house, on scratching items off my To Do list again.

Daffodils helped.

The house Eric Norgren currently had me papering was a remodel, already landscaped, and for spring, the owners had two half whiskey barrel planters crammed with daffodils flanking the front door. That after the gray of winter, the first thing to bloom should be these bursts of yellow cheerfulness has always seemed to me a terrific plan, surprising me anew, year after year. I made up my mind to plant some at the McBee house. You had to remember to do it in the fall though. That was the trick—having faith in spring.

Except for Eric coming around, I had been enjoying this job. The other guys on the remodel were nice, people I'd worked with before.

Skip Fenton, the carpet layer, used to give me a hard time when I first started papering. It's so silly, really. Women have been hanging wallpaper since it was invented, I'll bet, it's just that nobody ever paid them for it. But go out and start charging what the guys usually get, and everybody's feathers start ruffling. The first time I worked on the same job as Skip, we were halfway through a workday before he figured out I wasn't the lady of the house. That really threw him. He started grilling me about licensing and bonding and all. He used to hang paper himself and thought he knew it all. Well, it took a couple of years, but we were good buddies now.

Eric was getting worse all the time, though. Or maybe I was just more fed up with him. He never touched me on the job—I could have called him on that. It was his constant stream of remarks that wore me out. "I had a dream about you last night," he'd say, leering. If it weren't for the job offers he represented, I probably would have told him where to jump off months ago.

I was working on the living room of this remodel when he dropped by to check progress one day. He started in on how great the paper looked, then slipped into how I didn't look too bad either from this angle. Since I was up on a ladder and he was standing with his face about six inches from my rear, I didn't appreciate this.

I climbed down. "Eric, when are you gonna give it up?"

He grinned. "Give what up?"

"The thing is," I said, "persistence is only admired if you succeed in the end. And since you aren't going to, this is getting less admirable all the time."

"You tell 'em, Bets." Skip hammered down a length of carpet tacking.

"Just being a gentleman," Eric said, playing to his audience, Skip and the electricians hanging the new light fixtures. "Just offering my . . . uh . . . services. In case that farmer of hers needs some help."

"Oh, Eric." I loaded my voice with concern. "That's so thoughtful of you. But, honestly, I wouldn't feel right taking you up on it." I bit my lip with regret. "I'm afraid my husband is just so good in bed, I don't think I could stand it—watching you humiliate yourself trying to top him."

Hoots from the guys.

"I think that's a no," Skip called.

Eric's face went red in the gratifying way only a Nordic face can. "Can't help it, Skip. I admire a wife who sticks up for her husband like that, even when she has to . . . you know . . . smooth over the truth."

"I don't have to smooth over anything," I said.

"No? Well, what's this I hear about him winding up at the hospital? My ex works there, you know. Tells me he's been having a little trouble."

"What?" I turned to him slowly, my eyes blurring.

Eric smiled, seeing he'd hit home. "Yeah, had to get his equipment fixed, she says."

My face burned. For the lie in this and for the tiny, gossip-distorted grain of truth.

"You've got it all wrong," I said.

"He didn't have surgery?"

"Not for that and it's none of your business anyway."

I turned back to work, picking up a strip of paper I'd already cut. I looked at the wall, had trouble focusing. That jerk. I stood there. Damnit to hell. There were a lot of things in my life that I couldn't control right now, but this wasn't one of them.

I dropped the paper and turned to Eric with a wondering look. "I just realized something, Eric."

"What's that?"

"I'm through here." I picked up my paste bucket, carried it into the kitchen, and rinsed the remainder down the sink.

He followed me. "Hey, what are you doing?"

"Like I said, I'm done." I gathered my brushes and razors.

"What're you talking about? You've got two more walls and the ceiling border. That's gotta get done today."

"Oh dear. Well, you better get busy then, huh?"

"Come on. Can't you take a joke?"

Exaggerated surprise. "This was a joke?"

"Well sure."

"It's just a joke that you've been wanting to get in my pants for two years?"

"Well, I mean . . ."

"Silly me! I should have known that. Of course it's a joke. Because"—I laughed—"you wouldn't know what to do if I said yes, would you?"

"Hey—"

"So I've done you a big favor, haven't I?"

He glanced at the other guys, who seemed to be enjoying this. "Look," he muttered, "can't we forget this and get back to wallpaper?"

"Nope," I said cheerfully. "Don't think so."

"But I've got a schedule to keep here. Commitments I've made. You can't just walk."

"Oh yeah? Watch me." I marched out, then stuck my head back in the door. "Eric? I wouldn't whine like that if I were you. It sounds so wimpy."

To Do

Work

Measure at Forsyths
Wed—Wong
Ad to paper for McBee house
Hang curtains—McBee

Make med school appt.
Gil—check for "personal leave"
Bulb catalogs
Income taxes
Fix pantry door
Clean up orchard prunings
Hack blackberries
Visit Grampa

Chapter 34

Gil took his eyes off the twisty Pill Hill road long enough to glance over at Betsy. Not talking much. Bad sign.

"Doin' okay?" he asked.

She made a sick face. Couldn't blame her. This trip to the medical school in Portland had been hanging over their heads all spring—a day of hope and a day to dread. On the one hand the pump sounded good—an evenly paced, nature-mimicking delivery of hormones to encourage ovulation. Software, as one magazine article had put it, for a scrambled reproductive computer.

On the other hand, who could get enthusiastic about three weeks with a needle stuck in her arm?

"The needle probably won't hurt once it's in," Betsy said. "Right?"

"Naw."

Gil hated needles too. Maybe even more than she did. Oh, he'd go in for a tetanus shot if a rusty nail puncture looked so ugly Betsy wouldn't let up about it, but he hated watching anyone else get stuck. He always averted his eyes if he was with Betsy when they drew her blood, and he sure as hell didn't tune in to all those medical specials on TV she found so fascinating. Sometimes he worried what would happen if she *did* get pregnant. She'd want him in the delivery room—and he'd probably pass out.

They were almost up to the hospital-clinic complex now.

"Why do they always put hospitals on hills?" Betsy said. "To keep us humble? Like we're climbing up for our salvation? Maybe we should be inching our way up on bloodied knees?"

"Gimme a break."

"I will lift mine eyes unto the hills, whence cometh my help."

"Betsy!" He'd take silence over weirdness any day, thanks.

"We sang that psalm in junior high choir. Can you believe it? They'd never let them get away with that these days."

He glanced at her. She had her head resting against the window.

"I don't know why I'm always worried that somehow these people won't think I'm . . . you know . . . worthy," she said. "They probably don't give a hoot who deserves a baby and who doesn't. We're just numbers to them. All they want is good success rates. They probably don't care if you're the best candidate for motherhood since the Virgin Mary or some drug addict who's already had three abortions."

"Well, *that* might be stretching it."

He didn't understand where she came up with all this religious stuff. The med school made *him* feel like a lab rat in a maze—first find a parking place, then negotiate the labyrinth of halls and elevators. And just the fact that it was a hospital. Hospitals brought back too many bad memories for him. Like his mother-in-law's car accident.

Betsy had been such a basket case that first night, sitting out the long emergency surgery in the Shepherd of the Valley ICU waiting room. And then the doctor prescribing those Seconals for all of them. One, he'd said, or two if one doesn't put you to sleep. Betsy had popped that second capsule too fast; she could hardly stand up in the morning when they were supposed to go back to the hospital. That was the day Gil introduced her to coffee, urging it down her as she slumped on the stairs. What a nightmare.

After Shirley was transferred to the med school in Portland, they made three trips up here a week for months, most of them after he'd finished school each day. Heading home late at night, silent and exhausted, they'd pull into an all-night restaurant and order coffee. Newly hooked on caffeine, Betsy would down one cup, start chattering, and keep it up all the way back to Mary's Bend.

And then there was the hospital vigil for Betsy's father, this time in the cardiac unit waiting room at Shepherd of the Valley, this time with no happy ending. He mainly remembered Stephanie and Matt rushing in after their frantic drive from the coast, arriving just in time to catch the end of the doctor's we-did-all-we-could speech. Stephanie totally lost it.

Pain behind closed doors—that's what hospitals meant to Gil. Having to come to a place like this to make a baby just seemed . . . wrong.

Now, inside the imposing building, he and Betsy argued briefly about which hallway they'd turned down when they'd been here for their consultation four months ago. After an elevator ride or two (once it went down when they pushed up), they rounded a corner and stumbled almost by accident into the Ob/Gyn waiting room.

Betsy showed the receptionist the yellow plastic ID card she'd been issued in December. Then she sat down, picked up a magazine from a low table, flipped through it, tossed it back.

"I think I've just reached my waiting room magazine lifetime tolerance."

They looked at each other for a moment. He reached over and took her hand. Cold. He knew she hadn't slept much the previous night. She always claimed, with a certain resentment, that he could sleep through anything, but she was wrong.

He slouched lower in his chair. Minutes that were no doubt ticking off with the usual speed on clocks elsewhere seemed to click with painful reluctance on the big wall clock here. Sometimes it seemed to him as if these medical people felt compelled to schedule a wait, just to build suspense. Wasn't it bad enough for Betsy without her having to park herself out here for an hour-long sweat? He gave her a sympathetic look as she returned from her third trip to the rest room. He wasn't doing too well himself. He glanced at the clock again. Noon. His stomach rumbled.

Finally a nurse appeared—young, slim, fluffy blond hair. She led them down the hall, past the room where they'd had their consultation with the doctor last December. She held open the door of a small examining room.

Gil dropped into a plastic chair in the corner.

Betsy was supposed to climb up on the table and take off her shirt.

"Okay," the nurse said, going out, "let me make sure the pump is available."

Make sure the pump is—? Gil sat up. What the—? They'd taken off work, driven two hours to get here, sat in the waiting room until they were ready to pass out from hunger, and now, *now* this nurse was going to check to see if the damn pump was *available*?

"I thought this was all set," Gil said.

"It was. Damnit, why is it, every time—" Betsy broke off as the nurse returned.

"Another patient's using the smaller one, so we'll try this."

Warily, Betsy eyed the black box. They'd talked about a unit the size of a cigarette pack. This was more like a paperback book. Well, Gil thought, at least they had it.

The nurse set a plastic carrier on the table and started spreading out tubes, syringes, and vials of medicine, talking nonstop and in no particular order about how to use them and what to watch out for.

He clamped his jaw, striving for an expression more pissed-off than panicky. But Jesus. Air bubbles in the line? Wasn't that lethal? Maybe this treatment ought to be limited to couples with a year or two of med school between them. And where was the damned doctor? His head buzzed, watching the nurse chatter on. We're crazy, he thought, letting ourselves be led into this by someone who looks like she'd be more at home in a spangled dress, flipping letters for a TV game show.

Okay, so this was unfair. Just because the nurse was a dish didn't mean she wasn't smart, right? That's the line Betsy always gave him, anyway. He noticed she was never too quick to defend dishy blondes when she actually encountered them, though.

"Could you slow down a little?" Betsy said. "I don't think we quite got all that."

The nurse stopped. "Which part?" Genuine surprise. Her explanation hadn't been 100 percent clear?

"Well . . ." Betsy glanced at Gil. "The part about air bubbles?"

"Oh that. Well, that isn't going to happen."

"Oh."

She laughed. "Don't worry, we're not going to let you out of here without making sure you understand everything. Now let's get this IV going." She called down the hall and another nurse came in.

Thankfully, Gil thought, this one seemed less scattered. Or was she just heavier and less attractive? Oh what the hell . . .

Together the two nurses tied a rubber tourniquet around Betsy's upper arm and started tapping at her veins.

Betsy took one more look at Gil and shut her eyes. He stared at the floor, trying to space out. *Let's see, with the price of strawberries up this year* . . . He smelled the alcohol. They were swabbing her arm.

"A little stick here."

"A little stick," Betsy said. "They always call it a little stick."

"Here it comes."

"Ouch."

Gil winced with her.

"You okay?" the first nurse asked Betsy. Jodie, her plastic name tag read.

Betsy nodded, then laughed nervously. "I guess you guys wouldn't get very far with *Okay, here's a stab of burning pain.*"

"That bad, huh?"

Betsy blinked the quick, shocked tears from her lashes. "The anticipation's always the worst. I never mind how bad it is, as long as it's over."

They were still bent over her arm.

"You *are* done," Betsy said. "Aren't you?"

They weren't answering.

Gil leaned forward. "Something wrong?"

"Damn." Jodie backed away.

"Nope," the other one said, "that's not going to work."

Betsy stole a glance at her hand. "It's not in? You have to do it again?"

"Bad vein," Jodie said. "Let's try another."

Gil watched the color drain from Betsy's cheeks. Oh shit. Why couldn't it ever just go smoothly?

"What about getting a doctor in here to do this?" he said. "If you're having trouble . . ."

"No, I've done tons of these," Jodie said. "That's not the problem."

"Gil, you can wait outside if you want," Betsy said. "You don't have to watch."

He slumped down. Tempting invitation, but come on. Too chickenshit even to watch, and she's the one getting stuck . . . ? He couldn't admit to that.

"Okay, let's go again. Ready?"

Betsy took a deep breath and nodded. The needle pierced her skin. She winced. Jesus. Gil shut his eyes. This better work. But when he looked again, Jodie had backed off.

Betsy exhaled.

"It just won't thread," Jodie said. "Darnedest thing. I've never had this trouble before. Her veins just keep collapsing on me. If she's going to wear this for a month, we have to make sure it's in there good. You guys don't want to get home and have it popping out." She looked at the other nurse. "What do you think? Farther up?"

The other nurse shrugged. "Can't hurt to try."

"Wanna bet?" Betsy said.

Jodie looked at Betsy. "You game?"

Betsy turned to Gil.

"Quit if you want to," he said. "I wouldn't blame you."

She was looking beyond him now, her face wistful. "Isn't it amazing," she said, "how most people get babies strictly by having fun?"

"Yeah well . . ."

"If I quit now, it's like it was a total waste, you having that surgery."

Gil shrugged. Something oddly familiar and somehow disturbing in that logic. Wasn't that how wars dragged on, nobody wanting to admit that past sacrifices were nothing but waste?

Jodie was looking at him. "He had surgery?"

"Yeah," Betsy said. "Thanks to modern medicine this guy is simply loaded with millions of extremely vigorous sperm."

"Betsy!"

"Millions of sperm," she repeated sadly. "All of them pining for one crummy little egg." She turned to Jodie. "He could have died! He threw up under the anesthetic and the doctors said—"

"Betsy!"

"Honey, it's just a medical fact."

"Well, I didn't die," he said irritably. "So quit if you want. It won't hurt my feelings." He wanted her to quit. Suddenly he'd had enough, surgery or no surgery.

Jodie turned back to Betsy. "One more try?"

"Okay." She wiped sweaty palms on her jeans. "One more try."

But her veins weren't having any of it. Five minutes of stabbing and grimacing and swearing later, it was clear: The pump was out.

"Sorry," Jodie said as the other nurse left. "Like I said, we've never had this kind of trouble with anybody's veins before."

That's right, Gil thought. Blame the patient.

At first Betsy's face simply relaxed into the relief of knowing the pain was over for now. But any second, he knew, he'd be seeing something else. Because no matter what she'd promised about giving up when they got to the end of the line, it wasn't going to be that easy.

She turned to him, just beginning to register the awful finality, the complete loss of all hope, when Jodie spoke up.

"You guys could always try Pergonal."

Alarm buzzed through Gil. "No, now wait," he said, anxious to speak before Betsy could. "That's the litter medicine, right?"

With dismay, he watched Betsy turn toward Jodie like an animal sniffing something tantalizing on the wind.

"Litter medicine?" Jodie laughed and scooped up the used IV supplies. "Our record here isn't quite that bad. Just a couple of sets of twins. You wouldn't mind twins, would you?"

"Twins sound great to me," Betsy said.

This wasn't fair, Gil thought. This was dangling raw meat . . . He forced a note of calm into his voice. "We couldn't do this without another appointment with the doctor, though." He looked at Jodie hopefully. "Right?" Not to mention that the proposition of fooling with Pergonal deserved at the very least a long, private discussion between the two of them.

"Sure you could," Jodie said. "You already had your consultation. Your records list you as Pergonal candidates. And this would be perfect, because we always start Pergonal on Mondays and today's Monday. You could start right now."

Right now? His pulse quickened. This was getting completely out of hand. Damned if these two women weren't getting ready to plot the future without him. *His* future!

"Come on, Betsy. We agreed we didn't want to risk having quints." He waited. "I'm not making this up, am I? We did agree on that?"

"Well yes, but . . ."

"It's not the risk it used to be," Jodie said. "We have ways of monitoring it now. Ultrasound scans will show if you're going to pop too many eggs. If that happens we withhold the shot of HCG you need to trigger the whole business and *ta da*—no ovulation."

"Oh, HCG," Betsy said. "Just like I've been doing with the Clomid?"

"Right," Jodie said.

"But back to numbers," Gil said, "how many eggs are too many?"

Jodie doodled on their chart. "Well, usually if there are four or more eggs we recommend scrapping the cycle, but you never know. We had one woman whose scan showed five. We *strongly* recommended withholding the HCG, but she was so fed up with trying she just said, 'I don't care, I want that shot.' "

"And . . . ?" Betsy said.

"And she had one baby."

"One?" Gil said. "Come on. . . ."

"Well, each egg has only a one-in-five chance, so—"

"But you really can't guarantee we wouldn't have quints." Gil crossed his arms over his chest.

"Oh, Gil, for Pete's sake," Betsy said. "There aren't any guarantees in any of this. Haven't you figured that out by now?"

"Hey, do you mind if I find out what kind of numbers we're looking at here before we go running off half cocked?"

Betsy and Jodie traded glances in that infuriating way women do, as if being female made them closer than the fact that he happened to be married to one of them.

Jodie's voice was cajoling. "I think I pretty much *can* guarantee that you won't have quints."

Gil eyed her. "But what about triplets?"

"I'll take three!" Betsy said. "I'd rather have three than none."

"See?" Gil said to Jodie. "She's around the bend. Anyone who could talk like that about triplets—"

"No, I'm completely calm." Betsy's voice trembled. "You're the one who's freaking out. What she's trying to tell us is that we've got choices along the way, right?" She looked to Jodie for confirmation. "We're not risking quints with the first dose of medicine, right?"

"Right," Jodie said.

"Gil, if we don't try this, we're all done."

"Yeah." Sounded okay to him.

Betsy's face crumpled. "But, Gil . . ."

He looked at her. Was this the wife who'd said a hundred times she was anxious to get this over with and quit? Good God, she'd do *anything*. Who knows how long this could go on?

He sighed. "Is this *really* our last chance?"

He and Betsy both turned to Jodie.

"Pretty much," she said. "Unless they come up with something new."

They'd better not, Gil thought, flashing on a picture of himself tearing through some lab, smashing test tubes . . . Then he looked at his wife's face. Shoot. He'd never hear the end of it if he stood in the way of this one last chance.

"Well," he said. "Will you agree that five eggs is too many?"

"Yes," Betsy said. "Five is too many."

"Four is too many?"

She hesitated. "Okay."

"Three?"

"Gil!"

Damn. Why did she always have to be so stubborn? What

was so hard about picking a number and sticking with it? This whole thing reminded him of sending her off to an auction, and in this case, the idea of any "accidental" purchases was making him very nervous.

"Remember," Jodie said, "each has only a one-in-five chance . . ."

Two women, waiting for his answer.

"Twins is the most you've ever come up with," he said.

"On my honor," Jodie said.

"Well . . . what the hell."

Jodie brightened. "You want to go for it?"

"Hey, I just work here."

"Okay!" Now she was all smiles. Two more guinea pigs. More numbers to put on her charts. "I'll be right back with the stuff."

"Wow," Betsy whispered as the door closed. "But somehow she doesn't make it sound as scary as Dr. Lowell always did, does she?"

He grunted. Actually he agreed, but he wasn't about to admit it. "You've got to promise we'll quit if this doesn't work."

"We'll have to. There won't be anything else to try."

"How do I know you're not going to decide you want to do in vitro or something?"

"Gil! In vitro's for women whose tubes are shot. But they've still got to make eggs. So yeah, this is really it."

"Promise?"

She sighed as if he were some balky child. "If this doesn't work, I promise I'll start talking Korean babies or whatever, okay?"

"Well, okay."

She gave him a smile of relief and gratitude, then launched into a feverish summation of her new and hastily reorganized line of thinking. It was all working out for the best, she said. She could cross the pump off without having it stuck in her arm for a month. The Pergonal was bound to work, and even if it didn't, she just knew she'd be able to accept the final verdict better if she'd tried everything possible first . . .

Get it in writing, Gil was thinking. Get it on tape . . .

"So how much do you suppose this is going to cost?" he asked.

"Oh, it's not cheap," Betsy said. "But don't worry about it."

"Don't worry about it?"

"It'll work out."

"Betsy—"

She blew an impatient puff of air up at her bangs. "I got a loan from my mom, okay?"

Gil stared at her. "No, I'm sorry, that's not okay. I made it real clear I didn't want you to do that, and you agreed."

"Oh no, I didn't. I made it real clear I was determined to ask her if I had to."

"Excuse me? I don't recall that being made clear at all. And anyway, if you had any inkling this was going to go on and on and rack up more bills, why'd you go ahead and buy the McBee house? You'll have to put it back on the market."

"Oh sure, that'd make a lot of sense, now that it's finally ready and we're going to see some rental income."

With no good answer to that, all he could do was scowl.

"Look," she said, "I'm not going to let some dumb thing like money get in the way of having our baby. You might as well get that straight."

Gil thought of mother grizzlies, defending their cubs. It was that same ferociousness in Betsy, defending a life not even conceived. On anything else he'd have fought back, but that flash in her eyes . . . In the face of this . . . this fierceness, backing off seemed like nothing more than part of the natural order.

Jodie pushed the door open with her hip. "Here we go." She dumped a new load of paraphernalia on the counter.

"We forgot to ask you," Betsy said. "What are our chances on this? How many get pregnant?"

"We've been running forty percent. That's patients who stick it out for three or four cycles."

Actual numbers.

"That sounds pretty good," Betsy said.

Gil knew she was looking at him. He made a point of studying his callouses.

"Not bad," Jodie said, "when you remember these are

women who've tried everything else. Okay, now." She turned to Gil. "You've given shots before, haven't you?"

"Shots?" Gil looked up.

"Yes, we usually have the husband give his wife the shots each day."

"You mean, like *me*? I'd actually be . . . doing the part with the needle?"

Jodie looked from one to the other. "Is this a problem?"

Gil wished, at this moment, that he were anywhere else on earth.

"I suppose you could arrange to go over to your doctor's office every day," Jodie said, "but that might be—"

"No," Betsy said. "He can do it. Can't you, Gil? Please. Don't make me go through that every day."

He rolled his eyes. Nobody was *making* her do anything. Finally he said, "Well, okay." Wasn't that the bottom line through this whole thing? Him saying *well, okay*. Seemed like every time he said it, things got worse.

"So I take it," Jodie said, "you don't have any experience with hypodermic needles?"

"Only when I shoot up."

Jodie just looked at him.

"I'm *joking*," Gil said, dead serious. "No, I don't have any experience with hypodermic needles."

"Well, no problem. Nothing to it. Really."

"I just remembered something," Betsy said. "A rumor, maybe it's not even true, but . . . someone said you'd had a fatality here. A patient on Pergonal?"

Gil sat up. "Somebody *died* on this stuff?"

"I told you about that, Gil."

Not when it was a story that had anything to do with *his* wife.

Jodie didn't look up from the boxes of medicine she was putting on the table. "It's true. Three or four years ago a patient died. But she had other problems. We made recommendations that she chose to ignore. It was just—" She broke off, fluttering her hands as if to wave it all away, the details being too complex, irrelevant, or unpleasant to go into. "Pergonal is a very powerful drug. I don't want to minimize that. But we'll be watching you—your blood, your weight . . ."

She took a closer look at Betsy. "Hey, don't get green on me. You're healthy. I don't think you'll have any problem. Hyperstimulation is really pretty rare these days."

"That's good to know." Betsy was breathing again. "And after all, people die in childbirth, right?"

"Nice thought," Gil said.

"Well, I'm just talking about the risks, here. I mean, I could get killed driving up through this dumb Portland traffic, right?"

Jodie looked at Gil. "Funny way of giving herself a pep talk, huh?" She held up a little glass ampoule of the magic white power. "Okay now, whatever you do, don't drop these. Twenty-five dollars apiece. You'll start with shots of two ampoules and go from there. So you can see it's going to add up." She gave them a quick mixing demo. Then she picked up the hypodermic and turned to Gil.

"Ever play darts?"

Chapter 35

Heading home, we once again had hope. We had fear. We had several pages of written instructions. And we had a grocery sack Jodie had loaded with five hundred dollars' worth of drugs and syringes—just for starters.

Summoning what was, for me, a rare degree of restraint, I hadn't revealed to Gil my nervousness at this little experiment in marital cooperation, nor had I let on the true extent of my trepidation over the Pergonal itself. *Let me live through this*, I was thinking as I watched him load the hypodermic that first time. *Keep this concoction from killing me, and I'll accept any verdict, even No Baby.*

Gil held up the needle. "Now don't get upset, but before I give this to you, you've got to promise me something."

"What."

"If there're too many eggs, you agree you won't have the final shot."

"Gil, we've been over this . . ."

"But I'm not sure we settled on how many was *too* many. We need to be logical about this—make a decision before something happens that gets us all emotional."

"Gil," I said, "there's nothing to decide right now. If I get too many eggs going, *then* we'll decide."

"Okay, but promise—"

"The only thing I'm promising right now is that if you don't give me that shot, so help me, I'll give it to myself!"

Over the bathroom sink, we stared each other down.

"I must be crazy," he said, "aiding and abetting the passing on of genes like yours."

"The shot, Gil."

"I can just picture some teenage daughter with your mouth. Sass? Oh brother."

"I am standing here with my pants down. Do you mind?"

"Okay, okay. Says on this sheet I'm looking for the upper outer quadrant of the hip."

I slapped my rear. "Right here." I took a deep breath.

"What is it they always say when they do this? A little stick?"

"Yeah."

"Okay, here's a little stick."

I waited. Nothing. No pain. I tried to brace myself and relax at the same time which is, of course, impossible.

"Okay, here goes."

Still I waited. Poor Gil. This was harder for him than for me. Finally—*ping*.

"Am I hurting you?"

"No," I lied, gritting my teeth. "Almost done?"

"Yup. There." He pulled it out.

"All in and all done, as the auctioneers say." I craned around, trying to see. No blood gushing out or anything.

He fumbled the wrap off a little round Band-Aid and carefully smoothed it over the red dot he'd made.

"It really didn't hurt?"

"Well, it felt just like when the nurses do it." He looked satisfied. Good. He'd forgotten what I'd said about the nurses' shots.

The mixing of the medicine for the nightly injection soon came to feel like a sacred ritual we were performing, Gil masterfully snapping the glass vials, me drawing up the diluent and squirting it into the powder. Maybe his scare talk about quints had actually been no more than a cover for squeamishness, because once he found himself successfully managing the shots, he quit fretting about multiple births. And I certainly appreciated his competence. After all, it was sparing me a forty-five-minute squirm in the clinic waiting room each day.

So it was all clockwork—until my first blood test.

"This is the last thing I ever worried about," I told Gil after the med school phoned with the disappointing results. My estrogen hadn't risen at all. "Here we are agonizing about my ovaries blimping up and exploding and instead they're just lying there, dead, not doing anything. It's like I'm ninety years old on the inside or something."

"Oh come on."

"All these arguments about whether or not three eggs is too many, and I'm probably not even going to get one!"

I vaguely recalled Jodie warning us of this possibility, but it was a concern completely eclipsed, at the time, by our fear of the power of Pergonal.

My dose was now doubled. A hundred dollars in each hypodermic. An expensive habit.

I set out each morning on my holy mission, driving up the hill to the hospital as the sun rose over the Cascades. The secret was in my blood, and only the high lab technicians in Portland could discern it. The mysterious red fluid was drawn, the tube packed in a box and shuttled north, where unknown eyes somehow measured the level of the crucial hormone. Did they know, these white-coated strangers, what this number might mean in our lives?

No, they couldn't care and wonder about every vial of blood. Pretty soon they'd be as bonkers as I was. Besides, these were people who found blood infected with this scary new disease—AIDS, blood teeming with the white cells of leukemia.

Measuring estrogen wasn't life or death.

I knew that.

Unfortunately, my heart did not believe my brain.

Chapter 36

Maximum green, Gil thought, steering the truck along the coast range highway. Maple and alder were leafed out, lawns at the houses here and there along the road grew thick and uncut, fed by spring rains to lushness. Wild roses tangled in the ditches.

"Gil!" Betsy said. "That car's passing!"

"I see it." Gil slowed to let the oncoming car slip back to the other lane. Someday she was going to make him have an accident, startling him like that.

"Sorry." She clutched the sack of medicine in her lap. "But I can't help it. Because wouldn't that just tear it? If we had a wreck and smashed up the medicine?"

"If we have a wreck," Gil pointed out, "the medicine won't matter."

"Ha! Guess not." But she didn't seem to ease her grip on the sack, and he knew she was squeezing her eyes shut each time they met a log truck coming around a bend.

He followed the twisty curves, tunneling through the green of the overarching maples as the road ran alongside the Yaquina.

Just last evening Jodie had phoned with the news. Betsy's estrogen levels had finally risen. All systems were go—a modern-day version of the stars being in the right places. Today was the day for the triggering shot of HCG, the final arrow on that damned chart.

Okay, he could handle that.

Sure, why not?

A romantic night at Neskowin. He wasn't going to let it bother him, was he, the fact that they had bet twelve hundred dollars on him being able to come through?

They sailed past meadows of tender grass laced with daisies, hillsides of bracken fern and purple lupine. Against the mild May sky, the ridge-top fir spires pointed toward the heavens.

"One thing I'll say for you giving me the shots," Betsy said. "It has been kind of nice, hasn't it? Just keeping this between the two of us?"

"Sure." What a laugh. Between the two of them if you didn't count the nurses who drew her blood, the technicians who analyzed it in the Portland lab, the ultrasound technicians, the nurse at the medical school . . .

That afternoon they hiked out to the end of Cascade Head, to vistas of the edge of the curving blue earth, bracing, ocean clean air, hours and hours of Betsy spinning out her wishful stories—what they might name the baby, how they would bring the baby here someday and tell him or her the whole story . . .

She really was getting her hopes up, Gil thought, following her along the footpath. He'd tried to point out the danger in that to her, but her answer was always the same: that the only alternative she knew to getting your hopes up was constant, low-grade despair—a prospect she did not find appealing at all.

And anyway, how could he stop her?

She was always saying how wonderful he was in his willingness to go along with whatever she wanted, and, yeah, that probably was better than dealing with some of these husbands she'd been telling him about. That Greg what's his name, almost forcing his wife to have surgery, or the one who absolutely refused to get a sperm count and had developed an obsession with pumping up his muscles at the gym. Still, Gil worried that just going along with her stemmed from a certain laziness on his part, a detachment, a turning over of the whole issue to her. Maybe it would have been better for them both if he'd stood firmer, insisted on drawing the line somewhere. It was seductive to see her so happy and optimistic again, but he feared they'd pay for it in the end. And what did *he* really want to do? Sometimes he felt it took so much energy coping with *her* emotions, he didn't have a clue how he really felt himself.

On the way back, at the Neskowin store, they picked out a special bottle of wine for that night. Also two boxes of chocolate cigars with perforated *It's a boy/It's a girl* tabs—the proud parents were to tear off whichever they didn't have.

"Now this *is* jumping the gun," Gil complained good-naturedly as they went out down the wooden steps together.

Betsy smiled. "Did you see the way that checker looked at me?"

"Even if you do get pregnant, you'll never be able to stay out of the chocolate until it's born."

"So? I just want the boxes. I'm going to flatten them, see, and paste them in the baby books."

"Books? That's plural?"

"Gil! I know I chatter a lot, but don't you hear anything I say?"

Of course he heard her. He was always listening. It's just that sometimes he thought of it as . . . well, as a sort of background music.

"Here it is again, then: The last ultrasound scan showed I'm going to pop two eggs. We might have twins." She got in the truck.

He stood frozen a minute, then lowered himself into the driver's seat. "Really?"

"Oh honestly! Am I in this all by myself or what? Where have you been? This is *Pergonal* you've been shooting me up with, remember?"

"Well, I guess twins would be okay . . ."

She rolled her eyes. "You guess twins would be okay."

"There's no way there could be more, though, is there?"

Her voice sounded phony bright. "Thinking of holding out on me tonight?"

"Betsy." He stared at her profile. "Two eggs and that's it, right?"

"Well, actually . . ." She wouldn't meet his eyes. "Two that look real good and two that look sort of . . . possible."

"Possible?"

"I told you all this. Don't act like I'm being sneaky. I showed you where the ultrasound technician wrote down the size of each one."

"Come on. For two years now you've been waving scraps of paper with numbers and graphs in my face. I can't keep it all straight."

"Well, don't freak out on me. Each good egg has only a one-in-five chance of getting fertilized, remember? And those extra two probably aren't even viable. The chance of triplets or something is extremely small."

She was probably right. Numberswise, the risk wasn't *that* bad. Still, he thought he'd feel better if there weren't the slightest chance of fertilizing any more eggs than he could reasonably foresee putting through college.

Well, it was too late now. He knew his wife, the she bear. Back out now, buddy, and there'd be hell to pay.

At the beach house, showering and dressing to go out to dinner, they flicked on the radio news. The story they heard was straight out of Gil's nightmares, a broadcast from hell.

A woman in California was about to give birth to septuplets. She had recently been treated with a fertility drug.

Pergonal.

He and Betsy just looked at each other.

Jesus. He didn't know what scared him more, the idea of quadruplets, or the thought that this wouldn't work at all and they'd have to go through it all over again next month.

Chapter 37

Pain. Good, promising pain. Throughout this almost ceremonial day of preparation, my ovaries ached to pop those eggs.

That night we had dinner at a cliff-top restaurant overlooking the ocean—one of those places that aims for a degree of decorum with linen and dimmed lights, but falls short, thanks to the customers, who persist in showing up in running shoes and parkas, fresh from beachcombing.

We dressed up more than usual. I had on a long skirt and Gil gave his usual nod to formality—clean jeans, still dark denim, no worn spots on the thighs.

It had been a wonderful day—I would always remember it, no matter how things turned out. Look at Gil sitting there, dark eyes shining, so handsome with his ruddy cheeks and curly hair. Only two sips of wine and I was downright mushy.

"How about a toast?" I said.

"But we've already started drinking."

"So? Don't get so hung up on the details."

"Okay, go ahead."

"I thought maybe *you'd* make it up."

"Why would you think that?"

I laughed. "You're right. Why *would* I think that?" Gil would never be the one with the words. "Okay, how about this? *To us.*"

We clinked glasses.

"To life," Gil said. "New life."

"Gil." He could still surprise me.

While I gazed at him his eyes shifted to a spot beyond my shoulder and his expression changed.

"Don't look," he muttered, but it was too late. I'd already swiveled to see why he was fighting so hard not to laugh.

I snapped back around, stricken by the same urge.

A young couple, obviously prom-bound, was being led to the booth opposite us. They were so young, so awkward, so beautiful. Both wore white with touches of red—the ribbons edging the tiered ruffles of her *Gone with the Wind* gown, the roses on her wrist, his boutonniere and the cummerband he kept tugging at. Gorgeous. Too gorgeous. They looked like escapees from *Walt Disney on Ice.* You want to talk romance? This was it, shoveled on.

I couldn't look at Gil or it'd be all over. We'd be rolling in the aisle, giggling at their feet. Maybe even one glass was too much wine for me at a giddy time like this.

Finally I braved a smile at Gil, because of the young couple, because of us.

Who said planned sex had to be so grim? We gazed at each other. Maybe we looked like middle-aged fogies to Scarlett and Rhett here, but actually we were young lovers ourselves, kids with a thrilling secret. Who would guess that in my possession I actually had a scrap of paper documenting the presence and size in millimeters of two of my very own, highly promising, follicular candidates for babyhood? This wasn't *regular* planned sex we were heading for, this was going to be special sex, important sex, mystical, earth-shaking, egg-and-sperm-exploding-into-life sex . . .

Back at the beach house, I set the wine to chill in a bucket of ice. "I want this to be the last alcohol I taste in a long, long time, okay?"

"Ten-four." Gil arranged kindling in the stone fireplace while I closed all the curtains.

Then I slipped upstairs and donned the new peach negligee I'd made for the occasion. When I came down, Gil did a classic and gratifying double take.

"Gee, what's that?" He was used to flannel granny gowns.

I smiled. This was going to be good. Six months without charts had helped. We were both in the mood in a big way, baby making or no baby making.

"Want me to pour the wine?" Gil asked.

"Let's get the shot over with first."

One more shot, then, win or lose, at least I was free of getting stuck for a while.

I took the sack of medical paraphernalia and carefully set each item on the kitchen counter. The magic potion.

"Okay, now," Gil said. "The nurse said to just poke the needle right through this rubber stopper, right?"

"Right."

No more little glass ampoules to snap open; the HCG was packaged differently. Gil stuck the hypodermic needle into the bottle of diluent and drew up 1 cc. Then he put the needle through the rubber stopper of the bottle containing the powdered HCG. Pushing the plunger, he injected the liquid into the powder. Then he gently moved the bottle from side to side to mix it.

"So far so good," I said.

He began to draw the solution back into the syringe. Then he stopped and frowned at it, puzzled.

"The needle's not long enough."

"What do you mean, not long enough?"

"I mean, with this rubber stopper, I can't push it down far enough to get the stuff off the bottom. Were they supposed to give us different needles for this?"

"I don't know."

"Thought you were the expert."

I pressed my lips together to keep from snapping back. The soft focus on things had shifted to sharp.

Gil pulled the needle out. "How about taking the whole lid off? Maybe we could pour it into something else."

I tested it. "It's not made to come off. If we try to force it . . ." I trailed off, hating to put it into words. I'd brought loads of paraphernalia, even the unused Pergonal, although I wasn't sure why, but this one vial of HCG was all we had. If we spilled it . . .

"What if I give you half a shot? It's better than nothing, right?"

"Gil, we can't do that. We've got too much into this to fool around with half a dose."

Gil inserted the needle through the stopper again. "Well, maybe if you hold the bottle I can force it in a little farther."

I held the bottle and watched two tiny beads of sweat form on Gil's brow.

"Okay, I think I've got it."

I sighed, weak with relief. All the liquid from the bottle was now safely in the syringe. We widened our eyes at each other. Close call. I gave him a grateful smile. Not only had we almost screwed up the medicine, worse—we had almost started to argue—not at all conducive to the smooth progression of the upcoming activities. Well, maybe we could get the mood back . . .

Gil withdrew the needle. The little smile melted right off his face. I stared, heart thumping again.

The needle was bent.

"Oh great," Gil said. "I can't stick this in you!"

"Now take it easy." I fished another syringe from the sack. My hands shook. "See? You thought I was paranoid. Aren't you glad I was paranoid enough to bring lots of extras?" *Don't rub it in, you dummy. Do you want to spend the rest of the evening bickering?*

"Okay, but how are we supposed to get it from one syringe to another?" My champion vial snapper had disappeared, along with all traces of his former smug competence.

Cold panic iced my veins—one of those nightmares where the terrors occur as the direct and immediate result of your own premonitions. You're afraid the man walking down the street will grab you—he grabs you. You're afraid you'll fall off the cliff—you fall. And now I was thinking the unthinkable—we were about to blow it.

Think. *Think.* "There's got to be a way to do this," I said.

"Squirt it out into something, and then draw it back up again," Gil said. "That's pretty simple."

"But what do we squirt it into? It's got to be sterile, right? We can't just use a drinking glass. That'd be dangerous, right, if you injected me with something that wasn't sterile?"

"Yeah, probably."

"I do have the extra boxes of Pergonal. I guess we could empty out one of the bottles of diluent. That'd be sterile."

"Yeah, but if we open the package," Gil said, "we can't take it back to the med school for credit."

"Even if we don't touch the Pergonal?"

"Right," Gil said. "They're sticking their necks out to take anything back once they've let it out of their building. If the package is open, forget it. I'm not paying twenty-five dollars, just for a sterile bottle . . ."

Oh *please.* If he was going to start in about money *now* . . .

"Okay," I said, taking a deep breath and letting it out. "Let's try to transfer it from one syringe to another, then. Squirt it from one into the back of the other?"

Our hands shook ridiculously. The whole thing had taken on a surrealistic, this-can't-be-happening quality. Gil held the receiving syringe with the plunger removed. I put the bent needle of the loaded one inside it. I looked at Gil.

"Go ahead."

I pushed the plunger. Careful . . . careful . . . easy does it . . .

The stream of medicine from my hypo shot straight through his and hit the counter.

"Jesus!" Gil tipped his syringe back. The rest of the medicine splashed out.

We stared at each other.

No. Roll the film backward. Go back and let one of us point out to the other that a hypodermic needle is hollow. Give us another chance!

"Well, that's it." Gil tossed the syringe on the counter.

I sank to the linoleum, wrapping my face into my knees. This didn't really happen. I'd close my eyes for a minute and when I opened them Gil would say, "Surprise! Just joking, the real syringe is right here!"

I won't say my life flashed in front of my eyes, but my life as an infertile person did. The charts, the shots, the full bladder, the ultrasounds, the surgery, the tears, the hours in the waiting rooms, the careful sex . . . everything we had come through to get to this point and now . . .

No, this *couldn't* have happened.

But when I pulled myself up by the edge of the counter, it was all still there, the litter of hypodermic needles and medicine bottles, sprinkled with precious drops of HCG.

Gil pulled the wine from the ice bucket. "Glass of consolation?"

Adrenaline zapped through me. "Don't touch that!"

"Huh?"

"You might have to drive."

"What?"

"To get more medicine."

"Aw, Betsy." He went in the bathroom, rummaged a bottle of Mylanta from our overnight case, took a swig. "Maybe we should just bag it."

"Are you kidding?" I headed for the phone. "You think I'm going to give up now? After all we've been through?"

He sank into one of the armchairs. "Who're you calling?"

"Dr. Lowell."

He looked genuinely pained. "Don't do that." He made his voice oafish. "Gee, Doc, we didn't know there was a hole in the end of that needle."

"We panicked, that's all."

"You don't find this a little embarrassing?"

"Ha! If embarrassment was going to hold me back, I'd've quit all this a long time ago." I scribbled down the number from directory assistance.

"But why call *him*? Why not the medical school?"

"Because it's ten-thirty on a Saturday night. Nobody's going to *be* at the medical school." Then I added darkly, "If I know Jodie, she's out there right now, doing it just for fun!"

"Oh come on. You *don't* know Jodie."

"So what! I feel like being mad at somebody. Would you rather I got mad at you? Besides, I'm not sure anybody else at the medical school even knows who I am. And what if I did get hold of her? She can't order the medicine from a pharmacy."

"That's great," Gil said. "She can hand us a grocery sack of drugs that could kill you but she can't order them from a pharmacy."

"That's right."

"Geesh. I knew this was crazy . . . Does Lowell even know we're doing Pergonal?"

"Of course. I told you I phoned him. Remember? Because I thought it would be a good idea in case I had some weird reaction?"

"Well, nobody's going to be at the clinic, either."

"I know that, Gil," I said. "That's why I'm calling his house."

"What! You're not supposed to do that."

"I don't give a damn. I'm not going through all the rigmarole of talking to their answering service and *is* this an emergency and *is* he on call and—" At the other end, Dr. Lowell answered. I poured out the whole ridiculous story, including the cozy fire, the wine, and the negligee. He took the intrusion into his home life good-naturedly. Maybe too good-naturedly.

I put my hand over the mouthpiece and turned to Gil. "He's laughing his head off."

Gil rolled his eyes.

"Now he has to tell his wife because she wants to know what's so funny."

"It's none of her business!"

"Yeah well, I'm the one that called his house. And they're in the middle of her Save the Forests fund-raising party. It's only fair . . ."

Finally Dr. Lowell got back on the line.

"You're going to love telling this one in the lunchroom, aren't you?" I said. "You're going to tell all the Save the Forests people."

"I wouldn't do that . . ." Still laughing.

"Right." Okay, it *was* funny. At least it would have been if it weren't so serious. Not a matter of life and death, maybe, but a matter of life. Life with a capital *L.*

"Well, let's see here," Dr. Lowell said, trying to get a grip on himself. "I'm just wondering how important it is for you to have the shot tonight. I hate to have you ruin your weekend. Maybe it'd work just as well tomorrow."

"No! To heck with the weekend. I need that shot tonight. My last tests were yesterday. By tomorrow, who knows how high my estrogen might have shot up? They told me at the med school I've got to have it tonight. That's all there is to it."

"Okay. Well, try to relax. Have a glass of that wine. I'll check around and phone you back."

Try to relax! I hung up the phone and stomped upstairs, where I ripped off the negligee and pulled on my jeans. I had to be ready for action. We might be talking bold moves here; I didn't want to be caught standing around in a slinky nightgown.

Five minutes later Dr. Lowell was back on the phone. He'd struck out—not a cc of HCG on the entire central Oregon coast. It wasn't like stocking penicillin or Tylenol with codeine, after all.

This was our choice: scrap the cycle or come home for the shot. The emergency room staff at Shepherd of the Valley in Mary's Bend would be expecting us.

"Five minutes," Dr. Lowell said. "That's all the shot will take. A couple hours' drive each way. You could be back in Neskowin by two A.M."

"Aren't you forgetting something?" I said. "Like we're supposed to have sex? Like an extra two hours of driving isn't going to improve anybody's energy level?"

"I know, but I just hate to see you waste a great weekend . . ."

I signed off. Gil and I went upstairs and started throwing clothes in our suitcase. "I don't believe that man, Gil. He's always so concerned about things being romantic."

"I thought you wanted it to be romantic too."

"Sure, but let's get our priorities straight. The main thing is that it works."

I retrieved my negligee from where it had slid down behind the bed. I wadded it up. "Well shit." I looked at Gil. "It was going to be so good, too."

"Yeah." He watched me stuff the nightgown into my suitcase. "Um, Betsy?"

"Yeah?"

"Think you might wear that thing again some time?"

I stopped, pleased at this, in spite of everything. "Sure." I snapped the case. "Get that shot in me and I'll wear it in about two and a half hours."

"Hey, the night's young."

Sure. Young but getting old fast.

"What about the closing-up list?" Gil said. "Sweeping and vacuuming and all that?"

"Forget it."

"But didn't you say your aunt's got the house next weekend?"

"Priorities, Gil. Priorities."

Chapter 38

As we headed down the highway, I checked the gas gauge. "Have we got enough?"

He snorted. "We better. Won't be any stations open over the mountains."

Why did he have to make this sound like an accusation? I mean, take me out and shoot me. I'd tried to think of everything. Gassing the car before we went to bed had not been one of them.

"Boy," I said, suddenly remembering. "Can you picture Aunt June finding the hypodermic needles?"

"I threw them in the trash."

"Sure, but they're right on top."

"Think she'll notice?"

"Of *course* she'll notice. Women always notice those little clue-type things."

"Well, you could phone her and explain."

"Are you kidding? I'll just let her think we're drug addicts for a week or two. She'll love it."

We drove for a while without speaking.

Finally Gil said, "How come we were so stupid? All we had to do was turn that bottle upside down to load the syringe."

"I guess so. Well, like I said, we panicked. Now that I think about it, we probably could have sterilized some sort of container in boiling water."

"So why didn't you suggest it?"

"Why didn't *you*? Face it—this wasn't our finest hour. I don't know, maybe I was just stuck on thinking sterile had to be *certified* sterile from the pharmacy or something. You know, like the sterile vial out of the Pergonal packet?" I let this hang there a moment. "We could have used that, but, no, we had to worry about twenty-five dollars."

Silence.

I checked my watch in the glow from an isolated house along the way. Almost midnight. Wonder how the prom turned out. Actually, it was probably prom night all over America. If it's true that a million teenage girls get pregnant every year, some of them were going to get pregnant tonight. Without even trying. A few of them actually trying *not* to. And here we were, our little pickup hurtling along under the distant stars, chasing one small chance . . .

"Think that girl's going to get pregnant tonight?" I said.

"What girl?"

"The one at the restaurant. You know, those kids going to the prom? It happens, you know."

"Not in a dress like that, I'll bet. How's he gonna get her into the backseat?"

"Backseats," I said, struck by a little pang of nostalgia. "Remember backseats?"

"Remember sex where you *worried* about pregnancy?"

"Huh. Must have been some other life." My head throbbed. My stomach churned. These curves had never seemed worse and this whole thing was one big crummy joke. To think that after all this, at some point in the wee, exhausted hours of the morning, we were supposed to make love. *Had* to make love, or it was all for nothing.

"Gil, you missed the turn. That was it back there."

"I never go that way."

I sighed. "Of course you never go that way. It's a brand-new bypass and we're usually not coming from the coast, heading for the emergency room, are we?"

"Hey. Do you want to drive?"

This was the point where I usually shut up, but not tonight. "Do you want to run out of gas? The needle's on empty."

"There's always a couple extra gallons after the needle hits empty."

I hesitated, then blurted it out. "And it's been on empty for the last twenty miles."

"That's it." Gil swerved to the side of the road and slammed the brakes. "You drive."

"Fine." We switched places. I pulled a U-turn and headed back to the bypass. It would still save a few miles.

Mary's Bend was quiet; no cars out. We were alone in our mission. I gripped the wheel. Almost there. I could see the lights of the hospital at the top of the hill.

The car started to sputter.

"Gil!"

It stopped.

"Oh shit."

Gil sat, silent.

"Well, what?" I demanded. "Go ahead. Tell me why this is my fault."

"All right, since you ask. If we'd kept going through town, we might have hit a service station that was open."

"If you'd taken the right turn in the first place, we probably could have made it."

We glared at each other in the dimness.

"Oh for Pete's sake," I said. "This is so dumb. If we hadn't both panicked back at Neskowin, we'd be asleep right now. All those little sperm would be swimming along, ready to pounce on those eggs the minute they popped. Lotta good 'if' does us now."

He waited a moment. "So what do you want to do?"

"What are my choices?"

"Well, we can sit here all night griping at each other or we can hike up there and get the stupid shot. It's probably only eight blocks or so."

"And then what? We check into a room at the hospital? I can just see it—'Excuse me, we'd like to check into your emergency sex room.' "

"Hey, I don't know what's going to happen, Bets. Let's just take it one thing at a time."

We got out, locked the suitcases in the cab, and started up the steep sidewalk.

In the unflattering, bluish light of the emergency room, we waited our turn behind a string of minor athletic injuries, the typical results of a balmy spring day in a small college town. I should have felt grateful that this was the worst Saturday night had offered up for Mary's Bend, but mostly I was annoyed everybody had waited until the middle of the night to come in for problems that had obviously had their beginnings many hours ago in broad daylight.

"Five minutes," I muttered. "Dr. Lowell made it sound like people would be standing here with the syringe ready."

"They probably weren't anticipating a rash of serious Frisbee injuries."

The people ahead of us all seemed to take so long filling out their papers. One guy was trying to sign in a woman who lived with him. Slight hitch—he wasn't sure of the spelling of her last name.

I noticed two of the receptionists with their heads together. They glanced at me. I thought I caught a smirk. Haha. Real funny. Check this! Two people who can't make a baby without everybody else in the world being in on it!

"I think I'm going to throw up." I headed for the rest room. I gagged but that was all. Nerves. God, I looked horrible in the mirror. Who would ever in a million years want to crawl in bed with *me*? I wet a paper towel and wiped my face, tried to smooth down my hair. Poor Gil.

He was standing when I came back out.

"Okay?"

I nodded.

"Come on, they're ready for us."

We followed a young man back into a small room.

"We've never done this before," he said. "The way we figure it, we need three shots to get the dilution right."

"No!" My vehemence startled him. I tried to control my voice. "I've had lots of these before. It was always one shot."

"Hmm. According to the directions here—"

"Those aren't right. Didn't Dr. Lowell talk to you?"

"Yeah," Gil said, "this was supposed to be all arranged. He said it'd take five minutes. We've been waiting an hour."

"I'm afraid he didn't say anything about how to mix it."

"Well, how about phoning him then?" Gil said.

"Yeah, I'd like to, but he's not on call."

"Okay, here's the deal," Gil said. "My wife's had a shot every day for two weeks. She's hardly got a place left for *one* shot, much less three. And I ought to know, since I'm the one who's been giving them to her. I hate to see this have to be any worse for her than it already is. Can't you call him at home?"

I blinked at Gil. Quite a speech, coming from him.

"Sorry." The guy gave me a sympathetic look. "Tell you what. I'll phone whoever *is* on call." He went out.

I burst into tears. "I don't believe this."

Gil patted my shoulder.

"This is just . . ."

"Yeah, I know."

"I guess after everything else it shouldn't really matter but—oh, I'm sick of this! Okay, we have to spend a fortune, okay, we have to have the whole thing orchestrated by doctors. But is it asking so much that just once, this sort of medical junk could go right for us?"

The nurse or orderly or whatever he was came in again.

"Did you get him?"

He nodded. "Sorry. He said just follow the cookbook recipe."

"Oh great."

"Look," said the guy. "I know this is a drag. But I am known as the very best shot giver in this entire hospital. Trust me." He held up the three syringes. "Shall we get this over with?"

I nodded, resigned. He was trying to be nice. It wasn't his fault my body was screwed up. So, for what seemed like the twenty millionth time, I pulled down my jeans and braced myself against the examining table.

"Well, yes," he said from behind me. "You have had a few shots, haven't you? Okay, now, take a deep breath." *Ping.* "Take a deep breath." *Ping.* "Take a deep breath." *Ping.* "Okay?"

I sniffed, pulling up my pants and managing a smile. "You *are* pretty good."

Gil pretended to be wounded. "Better than me?"

"Oh hey, Gil. Giving the shots is nothing compared to what you've got to do now. That'll be the hard part." I turned to this guy I'd never met before. "We're supposed to have sex now, can you believe that? And our truck's parked at the bottom of the hill with no gas in it."

Gil tried to smile. "Wouldn't you love to say you got pregnant in a backseat?"

"It doesn't *have* a backseat! I want to be home. At the farm."

The orderly pulled out his keys. "Here. Take my car."

I stared at the keys. I stared at him. "Really? You'd let us do that?"

"Hey, this is a full-service emergency room. Besides, I'm not going anywhere tonight. Just bring it back by seven, okay?"

"So," Gil said, as we headed out. "Can we count this as something going right?"

At home we walked in and then just sort of stood there, as if we hadn't expected to make it to this point, as if we weren't sure what came next.

"Are you believing all this?" I said. "Because I'm not."

Gil set down the suitcases and gave me a crooked smile. "I can believe anything."

"You know," I said. "Actually, I can too."

He stooped over my open suitcase and started pawing through the clothes.

"Wouldn't this make a terrific story to tell the baby someday?" I said.

"Sure would." He pulled out the negligee and stood up, handing it to me. "So let's make a baby."

I knew he meant it by the way he couldn't quite say it and look at me at the same time.

He found the wine and poured it into jelly glasses. Wordlessly this time, we clinked.

I took mine into the bathroom, where I washed my face and put on the nightgown. I was looking better. I took another sip. Feeling better too, except—My reflection stared back from the mirror, big-eyed, surprised at recognizing the feeling that kept me lingering here instead of rushing upstairs.

I was shy. Can you beat that? I never would have guessed—you could be married for eleven years and still feel shy.

When I came out it was dark except for the light over the stairs. I gathered my sweep of skirt and started up. At the top, I pushed open the bedroom door. Gil had lighted a candle on the nightstand and it gave the room a golden glow. Naked, he was standing at the window, back to me.

"Gee," I said softly, shyer than ever. This was not, you might say, our typical tryst.

He turned and came toward me. No, he didn't call me darling.

Do you think I cared?

We stood there for a long kiss, the slightly-out-of-control kind that lets you know you are rapidly on your way to something terrific.

I pulled back and we shared a knowing smile. I loved the feel of him through the thin fabric. He'd never let me down—I wasn't worried about that. But it was so good to have it the way it used to be, so good to know the spark was still there. He lay me back over the bed and pulled up my gown. Then he grasped the backs of my thighs and pulled me toward him. My legs dangled over the side, my toes barely touching the carpet. My eyes were wide open, watching his face, watching that look of his that no one but me ever sees.

Only when it was over did I think about a baby, and what an amazing baby it might be, born of this. The night wind rustled the new oak leaves and billowed in the lace curtains. I thought about the black sky beyond the window. I shut my eyes and thought about the forces of creation, the power that keeps the stars wheeling, keeps us spinning through the universe.

I think I was praying.

Chapter 39

Four days later I picked up the ringing telephone. "Hello?" This one word traveled the lines across town to my mother, who instantly took my emotional temperature.

"Honey," she said, "what's wrong?"

One word! But she could tell. I summed it up. My temperature hadn't risen as it should have. The whole cycle looked like a wash. The money, the shots, the crazy drive . . .

"But don't you have to wait and see if you get a period to know if you're pregnant?"

"Well, the thing is, your temperature's supposed to shoot up right after you ovulate. It's been four days since the HCG shot and it hasn't gone up, so, see, I don't think I ovulated at all."

"Hmm, I never understand all this temperature business. But I wouldn't give up yet, not until you have a period anyway."

I sighed. "Sometimes hoping wears you out, you know?"

She proceeded to give me her standard, this-is-all-going-to-work-out-somehow talk, trying so hard to cheer me up that I felt incredibly guilty at not being able to oblige her.

"We did get some good news," I offered finally. "Amy's pregnant again."

"Is she." Definitely not the explosion of joy reserved for those with unblemished medical histories.

"Okay," I said, "*potentially* good news."

"Oh dear, I certainly hope it works out this time."

"God. It's such a long road for her. The whole thing. This time she won't be able to relax for a single minute until the baby is born."

"And then you think she will?"

"Well, you know what I mean."

"Once you're a mother, you never relax. Not completely."

"Yeah?"

"Well, look at me—I'm still worrying about you."

"I'm going to be all right, Mom." I laughed shortly. "That's what you keep telling me anyway."

"I know, but, honey, you're my daughter. I want better than 'all right' for you."

There was a long pause.

"Oh yes," my mother said finally. "I knew there was some reason I called. But—oh dear, I'm afraid this isn't turning out to be very good timing."

"Mom, what?"

"Of course you're bound to find out sooner or later . . ."

"Mom!"

"All right, all right." Still she hesitated. "Well, Laura's pregnant."

"You're kidding."

"No, June called me yesterday."

"You're kidding."

"Of course, she's thrilled. June is, I mean. Laura told her it was an accident."

"Oh right."

"You don't think so?"

"Well, obviously, Mom, I'm in no position to know, am I? But come on. She's made it through twenty potentially reproductive years without getting pregnant and now, just when her clock's about to tick out, she has an accident?"

"She says Barry's not exactly thrilled, but they're going to make the best of it."

"They're going to make the best of it." Swell. Oh, give me strength. The only thing worse than Laura insisting on the advantages of living child-free would be Laura, pregnant, proclaiming it heaven on earth.

Mom listened to my silence for a moment. "Oh, honey, I was so hoping you'd be pregnant by now too."

"Yeah."

"Have you decided whether you'll try the shots again?"

"I don't know, Mom. Twelve hundred dollars' worth of drugs and I don't even pop an egg?"

"Now, you don't know that yet."

"I know I wasn't pregnant plenty of months when my chart looked better than this."

There was a long silence.

"Well, honey, maybe it's time to think about adoption. Gil's willing, isn't he?"

"Sure, in theory. But wait till he sees those applications and realizes how they'll want to check us out, make us prove we aren't perverts. It won't be a pretty scene."

"Oh phooey. They'll take one look at you two and your farm and *know* you'd give a baby a good home."

"Thanks, Mom, but I don't know if you're allowed to use your own mother for a reference." I sighed. "I don't know, it's just going to take some gear shifting here. I've had this one goal for so long . . ."

"You'll work this out, though. When I think back, there've been lots of times you didn't get what you wanted. But you know what? You usually just got busy going after something else."

"But what have I ever missed out on that compares to this? Mom, I'm not going to have Gil's baby."

"Oh, honey . . ."

"And I was so sure this time would be it."

Of course I'd been sure every time. I realized now I had lived each and every cycle on the deep-down assumption success was at hand. I couldn't have continued otherwise.

"Sweetie." My mother's voice had gone small. "I just hate to hear you sound so down."

"Well, of course I'm down. Aren't I entitled to be?"

Oh, listen to me. As if whoever offers proof of the most misery wins. What's the point here, anyway? What's so great about proving you're entitled to your suffering?

The prize of happiness goes to whoever figures out how to *quit* suffering, right?

"I'll be okay, Mom. A lot of it's probably all these hormones. Everything seems to hit so hard. Like that story in the newspaper?"

"Yes, it's terrible, isn't it?"

"I just cried. Can you imagine, having to sit there and watch them die off, one by one?"

"One by one?"

"Yeah, the Frustaci babies. The septuplets."

"Oh. I thought you meant the floods in Bangladesh. Ten thousand dead, they're saying."

"Oh. Well, that's terrible too. Life stinks, doesn't it?"

"Actually, I think life's fine. It's death that stinks."

But what could you call what Gil and I had? It wasn't death, but it wasn't life either—the spirit of this reluctant child of ours suspended somewhere in between.

After I hung up I sat there and slowly, without enjoyment, ate the chocolate cigars, one after another. I trashed the empty *It's a boy/It's a girl* box. Then I put the special wine bottle out for the recycling truck with the pretty label I'd planned to save still on it. What a sentimental idiot I was! Could I actually have imagined that getting laid in a particularly memorable manner had anything at all to do with the cold hard facts of reproduction? Or lack of it?

"Maybe the people on *Donahue* are right," I told Gil. "Maybe somebody *is* trying to tell us something. Maybe I'm not meant to have babies."

That night I heard him down on the front porch, sitting in the swing, playing a mournful Cajun melody on his harmonica. I recognized it from one of his records. The French words probably meant something like "I'm going to beat my wife if she looks at another man," but the tune just sounded like pure lonesome heartbreak.

Chapter 40

"Hi, Grampa."

Fred Strohmeyer opened his eyes and craned his neck around. He tried to focus on the face. Aw come on now. He knew her. Knew it was a relative, anyway. Name escaped him, though.

"Well, sweets, if you aren't the perfect person to drop in on the old man today. Come around here."

She eased past the wheelchair where he sat and propped herself on the edge of the bed. "I brought you some of Gil's strawberries."

"Strawberries!" Gil. Gil and Betsy. Sure, he had it now. "My, those are dandies. Thank you so much."

"Would you like some now?"

"No, I'll wait until that little girl on the next shift can get me some half-and-half. I like my half-and-half with them. Always have. Well, I don't mind telling you, this outfit—they're negligent, that's what. Leave me sitting here in this chair for hours. Somebody promised to get me back into bed right after lunch and here I am. What time is it?"

"Uh, one-thirty." She stood up. "Shall I go get somebody?"

"No. Sit down."

Finally, a relative who cared about him, somebody who'd feel bad to know what terrible treatment he was getting. He began to spill it all out—how his legs ached, how the aide had crabbed at him in the whirlpool bath, the way it hurt so bad when he slipped down in his wheelchair in the dining hall and there was no one to haul him up straight again . . .

"I ask them to close the shades. The sun's too bright for me, see? Then at night I'll want them open and they'll say, 'Well, why?' But, honey, those are the stars out there going by. That's the moon in the sky. I don't want to lie here shut off. I want to be part of that. But these people here think I'm halfway nutty . . ." As he spoke, the tension in his muscles eased, flowed out with his words. He talked some more, went on to other stories.

"They admired my compost pile so much. Never saw anything like it, they said." He sighed. "That good clean smell of rich, healthy earth, ready to grow things. I'd mix that with a little potting soil . . . Aw, honey, sometimes I'd give anything to go back. Like to be out in my greenhouse, potting up some nice geraniums while I listened to those guys on *Coffee Break*. The rain'd drum on that old fiberglass roof, but inside, it'd be nice and warm and—"

"We're a lot alike," she interrupted.

He peered at her and saw she was smiling a sad sort of smile.

"I used to run that little GE heater," he went on, "and, honey, it was a dandy . . ." He told her all the details, proud of how well he remembered them. Nothing wrong with *his* brain.

He did his best to entertain her, but she did seem to stay for the longest time. Finally she stood up like she realized she was wearing out her welcome.

"That's right now. You better get on out of here." He didn't want to be rude, but it tired him, keeping up the small talk. "You've got things to do. You're busy. You've got to be. It all goes by too fast."

She stood there, stricken.

"I'm talking about time," he said. "Life! Or maybe you're too young to see that yet, how some of it goes by too fast and some's too slow. The nights here, when I ring that bell for pain pills and nobody comes . . ." He felt his face twist. "Criminy!"

She took his hand. Lord, those hands of hers—fingers that bent around anything she wanted to pick up, tendons and muscles strung together into such intricate machinery. Had he ever truly appreciated his hands?

"I think Mom'll be by to see you later," she said.

"Fine, fine. But now, wait. Who's your mother again?"

She looked startled. "Grampa."

Well, he couldn't be expected to remember everything, could he? He hated that look he'd get from people every once in a while—the one that told him he was way off, losing track again.

"It's not Shirley, is it?"

She let out the breath she'd been holding. "That's right." Everything knocked out of place by his forgetting settled softly back.

Sure, he could see it now. Something around the eyes. Or was it the way she cocked her head? "Okay, then. Well, you take care of that good husband of yours. Take care of those kids."

The air was strangely still. The out-of-whack feeling again. He could hear her breathing.

"Grampa." Her voice sounded funny. "I don't have any kids."

"Don't tell me that! Don't you try to tell me my memory's gone punk on me!" Christ! How did they think it felt, having your brain turn into a sieve, everything running out?

"I'm sorry, I didn't mean that. It's just that I . . . don't have any."

"Well, why not, I'd like to know." *Love to the kids.* That ought to be a safe remark at her age.

"Maybe you're thinking of Stephanie and little Jack."

"Say, that Stephanie's such a little sweetheart. And they *are* saying that little baby's my first great-grandchild. He's got my genes!" He looked at this other granddaughter again. "But are you sure you don't have any? You're not just pulling my leg? Thought sure you had a little boy and girl."

She shook her head.

"Well, who in the Sam Hill *are* those kids then? The

ones running around your farm?" He closed his eyes. He could see them so clearly. But maybe he was confused again. Lord, it did go so terribly fast. One minute you'd think you were remembering something about your grandchild, and then it'd turn out to be a twenty-five-year-old memory about your daughter. Well, maybe it didn't matter, keeping everybody straight. They were all one family, one generation after another.

He opened his eyes. "Kind of funny, isn't it, how life goes on."

But he couldn't see her face. She was standing with her back to him now, looking at all the pictures on his wall. Just wonderful how people always admired those pictures.

Chapter 41

The first morning light was glowing through the lace curtains two days later when I pulled the thermometer out of my mouth and got a surprise. My temperature had finally gone up. What the heck.

"So what's that supposed to mean?" Gil said, already pulling a pair of jeans from his closet hook, eager to get out to the fields.

"Maybe I ovulated after all. Maybe there's still a chance I could be pregnant."

No comment.

In the following days, he refused to be party to tentatively mounting optimism.

"I talked to Amy," I told him. "She says a friend of hers got pregnant using Pergonal and her temperature took a long time to go up too."

No comment.

It was dawn again a few days later when I recorded an ominous temperature drop. Ten minutes with the thermometer in my mouth couldn't raise it. Finally I dragged myself to the bathroom, dreading what I knew I would find.

Oh damn. A spot of blood. My eyes shut tight, then opened. Still there. I could hardly have felt worse if I'd been hemorrhaging.

I got myself fixed up, but then, instead of going out, I stayed in the bathroom to do my crying. *I'm never going to have Gil's baby*, I told myself. Then I sat there on the closed toilet lid and cried for being such a fool. And not just this last time, letting myself hope again. No, I'd been foolish from the start, daring to imagine that every good thing in life was naturally bound to come our way just because we were young and willing to work and because we loved each other so much.

Gil must have heard me. He opened the door and came in. He took a seat on the edge of the tub, where he could reach and encircle me with his arms, his knees clamping me too.

Now he would insist I stop crying.

"You don't have to hide and cry in here," he said instead. "At least come out on the sofa."

I didn't move. His arms felt so good around me. Braced for him to tell me I should stop crying, not hearing it, I stopped crying.

That afternoon he caught me pulling out the stash of baby things from under the brass bed.

"What's all that?"

"What's it look like?"

"Oh, hon. I *told* you not to. The last thing you need is . . . this stuff to cry over."

"Who's crying?"

He sighed, snagging up a tiny T-shirt. I saw something new pass across his face, something soft. "Gee," he said, "are they really this little?"

"That's the rumor." I couldn't stand it—that little shirt, suspended between his dirt-stained fingers. "Here." I snatched it away. "I think it's time to get rid of all this."

He watched me stuff it into a sack that also contained a folded length of yellow bunny flannel.

"Would it be easier if I took it?" he said.

"Yeah. Thanks. Take it down to the Red Cross."

"But . . . wait. Does this mean you're giving up on adoption too? Couldn't we use this—"

"No, this was part of something different. If we're going to think about adoption, I have to start fresh."

"Are you sure, hon. Maybe we—"

"Look, right now I just want this stuff out of here, okay?"

The next day Gil got the pale pink card from Marsha: a baby announcement.

"I don't believe this!" I said. "It *is* a conspiracy." I was counting back. "She must have known she was pregnant when she called at Christmas. Did she tell you?"

"Uh . . ." His eyes shifted. "Well, yeah, I think maybe she did."

"And you didn't tell me?"

"Well, obviously this isn't the sort of news that perks you up a whole hell of a lot."

"But why would she—" Then I had a thought. "Gil, did you tell her we were having trouble? Getting pregnant, I mean?"

"I might have mentioned it."

"You *told* her?"

"Well, she asked if we had kids . . ."

"You *told* her?"

"Gimme a break. You tell anybody you feel like telling. I told one person."

"Yeah, right. The very last person on the whole face of the earth I would want to know about this."

I'm not ashamed to confess that this was one birth announcement I tore to tiny bits.

Two days later, my temperature graph jagged up again. I stopped bleeding.

"This is weird," I said to Gil.

"What?"

"Well, look at my chart. I wonder if . . ."

"Betsy, don't. Don't do this."

"What?"

"Don't try to get me going."

"Just look at my chart."

"No, I *won't* look. I'm sick of your damned charts."

"Right," I said, stung. "And I think they're so much fun."

"Betsy." He hesitated. "Listen carefully: You. Had. A period."

"I know, but—"

"Get a grip, will you?"

"But sometimes women bleed a little even when they're pregnant. Amy knows a woman who—"

"Would you *please* sign off on this? Getting on the phone to everybody all the time, making each other crazy, hashing this stuff over and over . . ."

"I haven't talked to anyone in months!"

"Come on, you're on the phone to your mom every day."

"Well, okay, my mom."

"And Amy."

"*Okay!* And Amy. But if it wasn't for talking to other women, I'd be in the state mental hospital by now. Sometimes other women know more than those doctors anyway."

"You're grasping at straws! You promised to draw the line—"

"And I will. I'm as sick of this as you are. Sicker, I'll bet. But how can I know *where* to draw the line, that's the thing. Honest to God, I was ready to quit. Didn't I chuck that baby stuff? I don't *want* to get my hopes up. But my temperature's right back up there after being down only three days. I don't think that was a real period. My breasts are sore—"

"I don't want to hear about it."

"And I feel like I'm going to throw up."

"When are you going to figure it out? You don't get pregnant by making yourself throw up!"

"I'm not!" I said. "Anyway, what am I supposed to do? Ignore my body? I do have to keep walking around in it, you know." I took a deep breath. "I can't help it, I *feel* pregnant."

He gave me a disgusted look. "Since you've never *been* pregnant, how can you possibly know what it feels like?"

What was the use? Nothing I said counted anymore. I was a crazy person. For two and a half weeks since the HCG shot I'd been yo-yoing back and forth between hope and despair. No wonder I'd lost all credibility.

Still, I missed the old Gil, the one who'd light up every time I said I thought that maybe, just possibly this time . . . The one so quick to sing his happy little song about the cake in my oven, the one so willing to believe whatever report I handed down from the pedestal of my superior female understanding of these things.

I missed the old Dr. Lowell, too. In the beginning he'd been so quick to take me at my word. One imagined symptom of pregnancy reported and he'd be whipping out his due-date disk, speculating along with me, offering me a magic day in the future on which to hang my fantasies.

Now, when I phoned to ask for another pregnancy test, I got only skepticism.

"You did have a period," he said. A statement, not a question.

"Well, I bled a little, but it was only three days and very light."

"I don't know, Betsy . . ."

"And today I threw up."

A long silence. "Well, the test is easy enough. You can come in tomorrow morning if you really have to . . ."

They both thought I'd become a mental case, making myself throw up. Had I? Oh God, maybe I *was* losing my mind.

The next morning in the kitchen I informed Gil that my temperature was still up and I was going over for the test.

"Right," he said. "Go over there and make a fool of yourself."

"Gil."

"Can't you at least save us the embarrassment and do one of those home test kits?"

"It's too soon."

"Then wait."

"Gil, I *can't* wait. Can't you see this is killing me?"

He looked at the ceiling. "So how many preg tests have you had since we started this? Six? Seven?"

This was so unfair. He knew very well most of those tests were just to make sure I wasn't pregnant so I wouldn't worry about taking more drugs. I hadn't really thought I was.

"Oh God," I said. "Sometimes I feel like I'm in this all by myself."

"Gimme a break."

"Well, what's it to you if I get the test? You don't have to be embarrassed in front of the lab technicians. You don't have to get stuck with a needle."

"No, but I have to suffer through calling for the results with you, right?"

"No, you don't. Just stay out on your tractor."

"Okay, I will." He grabbed his cup of coffee. "But one thing—if it's negative, you've got to promise to believe it. No starting in again about the lab making mistakes."

He waited for my answer. I didn't give him one.

"I really don't want to hear about some woman in Tallahassee who was pregnant even when her lab test said she wasn't, okay?"

I swung open my folded arms. "Okay, okay." But actually I only meant okay about the woman in Tallahassee. As for the rest of it, I couldn't make any promises. Was getting a negative result going to make these symptoms go away? Suddenly I realized that's exactly what Gil thought would happen. Dr. Lowell too. Convince me I'm not pregnant and the symptoms, which I'm obviously cooking up out of pure wishful thinking, will evaporate.

Gil set down his coffee. "You know how you're always telling me you wish I'd say what I feel? Okay. I feel like a sucker. Every time you've told me you're just sure you're pregnant, I've believed you. Over and over. Then when you're not, I've got to do the crash-and-burn scene with you."

"Gil—" He'd been crashing and burning too?

"So if you're pregnant, great. If you're not, that's okay too. Really. But I don't want to go through this anymore."

"Well neither do I!" And then it hit me—this was it. If I wasn't pregnant right this minute, I wasn't ever going to be.

I drove up to the clinic and had my blood drawn, then went out on a wallpapering job to help pass one of the longest days of my life. I finished up in time to come home for the fateful phone call. Gil was conspicuously absent.

Well good. I didn't want him there when I phoned. If the test was negative, he wouldn't say the right thing, anyway. There *was* no right thing. No words could make this better.

I went upstairs, flopped on the bed and stuck the thermometer in my mouth. I checked my watch: 5:05. My breasts were tingling again. I *had* to be pregnant. If the test came back negative, it'd mean that not only was I not pregnant, I was also a mental case. Even if we somehow steeled ourselves to go on, I'd have to promise to let Gil and the doctor chart the course of treatment. I'd have to keep my mouth shut, not have opinions, not study books and talk to other women and try to figure all this out. I'd have to give up my mind and agree to be nothing but a body. It wasn't fair! It wasn't fair to have to be infertile *and* mentally incompetent.

I took the thermometer out. Silver mercury bar right up there at ninety-eight point six, shimmering promisingly. Shoot. I didn't care what the doctor said about my temperature the rest of the day being irrelevant, I'd taken it enough times to see there *was* a correlation.

I went to the bathroom and checked for blood again. Negative.

I looked at my watch: 5:15. I sat down in the rocker by the phone and took a few deep breaths. My heart pounded. My intestines writhed. Ridiculous! Get a grip. Why should this be so awful?

Maybe because everything had boiled down to this: positive or negative, win or lose, Betsy sane or Betsy crazy. In a few minutes I would either be richly vindicated or I would be labeled a hopeless mental case.

I can't do this anymore, I was thinking. I want this finished. I'll settle for steady, quiet happiness. Satisfaction with a wallpapering job well done, a neglected old house put right, a nicely turned compost pile . . .

I dialed the number I knew by heart. It rang. Ten times. Fifteen. Come *on*.

"Mary's Bend Clinic."

"Uh—"

"Will you hold, please?"

Deep breath. Out the kitchen window the sun flickered through the leaves. Please, please . . .

"Ob-Gyn. May I help you?"

"Yes, this is Betsy Bonden. I'm calling for the results of my pregnancy test?"

"Oh yes." A shuffling of papers. "I'm sorry—"

My heart clutched.

"I'm afraid the tests aren't back from the lab yet. Should be any minute. How about if we call you?"

I hung up and sank back into the rocker. I really did feel like throwing up. I jumped up and paced the house. Then I sat back down. For fifteen minutes I stared at the phone, willing it to ring.

And still I jumped, surprised, when it did.

"Mrs. Bonden?"

"Yes? *Yes?*"

"How are you this evening, Mrs. Bonden?"

Well, nobody ever starts a phone call this way unless they want money. "Actually," I said, "I feel rotten. Are you selling something?"

"Oh no." Indignant at the very suggestion. "I just wanted to inform you that you have been selected to receive a free—"

"No thank you." I hung up.

The phone rang again.

"I said I'm not interested! And I'm expecting—"

"Betsy? This is Shelley at the Mary's Bend Clinic?"

"Oh. Yeah. Gee, I'm sorry, I . . . you've got my results?"

"Yes, I do." One second expanded into an hour. I stared out the kitchen window. "Your test was positive. Congratulations! You're pregnant."

Positive. The leaves trembled in the light.

Positive. My eyes blurred.

"Positive?" I stood up. "Are you sure?"

"Yes, I'm positive it's positive."

My knees buckled. I let myself sink to the floor. The phone followed me with a crash.

"Betsy? You there?"

"Yeah," I said, righting the phone. "Sorry about that. Yeah, I'm here. Hey, I'm not crazy!"

An uncertain laugh. "Um, would you like to make an appointment for your first prenatal visit?"

"What? Oh, I'll have to call you back." Patches of sunlight flittered over the hardwood floor. "I can't even think."

I hung up and sat there. I wasn't crazy. The symptoms were real.

We were going to have a baby.

A baby.

Gil. I had to tell Gil.

I got up unsteadily, trying out my joy. Better let it wash over me slowly or it was bound to knock me flat.

I went out the back door and looked up at the sky. It was

bluer, I swear. That was the universe out there and I, Betsy Bonden, wife of Gil, future mother of somebody or other, was in favor with it.

Hot dog!

I hurried out toward the far field, where I could hear the low rumble of Gil's tractor. Every few steps a new joy would explode in me, like blossoms bursting open to the sun. My mother. She'd be so happy. Gil's parents. A cousin for little Jack. And Grampa Stroh—

It would be like this for months, I realized, all the suppressed daydreams popping back into possibilities again, everything from the most important, like telling Grampa, down to the trivial—the pleasure of looking through the wallpaper books with my own baby in mind.

My own baby.

At the start of the dirt road, I slowed down. I wanted to make it last, this moment we'd been trying to reach for so long. This was part of the baby's story, after all. A mother needed to remember these things. So drink it in and memorize every detail, the smell of fresh, growing things, the way the sun lit every living leaf, every blade of grass, every daisy nodding along the edge of the field. Now we were truly part of it all—life going on.

Even the arms of the oak trees dipped their branches to me as I passed.

Chapter 42

Twisting around on the tractor seat, Gil watched the auger spinning off loose dirt as he pulled it up out of the freshly dug posthole. Only a few more to go. Then he could start setting posts for the new boysenberries. Facing forward, he stepped on the clutch, disengaged the power take-off.

That's when he saw her coming. Damn. Dragging too slow for good news. Not that he ever expected good news anymore. Seemed like the best he could hope would be hearing she was ready to give this up and start looking for a baby to adopt. Well, whatever she had to say, she wasn't going to want to shout it over the tractor. If he'd learned anything in eleven years of marriage, he'd learned to spot a cut-the-engine-type conversation coming at him. He shut it off and threw an elbow over the seat back, watching her pick her way through the new berry starts.

She'd be wanting him to say something; he always hated that. *Next month for sure* just wasn't going to make it anymore, and besides being cruel, *I told you so* was no satisfaction, not when he'd been hoping against all evidence he'd be wrong.

He took off his cap, wiped his sleeve across his forehead. Maybe it was time. He couldn't stand to see her like this anymore. And what about him? She didn't exactly have a monopoly on craziness around here. What else could you call it when he stashed her baby stuff in the shed because he just didn't have the heart to dump it at the Red Cross? Damn that silly little shirt . . .

He swung down off the tractor. No, it was definitely time. She'd hate him for a while, might not talk for a week, but it'd be best in the long run.

Yeah, look at that. She was already crying. Damn. The whole thing just made him so mad. Swear to God, if he'd known how miserable they were going to wind up—both of them—he would have put a stop to this before they ever started.

"Aw, honey . . ."

"Gil."

"It's okay, Bets."

"No." She shook her head. "No."

Wait a minute. She was smiling.

"Betsy?"

She nodded.

He stopped in his tracks. "It was positive?"

Still nodding, she fell into his arms.

He stood stock-still for a moment, then he hugged her right off her feet.

When her toes finally touched earth again she pulled back, her face a sheen of tears. "You know how people always say that when you look forward to something too much, it can never be as great as you imagine?"

He sniffed. "Yeah?"

"Well . . ." She sniffed too, laughing. "That's a crock!"

To Do

Visit Grampa
Thank-you to Amy for flowers
Pick out nursery wallpaper
Make prenatal appt.
Start quilt
Check cloth diaper services
Maternity sale at Stork Shop
Strawberry jam

Check library for prenatal books
" bookstore " " "
Sat—garage sale Crib? Change
table?
Call Carla?
Call Laura?
Order daffodil bulbs
Fix pantry door

Chapter 43

On a cold January afternoon that was apparently passing uneventfully for the rest of Mary's Bend, Gil drove me across town to the hospital. My water had broken. My time had come.

At the emergency room door, a young man came out with a wheelchair. Guess who? The best shot giver at Shepherd of the Valley Hospital!

Recognizing him, we started laughing.

"You know those three shots you gave me?" I patted my huge belly. "They worked!"

A wink and a thumbs-up sign. "We aim to please." He settled me into the chair and steered it toward the elevator. "So what's it gonna be? A boy or a girl?"

"We're betting one of each," Gil said.

That's right—twins.

These children of ours—it was as if they had always existed in our minds and in our hearts. That winter morning, at the hour of dawn, they were finally delivered safely into our arms. A son and a daughter.

So let the cynics be cynical. Let the sophisticated types enjoy their ennui. If you can call birth any kind of ending, I'm here to say that happy endings are for real. Ask Carla with her new baby daughter. Ask Amy and Ed with their new baby son. Ask any man and woman who've broken their hearts trying for this. No, the hospitals don't actually feature heavenly choirs in the delivery rooms, but then, they don't need to. We hear the hallelujahs just the same.

Nobody lives happily ever after. I knew that. Our happiness might be only for this moment, a fleeting stop before we moved on to new griefs, new joys. But for people who've been stalled, moving on is, in itself, something of a miracle.

I remember the sun coming up over the Cascades that morning. I remember gazing into our babies' faces and thinking of something my mother used to say about coming to believe in God. And I remember looking at Gil and thinking that if there were any two happier people on the face of the earth at this moment, I couldn't imagine who they might be. Or how they could possibly have been more richly blessed.